years but it wasn't
until nine years ago that she decided to share her love of writing sexy, gritty stories with anyone outside her close family (the over-eighteens anyway!). This series is Zara's next step in her erotic romance writing journey. She looks forward to bringing her readers even more sizzling-hot stories featuring panty-melting alpha heroes and the women who rock their world.

You can learn more:

www.zaracoxwriter.com
Twitter @ZCoxBooks
Facebook: Zara-Cox-Writer

BLACK
Sheep

ZARA COX

piatkus

PIATKUS

First published in the US in 2017 by Forever, an imprint of Grand Central Publishing
This paperback edition published in 2017 by Piatkus

1 3 5 7 9 10 8 6 4 2

A CIP catalogue record for this book
is available from the British Library.

ISBN 978-0-349-41479-9

Printed and bound in Great Britain by
Clays Ltd, St Ives plc

Papers used by Piatkus are from well-managed forests
and other responsible sources.

Piatkus
An imprint of
Little, Brown Book Group
Carmelite House
50 Victoria Embankment
London EC4Y 0DZ

An Hachette UK Company
www.hachette.co.uk

www.littlebrown.co.uk

BLACK
Sheep

PART ONE
Axel

Chapter One

FUCK BYGONES

AXEL

Childhood sweethearts.

Even way back then, I despised the term. There was nothing childlike about what I felt for her. Even less was the implied sweetness of our connection. But we let them smile and label us as they pleased. All the while knowing and relishing our truth. She was pure sin, and I was the devil intent on gorging myself on her iniquities.

I lived for it. For her. The sexy, hint-of-sandpaper voice that could bring me to my knees. The limpid blue eyes that paralyzed me. The killer curves that made me want to destroy every other boy or man who dared to look at her sixteen-year-old body.

At nineteen, I was fully cognizant of my obsession, was aware that it was a live grenade destined to blow me apart one day. But I was ready to die the first time I looked into her eyes. As long as I died in her arms.

I should have known my end was near the day she called me by her special name.

My Romeo.

She called me that the day I took her virginity beneath the stars on the beach of our families' adjoining Connecticut properties.

My Romeo. As if she knew we were doomed. Perhaps she knew *I* was. Perhaps she'd known of the plan all along. Or she hatched it the day my father enrolled me at West Point. The day he embraced his grand and greedy plan to fatten his bank balance from war instead of just from common mafia mongering.

The irony was that I was the only fool in the piece. I may have accepted my role as Romeo, but her name wasn't Juliet.

No, the devil's siren went by the name of Cleopatra McCarthy.

And when it came right down to it, Cleopatra McCarthy was only too happy to watch me burn in the flames of my obsession. Happy to watch me die.

Childhood sweethearts. Fuck that.

Whatever we felt for each other was as old as dirt, filthy as sin. What I feel for her now is…too fucked up to name.

So now I watch her. She watches me.

Strangers. Enemies. Our hate sparks between us like forked lightning. Bitter, twisted. *Alive.*

There may be a wide dance floor between us and the sound of jazz funk blaring through the speakers inside the walls of XYNYC, my New York nightclub, but we may as well be cocooned in a little bubble of our own, merrily breathing in the fumes of our hate.

Eight years is a long time to drip-feed yourself poisonous might-have-beens. But I'm more than comfortable in my role of rabid obsessor.

I lean back, elbows on the bar, ignoring all around me except the woman tucked away in my roped-off VIP lounge. The elevated lounges offer a clear view without obstruction. The short black dress clings to her hips and upper thighs leaving her legs bare, the halter neckline and her caught-up hair displaying lightly tanned shoulders and arms.

The glass of vintage Dom Pérignon champagne in her hand hasn't been touched. Not a single inch of her voluptuous body has moved in time to the music, even though music is…*was* a great love, once upon a time. Even after all these years, I retain residual resentment that I had to share her with Axl Rose and Dave Grohl, watch her body twist in ecstasy that wasn't induced by me.

A waiter offers her a platter of food. She shakes her head and takes a step toward the black velvet rope that blocks the lounge. My bouncer steps in front of her.

She glares at him.

Without glancing my way, she reaches into her tiny purse for her phone. She sets her glass down, and her fingers fly over the screen.

My own phone buzzes in my pocket. I'm not surprised she has my number. Any member of my family could have obtained it by illegal means and given it to her. I take a beat before I pull it out and read the message. "I've been coming here almost every night for two weeks. You have to talk to me sometime."

I glance up, make her wait for a full minute before I reply. "Do I?"

Her nostrils flare lightly. "He wants an answer."

My mouth twists, and I swear the impossible happens, and I hate her even more than I did one second ago. "What are you now, his messenger?"

Her gaze flicks up to me before she shrugs, her bare, slender shoulder gleaming under the pulsing lights. "You've ignored all his emails and your brothers' calls."

"They're spineless assholes."

"Are you going to talk to me?"

"No."

"Then why keep me here?"

"I told you the terms of admittance. You come of your own free will; you don't get to leave until the club closes. That's in two hours."

"This is ridiculous, Axel."

My stomach knots just from seeing her type my name. "Then don't come again."

She looks up. Our eyes meet across the dance floor. Her hatred washes over me in filthy waves. I want to roll around in it. She holds my stare defiantly for a minute before she lowers her head to her phone again.

"It's not that simple. Please hear me out."

Again my stomach clenches, but this time it's accompanied by a crude little jerk in my pants that grabs my attention. "Please? You begging now?"

Annoyance flickers across her features. Her thumb hovers over the screen for the longest time. Then my phone buzzes. "Yes."

I didn't expect that. The Cleo I knew never begged unless it was to plead for my cock inside her. My mind circles around why she would do so now, and my erection hardens. A few crazed seconds later, I decide it's safer for my sanity not to know, and I settle back into sublime hate. "Too bad the first time I hear you beg has to be via text. Answer's still no."

"Axel, this is important. Let bygones be bygones and hear me out. It won't be more than five minutes. Please."

I'm doubly pissed off that I can't hear her say that word. I've waited a long fucking time to hear it. I'm even angrier that I can't cross the distance between us to ask her to repeat it. I put everything into the two words I text to her. "Fuck bygones."

It may be a trick of the light, but I swear she feels my new level of rage. Her lips part in an inaudible gasp as she reads my reply.

Turning away, she stalks to the private bar in the lounge. The waiter nods when she murmurs to him. He slides a shot glass across the counter and reaches for the premium tequila sitting on the shelf behind him. He pours. She picks it up and raises the glass to me before she downs it in one go.

I stride to the edge of the dance floor, hating myself for being concerned about the consequences of what she's doing. Then I remind myself that it's been years since I witnessed Lightweight Cleo topple over after one shot of tequila.

All the same I watch her, narrow eyed, as she downs another shot before heading for one of the velvet booth seats. There is the tiniest weave in her walk, and I have to clench every single muscle to stop myself from charging across the space between us.

The simple, undeniable truth is I can't.

Because of Cleopatra McCarthy, my life exploded in a billion little pieces. Pieces I didn't bother to put back again because I knew the exercise would be futile.

So for over eight years, I've lived with this new, permanently-altered-for-the-worse version of myself. A version I'm not in a hurry to reassess or remodel. A version that keeps me steeped in the obsidian fury that fuels my existence.

I stay on my side of the divide because to come within touching distance of her is to succumb to the carnage raging inside me. After all this time, I should have enough of a hold on myself to smother the compulsion.

I don't. If I did, I would've stopped her from stepping foot inside my club the first time she turned up.

But even worse than the control I sorely lack is the fact that I'm a glutton for punishment. Hell, it's the reason I run the highly successful and exclusive Punishment Club. In the handful of years it's been open, I've made over twenty million dollars in membership fees alone. Who the fuck knew there were crazies out there like me seeking to be exposed to the very thing they hate the most?

I derive a little perverse satisfaction from the fact that I'm granting them an outlet, even while I'm unable to find one for myself. I accepted my fate a long time ago. What haunts me can only be cured one way—by the moment I stop breathing.

"Macallan. Triple. Neat."

I reel back my thoughts and turn at the sound of the deep, raspy voice.

Quinn Blackwood.

He's not exactly a friend but there's mutual respect and acceptance of the otherworldliness inhabiting our blackened souls. It's what drew us to each other when we were placed in the same group for a brief time at West Point. Although Quinn never served, we kept in touch and ended up owning several nightclubs together, XYNYC being one of them.

Like me, he doesn't need the income. Like me, this place is one of many outlets for the demons that haunt him.

I make sure Cleo is still seated and return to the bar.

I watch Quinn knock back a large drink in one ruthless gulp. "You know there's a better blend in your VIP room, right?"

He slams the glass on the counter with barely suppressed violence. "Too far," he replies.

We're roughly the same height so, when he shoots me a glance, I'm well positioned to see the hounds of hell chasing through the jagged landscapes of his eyes. I don't flinch. I welcome the horde like kindred spirits. Our souls have endured more than enough to last us several lifetimes, and we both know it. "That bad, huh?"

His jaw clenches as he takes a breath. "Worse."

"Need any help?"

A dark shadow moves over his face, and he shakes his head. "It's done. I have what I need."

I don't press him for more information. Ours is not that kind of relationship.

I catch movement from my lounge, and my gaze zeroes in on my nemesis. She's risen from the sofa and is leaning against the railing once more, the untouched glass of champagne again in one hand. The bodyguards are once more alert, and a few of my errant brain synapses attempt to be amused by the glare she sends their way. "If you need anything else, let me know," I say absently, unable to take my eyes off the woman whose presence looms as large as the Sphinx before me.

I sense Quinn following my gaze, then returning to me. "Looks like you have a situation of your own that needs taken care of."

"Yeah." My voice feels as rough as it sounds. "Fucking tell me about it."

He doesn't nod or smile. Quinn Blackwood rarely smiles. But then, neither do I. Another thing we have in common. "Anything I can do, let me know," he says.

No one can help me with this. "Thanks," I say anyway.

He asks questions that bounce off the edge of my consciousness.

I shrug. I nod. I respond. But throughout, my senses are attuned to the other side of the room.

I barely register him stalking away. I click my fingers, and Cici, one of my waitresses, sidles up to me. I relay instructions, and she leaves, but not before she smiles in a way that ramps up my irritation.

I can't think about that now. I have more than enough to deal with tonight.

Four lounges from Cleo's, Vardan Petrosyan, the New York head of the Armenian mob, is downing expensive vodka like there's a drought coming. His unsavory presence sticks in my gut like a rusty blade, but since he's one of the many devils I've struck a deal with, I have to tolerate his company for as long as necessary.

He's been here going on two hours. I've ignored him for most of that time. Any longer and I risk pissing him off.

Men like Petrosyan demand fear where they can't achieve respect. I feel neither, and he knows it, but he's also aware I need him more than he needs me right now. So we both pretend I feel the latter.

I make my way to where he sits with his entourage. His minders stand in my way for the extra second it takes to make their point before they step aside.

The mob boss has a tall, slim blonde perched on each thigh. They both glance at me as I approach. I ignore them and focus on the short, stocky man with boxy features.

When he finally removes his wandering lips from one of the women's cleavage, Petrosyan stares at me with dead black eyes, a cold smile sliding across his face. "I was beginning to think you forget about me," he tells me in broken, heavily accented English.

"I wanted to catch you when you were feeling soft and mellow," I reply.

He barks out a laugh. "Nadiya, he thinks I'm soft and mellow. Do *you* think I'm soft and mellow?"

The blonde on his left immediately shakes her head.

"Feel free to check; let's make sure, ya?" he encourages.

She happily obliges by groping him brazenly. "No, Vardan, you are hard...everywhere."

He chuckles, his eyes a touch colder. "You see, my man, you waste both our time."

I take a breath and force a deferential nod. "My apologies. Do you have everything you need?"

He stares at me for several seconds. "No, not everything. But it is nothing that a little...negotiation cannot satisfy, eh?"

I've been expecting this—the obligatory extortion that happens every few months. Normally, I head it off by stating a few facts and figures, namely that I'm paying almost double market value for the service Petrosyan is providing me. This time, I don't.

Cleo's persistent visits are evidence that my plan is working. The fracturing Rutherford kingdom is developing even more cracks. And I'm willing to pay dearly for that.

"What do you want, Petrosyan?"

His expression doesn't change, but sensing a victory, he immediately turfs the girls off his lap. Once they've drifted off, he stands, adjusts his shiny suit, and rises up on the balls of his feet. But nothing can disguise the fact that I'm a foot taller than him.

"I want for you to tell me what you're doing with all the product you buy from me, for start. It's not ending up on the street or in clubs, I know that for fact," he says.

"And like I told you when we started this...partnership, it's none of your business." Although I owe him no explanation, I don't relish the idea of telling the mobster that every ounce of heroin I've procured from him for the last two years has been flushed down the toilet. That this isn't about taking over my father's business to make money for myself but to ensure the Rutherfords have zero business by the time I'm done with them. And if by doing so, I help take a few hundred kilos of drugs off the street...I mentally shrug.

Petrosyan's jaw flexes, but he nods. "Okay, then let's talk *our* business. Economy is in toilet. I need to raise prices—"

"Two hundred thousand a month. Fifty thousand dollars more for the same deal."

He looks off to the side, pulls on his cuffs, and then his fish eyes dart back to me. "I am thinking a cool quarter million has nice ring to it, no?"

"Fine. Deal. Are we done?"

Surprise livens his eyes for a few seconds before his gaze turns speculative. "You must really want to...how you say, shank it to my former business partner, hmm?"

"Yes, I must really want to *stick* it to him."

The turn of phrase baffles him for a second then he gives up in favor of confirming that I've really folded and given him a one-hundred-thousand-dollar price hike after a two-minute negotiation.

Now that he's satisfied, I turn to leave.

"I would sleep with gun under my pillow if I had someone like you for enemy," he states.

I look over my shoulder. He's watching me carefully. Trying to read the unreadable. "Then it's a good thing we're friends, isn't it? And you do sleep with a gun under your pillow."

He laughs. "Well, for you, I would make it *two* guns."

"You keep your end of the bargain, and you will never need to."

He catches the warning in my voice, and the laughter fades. "You keep up payments, and we won't have problem." He clicks his fingers for his girls.

Our battle lines redrawn, I return to the bar in time to spot Cleo raising a nearly empty champagne glass to her lips. My jaw clenches. Added to the two shots of tequila, I'm uncertain what the result will be. So I sharpen my focus with an even more vicious blade. Everything falls away as I saturate myself with her presence.

Every breath. Every blink.

I catch the moment her hips sway, ever so slightly, to the throbbing rock anthem.

The move resonates through me like the cuts of memory's blade. In an instant, I'm thrown back to the bedroom in the pool house I claimed the day I turned eighteen. It was the single thing I requested when my mother asked me what I wanted for my birthday.

The need to distance myself from my father had grown into a visceral, unbearable ache. My mother saw it. She granted my request, despite my father's firm refusal. It was most likely what earned her the black eye two days later.

I don't know because I didn't ask. It would've been useless to do so anyway. She would've lied. And I was too selfish, too thankful for the mercy of not having to live under the same roof as my father, to rock the boat.

So I claimed my tiny piece of heaven in hell. And it was there that Cleo danced for me for the first time. Where we celebrated a lot of *firsts*.

That particular memory flames through the charred pits of my mind. I don't fight it. Like the fleeting moments of pleasure and pain, it will be gone in an instant, devoured by the putrefying cancer that lives within me.

Sure enough, it's gone from one heartbeat to the next, and I'm left with rotting remnants of what once was.

"All taken care of, boss."

I snap my head to the side. Cici's standing next to me. Her gaze slides over me from head to toe before it settles on my face. She's wearing that special *do me* smile she's worn since she started working here six weeks ago. I made the mistake of fucking her as part of her interview process. I shouldn't have. I could pardon myself by making the excuse that her presence in my office that day coincided with the first call in three years from Ronan, my oldest brother.

Ronan. Daddy's boy through and through, right down to the pansy-assed ring on his left pinkie.

Like one hundred percent of our interactions, that call hadn't gone well. So I needed an outlet. It was either a fist through a wall or my cock in a pussy. I chose pussy. I refuse to make excuses for that choice. Because what's the point of having a black soul, of making choices that leave your hands permanently soiled in evil, if you don't fucking own it? But I do admit to a modicum of regret. She's not the first employee I've fucked, but usually I'm a little more circumspect with my choices. My blinding rage prevented me from seeing that ill-disguised, you-fuck-me-I-own-you light in Cici's eyes until it was too late.

Now, irritatingly, ever since our one encounter, the ever-growing stench of possessiveness clings to her every time she's in my presence.

She sidles closer now. "Is there anything else you need?" she says in a low, intimate voice. "I couldn't help but notice that both you and your friend are wound up tighter than a drum tonight. I...I can help relieve your stress...if you want?"

In the next minute, she'll find an excuse to touch me. I'm slammed with the smell of cheap perfume and shameless arousal. Because my senses are wide open and raw, I take a deeper hit than I normally would. Which makes me direct more anger at her than I know is warranted.

"Cici?"

"Yes, boss?" she responds with a breathy eagerness.

"Fuck off and do your job," I snarl.

She recoils with shame and turns red-faced toward the bar.

"Jesus, twice in one night. You'd think I have a disease or something," she mutters under her breath as she busies herself collecting a drinks order from the bartender.

I feel no remorse when she walks away in a huff. I don't give a shit what's got her ass in a vise or who else she's hit on tonight. Under normal circumstances, her feelings matter very little to me. Tonight, I care even less.

When she moves away, I exhale and glance at my watch. On Tuesday nights, the club shuts at three a.m. It's almost one. Two more hours to go.

I brace myself before I raise my head.

It does absolutely nothing to buffer the potency of Cleo's stare or the effect of the evil little smile I see playing at her lips when our eyes hook into each other.

She's under my skin, where she's lived for seventeen years. And she knows it.

Fifth Harmony's "Work" blasts from the speakers. The hard beat and dirty lyrics produce a lusty sway of her hips. The look in her eyes and the movement of her body are almost dichotomous. Her eyes tell me she hates me. Her body beckons me with the promise of transcendental lust.

I should retreat to my office where I can watch her from the relative safety of security cameras. Or walk the other upper and lower floors, greet a few VIPs who would love a personal acknowledgement from me.

Fuck that.

I stay put and nod tersely at a few regulars who are brave enough to breach the no-fly zone around me. When my bartender slides a glass of Scotch to me, I pick it up and down it.

Cleo and I play the staring game until she reaches for her phone once more. She toys with it for a beat before her slender fingers fly over it.

My blood thrums harder as I take my phone out and read her message.

"Stop this, Axel. Be a man. Come over here and talk to me."

My cheek twitches in an imitation of a smile. "You're not senile, I hope, so you wouldn't have forgotten that I don't rise to dares. Or taunts."

"Dammit. What do I have to do?"

Those six little words send all the blood fleeing from my heart. It turns harder than stone, and my vision blurs for several seconds. I cannot believe her gall. "You're eight years too late with that question, sweetheart."

Her head snaps up. She's breathing hard. She shakes her head. I'm not sure if it's denial, disbelief or a plea. It's probably none of those things. It wouldn't be the first time I've attributed a benign sentiment to her actions only to be shown the true depths of her traitorous heart.

My phone buzzes again. This time there's a single word on my screen.

"Axel."

A whispered caress. An entreaty. A demand.

It's a thousand other things. All wrapped in sugared poison. I push away from the counter, despising the knots in my stomach and the steel in my cock. I feel her gaze on my back as I stalk through the door next to the bar that leads to my office.

Shot after shot of adrenaline spikes through my bloodstream until dark, volatile sensation drenches me to my fingertips. My office door slams behind me, and I throw the bolt, as if locking myself in will prevent my growing insanity.

Already I want to tear the door off its hinges and rush back to the bar. I force my feet the other way and throw myself into my chair. High on the wall, the screens reflect the various areas of the club. My eyes zero in on her. I don't even fool myself into thinking that she's as defenseless as she looks. Her skin may look satin smooth, but it's coated with steel armor.

Deliberately, I shut off the feed to that camera and activate my phone. As I type, I silently urge her to accept my words.

"You're free to leave. Take me seriously and Do. Not. Come. Back."

As I power off my phone, the full extent of my weakness cannons through me. I don't want her to come back, and I don't want to hear her out for one reason alone.

She's here because of my father.

She's here on behalf of the man I hate more than anything else in the world. The man who made sure that, at nineteen, I would never have the option of redemption as long as I lived.

For a few years, I thought he would be satisfied with helping the devil stain my soul. But no. He's still after me. He's used his sentries in the form of my brothers, and now he's pulling out the big guns. I give him kudos for sending Cleo. With each visit, I've felt my edges crumbling away.

Despite everything I feel for her, I've tortured myself with the urge to give in. To hear that voice up close and personal. To smell her. Touch her.

Is her skin still the softest satin I've relived in my dreams?

Jesus.

I crave all of it even when I know it will be the last straw once she speaks the words she's been sent to deliver.

The Rutherfords and the McCarthys.

Once unlikely allies turned bitter enemies. Two dynastic families with feet firmly entrenched in underground crime. Drugs. Girls. Racketeering. Extortion.

Murder.

Between the two of us, we changed the course of our families' destinies. And I intend to change it even more. I intend to annihilate the Rutherford name until there's nothing left.

In a family of cold-hearted black sheep, I, Axel Rutherford, am the blackest. Abundantly despised by my three brothers, actively hated by my father.

She was the golden princess. Put on earth to test every single one of my hardened edges. And I happily burned away every last one for her.

But my reward wasn't forever with her.

Instead she turned away from me. And crawled into my father's bed.

Chapter Two

CRIME AND PUNISHMENT

The howls of hell's demons eventually stop once the club is empty of patrons. Stomach clenched, I turn on the monitors, zoom in on where she was. She's gone. The relief I should feel is painfully missing.

I stand, already punching in my assistant manager's number to let him know I'm leaving as I stride out of my office and out of XYNYC. In the city that never sleeps, the stale stench of humanity and rough sounds buffet me when I step out, but I welcome it as I walk the short distance to the underground parking garage where my black McLaren Spider waits.

Its throaty roar echoes the one prowling inside me so I slam my foot on the gas and revel in the squeal of tires when I skid onto the street.

Twenty minutes later, I park in another allotted spot beneath another building I own.

The Punishment Club started out as a sick private joke, a way to find a less hellish outlet during a period when time on my hands was an even more dangerous thing than the average death-wishing that was my constant reality.

In New York City, it didn't take long for it to become clear that there was an outlet for every problem. And very often, the more extreme the outlet the better.

When Black Widow, my now-manageress at the Punishment
Club, suggested we open the club for six months, tops, to alleviate
our boredom, it was done on a drunken shrug-fuck-it-why-not
basis. Six months turned to one year, then another. Now, the club is
bringing in nearly as much monthly income as XYNYC with almost
five hundred applicants creaming themselves to become members.

Unlike most underground clubs, there's nothing dungeon-like
about the Punishment Club. It soars into Hell's Kitchen's skyline
like the fat *fuck you* it is, right down to the giant red double doors
gracing the Victorian front entrance. Others cautioned a little discretion when it came to advertising the club's presence. I countered
with a *fuck no*, although I conceded to a less glamorous side entrance for the politicians and priests who didn't want their *shibari*-
while-wearing-baby-clothes addictions whispered about or publicly
witnessed.

I may be insane but I'm not stupid. Not when it comes to money
anyway. My acumen where money is concerned is what turned the
two-hundred-and-fifty thousand-dollar online gambling windfall
when I was nineteen into billions at age twenty-nine.

I enter the code in the wall panel, and the double doors spring
open. An elaborate, tiered chandelier lights the marble-floored
foyer. There are no whips or instruments of torture announcing the
true function of this place. In fact, as I walk down a short hallway and enter the main reception area of the club, the strains of
Evanescence-type music and the sound of clinking glasses would
fool anyone into thinking this is an ordinary club. To be fair, at this
time of the morning, most patrons are secreted away in their various rooms so the usual hints are well hidden.

Not so well hidden is the woman hanging right above my head
as I enter the heart of the ground-floor club area, completely naked
and bound with chains, her long red hair hanging free, and her
legs splayed open. Her eyes are fixed at a specific point on the ceiling, where a phallic-shaped bowl tilts hot, blood-red wax straight
between her legs. With each hit, she flinches, and tears spill freely
down her temples.

Although there are about two dozen members milling around, she's the only one receiving her punishment in plain sight. I sidestep the silver wax-collecting receptacle on the floor beneath her and make my way to the hostess's area.

The girl behind the desk looks up, her eyes widening a touch when she sees me. As I hand her my coat, I see her checking me out but she, unlike Cici, is careful not to engage me in conversation. She hands over the dark purple key card that will grant me admittance into the sanctum sanctorum six floors above.

"The Black Widow?" I ask. My voice is gruff, almost hoarse, but she hears me.

"On the third floor with a client," she responds, eyes of indeterminate color meeting mine for a second before she lowers her gaze. "She's almost done. Shall I let her know you're here?"

"Yes. Thank you."

"You're welcome." She nods and turns away. A waitress comes toward me with a tumbler of Scotch on a silver platter. I take it and knock it back then make my way to the private elevator. With a swipe of my card, the doors open.

Seconds later, I'm on the sixth floor. Black carpeting and expensively paneled walls muffle my footsteps as I head to the room at the end of the long hallway. On both sides, steel doors and soundproof walls seal away men and women giving in to their basest proclivities in the name of punishment. Some are as innocuous as a "teacher" forcing a "student" to read dense poetry. Others are...not.

The Black Widow is in charge of making sure we don't step outside the law or breach safety rules, but as owner of the establishment, I'm privy to all members' and potential members' punishment requests should I wish to see them. I've seen a few. Enough to know, were greed and money my priorities, my bank balance would be ten times fatter than it currently is since I've declined more members' applications than I've accepted.

Nothing much in this life makes my stomach turn. Not anymore. But even I know to leave some things alone.

Besides, with my years-long plan to bring down the Rutherford kingdom now approaching its crescendo, I don't need further distractions. Keeping people like Vardan Petrosyan on my side is more than enough work.

Standing in front of the cold steel door that is the entrance to my personal hell party, I hesitate. Would I be better off taking the safer route of getting hammered and sleeping it off?

No.

I'll only wake up in a worse state. A state where the temptation to slide behind the wheel of my McLaren Spider and hunt down my father may get too big to contain. It's happened before. I've stood over his bed and stared down at him. In the inky, soulless black of that night, homicide was as soft and seductive and deadly as a kiss. To this day, I have no recollection of how I walked away. What triggered me to step back? I don't want to know.

All I know is that the time to be back in that room isn't here yet. It's coming. But until then…

I reach out and touch the door. The cold from the steel seeps into my pores, chills enough to ground me in the present. With my left hand, I swipe the card again. I push the door open, take a breath, and step into the room.

"Lights."

Sensors heed my voice, and the room is bathed in soft light. I prowl forward into the windowless, drapeless room, my attention on the single piece of furniture in the space. Behind me, the door swings closed on a soft whispered click, sealing me into my prison. Three steps down and I'm in the dead center of the circular, sunken room.

Another few steps and I stand before it.

The chair is wide and low and squat, with four iron claws bolted into the floor. It could've afforded comfort if I'd allowed it. Instead it is stark, the cast iron back high and rigid enough to make my spine protest even before I've taken a seat. The broad metal armrests are also sturdy to accommodate the hours I intend to spend in the chair. Beside the front legs, two metal cuffs lie open, attached to titanium chains.

I stare dispassionately at them, wishing the sight of my bindings brought even a little bit of sunlight, a promise of redemption somewhere in my future. But even now, even in this place, all that echoes within me is…anticipation.

How can I yearn for the very punishment that should shame me? How can I—

My thoughts scatter as the door opens behind me. The click of heels pushes me into action. I toe off my shoes, followed by my socks. My shirt comes off next, then my belt. Wearing only my pants, I settle in the chair, my back to the icy embrace of the iron throne.

I feel her scrutiny long before I lift my gaze to her.

The Black Widow. Tall, willowy with jet-black hair that I suspect is cultivated for maximum effect, she's stunning the way an ice sculpture is stunning. Sharp green eyes peer at me from beneath long, mascaraed eyelashes. But tonight, her normal dark lipstick is absent, as is her all-black attire. Instead she's wearing a gray matron's uniform, complete with white cap, white apron and thick gray pumps.

I'm not aware that my curiosity filters through until she looks down at herself with a grimace.

"Senator Otis is downstairs. Tonight it's English-boarding-school-and-his-dinner-lady-serving-him-gruel night. I left him eating the slop and crying."

I nod, neither amused nor amazed. Her gaze slides over me before returning to mine. She knows better than to probe, but she's not afraid to stare.

Others might be foolish enough to believe it's softness they see in her eyes, but like me, nothing about her is soft.

We stare at each other in silence before I calmly lay my hands palm up on the armrests. Still in silence, she drops her gaze to the cuffs then back to me.

I nod.

With a graceful sway that hints at a deep sensuality I have no interest in exploring, she closes the distance to the chair and sinks down to pick up the first cuff. The click is loud, specifically designed

that way to add severity to the moment. My soul barely twitches.
The second cuffs secure me to the chair. I don't test their resilience.
I already know they won't free me until I desire it.

She stands back and stares down at me.

"How long? The usual two hours?"

"No. Longer."

"Four."

I shake my head, the sight of that *Please* on my phone screen
flashing across my mind. Taunting me.

"Five?" Her voice doesn't change, but there's something in there.
The tiniest hint of concern.

I stare at her. "Six."

"No—"

"Do as I say. Or I'll get someone else to do it."

I trust no one. But like I do with Quinn Blackwood, the Black
Widow and I share a special bond. Not one I would swear life or
death on by a long shot. But there's an…understanding. She's the
only one who's been allowed into my special room, the only one
who knows the ingredients of my sweet poison. The only one who's
seen what this room does to me. The longest I've been able to withstand is five hours.

Her concern is warranted.

I see her swallow before she reaches into her pocket. The small
remote is directly linked to the chains. She sets the time but hesitates before pressing the requisite button.

Boldly she steps up to me, and she slides her hands through the
hair at my nape. I jerk away but cannot escape her touch because of
the cuffs. She stops, staring down at me with narrowed eyes.

I'm on the edge. Hell, who the fuck am I kidding? I was born on
the edge. But tonight I'm a *whisper* away from annihilation and we
both know it.

"Are you sure about this?"

"Fuck no. Hell yes."

She opens her mouth.

"No," I preempt her.

"I don't have to stay here with you, but I can be outside."

"No. Press the button. Don't make me repeat myself."

"Axel..."

I close my eyes and shudder as my fists ball. I want to hear my name, but I don't want the voice to be the Black Widow's. There's only one voice I want to hear right now. One face I want to see. Cleo's.

"Do it and leave. Now."

"I will, but at least let me come back and check on you—"

"Say another word and I'll fire you."

Her eyes harden to ice chips. "Fuck you. Have your six hours if you want. But I'm coming back in three hours to check on you. Fire me then if you want."

With a defiant flick of her wrist, she sets the timer down between my feet, within touching distance.

The moment her back is turned, I kick the remote. It bounces against the last step and skids sideways halfway across the room. She hesitates, her back stiff, but she doesn't turn back around. In silence, she leaves.

The moment the door shuts, twenty projectors on the dark gray walls flicker to life. Large, small, and in-between, they take up every inch of the circular wall. If space allowed I would have had more screens put in, but I work with what I have.

Each one is set on a half-hour loop at full volume with a different video. With barely an inch between them, they could be one jumbled-up picture but I know each screen like I know the length of my cock.

I take a deep breath as the first reel plays on the middle screen. The chair moves, the wheels beneath the floor spinning it slowly around.

Fading sunlight dapples over a lake before the camera swings to the figure in the tiny white bikini fleeing a large wave.

The wave catches her, splashes up to mid-thigh. She shrieks. "*Omigod*, you're such a liar. The water is *colllllld*—What are you doing?"

"What does it look like?"

She approaches. Her hands come up to block the lens. "Stop filming me. I look fat."

A different hand reaches out to grasp hers, gently nudging hers aside. "You don't look fat, Cleo. You're perfect."

Feminine hands curl around a masculine one. Together they slowly lower until long-lashed, deep blue *knowing* eyes stare into the camera. "You're only saying that because you're in love with me." Sultry words whispered from between kiss-swollen lips.

"Yes, I'm saying that because I'm in love with you." Gruff, hopelessly young, newly broken voice, thick with seething emotion. "I'm also saying it because I have fucking eyes in my fucking head."

A naughty, goes-straight-to-an-eager-cock giggle. "You're so *bad* swearing all the time. Daddy says he'll paddle my behind if he catches me swearing."

A wobble of the camera before it steadies. "If he lays a fucking hand on you, I'll tear his fucking head off." A voice no longer gruff, hard with rigid purpose. Harsh breathing. "I mean it, Cleo. I see so much as a scratch on you, someone will fucking *die*."

A gasp. "You can't say things like that!"

"I can. I fucking am. Because you belong to me. I don't care who created you. You are mine. No one else is fucking allowed to touch you. No one is allowed to take you away from me, do you hear me?"

A bite of her lip as her nostrils flutter in a shaky inhale. "You're scaring me."

Deep, harsh breath. "Am I? Really? Tell the truth. Are you scared, Cleo?" Camera poised with intent, recording every flutter of her lashes.

A pause. A firming of plump lips. Then a shake of the head. Thick, vibrant locks frame her stunning face.

"Say it. I want to hear you say how it makes you feel when I say this to you."

"It...it excites me."

"That I claim you as mine?"

A shy nod.

"What else excites you?"

A flick of her gaze between the lens and the face behind it. "Come on. I can't say it on camera." She reaches out.

The camera angles away from her but remains on her. Focused. Rabid. "Tell me." The voice that will one day command hell itself.

"It excites me when you say that you'll do…all of that for me."

"All of what?"

"That you'll…tear his head off."

"I fucking will." A solemn promise. A brief pause. "You think I'm a sick psycho?"

"I think you're…you're…"

"What?"

"I think you're *effing* amazing."

"*Effing?*"

Pink color stains her cheeks. "Don't tease me."

"I won't if you say the word. The *actual* word, Cleo."

"I won't."

"Right. Then I'm not as amazing as you want me to think, am I?"

Blue eyes, opened wide. "You are."

"Then say it. You're not going to burn for it. It's just a word."

"I hate you when you're like this."

"You don't hate me, but fine. Don't say it."

The camera swings out to the lake, to the setting sun that's almost swallowed up by the orange water.

"You're *f-fucking* amazing. There. Are you happy?"

"Nope."

A crunch of footsteps in the sand before she steps boldly in front of the camera. "You're fu-fucking incredible and f-fucking amazing, Axel Rutherford."

"Am I?"

"Fuck, yes! Now will you stop being fucking mad at me?"

"I will if you stop saying *fuck*!"

An outraged yell before she lunges. The camera drops to the ground a second before grappling bodies swing into frame.

It shows a bear of a teenage boy in swimming trunks, his heart in his eyes, his arms slowly drawing her to him.

A voluptuous teenage girl who holds his world in her soft, deceptive hands.

She makes space for him between her young thighs and pushes his overgrown hair behind his ears.

"I can never be mad at you, Cleo. I fucking love you," he whispers.

She frames his face in her hands. "I love you, too. My Axel. My Romeo."

A long, endless kiss sealing his doom.

Another screen. Another camera, this one manned by Troy, his middle brother. Ronan stands next to their father, who's seated behind his massive cherrywood desk, elbows on armrests, fingers in a steeple. Despite being in his mid-fifties, Finnan Rutherford has little to no gray hair. He liked to brag that it was because he was planning to live forever and his body knew it.

Axel knew it was because his barber didn't just give him a trim once a month.

"You getting all this, boy?" Finnan barks.

"Yes, Pa," Troy responds. He pans around, stops at a chair occupied by none other than yours truly. The blood running down my nose is nothing compared to the pain shooting from my ribs.

One of the many brainless minders trained to follow Finnan's bidding looms above me, eyeing me with snakelike beady eyes.

"Good. Now, tell me again what has you in a snit, son?"

Bolton Rutherford, the comedian of the family, snorts from wherever he's watching this spectacle unfold. I don't know when Finnan decided it would be a fantastic idea to start documenting every event of his life. Considering he's eyeball deep in organized crime, it was one of his spectacularly stupid ideas. But here we are.

"I don't want to go to West Point," I gurgle, blood sliding from the corner of my mouth. The pain in my chest and throat is relentless, the hour-long beating having ruptured something I'm one hundred percent sure I don't want to know about.

"Why not?"

The camera is trained on me, ready to record my every word. I grit my teeth and remain silent.

"Because he's *in love*," Bolton jeers, then pisses himself laughing. My other brothers join in with various degrees of mirth. Troy religiously captures it all.

Including Finnan's nod to the minder.

The beating starts again.

At some point, I pass out, and I'm left slumped over on the floor, my blood pooling on the expensive Aubusson rug. The camera is set down but left running, whether by design or neglect, I'll never know. I suspect it's the former. Finnan Rutherford believes himself too clever to admit neglect. It records him eating lunch, making a few non-incriminating calls, even arranging to have flowers placed on Ma's grave.

But it's the next frame that makes me jerk in my seat, high in my present hell above Hell's Kitchen.

She walks in, dressed in white. An angel with tumbling hair. She barely spares me a glance as she heads straight to Finnan. They embrace.

"Did he agree?" she asks.

My father sneers in my direction. "Of course not. Heaven knows how an ass like that sprung from my loins."

Blue eyes I've looked into more times than I've drawn breath flick my way. Completely devoid of expression she regards me dispassionately before she dismisses me like the sack of shit I am. She sighs. "Leave it with me. I'll work on him."

He touches her … *caresses* her cheek. "You're a godsend, Cleo, my angel. I don't know what I'd do without you."

Her hands slide around his neck, and she presses the body I believed was mine against his. Even though their voices are muffled, I hear her clearly. "You will never have to find out. I promise."

The clanging sounds jerk my focus downward. The tendons on my arms stand out in my blind battle with the cuffs. The skin on either side of the tight metal braces is oozing blood, and my lungs burn with the need to break free and howl.

The words that will activate the fail-safe and summon the Black

Widow claw the back of my throat. I swallow them down. I'm nowhere near done reliving every one of Cleo's transgressions.

All the screens are lit up, each one playing a different recording of my spiral to sub-humanity.

But one screen remains dark. I'm not ready for that one last video. The faceless one that haunts me alongside hers and projects my suffering to another level. The one that makes me wish I were dead in one moment. Then glad I'm not in the next.

Dead means forgotten.

And I don't plan on forgetting anytime soon.

Chapter Three

GUNPOWDER AND LEAD

CLEO

For far longer than I care to remember, I've held the power of life and death in my hands. Between one breath and the next, the responsibility was thrust on me. A permanent state I have no hope of escaping. Not if I wish to keep the one remaining parent I have, my mother, on life-supporting machines rather than six feet under with my dead father. Machines that stay on or could be turned off in an instant, depending on which move I make in this deadly game of chess that is my life.

At twenty-six, I should be putting my actively pursued, proudly earned interior design degree to good use. Instead it's a front for my real vocation as Finnan Rutherford's companion. A career I didn't choose but find I'm now irreversibly immersed in.

I had to learn the game fast or risk losing my life through apathy. It's a good thing I'm a fast learner. I discovered that I'm an even better student with a loaded gun against my temple.

I've stood over too many graves and seen too many of the risks Finnan takes with others' lives not to have learned my lesson. So now I comply. I obey. I smile through the ravaging pain and the blood-red rage in my heart.

And I plot.

Revenge is the only thing that sustains me. It keeps me breathing, helps me place one foot in front of the other, and steers my compass true.

On the worst days, I wonder if everything I'm fighting for is even worth it. Those dark days I yearn to give in. But I can't. Not yet. Not if I don't want my mother's death and countless others' on my hands. Having finally accepted the responsibility of my birthright, I've also accepted responsibility for those in my care. I do this for the dozens who don't know that me staying on my knees is the only way they get to breathe.

Checking out would be cowardly. Although I haven't ruled it out completely as a last resort. For now, like the six prom dresses I tormented myself over choosing from what feels like a million years ago, I'm keeping my options open. The grim, otherworldly humor behind the sentiment almost makes me smile.

The oil-smooth door swings open behind me, wiping away every last trace of phantom humor. In the den where countless lives have hung in the balance, I fight the shiver that trembles up from my ankles.

In the half hour since my return from New York, he's kept me waiting in this room that reeks of violence and corruption. A deliberate act meant to establish my weakness and his power.

"You failed me again, my angel." The accusation is softly voiced in a deadly rasp.

I force my spine not to stiffen and take a breath. My gaze rests on the view of the immaculately kept Connecticut mansion grounds and encroaching dawn for an extra moment before I turn around.

Finnan Rutherford, the man everyone thinks is my adopted father but is as far from a father figure as the moon is from the stars, regards me from his impressive six-foot-plus height. Despite the early hour, he's fully dressed in a tailored white shirt and navy three-piece suit, his pinstriped Oxford tie neatly knotted. Not a hair out of place. Like his four sons, he's built of strong Irish stock with a square jaw, thick shoulders and smoky gray eyes always set with narrow-eyed focus. For the longest time, I was terrified of that stare, couldn't imagine that he didn't see into my soul and read the intentions in my heart. But I've learned to contain that emotion when in his presence, much like I contain all of my emotions these days.

I stride forward, slowly, and pause against his desk, my own gaze direct. "I warned you this plan would fail. You didn't listen. Don't blame me now that my predictions are coming true."

One dark eyebrow lifts. "Are you saying you weren't the right person to handle this? That I was wrong to think I could trust you to get it done?"

I swallow the kernel of terror that threatens to break free. I know better than to answer in the affirmative. "I'm saying I would've done things differently. Sending me to him almost every night for two weeks reeks of desperation," I say with a shrug, even though my heart is hammering. Finnan doesn't like his faults pointed out. But I'm done dancing around the issue. Or subjecting myself to another long night involved in a staring contest with Axel Rutherford.

Being forced to face Axel again after years of meticulous avoidance has been ten different kinds of hell. Doing it night after night from behind the mask of my rage has been crucifying. But the state of being that sustained me all these years did nothing to protect me from what seeing him again did to me.

What it continues to do to me. Even now, I can barely contain the trembling inside, the volatile electricity pulsing through me.

I wrestle down my emotions and watch Finnan cross the room to the drinks bar he had custom built two years ago. Like most of the prominent furnishings in the house, the initials *FR* are etched into the polished teak surface.

Finnan Rutherford is very much into branding. He placed his most intimate brand on me on my nineteenth birthday.

In silence, I watch him pour a shot of premium single malt Irish whiskey into a crystal tumbler. At this early hour, anyone would be forgiven for thinking he suffers from a drinking problem or that he's rattled by the outcome of another failed assignment. Or even that he slots his early morning drinking under the it's-always-five-o'clock-somewhere excuse.

But the shot is merely part of his morning routine, much like his twice-weekly kippers-and-boiled-eggs breakfast. Worse of all, Finnan does his most ruthless thinking fortified with that single shot of liquor.

He knocks back the drink, sets down the glass, and turns to face me. Eyes so much like Axel's, and yet infinitely different, drill into me as he approaches. There was a time when I made the game interesting for him by showing fear or retreating several steps backward to prevent contact. That time has passed.

I stand my ground, rigid and resolute.

His forefinger touches my cheekbone for a second, lingers, then traces downward to my jawline. I don't shudder. Or gasp. Or pull away. I don't lean into the caress to express false pleasure. Those are all wasted efforts, useless gestures I don't exert energy on. Every last reserve of my strength is saved for other things.

"You think I took the decision lightly to send you, my most prized possession, to *him*?"

Some women might enjoy being at the receiving end of such a blatant statement of ownership from one of the most feared men in the country. Others would perhaps protest, albeit diplomatically—unless they had zero self-preservation—at being labeled a possession. I don't react one way or the other because Finnan's words are the truth.

He owns me. In every way thinkable, save for a signed paper proclaiming me his chattel, I belong to him. Ever since I discovered the chilling and calculated way he dealt with my parents, I've accepted the futility of protest.

"No, I don't think you made the decision lightly. But it's clear it needs rethinking. Axel—" I stop, realizing that, although he features prominently in my thoughts—how could he not when he's the star player in my end game?—this is the first time I've said his name out loud in years. I'm not prepared for the onrush of memories that accompany uttering his name. I absorb the shock of it and take a frantic moment to regroup. "He dug his heels in the moment you sent Ronan."

Finnan drops his hand from my face and walks around to drop into the high-backed seat behind his desk. "Those two have been bickering like wet hens since they were in diapers," he says, his jaw tight.

A situation Finnan encouraged at every turn, steeped in the unfortunate thinking that pitting one son against the other would breed healthy competition. All it did was breed resentment.

Seated on his throne, he returns his attention to me. "Enlighten me then, my sweet. How would you have gone about bringing my errant boy to heel? Considering he was just as stubborn *before* I sent Ronan."

I wouldn't refer to him like he's a truant child acting out, for a start. I clench my gut as I recall the last look Axel gave me before he disappeared through the door behind the bar. "At this point, he's going to toy with whoever else you send after him."

"Whoever *else*? Are you taking yourself out of the running already?"

"I should never have been in the running." I can't prevent the angry bite in my tone from filtering through.

"If I didn't know better, I'd think you're questioning my judgment for the second time since I walked into the room. Are you, my petal?"

My sigh is as weary as the hand I massage my temple with. "I'm tired, Finnan. I haven't slept, and I've been forced to endure high decibels for hours. My head is pounding."

His head jerks up, and I almost see him scent the air. "Forced?"
Shit.

Anything other than his son's indifference will be seen as engagement. And there's nothing Finnan loves more than the getting under his last-born's skin. Even now, when every single day grows more precarious for the Rutherford empire, Finnan is most engrossed with discovering his son's weak spots.

In his eyes, exploiting Axel's weaknesses would be the quickest way to gain his attention and cooperation. It isn't a theory I disagree with, but with my own horse in this race, I prefer to keep any advantage I find to myself. Which is why I'm choosing not to tell him about the meeting I witnessed between Vardan Petrosyan and Axel.

"Ax—He kept me waiting all night. Then he threw me out."

Finnan's mouth twists. "That boy has always possessed the manners of a cockroach."

Not always.

There was a time when Axel would've paved a path of pure silk for me if I wished to walk barefoot across the world. A time when my every wish was his command.

Or at least that was what I believed.

That time seems like a distant, ethereal dream now, insane moments fashioned by witches and leprechauns for their hideous and *brief* amusement. A sketch they evidently grew tired of very quickly. Because why else would something so beautiful and rare have turned so ugly and savage so fast?

Was it even love? Wasn't love supposed to last forever?

I don't know. What I know is *hate* lasts a hell of a lot longer. Especially when it's fuelled as lovingly as I tend it.

Realizing memories are hell-bent on breaching my closely guarded vault, I straighten. As cute as my four-inch Jimmy Choos are to look at, they pinch something fierce after hours of constraint. I'm also in desperate need of a shower.

Most of all, I'm eager to get away so I can reaffirm my carefully laid-out plan. A plan that, for a single moment tonight, when my eyes met Axel's across that packed dance floor, I failed to prioritize.

That single moment of faltering drowns me in shame now as I wait to be dismissed from Finnan's den.

"Fine, go and rest. You'll try again tonight."

It takes every ounce of control to prevent my fists from clench-ing. "No."

"Excuse me?"

"I told you, it won't work. There's only one way you'll get his at-tention, and that is if you call him yourself."

His eyes turn arctic cold. "Are you sure you're ready for the kind of attention he'll receive from me if I have to track him down myself? Especially now I have confirmation that he's behind the Ar-menians' defection?"

My sharp inhalation gives me away.

Finnan gives me a small, cold smile. "What, you think I want him to come home just for a nice father-son chat?"

I shrug. "How would I know? You didn't tell me why you wanted the meeting."

"Because I know you're not as dumb as you want me to think."

I hold my breath and don't answer because I feel the icy fingers of his rage crawling over my skin.

Finnan leans forward in his chair, his jaw set. "I know he's in bed with that fucking weasel Petrosyan. I also know he's throwing money at the Albanians. What I've yet to fully grasp is whether he's idiotic enough to think he can get away with it or whether he's doing it to get my attention. Either way, what he's doing needs answering."

There's much more to it than that. For one thing, Finnan's recent troubles have had little to do with Eastern European drug lords, un-less they've started operating out of the Pentagon and the Capitol Building in Washington, DC. But I do know he's been trying to get back into the mob business, which he claimed to have walked away from years ago.

But I also know Finnan isn't one to let a slight stay unaddressed, no matter how small.

Vivid memories of the kind of violence he favors flash before my eyes. "I don't have feelings about him one way or the other except to say that my time is better spent elsewhere and not running another fool's errand."

I didn't intend to let the veiled insult slip. I can only blame my weariness. But my heart races as I wonder if I'll be taking my shower with one or two more bruises to add to the collection already on my body.

But Finnan remains seated. Calmly, he tugs open a drawer and picks up a remote.

My heart ejects itself into my throat. I haven't seen one of Finnan's videos in over six months. Of all his instruments of torture, this one is the most effective. It's probably the reason I've blocked it out, maybe even convinced myself he's grown bored of it.

But no. Evidently not.

He presses a button on his desk, and the panel on the opposite wall slides back to reveal a sixty-inch high-definition screen complete with surround sound for maximum viewing experience.

Fear rolls through me.

"Finnan, I didn't mean—"

"You seem to have forgotten what I'm fighting for. What we are *all* fighting for. I thought, since you're part of this family now, that you were on board with what needed to be done, but it's clear your motivation needs a tune-up. Watch the video, Cleopatra. I'm confident it'll help you gain some perspective."

I want to shut my eyes. Turn away. Cover my ears so nothing filters through. But of course, my gaze fixes on the screen.

The screen turns a mottled gray for a second before the frame settles. Against my better beliefs, words of prayer roll silently through my head.

Please, dear heaven, let it be me. Don't let it be someone I know. Don't. Let. It. Be. A. Child.

Recalling the one time it had been a child, I lose my bravado. My numb fingers grip the edge of the desk. "Please, Finnan."

"Watch." Ruthless. Barbaric. The single word is uttered with a relish that cuts through my useless prayers.

At the first sight of the teenager skating along a quiet suburban street, nausea punches upward.

Oh God.

Gary Gordon lives two streets over. He turns eighteen in two months and was just accepted into college on a football scholarship. I only know this because I managed to talk my ever-present bodyguards into letting me out of the house to go running last week when Finnan was out of town. Sheila Gordon was also on a run and wasted no time inviting herself to join me to brag about her son.

A son who, oblivious to the danger stalking close by, bobs his head to the music from his headphones as he rolls down the road.

The car speeds past him, turns the corner, and parks. Whoever is operating the camera—it can only be one of Finnan's men—reaches for a silver baseball bat lying on the passenger seat and exits.

"No." The word trembles from my lips. *Please, please, please.*

Gary rounds the corner and comes face-to-face with the camera-wielding thug. He stumbles off his skateboard then covers his embarrassment by flicking it up and catching it mid-air.

He pulls out one earbud as his gaze drops to the baseball bat. Apprehension crawls over his face a second before the video cuts.

Before my screaming senses can give in to the relief they crave, a close-up of a page with neatly typed words appears on the screen. The header is in all caps, the single word underlined.

<u>*EULOGY*</u>

I turn from the screen to the monster seated behind his desk, willing my legs to keep me upright. "You didn't have him killed. He's not dead." I have no basis for my assertion save for the need to *believe* it. The alternative is unthinkable.

"Pay attention," he says, his voice returned to its deadly softness.

Reluctantly, I refocus on the macabre words written for a child who could still be alive. After a few sick lines celebrating Gary's life, I force myself to return to the beginning. I notice the date set three weeks from now.

Relief punches through me, and my whole body trembles with it. "He's not..." I stop and swallow. "He's okay?"

"For the time being. He's joining his father and me for golf next week. I promised Bob I would teach Gary how to swing properly.

But I could just as easily be helping Bob arrange a double funeral for his wife and son if you don't get me what I want." He nods to the screen.

This time it's Sheila approaching the driver secretly filming her. The gun with the silencer is in his lap as he asks for directions, which she happily supplies. I detest the snooty, know-it-all house-wife, but the last thing I wish for is her death.

"Okay." My voice is as weak as my legs. I clear my throat before I say the words he wants to hear. "I'll give it one more try."

Finnan's smile is sinister personified. "I need you to do more than try, my dear. My son needs to be brought back into the fold sooner rather than later. Make it happen or Sheila and her son will only be the start of your worries."

I drag in a breath. "Okay, you win. I'll get you what you want."

With a flick of his wrist, the TV retreats into its panel. Finnan's features settle back into the twisted, deceptive affection.

"Before you think me unreasonable, I have another way to get you access to Axel." He slides a file across the desk. "That's a mem-bership to one of his clubs. Have to hand it to the boy, when he's not busy being a fucking pain in my ass, he has a half-decent brain. At least he did when he came up with the idea for this club." His gaze rests in the middle distance for a moment, a memory slowly hard-ening his face. "Shame he can't see that he owes it all to me."

I pick up the file. "Can I go now?"

He focuses on me. After a moment, he nods. "I'll let you exercise your discretion as to when you want to use that. But whatever you do, I want to hear from him by this time next week."

I stumble out of the den on weak legs. Shutting the door behind me, I gasp in a breath, the sound echoing in the long, silent hallway. My lungs burn, and my vision blurs. I'm crying. I lift hesitant fingers to my face, surprised.

Dear God, when was the last time I cried? The day I buried my father?

No. On that particular occasion, shock and horror were the paramount emotions. With my universe shifting relentlessly on its axis, there had been room for very little else. But I'd also harbored deep resentment against my father because I knew that, had he stayed put on his side of the mob divide in Boston, he would still be alive and my mother would be safe.

Michael McCarthy's greed was what brought us onto Finnan Rutherford's radar in the first place.

An upper-level Southie mafia jock from the roughest part of Boston, he rose in the ranks very soon after marrying my mother, the daughter of the head of the Boston Irish mob. The fact that my grandfather died shortly before that marriage happened isn't a fact I dwell on, even though I've heard the rumors that my father killed my grandfather to grab the throne and got my mother pregnant almost immediately to solidify his position. Except the empire he usurped was already on its last legs when he assumed the throne.

With the rise of Eastern European mafia outfits on the East Coast, not a lot of attention was paid to the once prominent, but now dying, Irish mob. My father made a few rash attempts to gain back that prominence, losing a few of his men through defection, a few more through old-fashioned shootouts, and a whole load of money and real estate in the process.

That was when he foolishly decided to look beyond his immediate borders and chose to make clandestine moves in Finnan Rutherford's New Jersey and Connecticut territories.

As Finnan took pleasure in informing me years later, he'd let my father encroach, slowly drawing him into his trap. Predictably, my father grew bolder, greedier, not realizing he was dealing with a much more cunning, even greedier opponent.

Ultimately, Michael McCarthy paid for his miscalculation with his life. My mother barely escaped with hers. That life still hangs in the balance depending on whether I toe Finnan's line or not.

Which leaves little room for stupid tears now. I swipe my hand over my cheeks and lurch away from the door. The sweeping staircase leading up to my room on the third floor feels like it's a million miles away. Halfway there, I stop and kick off my shoes. Scooping them up, I run the rest of the way. Attempting to flee my demons will only make them laugh louder, but I don't care.

In the false sanctuary of my room, I slam and lock the door, a useless action since I'll have no choice but to open it again should Finnan demand entry. I drop my shoes and the file on the floor. My dress and underwear come off next, and I stumble into the bathroom naked.

The scalding water pounds me for fifteen minutes before my trembling ceases. With a vicious twist, I yank the tap to cold and will clarity back into my mind.

Tears won't save me or any other person on Finnan's sadistic radar. For now, all I can do is find a way to give him what he wants.

Axel.

The full-body shudder that runs through me has nothing to do with the cold water. It's a physical manifestation of the raw hate that burns in my soul for the youngest Rutherford son.

I don't delude myself into thinking hate is the only emotion I feel for Axel. From the moment I set eyes on him, my sensation cauldron was set to overflow. Even at age nine, I knew that the boy with intense, unnerving gray eyes, staring at me from across the Thanksgiving banquet table in my parents' house, held my very existence in his twelve-year-old hands.

That boy grew into a man I was prepared to lay down my life for.

The man whose name I happily etched on my skin in a twisted fit of rebellion and ecstasy, never once guessing he was merely playing a role in my life. That the black sheep Rutherford was staging a sick, brutally evil game that was destined to end one way. With my father dead, my mother on life support, and my soul in tatters.

He succeeded. Then he walked away, leaving me at the mercy of those who were too eager to finish me off.

But they forget I'm forged from the same Irish steel Finnan Rutherford loves to boast about.

I step out of the shower and dry myself. In the wide vanity mirror, my gaze drops to the red patch of skin just above my right hipbone where his name once resided. Against my will, my fingers trace the four-inch arch, a tiny part of me wishing I could laser away my feelings for him as easily as I erased his name from my body.

But no. What was taken away from me needs to be repaid a thousandfold.

So first I will take care of Finnan. Then I will take care of Axel.

The man whose death is the only thing I live for.

Chapter Four

MAJOR SALVO

AXEL

Running an empire that operates on a nocturnal cycle means most of my mornings are spent sleeping or coming down from whatever ill-advised activity I indulged in the night before.

Yet I'm wide awake at ten a.m. The six hours spent in the punishment chair two days ago did nothing to take the edge off the raw insanity pounding through my bloodstream. Like every morning for the past two weeks, I prowl my penthouse apartment, sleep the furthest thing from my mind.

Not that I need a lot of sleep to function. My stint in the special branch of the army cured me of the need for several comforts I previously took for granted, while it equipped me with a whole new set of stomach-turning skills. Skills I was primed to excel at, according to my commanding officer, having seemingly acquired the basic building blocks of rendering mayhem at birth.

I switch off *those* memories and turn away from the Upper East Side view of a heat-hazed New York. Heading down the hall, I enter the room I converted to a private gym when I moved in. I ignore the gleaming dumbbells and head for the punching bag in the middle of the room. For the next hour, I pound the shit out of it, until sweat streams down my body. But my mind still churns.

My growl of frustration bounces around the room as I stand there, breaths heaving out of me. Tugging off the boxing gloves, I toss them across the room and press the heels of my hands against my eyes.

Immediately her image springs into my mind.

Cleo. With him.

Cleo. With me.

Please, Axel.

The clarity of her voice in my head makes my jaw clench. A different image slides into frame. Cleo, on her knees, saying those two words. Cleo, her stunning face captured in a mixture of innocence and arousal. The innocence is mockingly deceptive; I know that now, but my starved cock is on a mission and doesn't appreciate the rationalization.

Dropping my hands, I leave the room, shedding my sweatpants as I go. Even before I hit the shower, I'm fully erect. Cold water slams my face and neck as scalding water hits my back. I brace my hands on the wall and give in to a dark chuckle. Hell, even my preprogrammed shower function is as torn as my mind and body. Grimly, I reach for the shower gel, hating myself for thinking about her. But I can't stop.

Please, Axel.

My hands slow over my body, and my eyes drift shut at the image of small, greedy hands trailing up my bare thighs. My breath catches in eager anticipation. Her dusky-rose, sinful mouth begins to curve, the knowledge that she has me trapped, at her mercy, gleaming in her eyes. Insatiable for her, I drink in her expression even as I fall deeper under her spell.

She wraps one hand around me, the other tentatively reaching for my balls. The ingenuous move makes me even harder. Knowing that I was her first, as she was mine, is like no other feeling on earth. Her sharp inhalation at my hardness almost makes me smile, but my balls in her exploring touch wipe away any amusement. She literally has me in the palms of her hands, hers to do with as she pleases. I rock forward, sliding into her loose grip. Her fingers tighten reflexively, dragging a groan from my throat. Blue eyes darken as further knowledge dawns. Applying more pressure, she pumps me once. Twice. My full-body shudder makes her eyes widen.

"Omigod. That's so hot. Show me more, Axel," she breathes, her gaze darting between my cock and my face.

The eagerness in her voice almost makes me blow my load there and then. Clenching my jaw, I fight to stay in control. "Just keep doing that for now, baby."

"You like it?" A question filled with a little wonder and burgeoning power.

A harsh snort rips free. "You have to ask? Can't you tell?"

A sultry little laugh clenches my body with helpless need. "I want to make sure I'm doing it right. You stopped me the last time…"

Only because I wanted inside her tight, little pussy more than I wanted a hand job. "I'm not stopping you now," I say, my throat tight with biting hunger.

Her gaze returns to her task, her mouth dropping open as the veins around my cock thicken in her hand. Every desperate forward thrust brings me within inches of her delectable mouth. A frown of concentration darts across her forehead as her tongue slicks her lower lip. She leans forward, and the involuntary, ravenous little breath she takes pushes me closer to the edge. Fuck, I want those lips around me. I want to pull her up, turn her around, and slap her pert, little ass for torturing me like this. I want to rip off that thong she's wearing beneath my T-shirt and lose myself in the sweet heaven of her pussy.

Hell, I want so many things with her that it's all a crazy jumble in my head. But I stay put. Because this, too, is paradise on earth. Her thumb slides over my sensitive head. The single convulsion that jerks through me bumps my cock against her parted lips. We both freeze.

Wide eyes sweep up to meet mine. Her breaths emerge as shaky and hot as I feel. Slowly, she moves closer. Tastes me. The touch is gone almost before it happens, but the trace of pre-cum on her lips sends my temperature soaring higher.

Determination mingles with inexperience on her face as she continues to caress me. "I want to suck it. Please, Axel. Let me?"

Jesus. "Yes," I groan, dangerously close to the edge.

The bracing breath she takes pushes her plump breasts and tight nipples against the white T-shirt. Unable to help myself, I reach down and brush my knuckles back and forth over one rigid peak. Heat flares up her face, and she squirms deliciously before she closes her mouth over me in a bold move.

The sight of her pink lips enclosing the tip of my cock shoots sensation straight to my balls. A second later, her firm suction has me gripping her hair, holding her in place. Desperate for more. "Fuck, yes, just like that. Christ, don't stop."

My head drops as I fight to breathe. Her gaze is pinned on mine, absorbing my every reaction as she quickly acclimatizes to giving her first blowjob. Ever the quick learner, Cleo flicks her tongue over my slit as she sucks, her mouth closing more firmly on me, taking more of my cock.

"Shit, why did I think you wouldn't be a fucking natural at this?"

She smiles that Delilah smile as, empowered, she works me like an aficionado. Slow, smooth strokes grow longer, faster. Her mouth is almost as tight as her pussy as she takes me deeper, gliding her wicked tongue along my stiff length. Delirium beckons, and my fist tightens in her hair as I plunge into her mouth.

My cock hits the back of her throat, caressing the soft membranes that vibrate pure electricity against my sensitive head. Insanity encroaches. My legs begin to shake. I feel my balls tighten, and I know I'm about to blow.

"Cleo."

"Hmm…" She releases me long enough to lick me from root to tip before she swallows me again.

Pleasure drowns me. "God, Cleo…"

My groan is deeper than it should be. The tone of a man, not the boy standing in the middle of his childhood bedroom, receiving his first blowjob from the girl he loves.

My eyes fly open. Memory fades, and reality intrudes. I'm alone with my cock gripped tight in my hand. The slide of the gel aids my desperate, helpless pumps, but even with my eyes open, I see her face, feel her mouth around me, sucking harder with every plunge.

I'm at the point of no return, caught in the spiral of arousal I can't stop even if I want to. I stab at the cold shower button, turning it off and leaving only heat. Steam rises around me, shrouding me in my own erotic hell as I continue to stroke myself. Longer. Harder. Faster. Pre-ejaculate mingles with the gel, making me slicker, reminding me of the deep recesses of her mouth. I slam an open palm against the wall, the knowledge that she can draw such a visceral reaction from me pissing me off. But no amount of anger is enough to stop the motions of my hand or the dirty bliss that beckons.

Weeks of no sex have me on the tightest edge as I fuck my hand with all the finesse of a teenager. I grit my teeth harder but I can't stop the rough groans that rip through me as my balls turn hard as stone seconds before I erupt. My head drops against the tiles as thick cum shoots from my cock and splatters on the wall. The force of the climax draws further shudders through my body.

Unceasing, I keep up the strokes. Lost in euphoria, I'm not sure how long I stay propped against the wall, caught between the past and the present, hating myself, and hating her even more. Slowly, my spent erection dies, and a semblance of control returns.

By the time I turn off the shower and leave the bathroom, my thoughts are less chaotic than they've been for a while. Using Cleo for my unwilling self-pleasuring is a stupid fantasy, but what the hell, I'm no fucking saint. I'll take that for now.

After dressing, I head to the living room to pour myself a drink. The sound of my buzzer interrupts my mellow self-loathing. I freeze, gritting my teeth while toying with not answering. The buzzer sounds again. I slide my untouched glass of Patrón onto the coffee table and head for the intercom.

"Yes?" I snap.

"Sir, there's a Miss Widow here to see you."

If I were in the mood, I would smile at the game the Black Widow plays with my concierge by supplying him with a different name on each, albeit rare, visit. As it is, she's at risk of pissing me off, first with her clear reluctance to follow my orders in the punishment room and now turning up here unannounced.

"Send her up." The quicker I deal with her, the sooner I can knuckle down the exact details of how I will deal with Finnan and Cleo.

My already fucked-up sleep pattern notwithstanding, they both need to be dealt with. Quickly and decisively. Especially if my brand of self-prescribed therapy has truly stopped working.

I shove my hands into the pockets of my sweatpants as I head for the door. My black T-shirt doesn't cover nearly enough of the ink on my arms but the thought of anyone seeing them doesn't disturb me enough to waste time covering myself up. Besides, another reason the Black Widow and I work well together is she knows not to ask questions. Or at least she did before the other night.

For a moment, I contemplate whether it's wise to invite her up here. Despite my satisfactory hand job, my senses are still churning. With sleep out of the question, I crave the next easily attainable distraction.

Long, hard fucking.

The elevator pings its arrival as I toy with adding my manageress to my fuck list.

She steps out, her walk brisk and confident, unlike the practiced sexy swagger she reserves for the patrons of the Punishment Club. She's back in her usual all-black attire although she's dressed for the day rather than in her night leathers, and her hair is caught in a ponytail.

I observe her critically, note the firm, supple body beneath the black jeans and silk top. Her waist is trim, her hips and breasts eye-catching enough to tempt any red-blooded male. And yet my cock remains unmoved, my libido still firmly in the grip of a foolish fantasy.

Not sure whether to be concerned or irritated by the distinct lack of interest, I return my gaze to her face. "You better have a damned good reason for interrupting my sleep."

"Call me psychic but I had the distinct feeling you weren't asleep," she replies, her voice droll as she walks past me and enters the living room.

My irritation mounts as I kick the door shut. "Next time, rely less on nonexistent psychic powers and more on your phone. I don't pay you to waste my time."

A trace of emotion darts across her features briefly before she shrugs. "I was in the area and took a wild gamble. Since you're up, I thought we could get some work out of the way." She reaches into her slim-line briefcase and extracts a black file. "We have a new set of applications ready for approval including a couple of expedited ones. I wanted to go through them with you."

"They couldn't wait until tonight?"

"Sure, but why wait? You're up so I thought I'd make hay while the sun shone."

"A curiously bright outlook for someone who works best at night. Alone. Without the likes of your boss disturbing you. Weren't those your exact words to me a couple of weeks ago?"

She grimaces. "Damn you and your sharp memory. Okay. Whatever. So I came to check on you—"

"It's not your place to check up on me," I say impatiently. Her presence stirs another pulse of anger inside me at the further evidence of my inability to control Cleo's effect on my life.

Her lips purse. "It is when you entrust me with your care at the club and I fail you."

My teeth clench. "You didn't fail me."

Her gaze drops to my wrist. "Didn't I?" she says softly.

Her tone rubs me almost as raw as the deep chafing on my wrists. "This is none of your business, B. Don't forget that the reason we work well together is because we respect each other's privacy." It's the reason I call her B, short for Black. I have no idea what her real name is, and I have zero interest in finding out.

"I think I've earned the right to be concerned about you, Axel."

"Take it from me that that's a stupid move."

I admire her for not showing a single iota of emotion at my response. She stares at me for several seconds before she turns to admire the view. "I'll leave after you let me dress your wounds," she says eventually, her voice hard and implacable. "While I'm getting your first aid kit, you can make me a coffee and we'll discuss the applications."

"Leave the files—"

"No." Her tight-lipped smile most likely hints at affront. I don't have the capacity to decipher it. "You can find someone else to take care of you at the club if you wish. Until you do, I owe you a duty of care. That might mean fuck all to you but I take my responsibility seriously. And I take my coffee black. Thanks."

Throwing her out will be easier than blinking. But one of the reasons I placed her in charge of one of my most lucrative businesses was the ruthless warrior's instinct I sensed in her. Also her soul is deeply tainted. If I believed in having kindred spirits, I would claim her as one.

It's that respect that makes me turn toward the kitchen after I point her in the direction of the bathroom. The coffee is already brewed. I pour two mugs and bring them back to the living room as she returns with the kit.

Wordlessly, she sets up the antiseptic, and nods at me. Exhaling, I extend one wrist for her to tend.

"Now the other one," she says.

My right wrist is in worse shape, an inch-wide layer of exposed flesh covered in dried blood.

"Jesus, Axel," she murmurs under her breath.

"Save it." My tone is cold, the memory of when and why that particular injury occurred playing afresh in my mind. I was mildly surprised my wrist didn't break with the pressure I placed on it once that video started replaying for the fourth time.

The video of Finnan fucking Cleo was his present to me in my second year at West Point, two days after I informed my instructor that I wished to leave the program. After Finnan was informed of my decision, he ensured that any hopes I had of reclaiming what was mine were reduced to ashes. I stayed. I excelled. I became one of the US Army's most lethal weapons.

Then I used my skills the best way I knew how—to extract every last secret that Finnan Rutherford possessed so I could dismantle his kingdom.

The Armenians and Albanians were relatively easy to convince to switch sides. Money buys them their number one objective—power—and I have enough of it to make it worth their while. It's the reason Finnan's coming after me now. The parts of me that didn't wither and die in the far-flung places of hell where I dished out death and destruction in the name of my country welcome the deeply personal war headed my way. Another part of me is already mourning just how quickly it will all be over.

B's mouth purses as she dabs the cotton swab over my wound. "So, the applications. Unless you have an objection, I'm going to refuse the pilot who claims he wants to spank only women who look like his mother. Something doesn't quite jive with me about him."

I force my mind away from blood and gore and retribution to the present. "Fine."

Her gentle touch continues to soothe my ravaged skin. "And that prosecutor who wants six black cats eating sushi off his naked body? Yeah, that doesn't work for me. I'm not into bestiality," she states dryly, her mouth twitching in a ghost of a smile.

"Sure."

She nods and carries on listing the pros and cons of applicants without referring to the file, a testament to how good she is at her job. All I want is for her to be done.

"Okay, great. Two more came in this morning. I recommend we approve both of them. One is a girl who wants a replica of her boyfriend's old bedroom—"

"Enough." Taking the gauze from her hands, I throw it back into the kit and rise. "You've done what you came to do. It's time for you to leave."

"Axel…"

I shake my head, my patience at an end. "I meant what I said earlier. You're good at what you do, which is why you're in charge, but you're still expendable."

She takes a deep breath, stands, and gathers up the file. "Got it. But even at the risk of getting myself fired, I have to say this. I know a thing or two about paying penance. You spent six hours in the chair. And yet you're still wound up as tight as a fucking drum."

The reminder amps up my cold rage. "Watch it, B. You're two blinks away from becoming the sacrificial lamb in a chaos-fest you didn't ask for. Walk away. Now."

She tries to stare me down. "I hear you, although you should be warned that the last thing I am in any scenario is a *lamb*. All I'm going to add is this. Something isn't working for you. Find a way to take care of it. Before it eats you alive."

* * *

I tell myself that those parting words *aren't* the reason I'm standing against the wall that guards Finnan Rutherford's Greenwich, Connecticut, mansion at midnight when I should be at XYNYC. The outer perimeter alarm was ridiculously easy to disarm. In the darkness, I pet the pair of Doberman pinschers trained to tear intruders apart but that are instead licking my hand, and I stare at the towering colonial mansion. A fuck-off house to end all fuck-off houses, built to impress those easily fooled by loud and shiny objects.

I never called it home because it was never my home. It was a place of depravity, of misery and humiliation. A demeaning arena where brother was pitted against brother and blood was forced on unsuspecting hands.

I could end it all tonight. Walk into his den or bedroom in the east wing and wipe the man who sired me from the face of the earth.

But taking a life, no matter how necessary or secretly relished the act, is a burden that would drag my damned soul deeper into hell. I accepted that burden a long time ago but I'm not ready to make my move yet.

Not when the game is getting interesting.

Is that just an excuse?

Perhaps I want to make him suffer a little more? It could be this is the only thing that anchors me to this world. I haven't decided yet one way or the other. So I turn my attention to the south wing, where *she* sleeps.

Cleo.

Her name explodes in my mind like the deadliest IED. Beneath my hand, a dog whimpers, sensing my altered mood. I soften my caress and take a breath.

I linger for another ten minutes before making my move. And it's not back where my Spider is parked two streets over. The dogs accompany me, along with the devil that's been riding me for two long fucking weeks, as I head for the house.

The pool house where my false bliss started and ended is shrouded behind box-cut mulberry hedges to my far left. I don't spare it a glance. My focus is fixed on the kitchen doors located beneath the south wing terrace. To my knowledge, Finnan has never used that particular room in his house, believing it to be a woman's domain. It's the easiest point of ingress, the half a dozen or so bodyguards tasked to protect the property currently playing cards in the carriage house above the five-car garage, past one garden and a tennis court over to my right. With the abundance of cameras, guns and four-legged guard dogs surrounding them, they've grown soft.

I let myself inside and stop. I tell myself I'm acclimatizing to my surroundings, but despite the clinical purpose to my visit, I can't stop the influx of familiar scents that hit me. Tulips and orchids from the flower room adjoining the kitchen where Ma spent hours cutting and arranging flowers and prepping bulbs. I'm surprised the smell still lingers considering she's been gone for nine years. The scent of polished leather from the mudroom next to the flower room. Kippers and cured ham from the butler's pantry. The remnants of carbonara sauce. Bolton's favorite.

My favorite.

Jaw clenched, I shrug off the memories.

"Sit," I murmur to the dogs. They sag onto the checkered tile, heads on front paws, eyes on me as I cross the room. Quick, silent strides take me to the north hall. I stop and listen for signs of life. Nothing. I head for the security panel set into the wall. The screen shows empty galleries on all three floors.

I'm neither excited nor agitated as I climb the stairs to the second floor. Even the idea of discovery doesn't escalate my heartbeat as I make my way to the master suite.

Confronted with the huge double doors that once symbolized fear and oppression to me, I slow my steps, savor the moment. Reaching into my pocket I take out the pouch and the two items I need.

Wealth grants me access to gluttony and excess. Occasionally, it also grants me access to unsanctioned gadgets available only on the dark web, like the small tool in my hand that gives me a clear image of what lies behind the doors.

I pick up the outline easily.

One body. Not two. She's not with him.

The breath I didn't realize I held punches out of me, and I take a moment to ground myself.

He is prone and warm, and the steady beat of his heart is a bright outline on the screen attached to the gadget. It's almost nauseatingly heady, the power I hold in my hand right now. Even if I lose my own life pursuing this, this moment alone will make it worth it.

But I don't intend to die today. So I let myself in on silent feet, the doors he didn't bother to lock opening soundlessly. In the near darkness, I pick out the leopard-skin rug laid before the yawning stone fireplace and the moose heads mounted on either side of the giant scroll-edged mirror above it.

Reflection from a security light outside penetrates the partially shut drapes and casts shadowed outlines in the room.

I move forward until I'm standing over him.

My father.

The last old-school mob boss standing after an unscrupulous eradication campaign that saw his opponents fall one by one. But power and prestige weren't enough for Finnan Rutherford. Like all greedy men, the old dog always wanted more, whether *more* was available for the taking or not.

Unfortunately for him, he took it a step too far, and by drawing me into his thirst for power, he's unwittingly handed me the tools to destroy him.

I flip the gadget to camera mode, and I record for exactly ten seconds. Any longer in this room and I risk being overwhelmed by memories I can't adequately contain.

Even now, as I back away from the bed, the knife tucked into my sock burns against my skin. I ignore the sensation and set the camera down on top of the mantel where it'll be in his direct eyeline. I retreat as silently as I came. I should leave, but my feet take me up another flight of stairs to the opposite end of the house.

I shouldn't go in. I shouldn't. But my fingers find Cleo's door anyway. The cool wood does nothing to calm me.

Hell, it does the opposite. As I stand there like a motherfucking idiot, the useless organ in my chest dares to shake off its impending demise and flog itself back to life. Right along with my traitorous cock that twitches back to life. Before I can talk myself out of it, my hand reaches for the doorknob.

I turn it and push. Nothing happens.

Relief that she's barred to me, and therefore to him, quickly turns to disappointment. Both emotions fall away, and I'm left with the bitter taste of prey denied. Like the knife in my boot, the tools I used to break in burn a hole in my back pocket as I stand there, my hand on the door.

The effort it takes to pry my fingers off resonates like a long-forgotten pain inside me.

Almost on automatic, I reach for my tools. One minute later, I'm inside. Her perfume hits me first. Light and alluring, just like the one she used to wear. My breath stills when she sits up suddenly, her eyes searching the room. They zero in on me, and I smell her fear.

I deliberately step into the pool of soft light left by the illuminated vanity mirror in her bathroom. She sees me, and her eyes go wider. More shock, less fear. A little part of me breathes easier while the other part continues to question what the fuck I'm doing. Her gaze darts to the door, and mine narrows.

Before she can think about making a sound, I step toward the bed. "How this goes depends entirely on whether you do something stupid or not, sweetheart. So think carefully."

Her gaze returns to me, her hands gripping the bedcover. "What do you want?" she asks.

The sweetly sexy voice I knew as a teenager has grown huskier, draped with a wealth of womanly knowledge. It whispers over me, and I clench my gut at the effect as I move closer. "What do I want? Since you people seem to have no qualms about invading my life, I thought I'd return the favor."

"By breaking and entering?"

I allow myself a little smile. "That's what you're worried about? Not why I'm in your room? Not that I could be wondering what you're wearing underneath those covers besides that flimsy piece of silk?"

Her fingers tighten on the cover, but a second later, her chin lifts a fraction, exposing more of her sleek throat. "What makes you think I'm worried? There are guards outside."

"All of whom were too busy playing cards and watching porn to hear me when I waltzed in fifteen minutes ago. I guess standards around here aren't what they once were."

Something shifts on her face, a hard look she tries to hide as her eyelids descend. When I move to close the bathroom door, her gaze flies back to me. I sense her renewed agitation. "Still afraid of the dark, sweetheart?"

"No," she replies, but her voice echoes with the tiniest tremble.

The sick bastard in me revels in the sound. Perhaps I want a little payback for the weakness I succumbed to in my shower. Or perhaps I like finding her behind a locked door, the possible result of trouble in paradise owing to my machinations. Either way, that little notch of gratification intensifies as I walk toward her. Beams of light slant in through the open curtains, bathing the room and her body in moonlight.

The sheets rustle as she attempts to scramble away from me. "Stop. Stay the fuck still. If you make me come after you, you'll regret it."

She stops. I prowl closer, prop one knee on the bed, and slowly tug off my leather gloves. She watches my every move.

"What...what are you doing?" Again I hear the shakiness in her voice. The sound transmits straight to my groin, and my cock hardens.

I tuck the gloves into my back pocket and crawl onto the bed. Bunching one fist into the sheet, I yank it off her.

The thin material of the silk or satin or whatever the fuck she's wearing glimmers as she attempts to move away again. I crouch over her, planting my hands on either side of her shoulders.

"What the fuck did I say?" I mutter. My voice is low, harsh and rough, probably owing to the effect of the long, smooth legs rubbing together in the anxiety she's fighting. Probably owing to the fact that I've lost my goddamn mind. But the vulnerability she's trying to hide is turning me on more than I anticipated. And I'm in no mood to stop. "Take that nightgown off," I growl.

She stops moving, but the eyes that find mine in the dark spark with pure defiance. "No."

I smile. "Okay." I push back and rest my knees on either side of her hips. Then I reach for the neckline of her flimsy gown and rip it apart.

Her gasp echoes around the room before wrapping itself tight around my cock. Her hands fly up to cover herself.

"Stop." My command is deadlier than before.

Her face tells me she's thinking about disobeying, but slowly her hands return to her sides. Her submission makes me harder as my gaze travels over her supple body. Lush breasts, heavier than I remember, flat smooth stomach, the faintest shadow of a bush behind the covering of her panties.

I take all of that in, twice, my cock throbbing behind the prison of my fly. I want to grip myself, ease the ache, but I don't.

After a full minute of withstanding my scrutiny, she begins to squirm. "I...I don't know what you think you're doing but I'm not going to let you—"

"I'm not going to rape you. Hell, I don't even want to fuck you." *Fucking liar.*

Puzzlement drifts over her face. "Then what—?"

"Have you been fucked tonight?" My voice is rougher. Harsher.

She inhales sharply, and then her hair slides on the pillow as she shakes her head. Hers is the only scent I smell in the room. But she could've changed the sheets. Showered.

"Were you fucked last night?" I press.

Again, a negative answer. A third question hovers on my tongue. *When was the last time he fucked you?* "Why should I believe you?" I ask instead.

"What makes you think I care whether you do or not?" she throws back.

I look down her body then back up. "You think this is a good time to test me?"

She fidgets. The movement draws my gaze to her full, luscious breasts, and my breath truncates.

"You're not going to rape me, and you don't want to fuck me so I'm assuming you just want to humiliate me with a Peeping Tom moment before you go on your way."

"Is the thought of humiliation the reason your nipples are hard, sweetheart?" I mock, ignoring the saliva that fills my mouth at the sight of the tight peaks.

"I'm cold," she responds cuttingly.

"Sure you are." The room is ambient, the air-conditioning on a low setting. "I guess that's also the reason you're breathing faster?"

She squirms a little more, her legs twitching beneath me. "Is there a time scale on this creepy interrogation?"

"Your beauty sleep can wait a little longer," I murmur, my mind tripping over everything I shouldn't do. Everything I want to do. I move lower on the bed, past her tightly held-together knees. The view is even more spectacular. "Take off your panties."

Her breath shudders out. She doesn't move.

"You want me to help you?" I'd rather not. I don't trust myself to touch her. Ripping the nightgown off her was enough.

"I want you to leave me alone," she says, a little more breathlessly.

A trail of fire lights my blood. "I asked to be left alone too, re-member? But nobody seems inclined to listen. Why should I listen to you?"

She swallows, perhaps realizing, for the first time, the depth of my cold fury. "You want me to beg?"

"I want you to take the panties off. I prefer not to ask again."

Her torso trembles as she takes another breath. Then, excruciat-ingly slowly, her thumbs hook into the sides of her panties. A bolt of lightning shoots through me as I track the material sliding down her hips, exposing her pussy to my gaze. The sight of the trimmed bush makes me bite the inside of my cheek, killing the unwanted groan that threatens to erupt.

I'm angry that she's even more beautiful than I imagined, that her perfect body now belongs to my father. Her panties tangle at her knees, and I resist the urge to rip them the fuck off her. "Hurry it up, baby. I don't have all fucking night."

She raises her legs and shoves the panties off. They drop to her ankles. I hook my fingers through them and toss the scrap of lace over my shoulder. We go back to staring at each other. A shiver courses through her, her breath held as she awaits what comes next.

"Open your legs."

Her mouth parts on a gasp. "Ax—"

"Don't fucking say my name. Open your legs."

Her legs slowly part. In the moonlight, the folds of her pussy gape to my gaze—the perfect hood of her clit, the teardrop shape of her labia, the tiny hole of her cunt. The *damp*, tiny hole of her cunt.

I tell myself, had I not seen that dampness, had I not smelled her arousal a second later, I would've ended this fucked-up madness and left. But I see it. I *smell* it. The succulent scent powers from my nostrils to my groin, and I feel a touch of fluid stain the head of my cock.

My fists ball on my thighs. "Touch yourself," I instruct roughly.

Her whole body trembles. "Wh-what?"

"You want me to leave? Touch. Your. Pussy." I grit out the words, the red haze washing over my eyes convincing me I'm on the edge of my control.

She starts to shake her head. Her eyes meet mine, and she stills. Her right hand twitches for a second before it slides over her hip toward her mound. Long, manicured fingers drift through her silky bush, and her breath catches as she hesitates.

"Do it." I barely recognize my own voice, a savage hunger pounding through me.

Her middle finger grazes her clit, and she jerks, biting her lower lip to stop herself from making a sound. But I want her sounds. I want her exposed in every way.

"I know this is turning you on. I can smell you. Don't fucking fight it. Stroke yourself harder."

Her fingers glide downward, forming a V on either side of her pussy. On the upward stroke, one finger presses down on her clit. A shudder rolls through her, a jagged pant hard on its heels. She repeats the move a few more times, her body writhing on the bed.

"Faster," I instruct after a few minutes.

Her fingers circle her pussy, expertly strumming her clit on each pass. Making herself wetter. Moonlight gleams on her dripping cunt, driving me even more insane as the intoxicating scent of her pussy pummels me.

Her hips begin to undulate. Tiny little rolls at first, then more pronounced as she starts to lose herself in the rhythm. I drag my gaze up her body, to the tight nubs cresting her breasts. "Tug on your nipples, make them stiffer for me."

This time she doesn't hesitate. Her free hand cups one breast, squeezes, before she catches the nipple between her thumb and forefinger. One tug, and her back arches. "Oh."

I watch for a few seconds before my attention is drawn back down between her legs. She's even wetter, her fingers making decadent sounds as they move over her drenched sex.

"Slide one finger inside, fuck that filthy little cunt," I rasp.

Her mouth drops open. *Sweet Jesus*, those full, fucking lips, with their perfect Cupid's bow shape. She's possibly scandalized by my uncouth language, possibly even more turned on by my instruction. Either way, her middle finger caresses her hole before it sinks deep, the suction telling me how snug she is.

"Ah!" Her hips jerk off the bed, another shudder wracking her frame as her eyes squeeze shut.

Fuck. My cock throbs, furious at the punishment I'm putting it through. My hands clench tighter as more pre-cum soaks my boxers. "Open your eyes. Look at me as you fuck yourself."

Her drunken gaze stumbles to mine as her finger thrusts in and out, and the heel of her hand grinds into her clit.

"Slide another finger in."

She complies. Her rim of her pussy stretches, and I see the resistance, see how tight she is.

Jesus.

Her breathing quickens, her pants choppier. "Oh. Oh God."

"You're about to come, aren't you?" My tongue is so thick that I can barely move it to speak.

Her head rolls on the pillow, her eyes at half-mast as she continues to ruthlessly torture her nipple. "Yes," she moans through clenched teeth. Her fingers move faster, the sound of her fucking filling the room.

I'm a heartbeat from blowing my own load when her back bows and an agonized moan rips from her throat. Her fingers stay in her cunt, mindlessly fucking herself as a powerful orgasm plows through her.

I can't look away, can't do anything except curl my hand over my cock, stroking myself as I absorb her every shudder and moan.

When her convulsions die down, she slides her fingers out. Her gaze doesn't meet mine, and when she turns her head away from me, I allow it, content with the residual tremors that shake her body every few seconds.

When I'm certain I've gotten myself under enough control, I move up her body, still making sure not to touch her. "Look at me."

She turns reluctantly, mutiny once again plastered on her face.

"You hate yourself for this, don't you?"

"Yes." It's a tight admission, her panting breathing nowhere near under control.

"Good," I whisper, then lean down to speak directly into her ear. "Let that remind you to stay away. Because the next time I see you, this goes one step further. Understood?"

She doesn't respond, but I know she's gotten the message. I wait to catch another tremor before I get off the bed. I force myself not to take one last look as I leave the room. I'm halfway down the hall when I hear the distinct lock of her door behind me. I allow myself a grim smile.

My feet don't stop moving until I'm back in the kitchen. The dogs rise in unison and trot to my heels. We make our way back around the side of the house and across the lawn to the wall.

A tingle in my nape drags my attention over my shoulder. Her room light is on and she's standing at the window. The fact that she can't resist watching thrills me.

Whatever twisted roles fate may have chosen for us to star in, the savage power of our mutual feelings for each other will never diminish.

I watch her until another light comes on, its oblong shape reflected on the ground. It's out of my direct view but I know it's my father's room.

My gaze returns to Cleo's window, to the body framed there. Even as the guards tear out of the carriage house, my attention remains on her. She doesn't move. Neither do I.

Not until the dogs begin to bark. I let myself out, my stride lighter as I retrace my steps back to my car.

My beloved McLaren Spider responds sultrily to my touch, and I accelerate away, my cock still hard, my heart kicking harder. Feeling alive.

After years of skirmishes in the shadows, I've launched the first major salvo in the war with my father.

And the flavor of battle has never tasted so sweet.

Chapter Five

SABER-RATTLING

Finnan's next attempt at saber-rattling comes one night later, via Bolton this time. Of all my brothers, he's the only one I can tolerate for more than five seconds. There was a time when he leaned toward being a pacifist and therefore seemed more human than the rest of my family. Of course, that didn't last long. Finnan soon belted that perceived weakness out of him. But perhaps Bolton didn't lose it all. I wonder if this is why he's chosen to make the call.

"What the fuck were you thinking, breaking into the house?"

I focus on my brother's voice. At thirty-one with no clear job title, his role in the mob hierarchy is as an aimless lackey, his inability to stick to one job due to his suspected ADHD a constant source of ridicule from Ronan and Troy. There was a time when I felt almost sorry for him. That time is long gone.

I drift my fingers through the dozens of shirts hanging in my dressing room before settling on the gray silk. Saturday nights are the busiest of the week in any nightclub business, and with the rejuvenated buzz firing up my blood, I'm eager to get to work, perhaps even find a willing female to pound my restless energy into.

Despite returning home and jerking off one more time to the image of Cleo, my libido is nowhere near calm. I intend to find pussy tonight to help alleviate my need where the Punishment Club failed me this past week. There are a few attractive regulars at XYNYC who will more than meet the kind of action I'm looking for.

"Are you going to fucking answer me?"

Right, Bolton the Peacemaker was a figment of my imagination. "Sorry, I thought the answer was obvious," I respond lazily knowing it will needle him.

"Fuck you, asshole," comes the predictable answer.

I place the phone on speaker and set it down on the center island in my dressing room before I continue perusing my wardrobe. "Okay. You called to insult me. Consider me thoroughly insulted. If that's all…"

"You better not be thinking of hanging up on me."

"Insults and threats. Why don't we continue this conversation when you have some new material to offer?"

"Are you out of your mind leaving that little present for Pa?"

"It wasn't well received, I take it?"

"Do the Ferris wheels on Coney Island go round and round?"

"Sorry, you lost me." I inject as much disinterest in my voice as possible.

Pathetically, he rises to the bait. "You're trying to get yourself killed, is that it? FYI, the last guy who tried something like that lost both kneecaps."

"He must be more popular than I thought if people are breaking in on a regular basis."

"Dammit, Axel, you know how lucky you were to get away with pulling a stunt like that without getting seriously hurt?"

Fury spikes like the purest coke through my blood. "Do *you* know how lucky you all are that I showed restraint? That I've shown restraint for eight fucking years? Do you have any idea what I could've done to *any* of you last night? Be thankful you don't have a fucking clue, brother."

"You really think you're special shit, don't you, just because you were in the army?"

I stop myself from giving him a single example that will make his blood curdle. "I don't just think it, brother. Ask yourself this—if I wasn't 'special shit', as you so eloquently put it, would the old man be so fucking off his head for me? Fuck, don't answer that. Just tell me if there's a particular reason for your call. I have ninety-nine things I could be doing other than talking to you."

He swears a blue streak, exasperation in every expelled breath. My lips twitch with the unfamiliar urge to smirk as I button up my shirt.

"What's wrong with you? All the old man wants is to have a sit down with you," he finally says.

"There's absolutely nothing wrong with me. And we know what he wants. What he's always fucking wanted when it comes to me. He wants me to fall in line. He wants me to kiss the ring. And a *sit down*? Really? You've watched *The Godfather* one too many times."

"You don't think your own father deserves the respect of a face-to-face conversation?"

My whole body turns to ice, and my heartbeat slows to a dull, barely registering thud. "Respect? You *dare* speak to me about respect?"

Bolton hesitates. When he speaks again, his tone is less heated. "You don't know the damage you're causing by playing this game. Ever since you were a snotty kid, you thought you were above everybody else."

My jaw locks for a moment before I pry it open to speak. "No. What I *thought* was that I didn't deserve to be treated like an animal. Or used as a fucking punching bag when the old man had a less than stellar day. You think it was a brand of *affection*? That every time he broke a bone or gave one of us a black eye, it was because he *loved* us? It was abuse, pure and simple. And you would know it if you pulled your head out of his ass long enough to think for yourself."

"There you go again, treating me like I'm stupid. You don't know what the hell you're talking about—"

"I know he's running scared because his fucking empire is crumbling. I know he wants to meet to warn me off the Armenians and the Albanians. I have no intention of doing either. His time is over. No more requests for a sit down or anything else. We haven't had a single thing to talk about in ten years. Whatever shit he's got himself into—and trust me, I know enough—it's on him."

"Jesus, what the hell did he do to you that was so bad you bear a grudge all these years later?"

The finger poised over the red *end* button freezes, shock ramping through me. The thought that Bolton would ask me that…

I wait for the rush of blood clouding my vision to clear before I snap, "Do you have fucking amnesia, Bolton? Or are you just high as usual?"

"Fuck you, I don't do that shit anymore."

Maybe not, but I can't help but wonder what damage the heroin he snorted for years did to his brain. A hell of a lot if he can't remember events that should be seared with the hottest branding iron on all our souls. Events I haven't been able to get through a single day without reliving, even though there was a time when I did those white lines right alongside Bolton. Just so I could forget.

I drag myself back from my darkest memories to Bolton's continued censure, "I'm not like you. I don't hang on to things like a woman hangs on to her goddamn purse. Have you tried letting things go?"

"You're wasting your time and mine if all you called for is to preach hearts and flowers and forgiveness, Bolton. I've stated my terms. No more visits from *anyone*. No more fucking phone calls."

"Or what?" he snaps.

My silence is loud enough as I turn away to select a pair of tailored pants from the hanger. He's still there because I hear him taking deep breaths. Regrouping. Which is surprising. The brother I knew before would have hung up by now. For all his peacemaking tendencies, Bolton's short attention span is usually shorter when he's stressed.

The hairs on my nape sizzle to attention as I listen to him take another breath. "You may not want to know or care, but shit is heading south fast, brother. Putting yourself between him and the

Armenians was the wrong move. Now the fucking Albanians too? Jesus, Axel, the moment the Bratva get wind of it, they'll pull out too. Pa will go apeshit."

I'm counting on it.

"Things are getting unpredictable around here," Bolton continues. "For everyone. You think you're a fucking island because you washed your hands of us years ago? Well, you're not. Shit can blow back on you in a thousand different ways. When it does, don't say I didn't warn you."

"We're done here, Bolton. Goodbye." This time I don't hesitate to end the call.

* * *

Despite my need to forget, Bolton's words ricochet around in my head as the petite, curvy redhead I picked up an hour ago performs a curious switch between grinding against and climbing my leg. When my hand slides around her waist, her face all but lights with joy as her gyrations intensify.

I drain the shot of Balvenie whisky in my glass and nod to my private bartender for a refill.

"Are you going to put the drink down and dance with me?" the redhead whispers sultrily in my ear, long false lashes promising any- and everything I desire.

My free hand slides into her over-teased hair. I tighten my grip hard enough to get her attention. She stops moving, a soft gasp leaving her lips.

"Are you enjoying my VIP lounge, doll? Do you want to stay up here all night long?" I ask, struggling to temper my tone.

She nods eagerly. "Oh yes, I do. You have no idea how many times I've been here, hoping you would invite me to—"

"Then don't fucking talk."

Her mouth drops open then she blinks. "I...what?"

"You really want me to repeat myself?"

Her mouth clamps shut, and she shakes her head. Wide,

increasingly excited eyes slide from my face to my clenched jaw to the glass in my hand and back to my face. She's a closet danger whore, one I didn't spot before now. Before coming to XYNYC, I did a passing tour through my other three New York nightclubs.

Viper Red and Viper Black cater to the edgier clientele and I could've had easy pickings of women who welcome my darker proclivities. But for some reason, I wasn't in the mood for that.

My Harlem club, Playhouse X, was equally lacking. I realized why when I spotted a brunette with a passing resemblance to Cleo, and my pulse kicked up a notch. Furious with myself, I went with the redhead. Jerking off to Cleo's image is one thing; actively seeking her out in other women is unacceptable.

I stare down at the redhead, and I wonder if I picked her out of the many available women tonight because she managed to hide her true intentions until now. As I'm idly musing what I'm going to do about it, she sways closer, an eager smile curving her burgundy-colored lips. Her fingers tiptoe up my chest. After exploring for a short spell, she slides one hand over my nape, the other reaching for the glass of Dom Pérignon she's knocking back with almost comical greed.

She grinds against my thigh hard enough for me to feel her pelvic bone. Beneath her burnt-orange cocktail dress, her nipples pucker to hard, visible points.

I take a beat to collate her attributes.

Lush breasts. Perky ass. Fuckable mouth, if painted in too garish a color. I bend my head and inhale her scent. The smell of wet arousal hits my nostrils.

Ready, warm, willing pussy.

I wait for all of the above to pleasantly coalesce and work its way to the cock that was semi-hard a couple of hours ago. Nothing. Zero interest.

I haven't fucked in … hell, almost three weeks. It isn't an unthinkable record for me, but it is a disturbing one given that I didn't make abstinence a clear choice and fucking is a great and regular stress releaser for me.

Almost three weeks…

Ever since Cleo's first visit.

"Fuck." The curse is loud and vicious enough to earn a worried glance from the redhead, even though she's exploring more of my body than I've given her permission to.

Public groping doesn't make me uncomfortable, not when I've indulged in an orgy or three in less salubrious days. But she's stroking my limp cock, her eager little hand busy at my fly. I should be getting aroused. Except I'm not.

Her gaze flickers up at me, one side of her lip caught between her teeth. The titillation is a little too forced.

Or my cock has resigned its commission without bothering to let me know. "Hands off the junk until you get a green light, doll," I growl with enough venom to make her shiver.

Yes. Definite danger whore.

Despite her clear predilection, she heeds my warning and goes back to exploring my upper body.

I sigh inwardly. Time for her to leave. I'm looking around for one of my bouncers just in case she decides to become a handful, when she gasps.

"Oh, you poor baby. What happened to you?"

She's holding my right hand and examining my wrist with a mixture of curiosity and morbid excitement. A second later, she attempts to lift it toward her puckered lips. I jerk away before her mouth can make contact with my chafed wrist. The skin is still angry, and the wound crusted over, but like the rest of my body, that part of me feels lifeless. I experience a vivid urge to rip the scabs off just to feel some pain, just to remind myself why I shouldn't heed a single thing Bolton said tonight.

"It's time for you to go."

Acute disappointment drowns her features. "It's okay. I won't talk if you don't want me to. I can be obedient." One dark-nailed finger approaches my collarbone. "I'm *very* accommodating. Whatever you want, just say the word, and it's yours."

There's a rapidly building fire in her eyes, and again I'm alarmed by my extreme lack of stimulation. "Thanks, but no thanks."

I temper my tone because, as unreasonable as I'm feeling, this isn't her fault. The bouncer leads her away despite her protests, and I turn toward my private bar. Getting hammered as quickly and as severely as possible feels like a capital idea right now.

Except, no amount of whisky can disguise the fact that I'm still tracking the monitors way more than I should, that every woman in the club with a passing resemblance to Cleo snags my attention. Which in turn gets me more notice from women than I want. A problem I counter with more booze.

I finally accept that Cleo's heeded my warning not to return around two a.m. I also accept, as I jerk off hours later in my shower, that her obedience this time around has pissed me off more than I thought possible.

Chapter Six

RULES OF ENGAGEMENT

Now that I know exactly what Finnan wants, the battlefield becomes clearer.

Now that I know what *I* want, I don't hesitate in pulling my substantial resources into achieving my aims.

I thought I was done with her. That what she did to me would irreparably taint my desire for her. I've been proved wrong multiple times now. Turns out hate doesn't overrule every single decision of my life.

She placed herself in my orbit. She's staying until I decide otherwise.

Five days have passed since I last saw her. Four nights that I've jacked off to the memory of her sweet pussy then locked myself in the Punishment Club afterward.

I'm going to take her, but before I do, I'm going to remove one more Rutherford cornerstone.

I eye the man sitting in front me. "Do we have an agreement?"

The young Bratva lieutenant shakes his head. "We Bratva take loyalty very seriously. What you're doing…it's very disloyal to your father, no?" he asks in a thick Russian accent.

"I thought the Bratva didn't recognize blood ties, only brotherhood?"

He seems marginally impressed. "*Da*; nevertheless, what you're doing, it has potential to be messy, and Bratva—"

I hold up my hand. "Please don't tell me the Bratva doesn't do messy. We both know that's a joke."

His face tightens with affront. *Shit*. I swallow and regroup, choosing not to feel annoyed that my request to deal with the head of the Russian mob was answered with a meeting with a low-level lackey.

The lieutenant looks around my office then stares at a couple of monitors showing a packed club. "You run lots of nightclubs, successfully by the look of it. What do you want with guns, anyway?"

I choose my words carefully. "I have a lot of assets to protect. You help me protect them, and I'll make sure none of the mess lands on your doorstep."

He watches me for a moment before his gaze swings back to the monitors. I follow his gaze and see my three brothers stroll into XYNYC.

Fuck.

The lieutenant nods at them. "We talked about your father. What about your brothers? That one, Ronan, has quite the temperament. If Bratva decides to do business with you, how do you plan to keep *him* in line?"

It's a problem I'm well aware of. Ronan grew up expecting to inherit the very empire I'm actively dismantling. I know he's been going behind my back trying to talk Petrosyan and the Albanians out of dealing with me. So far, the lure of better profit has thwarted his efforts. But he won't take defeat lying down. I grit my jaw at the thought of going toe-to-toe with my oldest brother. "You don't need to worry. He won't be a problem."

The Russian shakes his head. "Before we even think about switching sides, we need better assurances."

"What would satisfy you?"

He doesn't immediately respond. He stands and buttons his jacket. "You will hear from us."

"When?"

"When you hear from us," he replies.

I exhale my irritation and stand to shake his hand. When he leaves, I sit back down and watch my brothers on the screen.

As instructed, they've been seated in my VIP booth and are being given premium service by my most trusted hostess.

Ronan, wearing a smirk, struts around like he owns the place, tossing back shot after shot of Balvenie whisky. He wears his thirty-eight years well, although a little wear and tear shows in the slight paunch clinging to his belly and the brackets framing his mouth.

Bolton sits brooding, thumbing his nose every other minute, his dark gray gaze darting after shadows that aren't there.

Troy, ever the ladies' man, is sweet-talking two girls on the edge of the dance floor. I watch him beckon the hostess. A minute later, he's offering champagne to the girls. Phone numbers are exchanged, and I'm fairly certain one or both of them will grace my brother's bed before the night is over.

I turn off the monitors and leave my office.

Bolton is the first to spot me. He surges to his feet, catching the attention of Ronan, who barks at Troy before his gaze swings to meet mine.

I struggle to remember a time when I felt any warmth or kinship toward my oldest brother. If there were such a thing as born enemies, we would be it. I have no inkling of the exact moment it began or the events that triggered it. All I know is he's hated me for as long as I can remember. And the feeling is mutual.

My gaze tracks left to Bolton. He nods stiffly, although his gaze is less cold.

Troy steps forward, and our eyes meet. If I had a heart worth salvaging, I would mourn the hardness I see in his eyes. With two older brothers forged in Finnan's image, Troy, the brother closest to my age, never stood a chance.

As if he senses my pity, his square jaw clenches, his eyes throwing challenges I have no intention of accepting.

"You wanted to meet. We're here. Tell us what this is about so I can get on with my night," Ronan says.

I shake my head. "I'm not discussing this here. I have an

apartment upstairs. We'll talk there. I only brought you into the nightclub because my meeting was running late."

Troy snorts. "Yeah, right. It had nothing to do with you wanting to rub your shady little operation in our faces or anything, right?"

"No, but you're free to think what you want. While you enjoy that premium champagne, of course."

He raises his glass to me in a mock salute. "Thanks. I will. And if this cheap little show bankrupts you, what with the economy being in the toilet and all, then all the better for teaching you to be a little humble."

I can tell him that with thirty-seven nightclubs situated around the globe, all turning a healthy profit, I'd sooner go bald overnight than go bankrupt.

I can also inform him that he'll need more fingers than he possesses to count the zeros of my net worth. But I don't have the time or inclination. I need them out of my way as quickly as possible.

"Let's get this over with," Bolton mutters, setting down his empty glass and thumbing his nose once more.

The tension in the elevator on the way up is thick. Bolton's incessant twitching tells me he's suffering the worst. By the time we exit, I'm certain my brother, contrary to his vigorous assertion otherwise, is still snorting shit up his nose.

I mentally shrug. As far as bearing crosses goes, his is one that might eventually kill him. Some of us are already dead.

In my apartment, they spread out on various seats in the living room.

"Drink?"

Bolton shakes his head. Ronan requests another whisky. Troy shrugs a nonanswer. I head to the bar and pour three whiskies. As I turn, I can't stop my mind from imagining Cleo here, instead of my brothers. My gaze tracks the room, conjuring up the many places I would fuck her. The couch. Up against the glass wall.

The floor, definitely. Maybe not the first time. Or the second. But her tight, little body would be pounded into that floor before I was done with her.

I hand the drinks out and retreat to the suspended fireplace at the farthest wall. "I'll keep this short. I know Finnan wants me to butt out of his dealings with the Eastern Europeans."

"And? You're gonna finally show this family some respect and do the right thing?" Ronan snarls.

I allow myself a stiff smile. "I am doing the right thing. I'm giving Finnan exactly what he deserves."

"Fuck you, Axel. What you're doing is giving Pa the finger, you useless piece of—"

"I'm not going to debate this matter with you, Ronan. I owed it to you to give you a heads-up. I'm telling you now that what's happening need not involve you three—"

"Wrong. You take him on, you take all of us on," Troy inserts.

I sigh. "Take off your fucking blinders for a damn minute, Troy. I don't want to fight you…any of you. None of what's about to go down need touch any of you."

"You want us to believe you're *protecting* us?" Troy laughs. "We don't need—"

"My protection. I know. But neither do you need to be caught in the crossfire that's none of your business."

Ronan discards his drink and stands. "You stealing deals from right under our noses *is* our business."

I swirl my drink for a moment before I meet his gaze. "The Eastern Europeans aren't the main reason Ronan wants to see me. I'm not going to give you the details. You can ask him, but if he hasn't told you yet, I guarantee you he'll lie. When this is all over, if you want to know the truth, maybe I'll tell you. For now, stay the hell out of my way." I harden my voice so there's no mistake that I'm being anything less than succinct.

"You have some fucking nerve—"

"This isn't up for discussion, Troy. Take my advice. Or don't."

Ronan's head snaps back as if he's just had an epiphany. "Fuck, you still have a stick up your ass about being sent to West Point, don't you?"

I struggle not to grit my teeth, any notion I had of warning him off the Bratva shelved. For now. "I've said what I wanted to say. Feel free to leave—"

"You're still salty because we didn't hold your hand while you ran around after that little slut?"

I stare Troy in the face, my fingers tingling with an inhuman itch to punch him. "I dare you to call her that one more time."

Troy loses a shade of color but the sneer doesn't leave his face. Ronan stares at me, a speculative light in his eyes.

Bolton scrambles to his feet. "Okay. You said your piece. We'll…uh, discuss it. Let you know how what we decide."

"You don't need to let me know," I reply, my eyes still on Ronan. "When the time comes, you'll either be in my way or you won't."

Chapter Seven

FIRST CONTACT

An hour after they leave, I head to the Punishment Club. Now that I've accepted that having Cleo again is the only thing what will appease the prowling beast inside me, my madness has throttled down a notch.

It's not a state that will remain stable for any appreciable time, even in the short term.

I haven't fucked in weeks. After watching Cleo come, and being unable to think of anything else other experiencing that heady sight again, the hand jobs are losing their appeal.

Yesterday, I contemplated accepting a blowjob from one of the many submissives in the Punishment Club. I discarded the idea a pathetic minute later, knowing that no one but Cleo would pierce the layer of sexual inertia blanketing me.

Until I have a firm commitment from the Bratva, I can't confront Finnan. Compared to Petrosyan and the Albanians, the Russians hold the upper hand in New York and New Jersey. As long as Finnan has their loyalty, he has a fair amount of security. Until that security is taken away, I can't make my move with Cleo. Anticipation has its right place in the right circumstances. My ultimate plans for Cleo, for example, keep my blood thrumming. Prolonged anticipation, however, shifts my mood in the wrong direction. As does silence from the source who should've delivered news by now.

I stop in a deserted hallway and pull my phone from my pocket. The email I'm expecting isn't in my inbox.

Growling under my breath, I head to the bar. B is walking the floor, all-black getup in place, her game face on as she chats with clients. With unwanted time on my hands, I take a moment to wonder what her deal is. Finding out will be as easy as making a single phone call. So far I haven't been tempted to.

She reaches me, sees my near-empty glass, and nods to the bartender. "Have another drink. And stop glowering. You're agitating my customers. Those who like that sort of thing are getting a free show. Those who don't might leave. Either way, it's not good for business."

I accept the drink without responding and take a sip. The liquor trails a fiery path down my throat but fails to warm me or come anywhere close to offering oblivion.

"Are you heading up?" she eventually asks.

"No."

She nods, and her gaze falls to my wrists. I'm aware she's brimming with more questions, but she remains silent.

After a few minutes, she leaves to make another circuit of the room, pausing to talk to a diminutive priest holding chains attached to a seven-foot giant's steel collar. I watch them, idly wondering which one of them is seeking salvation. Whether they will find it.

"Walk with me." B has returned to my side.

I swirl the golden liquid in my glass. "Why?"

One sleek eyebrow rises. "Because you need the exercise?"

"Is this another half-assed therapy session? Because I'll be less receptive than I was last time," I warn.

"It's…something. Not sure yet. But I get the feeling you'll be interested."

The need to tell her not to waste her time or mine hovers on my lips. But it's only eleven p.m. Sleep isn't anywhere on my horizon and hasn't been since the last time I saw Cleo. I could return to my apartment and spend the next twelve hours in my personal gym. Or

I can burn five minutes pandering to whatever the fuck B has up her sleeve.

Time is an endlessly fucked-up labyrinth right now so I shrug.

She heads for the elevators at the far side of the reception area. The stunning black girl behind the desk eyes me with thinly veiled interest. She's tall, shapely with a superbly toned body. I try to imagine her red-painted lips wrapped around my cock.

All I get is gray static.

"What is this all about?" I growl as I step into the elevator.

B presses the button for the second floor. The newbie floor. My barely awakened interest drops to zero.

"Our latest member has been here three nights in a row."

I shove my hands into my pockets, admitting that postponing a session with my punching bag probably wasn't my best idea. "That's unusual because?"

She notes my disinterested tone and holds up a manicured hand. "Bear with me. You trust my radar to be pretty accurate. But this one...I'm not so sure about. She either has serious mental issues I didn't pick up on or she's paying a hell of a lot of money to use our suite as a hotel room."

My jaw bunches. "We have clients who pay to sit in a white padded cell without food or water for twenty-four hours at a stretch. What's different about this one?"

"You'll see."

The elevator pings open. I suppress my rising irritation and follow her down the hall. Unlike the Gothic-bent decor on the upper floors, the doors and hallway are painted in lighter colors, with some rooms offering viewing windows for those with exhibitionist tendencies.

She leads me to a door that has a TV screen attached to the wall next to it. It's accessed by a special code known only to senior staff so newbies can be monitored. By definition, the Punishment Club is a place of extremes, but those new clients still need monitoring during the first three months after joining despite the waivers they're required to sign.

She enters the code. The screen flickers to life.

The woman is sitting on the rumpled bed, her head on her drawn-up knees, arms wrapped around her legs. Her long dark hair is obscuring her face but there are no visibly unsettling signs of distress. She's either sleeping. Or meditating. Or crying. My gaze moves from her to the room.

The large picture of the lone surfer at sunrise on the wall above the bed is the first strum on my wary senses. The bed frame and headboard also look familiar. The gray and white sheets. The red headphones draped over the studded armchair. The chair itself.

The distinct purple-foiled stack of condoms on the dresser.

My breath expels from my lungs in a harsh rush as I whirl to face B.

"Who is she?" The question is redundant because I already know the answer.

"I told you, she's our latest client. I tried to tell you about her when I came to your place—"

"What is her *name*?"

"Cleopatra McC—"

"What the fuck is she doing here?" My whole body clenches, her name a cattle prod direct to my core. I swing back around to stare at the screen.

B inhales sharply. "Wait a second. You know her?"

Yes.

No.

I slam my open fist against the door. On the screen, Cleo's head snaps up, her brows furrowing. The confirmation starts a throbbing in my chest.

Jesus.

"Hello?" She eyes the locked door, her face wary.

"Open the door," I growl at B. "And I asked you what the fuck she was doing here."

She frowns. "Pretty much the same reason everyone in this building is here."

Rage fires up my spine. "Be careful, B, don't fuck with me. Or the next button you push might just reap the results you least expect."

"I'm a big girl. I can handle it. I can also handle some answers right about now. So?"

"Open. The. Fucking. Door." I can access the door code from my laptop in my office downstairs. Or I can find an assistant to get it for me. Doing either will take too long.

My gaze flicks to the screen. She's risen up on her knees and crawled to the edge of the bed, her gaze still fixed on the door. "Hello?" Her voice is huskier than usual. As if she's been crying.

My gaze slices back to B. Her lips press together in a mutinous line.

"I'll open it. As soon as I get some assurances—"

"Fuck your fucking assurances. Give me the code to the fucking door, B. Right now. Or I'll find someone who will."

She stands her ground, her gaze implacable. "Tell me you're not going to do something…unwise, and I will."

I've fired people for less than the insubordination being displayed right now. But I need the door opened before my head explodes. I take a breath. "I know her. She's…" *Mine.* "I fucking know her, alright? Open the door."

She nods, skirts around me, and punches the code into the door panel. The door clicks. I grab the handle immediately, almost alarmed it might lock again before I can get in.

"I want the code to that screen disabled in the next ten seconds. No one watches her. No-fucking-one. Is that understood?"

"It's understood."

I nod. Inhale. I start to push the door open. A thought stops me dead cold. "Has anyone else been here? With her?" The words fly like bullets from my throat, even though I'm not sure how I'll handle anything other than a *no*.

"No."

A tsunami of relief shakes through me.

"Wait. Before you go in."

My grip on the door tightens. "Yes?"

"You should know…When she checked in three days ago, I brought her a complimentary drink. I won't go into too much detail but…like I said, she seemed a little off."

Hellfire licks a path through my chest. "Why? What's wrong with her?"

"Hey, I asked. She didn't feel like sharing. I didn't push. But that's the reason I've been keeping a close eye on her. All I'm saying is tread carefully—"

"You're overstepping. Again. Leave, B. Now." I've wasted more than enough time talking to her.

She obeys.

I step into the room.

A room that is an exact replica of my bedroom in the pool house ten years ago.

Of all the things she could've chosen as her penance, she chose a replica of my room?

Why?

A few million other questions pepper my brain, but Cleo's gaze is locked on me. Mine on her. Once upon a time, when my addled state didn't know better, I stupidly believed the phenomenon of our gazes connecting had the power to stop the world from spinning. That view has altered significantly. But the sensation lingers in the tunnel vision that makes me only see the rapid rise and fall of her chest. Her lack of surprise at my presence. The calm acceptance of what's to come.

She didn't seek me out, but she's here because of me.

She knows who owns this building, who owns the Punishment Club. All my businesses, from the trendy cocktail bars to the hard-core BDSM clubs, come under the Axel, Inc. umbrella. It wouldn't have been difficult for her to find this place. Although I suspect a different hand has facilitated her presence here. The timing is a little too accurate.

"Hello, Axel." Her voice is even, the rasp barely above a murmur.

I ignore the greeting and kick the door shut behind me. "What the fuck are you doing here?"

"Getting your attention any way I can." Her throat moves in a nervous swallow. I follow the movement, the thrumming in my body spiking to another level.

She shifts. My gaze drops, and I see what she's wearing.

A dark purple silk teddy and knicker set. The kind that leaves very little to the imagination. The kind that begs to be ripped out of the way so the despoiling can begin. The whisper-thin material hugs her heavy breasts, the flimsy straps doing a piss-poor job of supporting her. The panties hug her hips, their lace trim framing the mind-altering nirvana at the top of her thighs.

She shifts again, sliding one silky thigh against the other. At the edge of the bed, she extends one leg and steps down to stand.

Bare feet. Tumbling hair. Effortlessly sexy. Infinitely deadly.

The breath punches out of me. My cock stiffens, and my balls tighten as the monstrous need to fuck roars back to life.

The memory of her wetness saturates me, and all I can do is stare as she glides to a stop before me, enveloping me with her perfume. Her eyes swirl with all the emotions I'm familiar with. But tonight most of them have been dialed back to leave a fierce determination in the eyes that rise up to meet mine.

"Do I have it, Axel? Your attention?"

Far more than I'm comfortable with. "That depends on what you intend to offer as a sweetener. The promise of pussy is always a draw. Even tainted pussy, no matter how much it turns my stomach."

Her breath expels in a pained gasp.

I laugh, feeling zero remorse. "Did you think all it would take is risqué lingerie to have me eating out of your hands? Or eating you out? Did you forget that you're a mere pawn in this tiresome game? An expendable commodity?"

She reddens. A trace of a quiver touches her lips before she bows her head and wrestles for control. After half a minute, she lifts her head. "This is not a 'tiresome game' to me. You told me not to return to the nightclub. So I found another way."

I drag my gaze from her face and turn away as I look around the room. Not a lot of things stump me. But this one does. It takes several minutes before I can form the words to ask, "What the hell is so important that he...that you would join *this* club just to get my attention?"

"He wants you to come to the house tomorrow."

"That's not news. I know he knows I've made new deals with the Armenians and Albanians that cut him out. I have endless resources to ensure they never deal with him again—"

"That's not why he wants to see you."

"Fine. Tell me why."

"Finnan wants to talk to you about Taranahar."

Chapter Eight

CALL OF EXTRA DUTY

Anar Farah, Afghanistan
September 2011

I don't remember the last time I slept.

I don't care. Neither does my commanding officer. Turns out not needing sleep isn't a bad thing when you're a soldier.

Sure, a few chins were scratched when some pencil pusher discovered I was a raging insomniac who hadn't slept more than a few hours a night for over a year. After two half-assed medical consults and a hastily scrawled agreement to stick to a rigid sleep regime, I went back to not sleeping and not caring about not sleeping.

What I care about is keeping busy. My CO is totally on board with that too because there's plenty to keep you busy when you're geographically situated one hundred miles west of hell's butthole.

Except I've done nothing but sit on my ass for the past forty-eight hours. Or more accurately, I've moved from punching bag to bench press to skipping rope to punching bag in a sweltering tent. My body is drenched with grimy sweat. I smell like shit. I know this because the oldest member of my squad, the only man bold enough to state the obvious, begged me to take a shower yesterday.

I ignored him. Word quickly spread that Rutherford was in asshat mode, and no one has approached the exercise tent since, even though I know they want to burn off the restless energy that rapidly mounts when new assignments take forever to come.

When my feet grow numb from skipping rope, I throw it down and move to the speed bag. It pulses back and forth in a red and black blur, mimicking my mind. My racing heartbeat sings as I push my body to its limit.

In the land where a pocketful of cold hard cash can get me any drug of my choice, I wish for a moment that I still dabbled. Snorting a long line of coke, preferably off a stripper's taut ass, would go a ways toward ridding me of the images playing on a relentless loop through my brain.

A year has passed since Finnan sent me the video. No. Let's be precise. If there's one thing I've learned in this hell hole, it's that extreme precision is the difference between life and death. One small miscalculation will see you sent home in much smaller pieces than you arrived in.

So…

Eleven months, twenty-two days, sixteen hours and four… no…five minutes since my life flashed before my eyes in vivid Technicolor. To think I once believed taking a life would be what kept me up at night. Turns out those were destined to haunt my waking hours. My night hours were reserved for reliving my father fucking the love of my life. Doggy style.

My piston-fast fists smash against the speed bag in an explosion of deadly rage. It flies clean off the hook and bounces across the dusty floor. It would've kept going were it not for the booted foot that slams on it just outside the tent flap.

One large hand reaches down for it.

Captain Crunch, a member of my squad, aptly named for his ability to crunch hazelnuts with his abs during sit-ups, pops his head into the tent.

In the squad, where the men know to give me a wide berth most days, Crunch ignores the flashing fuck-off signposts, his incessant banter and wit always in operation whether I acknowledge them or not. Within hours of my arrival in the camp, I knew everything there was to know about Conrad Whitby.

Married to his high school sweetheart. Father to two-year-old twin girls he head-over-heels adores. Born and bred in Montana. Allergic to sesame seeds and avocado. Broke his nose in a bar fight the night before he shipped out. The list is endless.

He eyes me for a couple of seconds, his hands rotating the speed bag. I don't welcome the scrutiny or the state-of-mind probe coming so I turn away.

He sighs. "Yo, tough guy. CO wants to see you in the command center, stat."

I grunt without turning around, my gaze fixed on the dangling hook until he leaves. I rip the bloodied bindings off my hands and stop long enough to wipe the excess sweat off my body before I jog to the command center.

Situated in the middle of the camp, the building is housed in a special hack-proof structure that continues to baffle our enemies.

Within the structure itself, the CO's office is contained within a Faraday cage since all the laptops contain extra-sensitive material.

I approach his office, the rage eating away inside me nowhere near abated.

Colonel Jack Clarkson looks up, waves away my stiff salute and nods to the chair in front of his desk. A moment later, his head jerks back, and he grimaces. "Jesus Christ, son, are you allergic to soap or something?"

"No, sir."

The middle-aged man who can run faster, fight harder than any other man in the camp except me, wrinkles his nose in disgust. "Then why the fuck do you stink worse than my ex-wife's incontinent mutt?"

"Tough workout, sir," I reply.

He snorts. "The day a workout is anywhere near tough for you is the day we drag your ass out of here in a body bag."

I clasp my fists between my knees, barely able to keep my foot from bouncing. "Yes, sir."

He stares me down for half a minute before he drags his hand through his inch-long ginger buzz cut. "Word is you've been in the exercise tent for two days straight. Is there a new set of…issues I need to be concerned about?"

My jaw ticks with nervous energy. Whatever assignment I'm about to receive can't be retracted because of psychological concerns. I won't allow it. "No, sir. You have my word that I'm in top shape."

He stares at me for another minute before he slides across a single sheet of paper. "This is a two-man mission, particularly sensitive not just in circumstances but also time-wise." I speed read, absorbing the details.

Three war lords. Private family celebration. Vicinity of a small village. Opportunity to kill three birds with one strike. Cripple the enemy.

Anticipation flows, thick and fast, pushing away the memories. "I can do it solo, sir." Company means conversation. It also means responsibility for another life.

"I'm sure you can, but I'm sending Crunch with you anyway. You take point; he reports in every four hours."

"Yes, sir."

"Another thing. The reason it's time sensitive is because there's intel that the same job has been handed over to a private military contractor." His jaw clenches, and a wave of fury flashes across his face. "I have no idea what the jerk buckets in DC are thinking, auctioning off sensitive operations like these to the highest bidder." He raps his knuckles on his desk before he points a finger at me. "But this is one coup I'm not going to hand them."

"I understand. I'll…we'll bag this one, sir."

"Damn fucking straight, we will. Go get some sleep—hell, go do…whatever you need to do to be bright eyed and bushy tailed and ready to head out at zero three hundred." He pauses for a beat before he adds, "When you get back, if you're still in that frame of mind, we'll discuss future solo missions."

I stand and hand back the paper. "Very good, sir." I turn to leave.

"Oh, and Rutherford?"

"Sir?"

"Take a fucking shower before you head out. It'll be a damn shame if you blow this op wide open because the enemy catches a whiff of whatever the hell it is that's oozing out of your pores."

I pass Captain Crunch on the way out. He nods to me but keeps uncharacteristically silent. This time I look him in the eye and nod back.

Exiting the command center, I pause and take a breath. For now, the hell that haunts my days and nights is locked away behind the surge of adrenaline and anticipation of mayhem.

We head out at exactly zero three hundred, the Huey's rotors cutting almost soundlessly through the night air as we head west. Across from me in the silent cabin, the sergeant monitoring the drone sent ahead of us watches a five-inch screen with grim intensity. Next to him Crunch is checking the camera mounted on top of his helmet.

That camera is the main reason he's here, besides watching my back. We need video evidence of what's about to go down. Confirmation of the kills will make the suits back home incredibly happy. It will also hopefully fast-track my request to join the covert team my CO doesn't think I know about.

"Drop-off point coming up in T-minus five mikes," the pilot's voice feeds through the headphones attached to my helmet.

"Everything looks good," the sergeant says, his gaze fixed on the screen. "I'm picking up three armed sentries at the entrance to the compound. No other signs of movement."

I have no doubt more men will be awake and guarding the inside of the compound but I nod and double-check my ammo. If everything goes according to plan, I won't need to fire a single bullet. The three knives strapped against my thigh will be all I need. The Filipino knife play I perfected a year ago isn't strictly army regulation, but it's served me well in the past, and I intend to do whatever it takes to get this job done.

The Huey drops us off two miles from the compound, located

just outside the small village of Taranahar. In the pitch-black night, the only way I make out Crunch is through my night vision goggles.

"Stay sharp," he says, his voice controlled and calm.

I don't respond. My feet are already moving over the rough sand and stone terrain toward my target. The compound is situated on a small incline set back against a much steeper hill, a clever location that provides the perfect vantage point for spotting imminent threats.

"We take out the one in the middle first, then you grab the left guy, I take the right," Crunch murmurs into his mic.

"No, I'm taking all three."

Before he can argue, I spring from the boulder we're crouched behind and power at a full run for the men.

"Fuck! Wait!"

I hear him coming after me but I don't stop.

Perhaps a part of me wishes for an end to it all. Perhaps part of me craves more of the blood that was forced on my hands at nineteen. Or perhaps this is my fucked-up way of atoning for the lives I took that dark fall night four years ago.

Whatever.

My first knife finds the throat of the closest sentry. He drops like a sack of stones to the ground, clutching at his gushing carotid. My second finds the chest of the next guard. He cries out before I get to him, alerting the third in frenzied Pashto. I silence him with a push dagger, which I yank out a second before the last sentry raises his gun. With a flick of my wrist, my last knife embeds itself between his eyes. His gun drops a second before he does.

Crunch gets to me as I'm dragging the first body out of sight.

"Jesus *fucking* Christ. What the hell's the matter with you?"

"Got the job done, didn't I?"

"That's not what I'm asking, and you fucking well know it," he hisses, puzzlement and rage deepening his voice.

I dump the body against the towering compound wall and head for the second. "You want to stop and have a discussion about it?"

"The CO's going to knock your fucking block off when we get back."

"Not your fucking problem then, is it?" I reply, my voice even despite the elation filling my chest.

In the darkness, I feel his eyes probe me as he helps me hide the third body. "You gonna go lone wolf when we get inside too?" he demands.

"I'm gonna do what I came here to do. You do what you were assigned to do—watch my six and document the whole thing."

I retrieve my knives, turn from the bodies, and head toward the preplanned point of ingress. He's not happy, and I'll most definitely get chewed out for this once we get back and he makes his report, but right now his happiness matters very little to me.

For the next hour or two, the color red will wipe away visions of blond-haired, blue-eyed traitors and a million could-have-beens. I'll have new nightmares to sustain me, at least for a while before they too are smashed beneath the one betrayal that refuses to stay buried in the past.

I breach the east wall of the compound with Crunch tight on my heels. We clear the first floor, disposing of six guards. I keep one alive long enough to force the information I need out of him. With the location of the big players secured, I move silently through the large house, my gun tucked against my side, the blades in my fists an extension of my body.

The two younger war lords, brothers of the most powerful war lord in the region, die in their sleep, their throats slit before they can so much as shift from dream to reality.

The last target is the most difficult, naturally. He's situated behind bolted double doors at the end of a long, dark corridor, and it takes a few minutes to clear the rooms leading up to it to avoid being ambushed.

Once we reach it, I lay down my knives, crouch low, and go to work with my lock pick.

I hear the click of the final tumbling lock one second before a deafening explosion rips through the air, followed almost instanta-neously by an enormous plume of orange mushrooming into the dawn sky. Two more explosions follow in quick succession.

Crunch backs against me. "Shit! We're fucked. We need to bail. Right fucking now!"

But it's too late. One of the many wives we spared but left tied up has gotten free. She runs to the middle of the compound and screams at the top of her lungs. Rapid-fire Pashto rips through the compound, followed by running feet. Light floods the hallway, illu-minating us in vivid relief.

Behind the doors, I hear movement then the distinct recoil of a submachine gun. "Crunch, get down!"

I dive for the floor, grabbing his leg and yanking hard.

But Captain Crunch is dead before he hits the floor, face first, blood oozing from several wounds delivered by the bullets that just ripped through the wooden doors.

I mourn my comrade's passing for one single second before pure instinct kicks in. Both legs slam against the weakened door, smash-ing it inward and sending the man behind it sprawling onto the floor.

Rumored to be in his sixties, Ahmed Fahim is nevertheless lean and agile. He tries to scramble to his feet, but I'm younger. Faster. And by taking my friend's life, he's just added another grim purpose to my mission.

I kick out his legs before he can regain them even as my hands close over my knives. I scramble across the floor and jump on his chest, pinning his arms to his body. Once he's immobile, I jerk my gaze around the room, make sure there are no more surprises ready to spoil my two-minute party.

We're alone.

"You will not get out of this alive!" he spits at me.

"Maybe I will, maybe I won't. But one thing's for certain. You will *most definitely* not live through the next minute."

Piercing gray eyes stare back at me, his fate stoically accepted.

Perhaps it's a trick of the light. Or perhaps it's my raw

subconscious willing it into being. But I see my father's face as I stare down at the terrorist.

I feel a smile curve my lips.

His eyes widen, the first true sign of terror marring his features.

"See you in hell, asshole," I snarl.

The knife I plunge into his heart is deeply satisfying. Deeply personal. And in that moment, I accept that I'm damned for all eternity.

I cannot recall the details of my escape or the days that pass until I'm rescued from the caves nine clicks south of Taranahar.

But I know I help to retrieve Crunch's body from where I hid it outside the compound, along with the camera that recorded most of the operation.

As predicted, Colonel Clarkson rips me several new ones for going off script, but it's tinged with the solemnity of a comrade lost. I stand at attention in his office and take my dressing down through the low roar that has taken up residence between my ears.

He talks about me laying low for the next few missions. Then he talks about a possible medal of honor, my second in three years. I want to argue against the first and refuse the second. But I don't speak for fear the roar will disappear, letting even more harrowing images flood back in.

"Did you hear what I just said?" The question is fired at me from my left.

I turn my head to where Clarkson has paused in his pissed-off pacing. "I'm sorry, sir, no."

He sighs and rubs a hand over his three-day-old stubble. "I said, we got to the bottom of what happened to fuck up the operation."

I nod and wait for him to continue. He stares back at me, his gaze holding more than just questions. "Is there something you want to tell me, son?"

Tension of a whole different kind seizes my nape. The camera didn't record Fahim's last moments so the colonel can't know how much I enjoyed killing him. "No, sir."

"You sure?"

"Positive."

Clarkson retraces his steps, his face pensive. "The explosion that alerted the compound to your presence came from that private army I told you about. As expected, they half-assed their operation, or maybe they were fed false intel. Who the fuck knows?" He shakes his head, his expression tightening with fury and a hint of pain for a second before his professionalism slides back into place. "They bombed Taranahar village thinking it was the compound where Fahim and his brothers were hiding out."

Jesus. "Casualty count?" I rasp.

"So far…eighty-seven, half of those women and children. They're still counting body parts. We may never know how many died."

My breath shudders out. A peculiar discomfort lances my chest. I'm not sure whether to be glad I have a little humanity left or mourn its presence.

My CO turns and strolls back to his desk. He picks up his tablet and activates the screen. "As you can expect, this is causing all sorts of bonfires back in Washington. A shitload of keyboard bashers have thrown a lot of man-hours into tracking down just who the hell is behind this particular private military contract. A few names popped up. One in particular grabbed my attention."

"Yes, sir?"

"MMFR International."

The brutal rush of blood threatens to drown the roar in my head. The initials make sense.

MM. Michael McCarthy.

FR. Finnan Rutherford.

So does, finally, the long-forgotten meeting that took place in our house in Connecticut with the army general. It's too much of a coincidence to sidestep.

I recall Ronan's barely suppressed excitement when he told us that General Courtland would be visiting Finnan from Washington. That the Rutherfords were about to strike the deal of a lifetime, which would make us richer than our wildest dreams.

The voice booms into my head as if the old general is standing next to me. *Rutherford, as a father of sons myself, I commend you for a venerable crop of boys. I have three sons in the army.*

In response, Finnan preened as he shook his hand, naked greed shining in his eyes. *Thank you, sir.*

Courtland nodded. *No, thank you! Let's get down to business. Then you can tell me which of your sons will be the first to honor our great country.*

Finnan nods at Ronan to shut the door.

As he moved to do so, his gaze flicks to Troy, Bolton, and me, standing to attention just as he ordered. He looks at my brothers, sees the fear and respect he's instilled in them from birth displayed in their gray eyes.

Then he looks at me.

I know my defiance is displayed clearly. So is my contempt. My shame.

I also see the exact moment Finnan decides that I will be the one. It was like witnessing a bolt of lightning scorch the earth. For weeks I tried to dispel the fear that look struck in me to no avail.

Perhaps a part of me suspected all along that something like this would happen—me standing in front of my CO, a man of honor, with my family name soiling my skin. Or worse.

My gaze meets Colonel Clarkson's as he confirms my fears. I wouldn't stake my life on it, but I swear I see sympathy in his eyes. "I have to ask if the Finnan Rutherford listed in the file is a relation of yours."

Denial hovers on my tongue. I swallow it. "Yes. He's my…father."

Clarkson swears long and hard. "There's no way to sugarcoat it. There's a shit storm headed your way, son. There are many things capable of being swept under rugs from here to Ulan Bator. But I get the feeling this isn't going to be one of them." He stares grimly at me before he nods. "Dismissed."

The roaring stops by the time I make it to my bunk. Still fully dressed, I lie back on my bed and stare at the ceiling.

I'm back in my pit of hell. Only this time, it's deeper. Darker.

Stained with Crunch's death. Yet another life cut far too short. Along with countless others whose faces will join in the perpetual haunting I now know I'll never be free of. But now I know who's responsible.

My father.

So I close my eyes. And I plot.

Chapter Nine

COUNTER PUNCH

"What the fuck did you just say?" My voice bleeds pure ice.

The single pop that went off in my head a second ago may have been my imagination. Or it could have been my last connection with something human and salvageable tearing itself free.

Or, most likely, it could be that I've put my hand on her. I'm touching Cleo for the first time in eight years. I know in that moment that I've sealed my fate. Hell, who the fuck am I kidding? My fate was sealed a long time ago, my path set in concrete the moment her blue eyes sank into me that very first time.

All the same, my palm against her bare arm is incendiary. The punch to my gut is immediate. As is her audible gasp. A groan dares to rattle up from the depths of my being. I smother it and propel her to face me.

To her credit, she doesn't flinch or attempt to pull away from my punishing hold. "He wants to talk about Taranahar," she repeats. "That's in Afghanistan, right? Is that where you—?"

With my thumb, I silence her, refusing to allow the smoothness of her velvet-soft lips to distract me. I bend low until her face is a dozen inches from mine. "I'm the only one asking the questions, sweetheart. What do you know about Taranahar?"

Her nostrils quiver with the breath she takes. "I…nothing. Finnan isn't exactly great at sharing," she says in a low, steady voice.

No, he's good at taking. The deadliest of parasites, he doesn't stop taking until there is nothing left.

I don't know why I believe her, but I do. After all, wasn't it the way he treated my mother too? A body in his bed and a pair of hands to deliver his food? That was when he wasn't knocking her around.

That last memory isn't one I like recalling. Because no matter how I slice it, I know I should've done more to protect my mother instead of running away to the pool house at the first opportunity.

The reason why I did *that* is staring right at me, her face a flawless vision I can't seem to look away from. I suck in a steadying breath before my fraying control detonates. "I don't give a flying fuck about what Finnan is great at. Why does he want to talk about Afghanistan?"

"I don't know."

Finding out my father was responsible for the Taranahar massacre escalated the darkness in my soul to a whole new level. For the better part of a year after it happened, I was dragged before endless committees and probed as to whether I had connections to my father's military contracts. Clandestine hearings—thanks to Colonel Clarkson pulling every available string he could find in order to protect my identity should I be found innocent—where almost every single skeleton in my closet was dragged into the daylight. But I didn't mind them because I wanted my father to be brought to justice.

The foundation of my hatred for Finnan was sealed when I discovered the reason he sent me to West Point. I was merely another sacrifice in his grand plan. My father had looked into my eyes and, recognizing what I was capable of, set me on a path toward war profiteering for his own gluttonous gain.

Armed with the memory of General Courtland's visit to Connecticut all those years before, it took less than a week of trail-chasing to discover the truth. MMFR International had, in some way or another, benefited from every single one of my successful missions by providing additional support with arms or with personnel while charging the Pentagon millions of dollars for it. It also hadn't taken a genius to work out that General Courtland was the one sanctioning all those missions. Further investigation revealed just why the general was firmly in my father's back pocket. The good general supplied bad cocaine to an underaged prostitute in Michael McCarthy's stable while he'd been fucking her, and the girl overdosed. Michael McCarthy, seeing the opportunity to blackmail the general, brought the deal to my father, and between them they hatched the plan to make millions from the girl's death.

The Taranahar incident and resulting public outcry put an end to what could've been an endless revenue stream. I hoped they would lock Finnan up in the deepest, darkest hole and throw away the key. But the investigation had fallen apart, and years later, he still breathed free air. So I decided to seek justice my way, the way I've done since I learned what a truly despicable man it was who sired me.

There was a time I believed he deserved a quick, merciless end. But slowly dismantling his kingdom and watching everything he's worked for crumble around him has been even more satisfying.

And now he wants to talk about the single most atrocious act he's committed to date. And he's using her.

I refocus on her face. "Did you know?" I ask.

"Know what?"

I drop my hand and shove it into my pocket. Touching her while the beast rides me this hard is no longer a good idea. Hell, was it ever?

"Why he sent me to West Point?" The question I never got the chance to ask because I was too busy saving myself from the thousand cuts of betrayal. I wonder why I ask it now, why I believe it's a subject worth pursuing.

I open my mouth to tell her not to bother answering but her features undergo a startling transformation. Her face goes slack, and the light goes out of her eyes. It's like I'm staring at a marble statue. A stunning, utterly enthralling statue.

"Yes. I knew. He and my father were blackmailing General Courtland into giving them military contracts. But he was also grooming you to become his perfect little soldier." Her lips barely move with the words.

Then why didn't you warn me? The question blazes on my tongue, burns into my flesh.

"And you were okay with that, of course." I recall the video recording my brutal beating and the tender loving care from her that followed, where I swore that I wasn't leaving her to join the army. Where she listened, nodded, then fucked my brains out, after which she talked me into spending four years away from her arms. From her bed.

So she could take up residence in my father's.

"Of course," she concurs with a lifeless murmur.

A despicably pathetic part of me wants to understand the unfathomable. "Why?"

"He had something I wanted."

"You wanted to be a gangster's doll? What about it turned you on? The money? The power? Status? *Rough sex?*"

Her throat moves in a slow, smooth swallow. "All of it."

My vision fades out for a moment. I claw back every single ounce of control I can muster just so I don't do something stupid and infinitely satisfying. Like strangle her. "*Fucking Christ*, Cleo. Did I ever even know you?"

Something moves behind her eyes. Whatever it is that sparks to life inside her flushes her face with color, and when she speaks, her voice is thick, crackling with seething emotion. "You knew me as much as I knew you, Axel."

The thought never fully forms. It isn't analyzed and accepted. Between one heartbeat and the next, I act.

She doesn't make a noise, not a single sound as I propel her downward and backward with a less-than-gentle push. Her legs splay out from beneath her. Her back lands on the floor with a loud thud.

She catches herself before her head connects with the hardwood floor. That little act of self-preservation snaps something free inside of me. As if the confirmation that she can take care of herself makes any of this lunacy okay. As if seeing that is the ultimate permission I need to unleash the terrible beast prowling through my bloodstream.

Nothing about this motherfucked situation is okay.

And yet, barely a second after laying her flat, I'm crawling over her. Planting my hands on either side of her head. Pinning her down with my body. Long, shapely legs bracket mine. The soft, deep cradle of her thighs welcomes me to her false home. The flush of her skin. Wide, blue eyes no longer flat and dead. Each catalogue of her intoxicating attributes registers like a sniper's shot to the head, and my cock hardens to stone even as my brain loses all function.

The rush of blood to my cock almost makes me groan. I swallow the sound because the time when I groaned for this woman is long gone.

Her breathing escalates, and she begins to wriggle beneath me. "Axel…"

I allow myself a smile. "I believe I can tell the difference now between you and the girl I thought I once knew. This…this is who you really are, isn't it, Cleo? The devil's whore pretending to be an angel?"

She stares at me, her perfect face framed by the rich, glossy mane spilling across my floor. "I was never an angel. How could I be after you— What…what are you doing?" she asks with a distinct screech, her hands attempting to push me away as I grip her hips and press into her.

The heat from her hands fires me up even higher.

Harder. I roll my hips until my cock is fully settled into the V of her thighs. Her eyes darken into a deep, bottomless blue.

"Rough sex," I speculate. "Fuck, baby, if that was what you wanted, all you had to do was say. Do you know how difficult it was for me to hold back when I fucked you? How tough it was for me to stop from pounding that tight cunt every time you spread your thighs for me? You know how many dark fantasies I had about taking you so hard you would be sore for fucking days?"

She stills completely, the only movement her shallow breathing. "You didn't…you weren't…"

"Capable of it?" I laugh. "Are you one hundred percent sure about that? Think back. That night in the gazebo, after we were caught in the rain?"

Her breath hitches all over again. "Troy's beach party. You…you were drunk. That was why we ended up there instead of your room…"

"I wasn't drunk. I had one drink." I lower my head until her delectable mouth is one inch from mine. "One single beer while you wriggled that sweet little ass in my lap for three hours straight. I couldn't make it back to the pool house because my fucking balls were ready to explode. I wanted to teach you a lesson even though you had perfected the art of pretending to be so fucking fragile. And yet, tying your hands with your bra and securing your ankles to that post with my belt was so fucking easy, wasn't it? You were *extra* wet that night, weren't you? Whimpering while you pushed out that pretty little tush for me to ride, begging me to fuck you? How many times did you come that night?"

"I don't remember," she replies, her nostrils fluttering with agitation despite her cold voice. "Get off me." She attempts to push me off again, but I'm nowhere near done. I lower myself onto my elbows. Our stomachs touch. Her breath shudders out.

"I do. Many, *many* times. So many you had cum dripping down your legs."

Color surges into her cheeks. "If you say so."

"It's okay if you don't remember, sweetheart. You passed out after that last time, after screaming your lungs out. I carried you back to my bed in the rain. You were out for hours. Then you woke up and pretended it hadn't happened."

"Perhaps it wasn't as memorable as you thought," she snipes.

If I wasn't skating on the edge of madness, I would be amused. "It's all in my head? That's the defense you're going with?"

"It's the truth."

I shift my stance to her left, lower my head, and take another heady dose of her scent. The animal prowling in me roars its approval then pummels me with its need to ravage. "What about a few days ago? You only needed a little push to get yourself off, didn't you? What about right now? Are you going to deny you're as wet as I know you are or is that all in my head too?"

Her gaze sweeps down and away, and her lips firm into a thin, mutinous line.

"Not gonna answer? I'll find out for myself, shall I?"

Her rough gasp feathers my jaw as I capture both her hands and secure them above her head. I dislodge myself from between her thighs, ignoring my cock's demented snarling at being denied, and stare down at her.

She attempts to move away. I clamp my hand to her hip.

The bottom half of her lingerie set is already riding her hip. A firm tug is all it takes for more of her lower half to be fully revealed.

Her curvy hips and smooth, toned legs fire up a savage hunger in my already boiling bloodstream. Keeping my gaze on her face, I let my knuckles drift down the side of one thigh. A delicate shiver moves through her.

"Look at me, Cleo."

She ignores me. I caress back up again. Her mouth slackens a touch, her breath expelling in the softest gush.

"Look. At. Me."

Her gaze meets mine. Heated. Defiant.

"Are you wet?"

Her chin rises in mutiny.

I push her panties lower. My fingers slide over her stomach, my nails grazing over her smooth skin. The muscles quiver delicately beneath my touch.

I finally look down.

Fuck. The material clings to her taut skin, moves with her breathing and the restless movement of her hips.

Black lace panties with two dark purple bows resting on each hipbone.

Purple. Her favorite color.

I despise myself for remembering. I despise myself for a lot of things right now. Which is probably why my hand is a little too rough when I grip the fabric and drag it down, half ripping it.

"God, you're—!"

"Open your legs."

"No."

I drag the torn panties lower. "You think I'm going to force you? No, baby. We're going to stay right here on this floor, all night if we have to, until you show me that treacherous little cunt. Until I prove you the liar that you are. And while you think about that, I'm going to indulge myself with something else."

Wariness enters her eyes. Her wrists strain against my hold until she recognizes that I have the power here. "What?"

Back in Connecticut, I forced myself to resist. But tonight, tasting her was inevitable the moment I found her here. I recognize that now. Tasting her deep and long was always how I preferred it. Although a lot of things have changed, the way I take her plump, fuckable mouth isn't one of them.

I close my hand on her throat and fuse my mouth with hers, devouring her with ravenous licks and greedy bites. She whimpers, but I know she's not fragile. She never was. It was all a fucked-up delusion.

She never needed a gentle knight in shining armor.

So I become her marauder.

I savor the texture of her tongue, reacquainting myself with its rough slickness, before I suck hard on it. Keeping it prisoner, I bite on the tip. She jerks beneath me, a moan escaping our meshed lips. Then she opens her mouth wider, her greed for my kiss as powerful as my need for satiation on every level. My teeth sink into her lush bottom lip, drawing it into my mouth for a fuller taste.

Sweet fucking Christ, she tastes even better than I remember. Or perhaps now that I know who and what she really is, my darkness is ready to open itself up to hers. Whatever. I roll my tongue over and over on that juicy flesh, each lick pumping more blood into my pulsating cock. I'm harder than I've ever been in my life, my dick head already saturated with pre-cum. I press that aching part of my anatomy into her naked hip, my mouth hungrier with the need to taste what my cock can't.

She struggles against my hold, her need for more air transmitted in the heart thundering wildly against my arm. I don't let up.

An unhinged part of me wonders if anyone has ever died from kissing. Maybe we will find out tonight. I open eyes I don't remember shutting. Our gazes connect, and whatever she sees in mine makes hers flare wider in alarm. Her punchy breathing washes over my face in frantic waves.

She presses her neck into the floor, backing away from me. I follow, my mercy nonexistent. Vicious teeth sink into my upper lip. I taste my blood and her saliva.

The tip of my tongue sweeps over the rough cut. The sting of it is sweet bliss. But not nearly enough. I chase the fading pain while a single word pounds through my brain.

Again.

I ease off a fraction, long enough to croak between our mouths, "Again."

Her eyes are enormous pools of trepidation. Ferocious hatred. And wild anticipation.

Her gaze fixes on mine, and she slowly draws my lower lip between hers. She captures me between her teeth. Then, with a groan, she sinks her incisor into the corner of my mouth.

My skin splits, and pleasure twists through me.

The sensation that registers is like a white-hot spike through my brain. Or what I imagine it feels like to be struck by lightning. I can't breathe. Or think. I'm floating above myself like a fucking ghost, wondering why the useless asshole I'm staring at is writhing in bliss and agony.

But it strikes me that I've always felt like this with her. Like two people pulling at my center of gravity.

Motherfucker.

Another surge of pre-ejaculate powers up my cock. I feel it soak my briefs, and I struggle to catch my breath. My vision burns blood red as I dive in for another mindless kiss. She takes it. All of it, her whole body a live wire, twisting and uncoiling beneath me.

Sensations flay me. Her skin. Her smell. The wild flutter of her pulse. Time ceases to register, our only anchor to reality the beating of dark hearts.

As I gorge, another thought takes hold. I warned her to stay away. She didn't listen. Now I hold all the power here.

So I decide that perhaps dying can wait a little while longer. I've tasted hell alone for a decade. It's time to taste it with her.

I break the kiss and lift my head.

Her mouth is swollen, ruby red, tinged with the savagery of our kiss and my blood. From head to toe, she's racked with tremors, caught within the brutal grip of unexpended lust.

My gaze drops, lingering over the plump, inviting thrusts of her breasts, then lower to her hollowed stomach to stop at the neatly trimmed hair covering her sex.

Her unbelievable scent fills my head with every breath I take. Even with her legs tightly squeezed together.

"Open," I command, the sinister power of my arousal bleeding through my voice.

The stubborn look on her face tells me she doesn't want to, but the subtle twisting of her body implies otherwise.

The latter wins out. Her legs fall open. Her potent scent is like a hallucinogenic, robbing me of thought for innumerable seconds. Like the mind-altering drugs I once sought oblivion in, her essence pulls at me with unstoppable magnetism.

I pull her bound hands down onto her chest and slide lower on the floor.

"Wider," I snarl.

Her knees bend upward, and I'm rewarded with the sight of her soaked, glistening pussy. I bend my head and inhale. My taste buds leap with excitement. My tongue thickens, and saliva floods my mouth.

Need stabs at me with agonizing brutality. It would be so fucking easy to taste her, to slide that pretty pink piece of false heaven into my mouth.

But that isn't the aim here.

So I glide my fingers between her thighs, taking care to avoid, for now, the hood and hole that beckon me with a siren's temptation. Her heat wraps around my fingers, her drenched labia hugging my digits.

A ragged moan tears from her throat, directing my gaze to her face. Her cheeks and neck are flushed, her head thrown back, eyes clamped shut. The tightness of her jaw tells me she's fighting the sensation with every atom of her being.

Such a pity.

If only she knew that, from here on out, victory will be mine and mine alone. I increase the pressure on her sex, which in turn juts out her clit. The swollen nub pulses, screaming for attention. Another whimper escapes her throat. Her mouth opens and forms silent words.

"Got something to say, baby?"

Her eyes pop open, and she hastily shakes her head. I massage some more until her clitoris turns as ruby red as her lips and her thighs tremble uncontrollably.

Only then do I allow my middle finger free rein. I tap her once. Twice. Her hips twitch clean off the floor. I press against her. Dark satisfaction oozes through me as the engorged flesh greets my fingers. "There it is. There's that saucy, pretty little liar. How she weeps for me," I croon wickedly.

Her eyelids flutter. "Oh…*God.*" Her voice is a hushed, fervent whisper as if she doesn't want to admit to the ecstasy rolling through her.

I tease and torment. Her hips pump, chasing my finger when I withdraw. My gaze stays on her face. I can't look away even if I want to. So I absorb every drop of pleasure and shame she reveals.

The pressure in my cock has passed the point of agony. I'm one shiver from exploding. But then, so is she.

I wait. Watch. Her full-body flush tells me what I need to know.

I withdraw my hand, and with every last ounce of self-control, I lurch to my feet.

Her shock is undisguised. Hard on the heels of that is a thick, hate-filled sob that jerks through her. As if the sound fills her with further loathing, she balls a fist into her mouth and rolls to her side.

"Get up."

The rumble from her clenched jaw sounds like, "Fuck you."

I reach down and grab her waist, pulling her upright. She staggers like a rag doll for several moments before she gains her feet. One hand pushes at mine while the other struggles to pull up her half-ripped panties.

"Round two to me, I think."

Her head snaps up, dark turbulent eyes lancing me through disheveled hair. "Fuck you." This time the words are raw and succinct.

"No, thanks. Or at least not until a few things are repositioned to my satisfaction."

She stills. "What does that mean?"

I reach out and smooth her hair off her face, the need to touch still a rabid fever in my veins.

"It means, sweetheart, that things are going to play out differently this time. Trust me on that."

"What things?"

My fingers linger in her hair, and I feel a punch of satisfaction when she doesn't push me away. "You'll find out. For now, you will run back home to Finnan and tell him to *fuck off*. I won't be visiting the house, and I won't be having a conversation about Afghanistan."

She gasps. "Axel, please."

For the first time, I hear a stark note in her voice. It pierces the thick fog of arousal long enough for me to focus on other things besides the obscene cravings of my black soul.

Bolton's warning flashes in my head. Hot on its heels, B's final words before I dismissed her. The questions I'm fighting off rush back, the demand for answers undeniable this time.

I take a step back, fist the hands that want nothing more than to drag her close, sniff the opiate of her skin.

I make a one-eighty-degree turn around the room, fighting an unexpected punch of something shockingly close to nostalgia. I face her again, note how small and mouthwateringly breakable she looks without her five-inch heels and pulsating hatred. "I'm going to ask you a question now, Cleo. If you lie to me, I will know. So think very carefully before you answer."

Chapter Ten

GAME ON

Her expression turns leery. Then resolute. She nods. "Okay."

"Five days ago when I told you to deliver the message to Finnan, you said I didn't know what he'd do if I sent you back empty-handed. What did you mean?"

Her expression shutters immediately. She attempts to look away. I capture her chin, raising her face to the light.

"You will not hide from me, not when you stand before me a ready and willing sacrificial lamb. Tell me."

"Finnan doesn't like to lose, you know that."

"You're generalizing. I prefer specificity. *What did he do?*"

"He was…having a drink when I told him. He smashed the glass. I called the maid to sweep it up. She took a little too long, he said. He beat her…dislocated her shoulder."

That sounded like Finnan. Rage twists through me. About to let go of her, I sharpen my focus on her face. Her *carefully* blank face.

"What about you? You didn't say what he did to *you*," I press.

She shakes her head, or attempts to anyway. My firm hold of her doesn't give much room for her to wriggle away from my demands.

A spark of anger flares into her eyes when I don't release her. "Are you sure you want all the gory details, Axel? Have you never heard of discretion being the better part of valor?" she spits at me.

"I have. But let's not kid ourselves that any one of us comes even close to being worthy of either of those words," I snarl. "You obviously didn't *fuck* him happy or he wouldn't have sent you back to me the very next day." The words taste like hot ashes in my mouth but, at the same time, I want her to confirm their accuracy.

She flinches. "No, I didn't fuck him happy," she whispers.

My relief is unlike anything I've felt before. I have the answer to the question I despised myself for needing to ask. I should move on to other subjects.

Like why this room, for instance. I don't. "I'm waiting to hear what he did."

"It doesn't matter!"

"The fuck it doesn't—"

She drops to her knees, the swiftness of her action dislodging my hold on her. Her hands fall on her bare thighs, and she tilts her face to me, the perfect supplicant. "This is what you want, isn't it? Me, at your mercy? Groveling at your feet?" Her gaze lowers to my still-hard cock. "Is that what turns you on now?"

I have never been into power play in the bedroom. Never needed to establish my dominance over a woman. I have sex the way I want, the way that delivers pleasure to whatever woman I'm fucking. Sure, I like to control proceedings, but it's never a pre-planned routine.

The sight of Cleo, so readily submissive, open and vulnerable, slices open a sinister vein of need so voracious that I stagger backward. Even as my cock swells to raging proportions.

She sees my body's reaction. Her breath hitches, and her lips part. This time the image of sliding my cock between her lips powers bolts of lightning through my bloodstream. I can barely see straight.

An incoherent sound erupts from my throat. I'm not sure why the sound galvanizes her but she begins to crawl forward. But something about the way she's moving isn't right.

A warning tingles on my nape. "Stop."

This time, the fear in her eyes is raw and unfettered. Every other emotion is stripped away. As I watch, frantically attempting to decipher what my brain is transmitting over the blinding roar of my hard-on, she shivers. "You have me, Axel. I'm begging."

Potent words that should immortalize the flames of my retribution.

And yet...

My feet propel me back another step. "Stay there. Don't say another word and do not move a fucking inch."

I stagger out the door, slam it shut behind me. My fingers spike into my hair, and I pace, confused about why I'm confused.

A segment of my plan may have come to fruition earlier than expected but I meant it when I called her a pawn. She is by no means the grand prize in my fight with Finnan. Not when he's sullied her beyond redemption.

So...why...?

My phone buzzes in my pocket. Distracted, I fish it out.

Bolton.

Bolton!

My finger hits the *answer* button.

"Why does he keep sending Cleo back to me?" I bark into the phone.

A weird little chortle. Then a harsh sniff. "Hello to you too, brother. You'll be happy to hear that I'm in...or out...or wherever the fuck you want me to be. Are you pleased to know you have thirty-three percent of the brotherhood in your favor? Or should I say thirty-three point three three three three—"

"Why, Bolton?"

"Because she's your fucking Achilles heel, brother. Always has been. Always will be."

I don't waste my breath denying the absurd assertion. "Why does *she* keep coming back?"

"Because he makes her."

My vision blurs. When it clears, my hand is braced on the wall. "How?"

"Ask her—"

"I'm asking you! Fucking answer me."

Another drug-induced chortle. "Why? Why should I give you shit when you made it plain you've cut us all out of your life?"

"I don't want you caught up—"

"Boo-the-fuck-hoo. You think you're the only one who bleeds when he's cut? The rest of us bleed too. At least you got out. Be thankful for that. Some of us didn't get the chance. Did you ever stop to think about that?" He sniffs again.

He's high as a fucking kite and soaring higher by the second. But I recall that Bolton was most veracious when he's high. Unfortunately for him, his outpouring is possibly the worst-timed confession in history. Because I need answers about the woman on her knees in the bedroom behind me more than I want to hear my brother's complaints.

"Answer me, Bolton. How does he make her?"

"How you do think? He keeps her in line the same way he used to keep Ma in line. Only difference is, Ma had a ring on her finger and the fear of a Catholic God's retribution in her heart. Your little…piece"—he chuckles—"well, there's no way to put this delicately, she stays for the shits and giggles."

I stare at my hand on the wall. The shaking hand—

I snatch it down and ball it tight. "Let me get this straight. He treats her the way he treated Ma, and she stays of her own free will? Are you sure?"

"Hmm…wait…hang on." I hear a clunk then a long, telling sniff. A handful of seconds later, he's back. "Yeah…where were we? Right, of course I'm not sure. When have any of us been sure about what goes on in Pa's head? You want to be absolutely sure, I guess you need to ask her," he slurs.

I have no room for the heavy emotion attempting to drag me down. "You need to stop snorting that shit, Bolton."

He goes silent for a minute. "If you care that much, brother, then step the fuck up."

The phone goes dead. I shove it back into my pocket and charge back into the room. She's exactly where I left her.

"Get up."

She staggers to her feet, a glimmer of pain flashing in her eyes before she masks it. The hardwood floor couldn't have been comfortable for her knees. To her credit, she doesn't rub her skin or flex her limbs.

She takes it. As if she's used to it.

Motherfucker.

My gaze probes her from head to toe. Every visible inch is creamy perfection. Unmarred.

"Turn around."

Her eyes widen. "Axel—"

"Now, Cleo."

Slowly, she obeys. Despite the volatile emotions roiling inside me, I'm paralyzed by the sight of her. From tumbling hair to tiny waist to heart-shaped ass lovingly cupped by silk and lace, every inch of her is mouthwateringly decadent. A feast for any red-blooded male.

A feast for my father.

Wrenched off lust's edge and back to my task, I scrutinize her body with scalpel-sharp precision. Nothing.

Was Bolton lying? No. Granted, the baying of demons is deafening at the best of times, but I didn't get it wrong. Something is going on with her.

I shake my head, frowning. "Your hair. Sweep it out of the way. I want to see all of you."

Her fingers twitch. A minuscule action. Her right arm lifts and curls behind her head. Her fingers brush her left jaw before they hook the thick swathe of hair and brush the mass to one side. A further expanse of silky, unblemished skin is exposed.

She starts to lower her arm. That's when I notice that she's favoring her left side, that arm a little less flexible than her right.

"Turn around, Cleo."

She turns immediately, relief on her face. "Are you done?"

"No, baby, we're just getting started. Take off your clothes."

Her immediate loss of color tells me everything I need to know. "There's no need."

"There's every need. If I'm going to take what you're offering...if I'm going to *fuck you* tonight, then you'll need to be naked. Or were you hoping I'd settle for watching you finger your pussy again?"

She shakes her head. "I...we don't...I can take care of you."

Several dozen images of just how she can take care of me whizz through my mind, even as I shake my head. "For you to achieve that to my satisfaction, you need to take off what you're wearing."

She wants to refuse. A flare of her nostrils ends with a twitch of a grimace a second before her right hand grips the panties, yanks them down her legs, and steps to one side.

For the third time in less than a week, Cleo McCarthy's pussy is bared to me. Except, this time, the ferocity of my arousal is tempered by what she's hiding beneath her teddy. What I can already see beneath the black lace edging up her left side.

Three purple bruises, edged in sickly yellow along one side of her ribcage. Bile and self-loathing rise along with blinding fury. "*Motherfucker!*"

Her teeth clench, whether from pain or in reaction to my rage, I don't wait to find out.

Striding forward, I knock her hand out of the way, grab hold of the material between her breasts in both hands, and rip it in half.

Beauty. Indescribable beauty.

And ugliness.

I shudder at the sight of her. I shudder at the thought of what I did to her a few minutes ago on the floor, while she was wearing this suffering on her skin. "*Jesus Christ*, Cleo."

"It looks worse than it is," she blurts.

She stays for the shits and giggles.

The idea that she's defending him makes every cell scream with homicidal fury. "Is that why you can't lift your fucking arm or a take a full breath? I'm an ex-soldier, trained in combat and other types of shit you probably don't want to know about. I sure as fuck know what a fist or a foot to the ribs looks like."

Her lips compress, and her gaze slides away, and once again I'm left with trying to understand the incomprehensible. "Why? What the fuck is so special about a middle-aged thug that you can't walk away from?"

Because that is what he is.

Finnan Rutherford was a common *thug* long before he bought a plane ticket and left the rough streets of Belfast behind him. Bespoke suits and a thousand fancy dinners haven't changed his DNA. "Does he have something on you?"

"Haven't we had this conversation before?" Her stillness and the boredom she tries to inject into her voice is telling.

"He does, doesn't he?"

"Axel—"

"What is it?"

She pales. Her gaze flicks away then defiantly returns to mine. "It's none of your business."

"That's where you're wrong. All it'll take is a phone call to him to make it my business."

Fear skitters through her eyes, but her headshake is definitive. "He won't tell you. What he wants from you has nothing to do with him and me."

All it'll take is a phone call to call her bluff, but I don't trust myself to interact with Finnan right now. My repository for fucked-up bullshit is overflowing, and the sight of her battered body is too much to handle. I drag the tattered lingerie from her body with one hand while the other reaches for my phone.

B answers on the first ring. "Send up a first aid kit. Now, please." I hang up.

"There's no need—"

"I require your silence right now, Cleo. Look at me and nod your agreement to shutting the fuck up."

She swallows and nods.

The kit arrives in minutes. "Strip and lie on the bed."

When she's stretched out, I dig out the special cream and smear a large drop on my fingers. I don't know where the hell B discovered it, but the cream numbs while providing exceptionally fast healing. An extremely useful resource in a BDSM club.

Cleo flinches when the cool cream touches her skin. I struggle not to grit my teeth as I massage the medication gently over her abused skin and watch the tension slowly leave her face.

When I'm sure the numbness is in full effect, I gently probe her ribs. Her breath hitches, but from the swift pebbling of her nipples, I'm certain it's from something other than pain.

He didn't break a rib.

I cap the tube, toss it away and rise. The closet that resembles the one from my childhood holds three dresses. I pick the one that'll be least aggravating to put on and return to the bed.

"Sit up," I command.

She slowly rises and drops her legs over the side of the bed.

"How do you feel?"

The breath she takes is a little deeper. "Better. Thanks."

I hold out the dress. "Can you put this on by yourself?" I'm nearing the limits of touch-Cleo-without-exploding.

She takes it and eyes me. "Are we going somewhere?"

I bare my teeth in a sick smile that makes her eyes widen. I cup the erection that hasn't abated despite the lunacy that permeates the room. My vision blurs for a second. "I'm fucked up enough to still want to fuck you black and blue on top of your black and blue. Putting clothes on that body might help with that problem."

Her face heats up, and her eyes darken, and fuck if that doesn't ramp up my temperature even higher. She pulls the black and white striped dress over her body and stands. It glides seductively over her hips to rest just above her knees. I mourn the loss of the sight of her pussy.

She glances toward the closet. "What about…umm…panties?"

I raise an eyebrow. "What about them?"

"Am I going to wear any?"

"No. It's going to be a long trip. I'm leaving my options open on that score just in case I have an urge to finger you at some point tonight."

The moment she steps into her heels, I place my hand on the small of her back and steer her toward the door.

"You still haven't said where we're going."

"You know where the fuck we're going. Where we've been headed since you showed up. You've pushed hard and bravo, sweetheart, I've cracked. So we're going to Connecticut. To see your..." Every description of who he is to her sticks in my throat. Every reminder of who he is to me burns a path of rage through me. "I was going to leave him to stew for a while longer, but this," I drift a hand down her side, "has got my attention. So yeah, we're most definitely going to see Finnan."

I watch her intently, searching for signs of triumph.

But either she's mastered the perfect poker face in the last decade or whatever game plan she's pursuing isn't realized yet. She chews on her lower lip in the time it takes for us to reach the elevator.

"You should be happy, Cleo," I whisper in her ear. "*Ecstatic.*"

"Are you...Is he going to like what you have to say?"

I laugh, deeply and bitterly. In all this, she still only cares about *him*.

"That depends on whether he's grown wiser and smarter with age or not. Either way, it'll be an offer he won't be in a position to refuse."

PART TWO
Cleo

PART TWO

126

Chapter Eleven

FRONT-ROW SEATS

Axel's video was the first one Finnan made me watch. Those twenty-one minutes in Finnan Rutherford's study when I was seventeen changed my life forever. It also placed Axel's existence in my hands.

Because that life belongs to *me*. Only me.

I alone will determine when and how the life of the man who killed my father, and tried to kill my mother, ultimately ends. It won't end tonight. Not if I have anything to do with it. Not until he's faced every single atrocity he's committed.

I watch his rigid profile now as he accelerates his sports car up the long drive leading to the Connecticut property. In the early hours of the morning, despite the heavy traffic in Manhattan, the drive took a little over ninety minutes with little conversation save for a query as to which brand of water I preferred when we stopped at a gas station.

He returned with two bottles and uncapped one for me, even going as far as to produce a handkerchief to mop me up when I spilled a few drops.

Gentle. Sexy monster. Caring. Cold-blooded psychopath.

Detachedly, I wonder how many other personalities he hides behind that pulse-wrecking, drop-dead-gorgeous face. Since hearing the name, I've googled Taranahar a few dozen times. All the articles I came across recounted atrocities of unthinkable proportions, a few less discreet sites throwing in harrowing pictures of mangled bodies.

Atrocities Axel is elbow deep in. It's not a leap to pin such barbarism on him. He killed my father, a man he knew was dear to me. He tried to kill my mother, although he has no idea he didn't succeed. Has no idea she's lying in a hospital bed thirty miles from here, kept alive by my total compliance and Finnan Rutherford's whim and blackmail.

Gentle. Sinister. Devilishly beautiful. Murderer.

I drag my gaze from the many-faceted devil as he pulls up in front of the mansion. Grim jawed, he casts a mocking glance at the house he grew up in.

"A marked difference from the last time I visited. Shall we?"

He snaps my seat belt free and steps out of the car. I track his imposing figure, dressed in black designer pants, a light gray V-neck tee and black leather jacket. Despite the July heat, he looks effortlessly cool and sexy as he rounds the hood to open my door.

Chivalrous monster.

Somewhere on a dark night a million years ago, I swore I was done trying to figure him out. But as I take his hand and step out, as he keeps hold of my hand and pins my body to the car, I find myself desperately trying to read him, trying to understand where it all went wrong for him. Where it went wrong for *us*. Was there ever any hope or was I always completely doomed right from the start?

"Still so serious," he murmurs, his breath caressing my cheek. "Whatever he's holding over you must be huge if you look like I've brought you to the gallows rather than to the home you're mistress of." Despite his mocking words and the lazy thrust of his hips against mine, his eyes are knife sharp, vigilantly cataloguing my every expression. "Care to tell me what it is?"

"No. I just want this visit to be over and done with."

"Don't worry, it will be." He raises the hand still clutching mine, a curious fascination on his face as he slowly links our fingers. Palm to palm, heat singes from one to the other, as if trying to meld our flesh. "I'm not leaving here until I get what I want."

The sound of a bolt sliding back draws our attention to the double doors of the house. Still gripping my hand, Axel drags me up the short flight of steps, situated between two imposing columns, just as Ronan opens the door.

Although equal in height and stature, Axel cuts a more imperious figure, his military training adding a dangerous edge to an already menacing package. The two men face off for a charged minute before Ronan steps to one side.

Axel strolls in, conducts a sweeping inspection of the marble-floored entry hallway, the grand staircase and light oak-paneled walls. The drapes that hang on either side of the cathedral-like windows are monstrously heavy and haven't been changed in years.

"I absolutely loathe what you've done with the place," he drawls. "Is this the current trend these days? Perhaps I need to renew my subscription to *Thug Homes Monthly*."

A muscle ticks in Ronan's jaw. "The place hasn't changed since Ma died, and you know it. And is that all you've got? Cheap shots at the decor?"

Axel's mocking façade drops for a second, and he looks almost disappointed. "You stuck around, brother, despite my warning. You want to see what I've got? You just earned yourself a front-row seat."

Ronan swears under his breath before his gaze drops to our linked hands. "Good to see where your fucking loyalties lie, you little slut," he sneers at me.

In a split second, Axel transforms from bored guest to lethal weapon, ferocious brutality seeping from every pore.

"Call her that again, Ronan. I fucking dare you," he invites, his voice baby soft with absolute malevolence.

The change is frightening, curiously mesmerizing. I want to look away, ignore the eldest Rutherford son the way I've done for more years than I care to count. But this version of Axel—savage defender, blind champion—triggers a long-buried memory. One that captures my attention and refuses to let go.

Axel and I on a beach…a different version of casual conversation with dangerous subtexts folded into malignant subtexts.

I mean it, Cleo. I see so much as a scratch on you, someone will fucking die.

That was one of a few conversations in the same vein. I listened to them with a giddy little flame in my heart, convinced they fell from the lips of my one true love. The one who would protect me, cherish me above everything else.

I couldn't have been more wrong.

Axel told me he would kill for me. What I didn't realize was that he meant it literally. Or cold-bloodedly. Or that the victim he picked would be one who mattered to me.

Worst of all, that the life-changing event would matter so little to him that he could carry on with his life as if it never occurred.

I watch him square off with his brother now, and my heart shreds with hopelessness.

"She's not worth a one-dollar dare," Ronan tosses out. "She never was. Too bad you're too blind to see that."

Axel delivers a chilling smile I feel in my bones. "You see blindness. I see the final act in a script I couldn't have written better if I had a host of heavenly angels wielding the pen."

My heart lurches despite the fact that this is what I've wanted all along—the Rutherfords at each other's throats, destroying each other the way Axel destroyed my family.

Ronan is eyeing him, wariness I've only seen him exhibit around Finnan crawling over him. After a minute, having failed to decipher the cryptic meaning, his eyes narrow. "What the fuck does that mean?"

"Front-row seat," Axel repeats.

Chapter Twelve

THE DEAL

AXEL

A door opens at the far end of the hallway. I watch Ronan turn to face the approaching footsteps, his expression morphing into one of fear-tinged compliance.

I stay where I am, my back to my father, my hand gripping Cleo's tightly. Maybe too tightly. She flinches and tries to pull away. I turn to her. "Stay."

Whatever she sees in my face makes her eyes widen and her mouth close.

What I feel is naked loathing so depraved that I wonder how the lethal force of it doesn't consume me. Again, she tries to disentangle her fingers from mine.

I let go of her hand for two reasons.

Delivering pain that isn't sexually oriented or has pleasure balancing it out was never my thing. And I need *all* my functioning faculties to deal with Finnan.

More than the cold fear of walking into my first ambush in the urban battlefields of Fallujah, more than the harrowing nightmare

of waking up the morning after blood was forced on my hands...
this is going to be by far my deadliest battle.

And it's one I intend to win.

My abs clench with revulsion as I sense him behind me. As I hear
him breathe the free air that his greed has helped snuff out of so
many.

"Since it seems that you don't intend to grace me with your hallowed presence, I'm forced to come to you."

I turn. Face the embodiment of every evil that lurks beneath my
own skin. I don't make excuses for what I am.

"Are you going to stand there like a deaf mute, boy?" The distinct
Northern Irish brogue Finnan wears with pride curls around every
word.

"I find it saves me a lot of time and effort to contribute only
when there's actually something useful to say. You taking a walk
from your den to your hallway doesn't constitute a useful conversation topic for me."

The muted curse comes from Ronan, the shocked gasp from the
woman I intend to reclaim this very night.

Finnan smiles. A white, ample smile that slashes his weathered
cheeks. But only his lips smile. Eyes the same color as mine remain
flint hard. Coldly toxic. The way they've been every time he's looked
at me.

I used to think he deliberately withheld any show of positive
emotion until it was earned. Time and experience and the evidence
within my own twisted DNA has proven that he's incapable of it.

He fingers the cuffs of his dress shirt with almost bored strokes.
But although he seems well put together, there's a bagginess to his
clothes that suggests he's lost weight. Or lost the patronage of his
favorite bespoke suit maker. The millions he spent trying to keep
himself out of jail have taken a toll on his bank account. I know that
for a fact.

"You're still throwing those feeble fists like you used to do when
you were a baby, and your ma, God rest her soul, tried to give you a
bath. It does the heart good to see some things never change."

I let loose a smile of my own as the familiar promise of combat oils my limbs. "You know what does *my* heart good? *You*. Thinking everything that has led to this has been a tantrum. I implore you to keep thinking that way. Believe that there's even a single scenario where you triumph."

"I don't need to. You will do all of the heavy lifting for me. Same as you've always done." His gaze flicks to Cleo, and I hear her sharp inhalation. Whatever passes between them ends when his eyes return to me.

I barely manage to keep my fists from tightening. "Sure. I'm happy to do one last act of heavy lifting for you. Just call the undertaker and pick a box."

Behind me, Cleo makes another sound. A twisted projectile of noise. Broken, yet powerful in grabbing my attention. The urge to turn around blasts through me. But that is not an option, not when my horns are locked in battle. I keep my attention on Finnan.

Your move.

"You must get this wild death wish from your mother's side of the family. If memory serves, her brother, your uncle Paddy, was also one to run his mouth off without forethought. Right until someone put a gun in it." His eyes gleam with a sinister light that makes me think that *someone* was him.

"Is that someone still around? I'd love to teach him a neat little trick that I learned in Manila."

"Axel." Cleo's voice quavers, her warning getting lost in the maelstrom of emotions coiling through the room.

Finnan's eyes shift to her again. I have to lock my knees not to step in front of her and block his view. Blot out every image of the two of them together that has attached itself to my psyche.

All traces of mirth are now drained from his face. "We'll continue this conversation in my den. Alone."

Ronan steps forward, affront bristling. "Pa—"

I make one last-ditch attempt to save my brother. For what reason, I don't know. "Listen to the man, Ronan. And if you feel like making drinks, I'll take a whisky, neat."

His jaw juts out. "I'm not your damn waiter."

I shrug. "Fair enough." I turn back to Finnan. "Lead the way."

I don't look at Cleo simply because I don't want Finnan's eyes on her. I don't want to dwell on the bruises hugging her ribs. Not right now. Not if I want to stop myself from driving my fist into Finnan's face until he stops breathing.

What I do savor is the fact that she's naked beneath that dress. That when I'm done here, she'll be readily accessible for the taking. And I intend to take her for as long as this insanity rides me.

Finnan heads for his office. I follow. I hear her footsteps retreat, and I detest that I already miss her presence.

Unlike the other parts of the house, Finnan's den has undergone a change since I was last here. An elaborate bar now resides opposite the huge desk and chair from where he rules what's left of his corrupt empire. He doesn't cross to it or offer me a drink. Despite what I said to Ronan, I don't need one. I'm dealing with Finnan stone-cold sober.

He steps behind his desk and sits on his throne. "This ends now. I know you've been running around with the Armenians and those other Eastern European assholes. I've even allowed you to run your little nightclubbing circus for long enough. It's time to come home."

"That 'little circus' was valued at eleven figures at my last audit. I'm sure one of your minions can verify that for you if you don't believe me. But let's not dwell on that for now. Or even on the fact that you believe you can order me around. This 'home' you wish me to return to, what do you foresee my purpose here being? Exactly?" I snap my fingers a second later. "Oh wait, could it be some hare-brained idea that I might help you with...something?"

"Watch yourself, boy. Need I remind you about that little video I have on you?" His voice has dropped to a pitch that terrified me a lifetime ago.

Now the urge to laugh is only halted by the permafrost weaving through my core. "I wondered when you would play that card. Is that supposed to terrify me?" I taunt.

"It's supposed to bring you clarity. Remind you that I've dealt worse a hand for lesser insults. I'm giving you the chance to focus your mind on what's important."

"Believe me, I'm focused. Are you though? Because I could've sworn this whole tiresome song and dance these past weeks has been to get me here to talk about a different subject entirely."

His shrug attempts a nonchalance that doesn't quite hit the mark. "Sure. Let's discuss that small business at Taranahar," he says.

I take a slow, steady breath. "You mean the one where your merry band of brainless thugs slaughtered over a hundred people?"

"There was never a definitive count."

"That's the thing with dropping half a dozen bombs on a village the size of three city blocks, *Pa*. After a while, they stopped counting body parts."

His lips curl. "From the way you speak, anyone would think you were on their side. Don't forget they bombed us first."

The inhumanity of that statement staggers me for a moment. "I haven't forgotten. But I'm on the side of not blowing people up for money or power."

The first sign that I'm getting to him is the hand that fists on his desk. "Life isn't all pansies and Kool-Aid. I thought I taught you better than that. Clearly my lesson didn't do enough."

A tremble rolls up from my feet. The breath locks in my lungs as images of bloody baseball bats, knuckle dusters, tire irons, and other instruments of mayhem flare across my senses. I count to ten to stop from lunging across the desk and adding to my own body count. "You think it's okay to teach your child a life lesson by forcing him to take a human life?"

"If he wants to succeed in this world, yes! What kind of world do you think you live in, boy? Take a look around you. The whole fucking world is eating itself."

"And so your solution is to help things along by blackmailing a general so you can bag millions along the way?"

His face twists in a mask of contempt. "Why the hell not? If McCarthy and I hadn't taken the opportunity, someone else would have. Whatever else he was, Courtland was a patriot, and he was not afraid of a little sacrifice in order to stick it to the bastards who bombed this country."

"And what about the other sacrifices that had nothing to do with the war? What about the girl he killed in McCarthy's brothel?"

He doesn't seem surprised that I have all this information at my fingertips. He merely shrugs. "Collateral damage that facilitated a smoother relationship."

A red haze rises before my eyes. "She was someone's daughter!"

"She was a whore," he clarifies, as if that justifies everything. "The only thing that mattered was that Courtland was a top-level army bureaucrat who happened to be in the right position to gear us up for long-term success. He handed me…*us* the deal of a lifetime. You think I should've walked away because one whore snorted the wrong shit up her nose? My ma didn't birth me to be a wimp! She taught me that survival was everything. She beat it into me as many times as was necessary for me to learn that lesson. But you, a son of my ribs, want to be coddled for the rest of your life after one unfortunate incident?"

"So survival is everything, even survival against an enemy that doesn't exist, isn't that right? You used to see shadows everywhere. Clearly that hasn't changed. Tell me, is it your paranoia that has you now making up a mother who doesn't exist? You grew up on the streets of Belfast after you were tossed out of the orphanage for beating up another child, remember? Presumably a child who was helping the world eat itself?"

"Enough with this nonsense! I need the Taranahar issue to go away. You're going to help me."

I could ask him how he imagines that would happen in a million years. But that isn't how this game will play out. I don't smile. I don't posture. I stare at him a minute before I ask. "How?"

The fact that I don't immediately tell him to go to hell stuns him for a moment. He regroups quickly although his gaze remains wary. "People get excited when the term 'war criminal' is tossed around. I need you to work with my lawyers on getting the excitement to die down, and preferably get the indictment thrown out."

"How?" I ask again.

"You have a Bronze Star Medal and a Distinguished Service Medal, plus a personal commendation from the president and useful contacts in the military. I need you to be the public face of my case when the time comes. I'll take care of the smaller behind-the-scenes matters. I'll even forgive this nonsense with the Armenians and Albanians, as long as you put a stop to that too."

Bile rises up my throat and floods my mouth. I swallow and force myself to speak. "What smaller matters?"

He rises and strolls to the bar, the confidence that I'm right under his thumb where he wants me easing his tension. "Nothing you need to concern yourself about." He reaches for the bottle of Irish whiskey and pours out two glasses.

I force myself to take the one he offers me. I raise it to my nose and sniff the less-than-premium brand he drinks these days before I twirl the glass. My interest in the drink is enough to satisfy him. He turns away, downs his shot, and returns to the bar to refill his glass.

"You do this for me, and you have my word the video will be destroyed," he says as he sits back down.

His word. Cheaper than the drink in my hand. I pretend to think it over.

A full minute passes before he leans forward, my silence taken for acquiescence. "There's a place for you back in the family, boy. Do this for me, and it's yours."

I nod.

He sits back in his chair. Smug.

"War criminal investigations can drag on for years, what with the red tape of international jurisdiction and all that," I venture. "They cost millions too, as I'm sure you found out with the first investigation."

He shrugs. "As long as I'm not sitting in some black hole of a maximum security prison, it can take forever for all I care."

"It's going to put a strain on my time. On my business."

"So?"

"So, I'm going to need…more."

"Define 'more.'"

Tension ramps back up my spine, thicker than before. I raise my head, look him in the eye. "Cleo."

The expression that creeps across his face makes my skin crawl. The need to speak her name in his presence makes me want to pummel something.

"She told me I was wasting my time sending her to you," he muses, a repulsive smile curving his mouth. "You'd think she'd have picked up by now that I know what makes my own son tick."

"Is that a yes?"

"You return her to me when this shit is over. I'm not finished with her yet."

"If you still want her when I'm done with her."

His teeth bare. "Unless you're superhuman, you won't be able to wear her out that easily. Trust me, I've tried."

The manic wave is cresting too fast. I need to leave. But I need answers. "I also want to know what you're holding over her head." Fuck. I realize my slip the moment the question leaves my lips.

Finnan's smile widens. "She didn't tell you?"

My jaw clenches, and I remain silent.

"I'll tell you what, show me some evidence that you're on the Taranahar case, and we'll come to an arrangement about your precious girl."

I stride to the nearest surface and dump the glass still holding the liquor. I'm long past saturation point. The brutal need to take vengeance snaps at the anchors of my control as I head for the door.

"I'm leaving. And I'm taking her with me." I grab the handle. Yank it wide open.

"You'll meet a little resistance but I'm sure you'll bring her round eventually. Oh, and remember what I said. I want her back."

I look over my shoulder. His expression is still smug. I can't resist the urge to wipe it off his face. "What makes you think she'll want to come back to you when I'm done using her?"

He shrugs, his demeanor remaining the same. "She may temporarily share your bed, but she'll *always* be mine. I only need to crook my finger for her to trot back to my side."

My brain screams at me to let go of the door. To rip and maim and smash and burn. I grip it tighter, pull the door wider.

"Axel?"

The change from *boy* to my name is probably what stalls my feet. Even if I bothered to recollect the last time he used my name, it would be a futile exercise.

"What?" My voice bleeds blackness I won't be able to restrain in the next ten seconds.

"We have a deal. Attempt to double-cross me at your peril."

Chapter Thirteen

SPECIAL DELIVERY ... OR NOT

CLEO

The futility of pacing finally drives me to the shower half an hour after I retreat to my bedroom. But standing still under the torrent of hot water doesn't stop my racing thoughts.

The two men who destroyed my life are locked in a room, colluding two floors beneath me. I don't delude myself into thinking somehow I will escape being caught in the middle of whatever sinister arrangements are being hammered out.

I'm not leaving here until I get what I want.

All I can think about is how to survive the impending hell long enough to finish the job and save my mother.

Because hell *is* coming. The look in Axel's eyes promised it. The ferocity with which Finnan pursued this meeting and the way he looked at me downstairs confirmed it. I will be collateral damage at the earliest opportunity. Or a sweetener to seal the deal the second it's required.

What I don't know is who will emerge the victor in this round. Finnan has innumerable aces up his sleeve. Including the video whose existence confirms the solid reality of monsters.

But Axel was... *is* the most cunning man I know, otherwise he couldn't have deceived me so completely. Couple that with the extra edge the army has honed into him and every fear that lurks in my heart is ramped up another thousand degrees.

I shut off the water and step out of the shower. My body is as clean as it can be with Finnan's brutality still stamped on it. Before the attack, he hadn't touched me in months, his preoccupation with Taranahar relieving me of his interest. Even as I threw myself between him and the maid, I knew it was a bad idea. But my conscience and my heart couldn't withstand letting him traumatize another human being. Not when I could stop him.

My fingers trace my midriff. Axel's cream has worked wonders. The muscles that were screaming before now merely throb with each heartbeat. The ribs that were on fire no longer deliver agony with every breath I take.

Grabbing a towel, I pat myself dry then sit in front of the vanity. I avoid my gaze in the mirror as I apply moisturizer over my body. I also avoid acknowledging the sneaky little tingle between my legs that has resided there ever since Axel walked through the door at his macabre club.

Yes, I'm ashamed I writhed at his erotic command and momentarily set aside my goals for a taste of what his touch promised.

I release my hair from its knot and brush it out, taking refuge in the mundaneness of the act. When my scalp begins to tingle, I drop the brush, rise, still naked, and leave the bathroom.

Axel is leaning on the wall next to the door leading to my dressing room, arms folded, legs planted. A dark overlord bringing nothing but chaos and destruction.

My gasp fades to silence as we stare at each other.

I can attempt to pass him, get some clothes to cover myself. Or retreat back into the bathroom and grab a towel. I do neither.

The seconds pass, and I accept that there's no use rushing to cover myself. He's seen me naked more times in the last week than anyone else has in a long time.

But still he looks his fill. Bold eyes burn a path down my face, my throat, my breasts. He lingers there for an age, compelling my nipples into painful peaks until, satisfied by my reaction, he continues tracking a course down my body. His jaw clenches when his gaze drops to my bruises. But the slit between my thighs soon draws him away.

Axel lingers the longest at my pussy, his nostrils flaring as he scents me audibly from across the room. The raw, animalistic nature of it weakens my knees while keeping me locked in place. "I double-locked the door. How did you get in here again?"

It's false security, locking my door in a house where I'm a prisoner, but it's one I cling to nonetheless. Staring at him, watching his powerful arms drop as he prowls forward, that security dissipates faster than a snow cone in hell.

"I picked up a lot of tricks during my time in the army, sweetheart. Infiltrating places I'm not supposed to be was a job requirement. Especially in my last year. Remind me to tell you about it sometime."

The connotations of that spike panic inside me. "You say that as if we'll see each other again anytime soon." I know we will. But my intention was for it to be on my terms.

He doesn't answer immediately. Instead, his gaze conducts another sizzling scrutiny, this time from the feet up, lingering again at my now-throbbing sex.

Then he walks around the room, taking his time to run his hand over the silk scarf draped over the armchair next to my dresser, my bottle of perfume and the gilt frame holding the picture of Saint, the dog I lost when I was twelve.

His touch is clinical, devoid of emotion. Not so the face he presents to me when he's done fingering my things. A face etched with naked, savage intent. "Did you think we would not? Shame on you. Especially after everything you did to ensure this very outcome?"

He starts to cross the room.

I take a step back.

"Stay," he growls.

Downstairs in the hallway, the word was filled with icy command. Here, now, it's no less domineering, but there's an added inflection to the order, a warning that promises anarchy if unheeded.

I kill the tortured sound that rises in my throat. And take another step back.

His hand whips out, capturing my arm. The restraint isn't painful or unbreakable, but the fire from his hand brands me, spreads like wildfire until my belly quivers with the shock of it.

"One of the many lessons you'll need to learn, *fast*, is this: when I say stay, you *stay*."

Panic escalates. "Why would I need to learn anything? Isn't your business in this house concluded?"

"My business with Finnan is. My business with you is just starting."

"No. We don't have anything to—"

"Are you really going to say that, Cleo?" he cuts across me. "Did you really imagine that all you had to do was deliver me to him and you and I would be done?"

My mouth dries at the sight of the unholy blaze in his eyes. "What…why…" I swallow and try again, hating my brain's inability to form coherent sentences.

"The words you're looking for are 'when.' 'Where.' 'How.'"

I open my mouth but no words emerge. I can only stare as one broad thumb trails over my skin, the lazy caress belying the frenzied look in his eyes.

"The 'when' is right fucking now. We're leaving this shit hole in the next five minutes. The 'where' is wherever I damn well decide. The 'how' is also my choice, although you should know the first time will probably be with you on your knees. Fucking a woman from behind is the surest and most satisfying way I get off. And I'm not ashamed to say, I need to get off pretty damn soon."

My heart drops to my stomach, even as my temperature rockets. "Axel—"

He nods approvingly, his head dropping to sniff the curve of my shoulder. "That's it, baby. Keep saying my name in that terrified little voice. Even if it's as fake as fuck, I guarantee you it'll always get me rock hard." He lingers, the very tip of his nose brushing my earlobe as he inhales me some more.

I stanch the shiver that curls up from my toes and summon every ounce of strength into my vocal cords. "I'm not leaving with you. I can't. I *won't*."

Every cell in his body seems to clench with rigid fury. I can't succumb to my terror because what Finnan might do to my mother if I leave without his permission is even more terrifying.

"You misunderstand me, sweetheart. This isn't a negotiation. I've already done that. You are my prize. So you see, there's no fucking way I'm leaving here without you."

Shock hits rock bottom and bounces hard, birthing pure anger. "Well, that's too damn bad. I don't give a flying fuck what you agreed with your father. I'm not leaving this house." Not when it means leaving the fate of precarious lives in Finnan's hands.

Axel's eyes turn into ice chips. "There's something Finnan wants more than anything else. Even more than you. I have the power to give it to him. In exchange for you." His gaze drops to my ribs, his chest rising on a furious inhale. "How do you think it'll play out if I walk out of here, *alone*?" he rasps with a voice that's barely human.

My brain scrambles in frenzied alarm. In the end all I can do is appeal to the monster before me. "Please…"

If anything, that drags the beast closer to the edge. My knees sag. His other hand grips my arm, holds me up to the lit fuse flaming in his eyes. "Beg for him one more time," he dares me.

I shake my head quickly. I can't leave my mother. I can't trust that Finnan won't turn off the machines keeping her alive the moment my back is turned. "I'm not begging for him. I'm pleading with *you*!"

A muscle jumps in his cheek as he stares at me. "Tell me why you want to stay so badly. Tell me what he has over you."

So Axel can find my mother and finish what he started? "No."

His gaze freezes over. "Then stop pleading. There may be other pleas I choose to accommodate. Leaving here without you isn't one of them."

His hands move up to my shoulders, the caress imprinting, marking me, attempting to change what can't be changed.

But despite that knowledge burning in my heart, my body responds to the caress. Already tight nipples strain further, my breasts growing heavy as liquid fire pools between my legs. My body heated the moment I spotted him across the room. Now, with his hands on me, his earth-and-spice scent engulfing me, my pussy swells, its slickness saturating me.

Sharp gray eyes track down my body, absorbing the change. His full lips part, his breath a light pant as his hands drift down my throat. Long fingers trace my collarbone, the hollow where my heart races. The valley between my breasts.

Then, as if he can't help himself, one hand spears into my hair, holding me still, while the other cups my breast. Kneads. Teases my nipple with a distinct lack of gentleness.

My deep, helpless shudder rips a feral sound from his throat. "Fuck." His warm breath washes over my upturned face. "You've filled out in all the right places. I'm going to enjoy fucking every inch of you. I'm going to relish reclaiming what was once mine. Then I'm going to return you to him, broken beyond repair."

The clinical outline of what he intends to do to me freezes my heart. Enough to stall the encroaching fear. Enough so I can look him straight in the eye.

"I never belonged to you." Not this version of Axel anyway. I belong only to the boy I once thought he was. The boy who was only ever real in my imagination.

"Maybe not. But you gave yourself to me first. I was the first man to fill that snug little cunt, to come inside of you, watch you stagger around all day, dreamy-eyed with my cum inside of you. That gives me rights, baby, whether you like it or not."

"Well, you're going to be sorely disappointed if you're counting on me being dreamy eyed again."

"Dreams are for assholes. I much prefer the reality of hearing you scream my name as you plead for mercy. Mercy you won't receive. Not until I've fucked you till you can't stand up straight. That is also *your* new reality. Accept it."

My mind spins with his words and the situation I can't immediately figure a way out of. One minute ticks by. Two.

My choices are nonexistent. For now.

He watches the fight go out of me with grim satisfaction. Giving my breast one last squeeze, he releases me. "We're leaving."

He casts an eye over the room, and whirls back to me, jaw clenched, his frame brimming with electricity. "And you won't bring anything he's given you. Not even a goddamn toothbrush."

I snort. "You expect me to go out naked?"

He freezes for a moment, eyes narrowed. The next instant, he shrugs off his leather jacket, drops it to the floor, and tugs his T-shirt over his head.

The unexpected display of chiseled, hairless chest, ripped abs, and golden skin fills my vision. My breath shortens, but the sight is nothing compared to what seeing his tattoos does to me. One elaborate design is a mesmerizing blend of words and symbols, some Celtic, others Japanese. They flow from his left ribcage, up and around his back, and over his shoulders. Around his belly button is a perfect symbol of yin and yang surrounded by vicious flames. On his muscled right arm, four letters spell *live* from top to bottom. On his left, the same letters from bottom to top, *evil*.

My jaw drops, and my hands fly out to brace myself against the bathroom doorway. Every promise of the physical specimen he would become was there in his late teens. But I'm still nowhere near prepared for the magnificent end product. From the top of his disheveled hair to the killer boots gracing his feet, I'm helpless against the potency of him.

So I stare. Gorge until my lungs scream for me to take a breath.

Self-preservation kicks in, and I know I can't watch that stunning perfection without spontaneously combusting so I shift my gaze to the T-shirt he's holding out to me. I must look brainless because he shakes the fabric at me. "Put this on."

"You can't be serious. I can't go out like this."

He takes my hand and slaps the material into it. "You can. You will. It's the choice between my shirt or you being naked."

"Dear God, you're insane."

He doesn't shrug off the slur. Or laugh it off. He stares at me, a peculiar light in his eyes. "Yes, I am," he says simply.

I'm not sure what to make of that. Not sure what to make of anything that's happened here in the last fifteen minutes.

Hands shaking beyond my ability to control them, I pull the T-shirt over my head. Immediately, I'm overwhelmed by his scent. Up close and personal, I drown in the warm spice of him. The cotton slides over my sensitive breasts, eliciting another shudder that shoots straight to my pussy.

Quickly digging my arms through the holes, I tug the shirt down. It falls to my knees, a respectable cover were it not for the fact that everything about this is fucked-up wrong. Especially the light in Axel's eyes as he drags his gaze over me.

My breath strangles all over again, my senses poised for what he'll do next.

He bends and scoops up his jacket. I force my gaze from his rippling muscles as he shrugs back into it and zips it halfway up his chest.

Dear heaven, if anything, he looks even more potent.

Desperate to escape the madness rampaging through me, I start walking toward my dressing room.

"Where the hell do you think you're going?"

"I need shoes, Axel."

"Not. One. Fucking. Thing."

Striding to the door, he yanks it open and looks pointedly at me.

I can do without shoes. Absurdly enough. But there are vital phone numbers I can't leave without. "Please. My purse. My phone."

Tension ripples his jaw. "You can bring your phone, but that's it. You won't need your purse."

He's a powder keg ready to explode. I rush to my bedside and dig my phone out of my purse while he bristles and catalogues my every move.

Because I can count on the fingers of one hand the things that mean a damn to me in this room, my feet don't drag as I exit.

He slams the door loud enough to wake the dead. His fingers circle my wrist, and I'm propelled down the hallway to the stairs.

When we're halfway down, Finnan appears at the bottom of the stairs. Although he doesn't break his stride, Axel moves in front of me, his bulk almost obscuring my view of Finnan.

"I came to wish you Godspeed. But also to tell you you're welcome back here anytime you want. *Both* of you."

We reach the last step, and Axel places his body directly in front of mine. "You shouldn't have bothered," he snaps. "Get out of my way or I'll be happy to assist you."

Finnan steps away with a smile. One I haven't seen in a while. One that says his power has been restored. My heart quakes at what that means for me. When Axel makes tracks for the door, it leaves me free to probe deeper into Finnan's expression.

What will it cost me to leave here tonight with Axel?

The question burns on my tongue but I dare not ask. Not in front of the man responsible for putting my mother where she is. Finnan stares back at me, offering me nothing while his smile grows.

I open my mouth, prepared to damn myself by asking, no, *pleading*, for my mother. "Finnan—?"

A hand captures my nape and my personal space is once again filled with Axel. "Do not speak to him. And stop *fucking* looking at him!" he hisses with fire and ice.

His hand stays on me until we reach the open front door. Then he sweeps me clean off my feet in one smooth move. Powerful arms hold me tight against his body effortlessly, as if I weigh nothing, as he walks swiftly down the steps. As we near his car, the door slides upward. He puts me in the seat, slots in my belt, and slams the door back down. He rounds the hood as if the devil himself is snapping at his heels.

Two seconds later, Axel Rutherford is accelerating down the driveway. Speeding me away from one hellish prison to another.

Chapter Fourteen

LEWD CONDUCT

The time on the dash reads 3:47 a.m.

Forty-two minutes since I was passed from one captor to another. For most of that time, Axel hasn't spoken. Outside, the landscape whips past in the predawn gloom. He stuck to I-95 when we left Greenwich until five minutes ago when he veered off the highway. Now, with only the occasional property flashing past, I have no idea where we are.

His T-shirt covers my thighs and knees, but my bare legs and feet remind me of my truly vulnerable state. I clutch the phone tighter between my hands. It's my only connection to my mother's doctors. My only means of help should I need it.

The idea is laughable. I have the phone only because Axel wishes it but I'm still grateful. Images of my body being found in a forest wearing his T-shirt or heaven forbid, nothing, flash through my mind.

I look around and see nothing but dark trees whizzing past. A shiver courses through me.

"You're not cold," he states from beside me, drawing my attention to him.

The hand controlling the wheel is relaxed now, his other arm propped against the door. He's a lot less tense than he was when we left Greenwich but I don't fool myself into thinking all is calm.

Instead I concentrate on his statement. "I'm not cold." The buttery-soft seat is warm, the temperature in the sports car pleasantly ambient.

"You must be shivering for another reason then."

The statement, softly voiced, nevertheless holds steel and demands an answer.

He's not getting the contents of my darkest fear. "It's not every day I'm kidnapped from my home and flung into a car wearing nothing but a borrowed T-shirt. I'm allowed some sort of reaction, aren't I?"

His mouth twitches for a nanosecond. "The T-shirt is yours to keep."

"And the kidnapping? Are we going to address that?"

"What's to address? You're mine now. End of story."

"Axel—"

"And if you stare at that phone one more time, it's going out the fucking window. You even *think* about calling him, I will crush you so hard you'll cease to exist. Is that understood?"

The stark words rob me of breath. This time my shudder originates from fear rather than the macabre conjuring of my brain.

"Answer me, Cleo. And for fuck's sake, stop shivering!"

"Yes. I…I understand." My voice is little more than a whisper.

I feel his gaze slant to me. Probe me.

"Motherfucker!" He wrenches the car down a dark road and floors the gas for half a mile before he brakes sharply before a semi-circle of red maple trees. "What the fuck's the matter with you?" he demands after he kills the engine.

I glance frantically around me. We're alone, with no other signs of life. "Why have we stopped? Where are we?"

Narrowed gray eyes shift from my face long enough to stab a finger in the middle of the car's satellite navigation. The pin on the map zooms in. We're on the edge of a park near New Rochelle.

"Cleo?"

I shake my head, my hand clenched tight around my phone. "Nothing's wrong. Can we...can we go please?"

Growling, he pries the phone from my hand and tosses it in the back. "Not until I get some answers."

"I told you, there's nothing wrong—"

"What the fuck does he give you that no other man can, Cleo?" The question jerks from him like a missile, straight into my chest. "What's so damn special about him that he would do this to you," he grabs the hem of the T-shirt and flings it up to bare my ribs, "and you still stay?"

He doesn't know your mother survived. As far as he's concerned, he finished the job that night. If you have any brains in that head of yours, keep that to yourself.

Finnan's words tear across my mind.

"Something you can never give me."

Scalpel-sharp eyes rip into me, his whole body once again lashed with lethal tension. "And what is that?" he asks. There's a strange note in his voice that, from any other man, I would attribute to vulnerability.

Axel Rutherford is incapable of that state of being. All the same, I have the upper hand here. For once, I have something he seems to want. Something I don't intend to give him.

I allow a slow, mysterious smile to curve my lips. "Why should I tell you? You seem to think you have all the power here. This one is my secret to keep. But take my word for it. You can *never* give me what he can."

The muted growl of a charging predator fills the dark space a second before he pounces. My seat belt is whipped from my body and he yanks me from my seat. The moment I'm sprawled across his lap, his fingers grip my hair.

He brings my face up to his. Holds me there, nose to nose, as his harsh breaths wash over my face. As he shows me the rampant madness churning through his eyes. "Maybe not, baby. But I will give you a whole *fucking* lot more."

Hot, firm lips slant across mine. Anger. Hunger. Nuclear-grade lust feeds into the kiss long before his tongue demands entry. Once he gets it, he rams deeper, rocketing the volatile dalliance to a whole new level.

It takes a minute to realize the rock I'm clinging to in this insane storm is his shoulders, that my very refuge is also my destruction.

I try to scramble free. His grip tightens until my scalp tingles. "*Stay. The fuck. Still.*" The words are smashed against our meshed lips, little more than a rumble from his chest.

I should heed the warning. But my mind is in free fall, the darkness both inside and out bloating my fears to uncontainable dimensions. Using his shoulders as leverage, I pull back. Our mouths part with a loud, rude suction that, absurdly, drives carnal need straight between my thighs.

"No," I manage, even as my body screams *yes*.

My crazed monster merely grins. "You don't get to say no to me, sweetheart. Not when I can already smell how badly you want me."

His mouth recaptures mine, tongue and teeth delivering pleasure so concentrated that my fear begins to melt. Other thoughts encroach.

He's so good at this.

How?

Who?

Where?

When?

A vicious volt of discomfort rams through me even as his pheromones bombard me. *What the hell*…

Recalling the crazy little move that set him alight at the Punishment Club. I nip at his mouth. He jerks beneath me, breaking the kiss to stare deeply into my eyes.

"There's my little cherry bomb. *Again*," he growls.

I dive back in, the hands that pushed at his shoulders a minute ago twisting into the leather, folding into the hair at his nape.

One hand grabs my hip, attempting to situate me more firmly in his lap. My head bumps the roof, and my ass hits the steering wheel.

I'm still sideways, the top of my hip cradling the monstrous erection tenting his pants.

"Fuck it." He slaps a button, and his door rises into the air. He steps out of the car with me still in his arms. Straightening, he just looks at me. In the still, dark night, the only sound is our ragged breathing and the scurrying of forest creatures. In the air, the scent of maple mingles with earthy spice and a well-oiled engine.

Stomping around to my side, he sets me down on top of the low roof. A sultry breeze whispers over me while the expensive car warms my ass.

All around me, shadows. "What…what are you doing?"

One firm hand pushes me back and holds me down. The ambient glow spilling from inside the car casts enough light for me to see the bald hunger on his face and the menacing hulk of his body.

My heart leaps into my throat. "Axel…"

His free hand runs over my body from shoulder to thigh, cupping my breast along the way. A helpless thrill of lust fires through me.

"I was going to wait till we got back to New York. But then you decided to go ahead and fuck with my mind. Didn't you, sweetheart?" His hand creeps beneath the T-shirt to grip my upper thigh. His fingers conduct a lazy circle inches from my burning core.

Sensation sizzles through me. Dark and carnal and so powerful that I can only shake my head.

Fierce eyes pinned on me, he draws my leg slowly, inexorably, over one shoulder. The T-shirt falls to my waist, exposing my lower half to a summer night and a monster's regard.

"Stay."

This time I heed the warning. He grabs my other leg and flings it over his shoulder. His hands capture my waist, his thumbs digging into my hipbones. The action causes my hips to jerk upward, offering my scent and sex to him. He looks down, his lips parting in a rough pant.

"I'm going to shave every wisp of hair off this pussy. Tomorrow," he rasps. "Right before I eat your bald cunt again. Then you're going to spend every moment you're with me without panties. I want this pussy available to me whenever the mood takes me."

A strangled sound of raw need erupts from my chest. My hands slide on top of the sleek car, flailing uselessly with nothing to hold on to. I watch his head descend. Slowly. Torturously.

Then he blows gently on my sex. The sensation is so unexpected, so intensely thrilling that my whole body shudders. Before the tail end of my shiver dies off, his tongue swipes at me.

Bold. Possessive. Full-on.

The broad kiss devours me from hole to slit, then his pointed tongue flicks with mind-melting expertise over my clit. Then he repeats the action.

Sensation rips me wide open. "Oh…*Oh*…"

His hands leave my waist, sliding beneath my body to lift my ass off the roof. He holds me effortlessly aloft, his thumbs sliding on either side of my pussy to part me wider.

He deepens the kiss, savors me so thoroughly, I can't stop the moans that erupt from my throat. My body, unaccustomed to pleasure on such an intense level, coils with acute anticipation as Axel continues to pleasure me with unrestrained decadence.

When pre-orgasm wetness slicks my body, I feel him tense for a second before a shudder ripples through him.

"*Fuck!*" The curse is torn from his throat. If he had a soul, I would imagine it stemmed from there too.

His movements grow more feral, his mouth and nose buried deep, scenting and lapping every drop of pleasure from me. The knot in my pelvis coils harder, my back arches off the roof, and I'm ready to detonate. "Oh God!"

His head snaps up.

"Cleo." My name is a sharp bark. I lift my heavy head off the roof. "Look at me. Do not take your eyes off me for one fucking second when you come."

"I…okay…please…Axel."

"That's right. You say nothing…*scream* nothing but my name."

"Yes. Don't stop. *Please don't stop*."

He licks me again, groans deep as he sucks my whole pussy into his mouth. "*Jesus*, you taste…fuck."

The rush and the roar build to a breaking point. I know I'll forever be damned for the pleasure I take from the monster who ruined my life. But I can't think, can't function beyond the bliss bearing down on me.

His eyes pin me, absorbing every twitch and tremble, gasp and moan.

"Axel." It's not a scream but a whisper.

"Fucking give it to me. Everything."

"Oh…Oh…*Axel*." The deepest, darkest, headiest orgasm rolls through me, singeing me from head to toe. My limbs jerk like puppets, my thighs squeezing the jaws of my psychopathic captor.

"Yes…holy fuck." His tongue quickens against me, staying true to his word and lapping up everything I have to give. When his gaze drops from mine, I sag back against the roof. I'm not sure if the stars above me are the real thing or a byproduct of my bliss.

A minute passes. Two. He eventually trails his lips along one inner thigh, then the other.

His hands leave my body, and I hear his zipper lowering. My gaze drops as his jacket comes off and is tossed onto the hood. His ripped, superathlete's body is exposed and framed against the shadowed trees.

"My turn."

Chapter Fifteen

P OR A

Oh God.

I tell myself there's no way to stop this from happening. That I'm caught between the rock of a merciless father and the hard place of a demon son. But a part of me rebels against that complete damning. The part of me that remembers Axel's look of anguish when he saw my bruises earlier. His gentle hands as he tended to my ribs.

I hate the recollection. I don't want to explore the tiny voice that says he'll stop if I say no. Because the probability is high that, if that happens, my fate will worsen. My heart rushes to embrace that reasoning. Because given the choice between one devil and another, surely the devil who takes time to draw pleasure from my body before he takes his is better than the one who uses violence?

I shake my head, quelling the dissenting voices in my head. I know which side is winning. The side that already has me panting on top of his car like a bitch in heat.

A clack of his belt, then the distinct sound of another zipper lowering.

He pulls my knees up and apart, exposing me more widely to the night air and his gaze. For a long moment, he stares down at me, one hand pushing his pants and boxers off his hips.

I look down as his cock springs free. My mouth dries. I'm not sure if time and distance has distorted my memory but the boy I knew and the man I'm looking at could be two separate beings.

Because where the Axel of youth and imagination was seriously impressive, the man before me is dauntingly overwhelming.

Even without the benefit of adequate lighting, his length and thickness trigger a quivering deep in my belly. As I watch, he grabs and strokes his cock with his left hand, slowly, lazily from root to tip. The drop of pre-cum that pools at his crown catches on his forefinger and is spread along his length on a downward stroke, leaving the underside of his heavy rod glistening.

The word tattooed on his arm ripples with intent as hooded eyes climb up my body to my face, his hand still leisurely pumping his cock.

"Take off the shirt," he orders, his voice pulsing with power and need.

My hands are heavy as I move to obey. Somehow I get it off, idly sense it sliding down the hood to join his leather jacket.

Fully exposed to the elements, my nipples harden to painful nubs.

His lips part, and I catch the hungry flick of his tongue over his lower lip as his gaze latches on to them. "Cup those tits for me," he rasps. "Offer them to me. I want to taste."

My hands slide beneath the heavy globes, and my moan catches me off guard. An existence steeped in unrelenting fear and bleakness doesn't leave much room for exploring one's own body, and I can barely contain the new sensations drowning me. Heart slamming against my ribs, I squeeze and lift my breasts to him.

He falls forward, one hand braced on the roof as he lowers his head. His tongue swirls over my areola for charged, mindless seconds before he sucks the tip hard into his mouth. The power of his suction hollows his cheeks. Within his warm mouth, he flicks his tongue against the sensitive peak, driving me out of my mind.

When I imagine I'm about to explode, he transfers his attention to the other peak, repeats the madness. Back and forth, he ravages my breasts. Mouth, tongue, teeth collude to drive me insane. Between my legs, my slickness intensifies, my clit screaming with the need for attention.

As if he senses it, his cock nudges against me. Apprehension ramps up high. He's big. Too big.

"Axel...I..."

He lets go of one nipple, kisses his way to the other straining peak. "Shh. This is happening, baby. No turning back now."

Despite the dark promise, he doesn't enter. Instead he slides his broad length up through my gathering cream. The engorged veins circling the underside of his cock bump over my clit. Over and over, until I feel my liquid mess coat my ass.

That's when he pulls back a fraction, and his fingers find me. He caresses my hole for a handful of seconds before one finger slides into my snug channel.

I gasp at the alien sensation while, above me, the considerable resistance he meets produces a vicious hiss.

"*Fucking Christ*, you're tighter than a goddamn drum." He pulls out, and pushes back in.

My breath strangles in my throat, and my eyes begin to roll.

"Eyes on me," he commands from between clenched teeth as he pulls back out.

Our gazes lock. I glimpse rapacious hunger. Barely leashed control. And a looming question I don't want to answer.

He finger-fucks me with single-minded intent, his eyes consuming my every reaction. His mouth returns to my breast, his tongue wickedly lapping at my nipples as he adds one finger and attempts to slide them both into me.

My body jerks at the pressure.

"Stay still."

I swallow a fresh dose of trepidation. "I...can't."

He tries again. My slickness eases his way, but the pressure knocks the breath from me.

Dear heaven, if he can't get inside me with his fingers, how on earth am I going to take his cock?

As if he hears my wild thought, he curses again. "*Not* fucking you isn't an option, Cleo. So you need to stop tensing up." The bite of frustration in his voice tells me he's reaching the edge of his endurance.

His fingers move again. Deep. Deeper. He twists his digits and strokes upward. Electricity zaps me from ankle to temple, and my hands fall away from my breasts.

An unholy gleam enters his eyes as he repeats the action. My startled cry precedes a rushing sensation that feels like an orgasm. But not.

"*Motherfucker*, did you just *gush*?" His voice is strangled, his nostrils flared wider than I've ever seen them.

A different heat engulfs my face. "I…don't know. I've never…"

"You've *never*?" Rabid eyes dig into me, demanding the truth.

I shake my head immediately, cringing when I feel the liquid spread. "No. I'm sorry," I whisper.

A harsh, incredulous laugh barks from him. "You're fucking *sorry*?"

"Please— *Argh!*"

A cunning twist of his fingers and electricity sizzles again, setting me aflame. The rush barrels through my pelvis again. Soaks his fingers.

"Jesus Christ." His eyes squeeze shut a second before his head drops between my breasts. His body expands on rough, choppy breaths.

What is happening? "Axel?"

The sound he makes as he lifts his head is pure wild animal, the look in his eyes frenzied as his beast rises. Rough hands hook under my knees and grip my hips to drag me to the edge of the roof. With my ass hanging over the edge, he rests his steel-hard cock against me.

"Sorry, sweetheart. This is going to hurt." The apology is couched in raw, unwavering intent.

Even with a dozen armies, I know I won't be able to stop him. The shrieking voice inside mocks my feeble attempt to deny that I want this too.

His broad head pushes into me, his hands bearing me down to receive him. Pain slashes through pleasure, iron-hot and spine-stiffening. My scream rips through the night.

"Fuck!"

My head jerks from side to side, and I throw out bracing hands. "No, Axel. I can't."

He freezes, loud breaths tearing from his throat. Then he leans forward until our lips are an inch apart, our eyes fused. "You're going to take me, Cleo. Right here. I'll leave the choice to you whether I stay in your pussy or take your ass. But one way or the other, I'm coming inside you."

Before I can respond, he's kissing me. Deep, carnal. Mind melting. His hips don't move, and the tip of his cock stays buried inside me. My hands are braced on his chest as the deep, erotically charged kiss continues.

I don't recall commanding them, but my hands move. Explore hot, rippling muscle. His strong neck. The thick, silky hair at his nape. I can barely think when he kisses his way along my jaw, down my throat, and up to my ear.

"Pussy." Deep voice wrapped with hard arousal. "Or ass."

The idea of all that relentless power in my back channel makes me shudder with an emotion I can't swear is one hundred percent terror. My already stretched pussy clenches tight around him, a shocking, greedy ripple starting deep inside.

His teeth sink into the curve of my shoulder. Hard enough to leave a mark. "Fucking do that again and all bets are off," he warns with a guttural rasp.

"Axel—"

"Pussy. Or ass."

The rippling intensifies, aided by the hunger building with each second. A whimper falls from my lips. He devours it with his own lips then raises his head to pierce me with fierce eyes.

My time is up. I'm nowhere near ready to take him with any other part of my body than where he already is.

"P-pussy," I stutter.

He pounces on the word, kissing it straight from my lips.

I hold my breath. But he's still not satisfied. Because seconds drag by and he doesn't move.

"Wh-what?"

"Say it again, Cleo. Beg me to fuck your pussy."

Echoes of the past sprinkle across my fevered mind. But where his demand for dirty words was glazed with mirth when we were young, every atom of his being is deadly serious right now.

I don't want to beg. A part of me wants to look back on this moment and absolve myself of this madness.

But where discomfort reigned, dirty anticipation and raw hunger smash through, digging their vicious claws in. When my hips roll of their own accord, he hisses.

The arms hooked beneath my knees spread me wider. "Say it!"

"Fuck me! I want you to fuck my pussy," I blurt in a surrendering rush.

Pain wrapped in unforgettable pleasure wrapped in raw lightning. That is the only way I can describe the feel of Axel plowing into me.

My scream blisters my throat. His animal grunt summons the beast. He waits a measly handful of seconds for me to adjust to his monstrous size before he withdraws and thrusts back inside me.

"Sweet mother, you feel unreal," he groans through a shudder.

I want to confess that yes, I feel unreal. That nothing about this should feel okay. In my heart of hearts, I know it's not. The loathing that has fuelled my existence for so long hasn't disappeared. It's just buried beneath the monumental tsunami of pleasure rolling through me.

As soon as he's done, as soon as I find my voice and brain again, all will be well. Until then...

He fucks me with savage, exquisite expertise, each thrust yanking me to a higher plane of bliss. My body slides across the roof until my head hangs over the driver's door. With a growl, he pulls me back down until my ass is over the edge again. He clutches my buttocks and guides me onto the relentless power of his cock.

Through the haze of pleasure, I look down, and my breath catches at the sight of his cock sliding inside me.

The strangled little sound I make seems to turn him on. Unbelievably, he thickens further inside me. One hand slides between the roof and my lower back, holding me still.

"You like that, baby? Like seeing your tight little pussy devouring my cock? You like seeing me sweat just to get half of my cock inside you?"

Although the sex was phenomenal, filthy talk never featured in our adolescent coupling, except for that one night in the gazebo, the night I received a taste of the real Axel and chose to ignore it. Hearing the vulgar words fall from his lips, I'm ashamed by the extra kick of electricity they deliver to my body.

I catch my lip between my teeth before I blurt out the *yes* scrambling up my throat.

"Not gonna answer, huh?" he asks after a dozen lethal pumps hurl me to the edge. "Watch me, then. Watch me make it so you can't fucking walk tomorrow without feeling me inside you."

He drags me lower, urgent hands yanking my hips to meet his rough penetration.

"Axel!" My flailing hands find his shoulders. My nails dig in, desperate for something to hang on to as my world begins to disintegrate around me. "Oh God…I'm…I'm coming!"

"Yes." The single word is yelled through clenched teeth, his piston-fast orchestration of our lower bodies hurtling us at lightning speed toward combustion. Ecstasy bursts out of me in a million sparks of energy, dragging an endless scream from my soul.

Seconds later, he slams into me, a furious groan tearing the lid off his control. Blistering heat sears my insides as he shoots his semen inside of me. Powerful. Endless. His whole body trembles with his release.

I'm weak as a newborn kitten. But evidently, he possesses excess energy because he tugs my legs around his waist, plucks me off the roof, reverses our position and enfolds me in his arms while keeping his cock fully embedded inside me.

He leans back against the car, his head buried in my neck. I rest my spent body against his chest.

Above our heads, the sky begins to lighten. Birds tweet, underbrush creatures scurry, ushering in a new day.

An age passes without words spoken before he straightens, carrying me with him to where I discarded his T-shirt.

He hands it to me, nodding at me to put it on. I pull the material still holding his scent over my head while his hands hold me tight against him and I continue to throb around him. Still in silence, he walks us to the passenger side.

He hesitates beside the door, his eyes piercing mine. It's as if he doesn't want to disengage. When he eventually does, we both smother groans.

He places me in my seat without my feet touching the ground. He crouches next to me, and the effort it takes not to stare at or hungrily inhale his sweat-damp body makes my eyes water. He pulls my seat belt across my uselessly weak body then tucks a swathe of hair behind my ear before he kisses my temple. "Look at me, baby."

I don't want to. I just want to close my eyes and will myself back to a time before the McCarthys imagined that getting involved with the Rutherfords was a good idea. Before my father and my mother's thirst for *more* uprooted us from mundane hell to the devil's playpen.

But his low voice, his body bleed immutable, savage authority. And for now, I'm his.

So I turn my head and look into haunting eyes.

"My name on your lips, my cum inside you, every single second of every single day. That's the way it's going to be for you from here on out."

Chapter Sixteen

ANOTHER WOMAN'S SHOES

"You can't keep me forever, Axel."

Lust cooled. Purpose restored. The flame of retribution rekindled in my heart. The shaky yet controlled words don't elicit an immediate response. Nor does he bother to zip up the leather jacket he shrugs back into. He stands, tucks his semi-hard cock back into his boxers, and zips up with sickening composure.

Sliding behind the wheel, he revs the throaty, powerful engine, executes a perfect U-turn and accelerates back down the deserted road. His body now loose and relaxed, he rests a wrist on top of the wheel.

"Don't delude yourself, baby. I don't want forever. What I do want is answers. Answers you'll give me before this thing is over." His voice reeks of arrogant assurance.

"You sound very sure about that."

He shrugs, a ghost of a smile whispering over his mouth. "I was sure you would let me fuck the hell out of you when I turned onto that road. And now there you sit, wearing a just-thoroughly-fucked glaze in your eyes and gorgeously flushed with my scent all over you."

Heat spreads up my neck. "If answers are all you want, you should've just said so and spared us both a hell of a lot of time."

"I think we just established that answers aren't *all* I want."

After the darkness of the park, the bright lights of the highway blind me for a second but my eyes adjust, and I stare at the profile of the man behind the wheel.

"You can have any woman you want, Axel. Why me? Why force this…*thing* on me?"

The questions seem to give him pause. Or perhaps he doesn't intend to answer. He changes lanes and steps harder on the gas, a blatant disregard for the rules of the road stamped into every gear change.

It's only when light traffic forces him to ease up that he casts me a sizzling glance. "Besides the fact that you make me as hard as a fucking rock just by breathing in my direction, there are a few things you need to atone for."

"Things like what?"

Another blithe shrug, despite the stiff clench of his jaw and when he speaks, his voice is granite hard. "The small matter of eight years of my life."

Shock powers my breath out of me. "What?" My voice is a ragged croak.

"You're not deaf, sweetheart."

I frown, wondering whether the madness that seems to dog us has finally addled our brains. "How…?" I stop. Shake my head. *Regroup.* "How the hell did you arrive at that wild and amazing conclusion?"

"Very easily. With irrefutable video evidence. You know the one."

"Video…?" A block of ice lodges itself in my chest. That sounds a little too much like a Finnan-made version of hell for it to be a coincidence. I open my mouth to ask for verification then absorb his whole answer. "What do you mean, I 'know the one'?"

The languid man who slid behind the wheel like a sated predator is gone. In his place is the snarling beast I recognize. "You knew his sick little game of filming every Hallmark moment. You knew he was recording what took place in his office the day he threw the let's-convince-Axel-with-a-little-grievous-bodily-harm party for me. What, did you forget to turn off the camera after you were done?"

The ice spreads further, numbing me from head to toe. "God, you think I enjoyed knowing that was happening to you in there? That I condoned it?"

His mouth twists in a macabre smile. "Nice try, sweetheart."

"Axel—"

"I saw you! On video, offering to 'take care of me.' You want me to recite it word for word for you? Or maybe you'd prefer to watch it again, with popcorn and a giant cocktail thrown in?"

The blood drains from my head, and the hand I lift to my head shakes uncontrollably. "He filmed that?" *Of course he did.*

A grating laugh barks from him. "That's what you're worried about? That you were caught on camera?"

I rush to speak before I can think it through. "Axel, I can—"

"Explain? Really? You have an excuse for sticking to your word and offering me three days' false sanctuary of pussy and sympathy before helping him ship me off to West Point?" His voice is a deadly dagger wrapped in soft velvet.

I open my mouth again, then realize no, I can't explain. Stating my reasons why will bring everything I'm fighting for to one brutal end. "I…I didn't want him to keep doing…that to you." A partial truth. Despite knowing the extent of his cold-bloodedness, the sight of Axel beaten to a pulp still wrenched at the part of me that insisted on remaining innocent.

We exit the highway. He stops at a red light, the less-than-smooth stamp on the brakes testifying to his shredding control. Eyes the color of frozen ice chips find mine in the dark. "You're a fucking liar, Cleo."

There is no way to escape the cold, bald indictment. But I can't keep silent. "You thrived in the army, hell, you positively excelled. I may not know much, but I know they don't hand out medals on a whim. You may not have wanted to go, but in the end, was it all so bad?"

His ragged hiss stops my breath. The knowledge that I've touched a nerve, perhaps one so raw it's a live grenade, smashes through me a second too late.

A horn blares behind us. His eyes don't budge from me, nor does he attempt to move. Not for another charged ten seconds. In those seconds, I see a thousand howling demons leaping through his eyes.

"The beating was nothing. I could've withstood ten times worse." His hand rises, and two fingers toy with my hair, twisting, smoothing, tucking, all while horns blast and cars swerve past us and drivers hurl abuse. "But you used this," he traces my lips, his touch whisper soft, "and this," his hand drops to my lap, dives beneath the T-shirt to stroke my pussy, "to change the course of my life. That deserves a reckoning, don't you think?" He withdraws and calmly sets the car in motion.

As if he hasn't just shown me the underbelly of his psychopathy. As if he hasn't just left me gasping.

"Axel—" I stop, my mind blanking in the face of that casual damning. Clearing my throat, I attempt to speak. "You can't lay the blame for…all of that on me."

"No, not all of it. But you're one of a collective, sweetheart. Everyone else will get what's coming to them."

Oh God. "What does that mean?"

He doesn't respond.

"So tell me what you would've done if you hadn't…if the army wasn't…"

"Rammed down my throat? It's okay, you can say it."

Except it isn't okay. Not by a long shot if the hands clenched tight on the steering wheel are an indication.

"Same thing you would've done, I suspect, if lust for power hadn't made you decide that being Finnan's whore was more your speed; I would've chosen my own fucking path."

I flinch. "I'm not his whore."

"Then you've done something with that interior design degree you were so giddy to achieve?" he asks.

My lips firm, shame and rage boiling my insides. "You would've found your own path? Really? When the two of you are forged from the same damn fire you may as well be one person? Isn't that why you're both so intent on destroying each other? So there can only be one to assume all the power?"

His thighs bunch in latent aggression as he navigates early-morning New York traffic. "I'm nothing like him."

The hollow in my shattered heart mocks me as I sit there, knowing he is *exactly* like his father while wishing he wasn't.

"You have the power to do *so* much, Axel. And yet here we are," I say, my voice bleeding emotions I can't stem.

He guns the car through an amber light then turns sharply down a ramp into an underground parking garage. He pulls into a private slot and kills the engine. Silence engulfs the car for tense seconds until he turns to me.

"No, darling. We're here because *you* had the power. And you chose to abuse it. You chose the wrong fucking team."

I don't get the chance to ask what power he's talking about because he pulls out his phone, conducts a terse conversation with someone called B, then hangs up. He turns his undeniably magnificent body toward me. Even seated, the chiseled perfection of his abs is on full display through his open jacket. The shameful throb that never quite abated kicks up again between my legs. I drag my gaze away, hoping not looking at him will help allay his effect on me.

I can't do anything about his intoxicating smell, which is filling the car. So I search for a distraction. Remembering my phone, I turn and look for it. The car is a two-seater with very little space behind the seats. But my phone is nowhere in sight.

"Looking for this?"

I glance over to find him clutching my phone.

I hold out my hand. "Yes. Can I have it?"

He slots it into his jacket pocket. "In good time."

I throttle back the panic that rises. "You can't withhold my phone from me, Axel."

Gray eyes narrow with sharp intensity. "Who are you calling at five in the morning?"

"No one. But that's not the point."

"Isn't it? Imagining you have any power here, at all, is only going to bring you disappointment, baby. I advise you to dial down your expectations."

"I'm not cowering before you just to give you a cheap thrill," I snap back.

A lazy finger drifts down my cheek, leaving a path of heat. "Don't sell yourself short. Not now. Not when I've paid such a heavy price to have you again."

"What did you pay?"

He taps me on the nose. "Don't concern yourself about it. Just know that nothing you give me will be considered cheap."

A weary sigh bursts free before I can stop it. "Axel—"

The click of heels halts my response. I twist in my seat to see a familiar figure striding toward us. It's the woman who approved my application to join Axel's club. The club that grants individuals their darkest fantasy atonements on a plate.

When Finnan handed me the file, I was too distraught to look at it. I didn't read its contents until twenty-four hours later, when his warning that I needed to step up my game *or else* forced me to. At first, the depravity behind the concept turned my stomach. Until further investigation mitigated my preconceptions.

First of all, no one is forced to do anything they don't want to.

Second, nothing that risks life or safety is permitted.

Third, all acts that stray toward the unconventional are carried out in a supervised environment. While I didn't know what that entailed, my imagination stopped its wild and desperate spinning.

I'm fully aware how less scrupulous places than the Punishment Club operate. My father had been an owner of two of those clubs when we lived in Boston, before he was lured to Connecticut by Finnan Rutherford. Finnan supplied him with girls. I know about this because I heard him arguing with my mother about what went on there. He eventually sold the club when a customer accidentally strangled himself during autoerotic asphyxiation.

My seat belt snaps free, dragging me back to the present. Axel's gaze rests on me, but he makes no move to get out. When the footsteps halt beside his window, he lowers the window and takes the bag she hands him.

She bends and scrutinizes my face with sharp, intelligent green eyes that hold a touch of concern. She's about to speak when her phone rings. Digging into the back pocket of her tight leather pants, she pulls out a sleek phone and walks away.

Axel reaches into the bag, pulls out a coat, and tosses it in my lap. "Put it on."

I eye the garment, a rebellious fire igniting inside me at the thought of wearing something that belongs to another woman. His woman? "Why?"

"Because we're walking through a club filled with depraved, desperate assholes. Your body isn't going on show for them to fucking salivate over."

I want to ask him why he's brought me here then, but I already know the answer. This is to be part of my punishment. The ironic thing is that I set the ball rolling myself.

I take the coat and shrug into it.

He finally steps out and comes around to open my door. I notice the other things he's holding. The highest pair of fuck-me shoes I've ever seen. They're black patent leather with lethal-looking silver studs down the back.

They aren't tacky, but the fire inside me, which is taking on a decidedly green tinge, ramps higher. "Those are—"

"Likely the most harmless shoes B owns. She's your size so they should fit." He crouches next to the open door like he did in the park and reaches for my foot.

My breath catches as he cradles one ankle and slips the shoe on then repeats the action with the other. Although casual, almost gentle, his touch still races fire up my legs to my core.

I'm still fighting to pull air inside my lungs when he surges to his feet and holds out his hand. I take it, battle with yet another dimension of sizzle stemming from his touch, step out and struggle not to topple over in the sky-high shoes. He catches me as I pitch forward, steadying me with both hands at my waist.

"You okay?" he asks with a raised eyebrow once I regain my feet.

I nod, temporarily unable to speak because my borrowed heels elevate me closer to his fierce, unnerving regard. And at this height, his full, sensual mouth is so tantalizingly close that mine tingles wildly.

We freeze in place, my gaze on his mouth, his on mine, for seconds. Or minutes. Until the sound of agitated heels pacing closer shatters the erotically charged standoff.

The hands at my waist move. He fastens the stylish summer coat with the single button, and although I'm not thrilled to be wearing another woman's clothes, I'm grateful for the cover it provides.

"Come on." His hand catches mine, and he leads me to the waiting elevator twenty yards away.

"—no! There's nothing to discuss. Stay the hell away from me. I mean it."

We both turn as B hangs up and crosses over to join us. She takes one step inside, and her phone rings again. Her elegantly manicured fingers curl around the device and a look passes over her face, gone quickly before I can decipher it.

"You coming?" Axel demands with a bite of impatience.

She eyes him. Then me. Then she looks down at her phone. Shaking her head, she backs away from the doors. "No. You two go ahead. I'll grab the next one."

As she turns away, I can't help but notice she's decidedly paler than she was when she approached the car. But her shoulders and spine bear the hallmarks of one pissed-off female when she stalks away in heels even higher than mine.

"What's up with her? Is she okay?" I ask.

Axel hits the button for the first floor without taking his eyes off me. Darkened eyes full of intent. "B can handle herself. Which makes it very easy for me not to give a fuck."

The moment the doors slide shut, he backs me against the wall. His scent, his size, the heat emanating from his exposed skin all crowd into me, feeding the frenzied madness that seems to be a hairsbreadth away.

"I like you small…A delectably fuckable handful I can manipulate on my cock any which way I choose. But I like you in these heels too." He raises my hand and plants an open-mouthed kiss in my palm before dragging it down to rest on his iron-hard erection. He covers my hand with his, pressing our fingers so I feel every thick ridge.

"You feel how fucking hard I am right now? I'm imagining how easy it'll be to slide my cock into you. You won't even need to bend over to receive me." Hot, vulgar words, crooned against the corner of my mouth before he licks the curve. A casual flick of his wrist, and the coat falls open. Heated eyes drag up and down my legs, and a hoarse sound escapes his throat.

"You're not…I'm not doing…*that* with you while I'm wearing another woman's shoes."

One brow rises, and there's brittle amusement in his eyes. "Jealousy looks…interesting on you."

The pulse of dark satisfaction in his voice makes my teeth clench so hard my jaw aches. "I'm not jealous."

His hands trail up my thighs, teasing through the dampness still very much present between my legs from our mutual release. "Am I misremembering an incident where you threatened to 'beat the shit' out of a waitress who smiled at me as she took our order? Or when one of Troy's girlfriends *accidentally* got shoved into a pool for brushing her tits against me at a pool party?"

In hindsight, a shockingly foolish period in my life I want to take back and crush to oblivion simply because it makes everything that followed so much more devastatingly bleak in comparison.

"Yeah, well, that was a long time ago, before…" I press my lips together to stop from saying something that will come back to haunt me.

The fingers playing dangerously close to my labia freeze. "Before?" The satisfaction is gone, in its place a tightly knotted cluster bomb that can go off at any second.

Before I knew the true depth of the darkness in your soul. Before I found out you were capable of cold-blooded murder.

"Before real life got in the way."

"Real life," he breathes, and I swear I see dragon's fire flaming from his aura. "And what we had before this 'real life' was…?" His voice is deceptively casual.

Behind us, the elevator doors open, but he doesn't move. Over his shoulder, I see four people waiting to board.

"Axel, we're here. There are people waiting…" I venture.

His eyes don't move from my face. "I asked you a question," he spits out. "What did we have?"

"Nothing more than unsustainable dreams spun by horny teenage idiots?" I hiss under my breath. We're gathering an audience and although his large body obscures most of mine, it doesn't take a genius to work out where his hand is situated.

I hear whispering before one man dressed in a shiny PVC boiler suit clears his throat.

Axel removes his hand, unhurriedly buttons my coat before he steps back. His face is the taut mask of a stranger and the hand that grasps mine is painfully tight, his control barely leashed.

The man in the suit receives a withering look that makes him take a hurried step back once he realizes whom he dared to disturb.

We enter the main reception area of the club and the first true taste of what goes on here hits me in the face. Even this early in the morning, the scene is so shockingly decadent, my jaw drops open.

In the city that never sleeps, apparently neither does the craving for punishment.

In a private alcove, two scantily clad women are openly flogging each other, the sting of the whips drawing sobs with each blow delivered; a middle-aged man in a three-piece suit is crawling across the floor, shaking his head and muttering *shame* over and over; a young man, barely over twenty-one, is seated in front of a video game, his severely bloodshot eyes glued to the screen as his fingers fly over the handheld console. Occasionally, he sips from a mug labeled *Rat Poison*.

Unlike the last time I was here, there are no nude clients or lurid sex acts being performed, for which I thank my lucky stars.

I follow Axel as he walks to another private elevator. The stunning black woman behind the desk openly eye-fucks him as we pass. He doesn't acknowledge her. Her gaze shifts to me, and whatever she sees in my face makes her eyes widen a touch.

His mocking reminder of my possessiveness over him once upon a time rises to slap me in the face. I want to tell her I have no claims on him. I don't straighten the frown I sense on my face, and when the words lock in my throat, I tell myself it's because I don't care enough to utter them.

We enter another elevator. This time he doesn't look at me or move in on me. He faces forward, jaw locked, although his hand doesn't release mine.

I'm not sure why I'm surprised when he hits the button for the second floor and walks me back to the suite I rented.

Did I, on some subliminal level, imagine he would whisk me to his personal domain now that I am supposedly his?

No, this is a far better fit. The reason I had the club make a replica of his pool house bedroom was so I had an inescapable reminder of my dangerously naïve past. The grief and horror that burn in my heart are adequate reminders, but the visual evidence is a useful stimulus.

He punches in the code and pushes the door open. I enter and my chest tightens as I'm slammed by the very thing I craved a moment ago.

Behind me, Axel hulks in ominous silence. When it becomes too much to bear, I turn and face him.

His face is hewn from stone, his eyes so dark and stormy that the gray looks almost black.

"Now what?" My voice is a hoarse, shaky mess I thoroughly detest.

He kicks the door shut with his foot and shrugs off his jacket.

He prowls forward, tossing the leather without looking where it lands.

"We're going to take a shower. I'm going to fuck you again. I'm going to feed you. Then we're going to talk about this." He indicates the room with a slow twirl of his finger.

Chapter Seventeen

BATTLE STATIONS

AXEL

Nothing more than unsustainable dreams spun by horny teenage idiots.

I can't get the words out of my head. Which is absurd considering I have endless proof of her heartless duplicity. It's why she's here, after all.

So why the fuck do I want to smash my fist into that damn painting I once loved so much? Why do I want to destroy every piece of furniture in the room?

I inhale. Slow. Steady. Slow—

Fuck it.

My boots come off with vicious kicks. Her little gasp is music to my ears. I want more. I *will* have more. Preferably when I'm balls deep inside her treacherous little body.

"Take off your clothes."

Either she's resigned to her fate or she's eager to be rid of the borrowed clothes. I don't care either way. The coat is discarded, and the T-shirt and shoes come off faster than they went on. In a heartbeat, she's naked. Her beauty punches me in the gut.

Christ, she's beyond gorgeous. From her tumbling hair to her swollen lips to that immoral little triangle at the top of her smooth, shapely thighs. The triangle my cock is burning to fill. And her breasts. Fuck me, those tits were the subject of my wet dreams long before I ever got to taste what was between her legs.

I force myself not to look at the bruises on her body.

I force myself not to ask *why*.

I force myself not to wonder, for the millionth time, how I got it so wrong.

I've driven myself insane for far too long.

Tonight, my cock overrules every single thought. I unzip my pants and push away my remaining clothes.

Her gaze drops to my erection, her mouth parting on a cute little pant that has my balls tightening with the raging need to fuck. Her thighs do that twitchy, slidey thing that drives me nuts. I close the distance between us, slipping my fingers into her hair.

Her head tilts up, way up, and I realize, despite what I said in the elevator about the heels, that I prefer her like this. Petite. Breakable. *Mine.*

I fist her hair, drawing her head back, exposing her face to me. Her nostrils quiver with a false vulnerability and her bewitching blue eyes darken with a peculiar light that reminds me of the guileful heart I'm dealing with.

I drop my hands to her shoulders and turn her around. "Bathroom. Now," I rasp.

She obeys. Her plump, heart-shaped ass taunts my cock as she walks. I resist the urge to turn that glorious skin pink and stalk after her.

Like in every suite in the club, the adjoining bathroom is fitted with every amenity and luxury. The fees I charge demand nothing less than the best. I bypass the Jacuzzi bath and head for the large shower cubicle. The shower is fitted with half a dozen heads ranging from a gentle spray to jet stream. I select a middle range and turn back to her.

She's gathering her hair to her crown, her movements slow and sultry, her eyes watchful.

"Leave it. It's getting wet whether you tie it or not."

She lets go, and it tumbles back down, half obscuring her face and breasts.

Un-fucking-satisfactory.

I stand with my back to the spray, the jets beating down on my shoulders, licking down my front. I want her tongue to do the licking. With special concentration on the throbbing organ between my legs. "Come here."

She places one foot tentatively in front of the other, the movement of her hips rolling into her slim torso. Hell, even the way she moves sets me alight.

Cleo McCarthy is built for fucking. Dirty, bed-breaking fucking. The kind I only managed to deliver once during our time as *horny teenage idiots.*

Don't think about that.

She arrives in front of me, and I clench my gut against the urge to desecrate her completely. Right fucking now.

I reach for her and turn her so the water hits her body. Her hair is drenched in seconds, plastering the lower strands to her breasts. I move the wet tresses out of the way and pass my thumbs over her erect nipples. They're dark pink from when I sucked them earlier. Heat washes up her chest, and the gasp I crave bursts from her lips.

"You like that?"

Heavy lids sweep down. "Hmm," she moans.

I let her get away with hiding her eyes from me and reach for the gel on the shelf. There are other special blends bought by B that I could use to enhance her mood, but I resist the urge to play dirty. For now. She may have been up all night, but she's not passing out until I'm good and ready.

I rub the gel between my palms then caress her neck and shoulders, arms and back. When my palms cup her breasts once more, she rewards me with another moan, her head bowing forward as pleasure washes over her. I wash her front, sinking down to wash her thighs and calves.

"Turn around."

She presents me with her back. From my position, I'm eye level with her wet, spankable ass. My palm tingles with the need to paddle her. But I want to be inside her when I do. So I concentrate on lathering her skin instead.

When I'm done, I tug the detachable shower head off the wall and train it on her body. I watch the water slide over her, and a dark pang washes through me. Fuck, I'm jealous of the goddamn water.

I want to laugh.

I want to roar with rage.

I want to fuck until I explode into a million pieces.

This is what she does to me.

What she's always done.

With her, I'm as changeable as mercury. The only constant is the junkie-strong need to have her. The verdict is as damning now as it was a decade ago. I'm salivating by the time I reach her pussy. "Brace your hands on the wall and open your legs."

Once again, she complies without speaking. Her silence doesn't worry me. Her body tells me everything I need to know when I aim the shower head between her legs and she shudders. When my fingers find her, she's as slippery as an eel.

Ready. So fucking ready.

Rising to my feet, I let go of the shower head, change positions, and slip my hand down her belly to tease her clit.

"Oh…"

One finger teases her hole, tests her scorching heat. A loud whimper escapes her.

"You feel empty, baby. Would you like me fill you up again?"

A groan rips from her chest. "Hmm."

My hand clenches on her ass, kneading her flesh. "I need the words, Cleo."

She pushes into my touch. "Yes, f-fill me up," she gasps against the wall.

As much as I relish the temptation to take her from behind, the memory of how she felt on top of my car, her legs tight around my waist, wins the position stakes. I catch her around the waist, and carry her to the bench inside the cubicle. Propping her up, I move between her legs, my supereager cock already poised at her opening.

The promise of bliss already clawing through me, I open her wider.

One small hand lands on my stomach. "Axel, wait."

My insides clench. "Hell no."

Her face scrunches, and she takes a breath. "Please."

The phenomenon of Cleo begging is a new but hellaciously delicious concept. Images of her doing it while on her knees rush through my mind. Pound through my cock. A bead of pre-cum leaks from me, insolently tastes her pussy. Connects us on a chemical level. The sight of it nearly knocks me off my feet.

"Please, Axel." She repeats. The curious note in her voice stops me.

I drag my attention from between her legs. "What?"

"I...you're not wearing a...condom."

I possess a million flaws, but I'm not sexually irresponsible. I've never taken a woman before without protection, not even Cleo when we were *horny teenage idiots*. I have monthly checks like clockwork. And I had protection in my wallet when we fucked in the woods today. Protection I did *not* use because I forgot.

I haven't fully grasped this zealous need to fuck her raw. A part of me doesn't want to analyze it for fear another layer of mania will present itself with malicious glee.

Whatever it is, I've crossed the line. I've tasted the ultimate high that lies between her legs. There is no going back.

"I'm clean. I can prove it to you if you need. And you're on the pill."

Blue eyes widen. "How...how do you know?"

"I had a little time on my hands in your bedroom while you took your shower."

Her breath catches. "You went through my things?"

My gaze drops to her pink pussy, her delectable opening flowering around my impatient cock head. Unable to resist, I drag my thumb over her aroused clit. Her hot shudder cements my decision.

"Yes." I feel no remorse, and my voice holds no apology.

She looks puzzled for a moment as she struggles to speak through my continued caress, even as her nipples jut out harder, scream for my mouth. "But, aren't you worried that you'll…Aren't you worried about me?"

"On a grand scale of things, no. I lived in the roughest part of Manila for nine months and trained with assholes who delight in ripping limbs off just for sport. I served in every hell hole imaginable in Afghanistan. I'm still alive. If the way I'm destined to leave this world is courtesy of this exquisite piece of heaven in hell between your legs, I'm *all* for it."

"You won't…I haven't…" She stops and bites her lip.

I take satisfaction in the fact that she's reluctant to bring *him* here. She's beginning to understand that I won't abide it. That'll make her transition so much easier.

It pleases me enough to bend and taste her lips. "Tell me you're clean and I'll believe you."

The look that rushes over her face is unexpected. A touch of relief. "I'm clean."

"Glad to hear it. But even if you weren't, we all have to die of something, baby," I lean in and mutter in her ear, unable to help the darkness that drips from my soul. She exhales sharply, and her face pales. Her eyes grow haunted, wary as they rest on me. It's unfortunate timing perhaps, but she needs to know. It's inevitable that she will be touched by some of it. "Some of us have surrendered to that end being less than the peaceful one innocents deserve. So, rest assured that this…" I probe her with a shallow push, "will be a fucking deliverance."

I grab her hips and plunge into her, unwilling to wait, unable to resist.

Her scream echoes in the rising steam and her small hands grip my biceps. I withdraw, slick and wet with her essence, wrap her legs tighter around my waist, and fight my way back inside her.

I fuck her with long, sublime strokes. Her cries fill my ears and attempt to probe the darkest corners of my existence. She's the purest drug, the highest high. Nothing I've had in my doomed life comes close to what I'm experiencing with her.

Her face is no longer pale, but her eyes are squeezed tight. I open my mouth to command her to show herself, but I'm rewarded in a different way.

"Axel, oh God…"

Her warm gush drenches my cock and balls. The decadent suction when I thrust back inside propels me to the edge.

"Yes. Oh, yes. Fuck!" Stars explode across my vision. Sweet Jesus, the intensity of it, *of her.*

I want…no, need her closer. Picking her up, I stalk out of the shower and into the bedroom. We fall, wet and irreparably altered, onto my childhood bed. Still connected but destined never to fit.

I punch every extraneous thought away and ride the rapture sizzling up my spine. Her hands move from my arms to my shoulders, into my hair. Nails drag across my scalp, and a groan tears free.

Her legs are spread wide. I press one knee into the bed and slam into her. My teeth grit, unable to get over how hot, how glorious, she is. "Damn, you're so small. Tight as a fucking fist."

A glazed look enters her eyes. "You…fill me up."

"Not enough, baby. Not nearly enough," I reply, my voice a useless croak. I have more to give but any more and I risk hurting her. I have too many plans for her to allow that.

But what she can take, I give in abundance. Until her breaths begin to fracture. Until her arms fall back and her head thrashes on the bed. "I feel…I think I'm coming….oh."

A firm grip in her hair halts the frenzied move, centering her for my attention. "Stay still, baby. Breathe."

Her panting escalates. "I can't." Her face contorts as I spread both knees and plow into her. "Oh God."

"Let go, Cleo. Look at me and give me what I want."

Her mouth parts on a final O of bliss. Then wild, sweet convulsions jerk through her body. I feel her climax rippling along my length, her muscles squeezing in ever tightening circles until she explodes.

"Fuck," I groan. White heat flares across every single nerve ending. Glorious pressure pulls in my balls for a deliciously long moment. Then I erupt like a fucking fire hose.

I'm drained in seconds, my mind firing with a million stars before it goes blissfully blank. I come to with my face buried in her shoulder, our bodies lying side by side. I'm still embedded in her. Despite knowing there are other, important things to tend to now the sex is out of the way, I continue to lie there, on familiar yet alien sheets, her soft weight in my arms, my pulse still wild.

"Axel..."

I tense, instinct warning me I won't like what she has to say.

"Breakfast," I preempt her. "I'll order room service." I keep a team of chefs on the premises so food can be easily taken care of.

She shakes her head. "Not hungry. Too tired. Later," she murmurs, her voice slurring.

No. Answers. You need answers.

"Cleo."

But she's already asleep. I grit my teeth and pull out of her. She shudders and moans in her sleep but doesn't wake.

And in the early morning light, I drop back next to her, my mind teeming with even more questions.

Chapter Eighteen

TOTAL RECALL

Despite the languid exhaustion prowling through me, I don't fall asleep next to her. For one thing, sleep is the furthest thing from my mind. For another, I don't trust myself on so many levels when it comes to her.

Hell, even now I can't tear my gaze off her. Impossibly, she's more gorgeous in sleep. Maybe it's because I can't see her eyes, can't hear that voice that promised to *take care of me* for Finnan. With her gloriously rich hair damp and just-fucked messy, her long lashes fanning her cheeks and her face devoid of makeup, I search for a whisper of the semi-innocent, sexy, shy girl I once knew.

Had she ever been there? Was it all a cover?

She gives a low moan and mumbles something in her sleep. My name? *His* name?

The renewed churning in my brain launches me out of bed. I sit on the edge, teeth gritted tight against the need to growl. Or wake her to demand answers to the questions plaguing me.

The hand I reach out to do just that hovers over her shoulder for a long second before I change direction and tug the covers over her.

There are others who owe me answers. Answers I won't get sitting here, staring at her like the horny asshole she labeled me.

Silently, I dress, leave the room, and head up to the sixth floor.

There are no signs of life in the hallway at this time of the morning, for which I'm thankful. I reach my suite and command the lights.

The spotlight falls over the metal chair.

Is it really only less than a week since I indulged in that useless six-hour bender? My gaze drops to my wrist. It's completely healed, although a few scabs remain here and there.

All the screens are blank. I don't intend to activate all of them. Only one. I head to the concealed bar set into the wall and grab a bottle of water. Then I check my phone for messages. Nothing.

I'm acutely aware that I'm delaying taking a seat in the chair, delaying the inevitable. I drink the whole bottle, my gaze finally resting on the screen on the far right.

Sitting down in the chair, I pick up the remote. My hand is shaking. I don't clench it or stiffen it to stop its damning tremble.

I deserve this. All of it.

The beginning of the video is laughably banal.

Early fall in Connecticut is the most beautiful time of the year. According to Cleo McCarthy, at least. Which means it was naturally my favorite time of year too.

The late-afternoon sun glints off the twenty-five-foot pool that fronts my pool house. The person manning the camera doesn't pause to appreciate the russet-tinged leaves or the beginnings of a glorious sunset.

His hurried footsteps approach my sanctuary, bursting in without knocking. He bypasses the messy living room and flings open the bedroom door.

I'm sprawled facedown on the rumpled bed, naked except for a pair of Calvin Kleins.

He kicks the side of the bed with a heavily booted foot. "Hey, Axe-hole, it's almost noon. Time to get up. Pa has a job he wants you to take care of."

I jerk up, my stubbled face going from startled to pissed off in a nanosecond. I roll away from my noxious, uninvited visitor. "Stop pointing that fucking camera in my face or I'll make you eat it."

Troy's mocking laughter. "You look like crap. You've been knock-ing back that shitty tequila again, haven't you?"

My gaze slides from the camera, and I leap off the bed in a vain attempt to hide my true state. "Fuck off, Troy."

He follows like a damn bloodhound. "Oh…wait! What you hid-ing, baby brother? Go on, tell me. I can keep a secret."

I round on him, my anger flaring in my bloodshot eyes. "Jesus, I'm fucking warning you. Quit with that thing." My chest rises and falls with uncontrolled breathing that I can't regulate, probably due to the other, illegal substances coursing through my veins.

He retreats a few steps until I head into the bathroom. The mo-ment I slam the door, he turns the camera on himself and waggles his eyebrows. "Methinks the baby bro doth protest too much. Either a) it's his time of the month, or b) he's hiding something. I don't know about you, but I vote for door number…two. Shall we find out what he's hiding?" He nods eagerly in agreement to his own question.

He starts opening and closing dresser drawers, closets. In the nightstand closest to where I sleep, he discovers a stack of condoms, and he smirks into the camera. Pillows are tossed, and my gym bag is turned upside down. He toes the contents, grunting in disap-pointment when he doesn't find anything. He circles the room with the camera then points it at the bathroom door beyond which the shower is running.

"Okay…" he muses. "One last try and then, sadly, I'll be forced to concede he's as boring as he's been begging me to believe." Once again, he approaches my bed. He climbs onto it with one lunge. Now level with the huge surfer painting hanging above my bed, he runs a hand along the top of the frame, down the sides, and across the bottom. He lifts the wooden frame and peers behind it.

Finding nothing, he tramples across the bed to the right side.

About to hop off, he hesitates, leans forward, then lets out a tri-umphant laugh. "Fuck yeah, jackpot!"

The large black lamp on my nightstand has a cylindrical shade. On the inside is a baggie taped to one side. Troy turns on the lamp and positions the camera to perfectly capture my hiding spot. Reaching inside, he rips off the bag containing the white powder and holds it up properly to the lens.

"Oh, Axeeeeeeeel!"

I yank open the door, see what he's holding in his hand and rush out of the bathroom. "The fuck are you doing, going through my things? Dammit, give that back."

He holds my stash out of reach. "No, no, no. Possession is nine-tenths of the law or some fucking bullshit, right?"

"Not when you're in my room, asshole." I lunge for the coke but he steps back into the middle of the bed.

"Tell you what. You want this back, you have to earn it."

My face congeals with boiling rage. "Fuck you!"

"Ah…no. I believe the fuck delivery is now firmly in your court. Your move, sunshine." He shakes the bag in front of the camera.

I grip the towel around my waist tighter, my gaze moving from the camera to the coke.

"What the hell do you want?" I hear the compliant tone of a burgeoning addict in my voice.

"Like I said when I got here ten minutes ago—ten minutes of my life I'm never going to get back, by the way—Pa has a job he wants you to take care off."

"Hell, no. Tell him thanks, but no thanks." I turn around and head back into the bathroom.

He follows. I grab my razor and look up into the vanity mirror. Our gazes clash.

"I'm not your fucking messenger boy." For the first time, the jocularity drops from Troy's voice. "I'm even less inclined to act as your carrier pigeon when the last time I tried I got this." In the reflection of the mirror, he taps the inch-wide gash on his chin that is still healing. "You're fucking coming or I'm going to tell your little girlfriend about your nasty new habit. Let's see how hot Cleo Spitfire is for you when she realizes you're snorting shit up your nose. You do know that two overdoses in her father's clubs is one of the reasons they hightailed it over here, right? You're not going to be her darling boy any longer when she finds out. In fact, I'm going to go out on a limb and predict that she'll drop you like a fucking stone."

Fresh rage spikes my body. "Go ahead and tell her. I fucking dare you."

He shrugs. "Alrighty, then." He pulls his phone from his pocket. Flips it open.

I drop the razor and lunge for the phone. "Jesus. Okay! I'll run whatever the hell this errand is. Afterwards, I'm changing the fucking locks to this place."

When Troy slides his phone back into his pocket, I return to the vanity. In the reflection, I catch a wave of bitterness cross his face. "You can't. You may think you've escaped to your own personal paradise, but you're very much a puppet on his string. Just like the rest of us. So man the fuck up and stop whining at every little thing."

"I'm no one's fucking puppet. And all this is going to be behind me. Very soon."

Through the mirror, I watch the camera lower a touch, and Troy's eyes narrow on me. "The fuck's that mean?"

In the chair in the Punishment Club, I close my eyes for a moment, foolishly wishing I can go back in time and shut the fuck up. That my cocky, coked-up and hung-over nineteen-year old self can find a little bit of self-control and not give in to the need to gloat.

"Online gambling. My fucking ticket out of this slime hole."

"You mean that poker crap you keep going on about?"

My smug eyes meet his. "I've made over thirty-seven thousand in five days doing 'that poker crap'. And tons of money doing other 'crap'. In one month, I can make a cool half mill. And you know the best thing? None of it requires breaking an old man's arthritic fingers. Or putting a liquor store owner in the hospital."

"You're still breaking the law. You're nineteen, Axe-hat. You can't gamble in Connecticut until you're twenty-one."

I shrug and pick up my razor. "It's a small technicality I can live with."

His gaze stays on me, gray eyes, similar to mine, turning pensive.

"Well…whatever. Hurry the fuck up before Pa sends Ronan. That dude's ornerier than a box full of wasp-stung frogs."

"Get the fuck out of my hair, and I will."

"You better, or this cheerful bag of shit lands on Cleo Baby's doorstep." He starts to back up then stops. I know whatever's coming will blow the top of my head off even before he speaks. "Hey, you know with her parents missing and Pa stepping up to adopt her, she's going to be our sister, right? So *technically*, by messing around with her, you're committing incest?"

I lose all interest in shaving. "Christ, were you born a full-fledged asshole or did you practice really, really hard?"

He shrugs. "Would rather be an asshole than a fucking perv."

"Why don't you go and do something useful then, asshole. Like find a fucking dictionary?"

"Nah, I'd rather go and tell the old man you'll be there in three minutes and watch him time your ass."

He leaves.

"And FYI, I haven't done anything with her yet," I call after him. He doesn't respond.

The footage cuts to Finnan's office. He's seated behind his desk with Ronan standing to one side, as usual. His instructions are simple enough. "Bolton, you go pick up the Ferrari from New Jersey with Axel. Ronan and Troy will take care of the Camaro."

Finnan casts a glance at Ronan. A look passes between them.

"That's it? We're just picking up a car?" The relief in my voice is palpable. I don't need to stand around and watch Ronan deliver a knuckle-duster sandwich to a waiter who skimmed a hundred dollars of an evening's take. Or Troy taking a sledgehammer to a food truck because the owner is two days late with his monthly "stipend."

The look in Finnan's eyes mocks me. "Yes, boy. That's it. It's only a classic car worth three hundred and fifty thousand dollars, so by all means, treat it like a goddamn Sunday afternoon joy ride."

My temper flares. My fists bunch. At the far side of the office where he does his best to appear invisible, Bolton catches my eye and shakes his head before his glassy gaze returns to the carpet. I throttle down and take a deep breath for two reasons.

One, if I succeed in pissing the old man off the way I'm dying to do, he'll find something more unpleasant for me to do, which, depending on what it is, might mean I don't get to see Cleo tonight. Missing the chance to see her is not an option.

Two, I may be hungover and still a little high from the lines of coke I did last night, but even from across the room, I can tell Bolton is strung so high, he's halfway to the fucking moon. No way can he handle driving a sports car with a powerful engine like a Ferrari without smashing it into a tree and getting us both killed.

I take a step back, lower my head, and fold my hands in front of me. The compliant gesture satisfies Finnan. He issues final instructions, and I nod.

As we turn to leave, he clears his throat. "One last thing, Troy?"

"Yes, Pa?"

"Take that camera with you. Make sure you get everything on film. If we need to, we'll use it to teach other assholes a lesson that you don't mess with the Rutherfords."

"Yes, Pa."

The next clip, the one with only Ronan and Troy, flashes onto the screen. My eyes refuse to blink, my stomach turning in on itself at the look on Ronan's face as he does what he relishes.

A warehouse with grimy windows and rusting car parts.

A man on his knees, a black cloth over his head hiding his identity. The suit he's wearing is soiled and ripped and two sizes too large. Either he's lost weight or the clothes don't belong to him.

Ronan circles him slowly, a menacing figure wielding a baseball bat.

"It's the end of the line for you, I'm afraid. I'm told you've become a strain on our resources, and these days we're all about *streamlining*."

The muffled sounds that come from beneath the bag tells me he's gagged.

"What was that? Sorry, I can't hear you."

More incoherent noises.

Ronan sighs dramatically. "It's okay. We don't need to have a conversation. We're strangers after all. I don't know you, and you don't know me." He looks at the camera and winks. "This is merely a necessary dance before the final goodbye. But kudos to you for doing the right thing for your family." He taps the bat lightly on the man's left shoulder. He flinches out of the way. "Although I don't know quite what that was. I was asked to tell you that the account numbers and the corresponding sums all check out. And for that, no other members of your family will suffer. That's good news, right?"

Rough, urgent sounds.

"Sorry, this is out of my hands. I follow instructions. Same way you should've."

A frantic shake of his head. Quick shuffling on his knees, as if he has any hope of getting away. For a split second, Ronan appears almost remorseful. Then his face hardens. "You brought this on yourself and on your family. Did you really think you could get away with disrespecting the Rutherfords?"

The man moans and shakes his head continually for a full minute. Then, perhaps knowing his fate is sealed, slumps onto his heels.

The first blow from the bat breaks his arm, a guttural scream echoing through the warehouse. The second is a roundhouse to his chest. He falls over groaning in agony. The third strikes his temple.

He stops moving.

Ronan tosses the bat and grabs the man by the shoulders. The camera follows as he drags him to a sky-blue car with classic lines.

A Camaro.

The trunk is already open. And there's someone else in there. Someone less hurt than the man, if the frantic wriggling beneath the tarp is any indication. The shape of the body and the pitch of the moans tells me it's a woman.

The man, now moaning again, is tossed in with her, and Ronan slams the trunk shut. The camera stops recording.

The next shot flickers into life, and the remote drops from my numb hands to the floor. Regardless of how many times I watch, the agony and rage and remorse are as fresh as the first time Finnan made me watch it.

A deserted parking lot behind a block of boarded-up properties in a shitty part of Bridgeport. Troy leaning against the Camaro, once again manning the damn camera.

I step out of the SUV driven by one of my father's security guards. My expression is beyond pissed. "What the hell are we doing here? I thought I was supposed to drive the Ferrari back to Greenwich?" Having to hand over that sweet ride to one of Finnan's goons to run *yet* another errand is frying my last nerve.

"Don't worry, this will be quick," Ronan says. He nods to the driver, who steps to the back and returns with a jerrican.

I smell the kerosene from five paces away. "What the fuck are you doing? That car is worth seventy thousand. Easy."

"Not everything is about money, baby brother. This is about principles," he replies.

I back away when the driver silently holds out the fuel to me. "Fuck no. This is a '69 Camaro. If any of you ignorant assholes want to torch a piece of prime American art, you do it your goddamn self."

"For fuck's sake, Axel. Torch the damn car and let's get the hell out of here already." This from Bolton, who's been finding reasons to head to the restroom every chance he gets. Unfortunately, he hasn't been able to in the last ninety minutes, and he's twitchier than a jumping bean.

"Yeah, Axe-hole. All this bitching is keeping your piece of ass waiting." Troy.

I look at the car. At my brothers. I shake my head, wondering for the umpteenth time if I'm adopted. I grab the kerosene and head for the car.

"Wait!"

"What the hell for? Isn't this why I'm here—?"

I stop when Ronan holds up his hand in warning. He turns up the illegal police scanner we all carry on outings like these. Then curses under his breath. Troy jerks to attention, his glib mood gone.

"Two patrol cars are headed to a property on the next block. A bonfire is sure as shit going to get their attention." He turns to me. "Change of plan. We're getting the hell out of here." He tosses something to me, and I catch it mid-air.

Keys. "I'm driving? Why me?"

"Because you're the fucking petrol head with a hard-on for 'prime American art,' apparently. And because I said so."

Again, I want to argue. But this whole errand thing has already taken too long. And Cleo has been sending me increasingly descriptive texts in the last hour. The last one was particularly dirty, involving my bed, my favorite baseball T-shirt, and a heavy hint that she wasn't wearing anything else.

I yank open the door and slide behind the wheel.

"Head to Bearwood Lake. We'll follow," Ronan says.

Bearwood Lake. Damn stupid place to torch a car but also the most likely place to be deserted at this time of day—just after sunset when it's too early for the nocturnals and the mosquitos are out in full force.

I put the car in gear, take a second to appreciate the sweet engine, and drive out of the parking lot. We arrive at the lake twenty minutes later. The weeping willows provide good cover as I circle to the far side of the large lake. Rarely used because of the steep banks surrounding it, it was nevertheless a good make-out spot during the summer but deserted at other times of the year. Behind me, the SUV rolls to a stop. I follow suit a little further on the bank, my nape tingling with fuck knows what as I get out. Troy's camera is still trained on me.

When my phone vibrates in my pocket, I jump. "Yes?"

Troy. "The big man says we're not going to torch it. You're going to drive it into the lake."

"For fuck's sake!"

"Hop to it, brother. Time and tide and all that." His tone sounds forced, the usual resident assholery lacking.

I take a moment to admire the car's classic lines, and silently mourn its impending demise. Then, after putting it in neutral, I give it one giant push and watch it roll toward the brackish water.

A second camera that I hadn't been aware was filming from the SUV tracks Troy and Ronan as they walk up on either side of me. Troy's camera is trained on the sinking car. His face is devoid of emotion, his jaw rock hard. I start to frown. A second later, grim resolution tightens his face, and he turns the camera on me.

I step away. "I've done my part. Can we fucking go now?" I snap.

Ronan watches the bubbles swallow the car until it's almost submerged. Then he turns to look at me. "Yes, brother. We can go."

When we get to the SUV, Bolton is nowhere in sight. Apparently the lure of a restroom on the other side of the lake was too strong to resist.

I slam the door and don't give the sinking car another thought.

All I want is to get home to Cleo.

I lied when I told Troy she and I weren't fucking. My soul was damned to hell the day I laid eyes on her because it was the day I vowed to make her mine at the very first opportunity. Waiting until the law gave us permission to turn our relationship physical was never going to happen. I've owned Cleo McCarthy's tight pussy for months now.

I ignore the shared looks between Ronan and Troy as we leave Bearwood Lake.

As I leave the site where I became a double murderer.

Half an hour later, I'm in her arms.

Things take on a weird vibe after that day. Bolton embraces his addiction and resides in a near-constant state of drug-fueled euphoria. Ronan redoubles his efforts to become Finnan's Mini-Me. Troy remains Troy, only worse.

Three weeks later, Finnan announces that he's taking Cleo to her birthplace of Boston to finish processing her transition to be his ward. My request to accompany her is flatly refused. Something about the whole thing fucking stinks, but I hang on to the thought that, once she's back in my arms, I'll never let her leave.

Besides, I intend to use the time she's away to double the two hundred thousand sitting pretty in my gambling account. The minute she turns eighteen, I'm marrying her and leaving this shit hole behind.

She's gone for six agonizing weeks. She returns two weeks before my twentieth birthday.

And the girl I've loved since I was twelve is gone.

In her place is a cold, heartless stranger.

Chapter Nineteen

FADE TO BLACK

The screen fades to black, and my vision darkens along with it.

I can't move. I can't think of anything else besides the faceless strangers whose blood drip from my hands.

Of families who will never know the truth. The fact that *I* will never know is a punishment I bear along with my innumerable sins.

But whereas I can never contemplate closure, I crave it for my victims. Have craved it for almost a decade.

I open my eyes, stare into the shadows that live within me and without. I reach down for the remote. One more time for the fathers, mothers, sisters, brothers, sons, and daughters who are missing two people unfortunate enough to be caught in the Rutherfords' web.

Before I can hit *replay*, my phone buzzes.

The dead organ in my chest attempts to leap. There's only one phone call I'm expecting at this time of the day. Everything else was diverted through executive assistants, attorneys, and minions.

"Any news?"

Detective Mac Malone pauses for a beat before he answers. "Nothing new worth breaking out the single malt for."

Bleakness I have no hope of stemming claws through me. "Then why call?" I snap.

"Not so you can have the satisfaction of shooting the messenger, that's for sure. I said I'd check in. That's what I'm doing."

"I'm paying you to do more than check in, Detective." The cold blade of my disappointment is poised to strike. And considering just how much I was expending on the bent cop, the treatment was deserved.

"Yeah. I'm aware of that." His tone is less willful.

I take a moment to remind myself why I picked him.

Growing up in a family such as mine exposed me to the reality of greed and corruption from a very early age. By the time I was ten years old, I could spot a bent cop from twenty paces; I could negotiate, bribe or threaten my way out of just about every situation by the time I hit puberty. It was only when I grasped the true extent of Finnan's ruthlessness that my family name became an anchor around my neck.

But those early years of training came in handy when needed. The end result was Mac Malone. Weighed down with two alimony payments and crippling gambling debts, he was ripe for the plucking when I needed serious work done after four private investigators hit a dead end.

"So?" I press.

"My contact at the Bureau is still drawing a blank on those accounts. Without a name of a bank or an account holder's details—"

"If I had those details, do you think I would've sought out your services?"

"Look, I'm just saying we started this thing with one needle buried with a million needles in a haystack whose location we don't know."

"And five years later, despite countless promises, you haven't found the haystack. If I didn't think you knew better, I'd think you were using me as an ATM."

The middle-aged man sighs wearily. "The money's great, sure, but beating my head against this particular brick wall is beginning to give me a concussion."

"Say the word, and I'll sever ties," I reply coldly.

"No! There's no need for that. If you would let me talk to the other individuals who were present—"

"No. Finnan is the one who issued those orders. I'm the one who drove the car into that lake. This is on the two of us. No one else. The man and woman were picked up in New Jersey in a sky-blue Camaro. Surely that should've yielded some results by now? You have the date and a starting point."

"You assume they were picked up in New Jersey. I'm digging through traffic camera footage for where you say the Camaro was picked up. But you have to allow for the fact that it's been almost ten years," he says, the way he's been saying for far too long.

My black temper frays as I stare at the blank screen that epitomizes the conversation I'm having.

"What about Bearwood Lake? It's a public park. Surely someone would've seen a two-ton Camaro being dredged from the lake bed and taken away?"

I receive a dark, cynical chuckle. "With respect, sir, you were a soldier once. You're also a Rutherford. So you know any desired result can be achieved with the right amount of incentive."

"And yet you don't seem to be incentivized to achieve mine. You have one week to find me something, Detective."

I hang up and slide the phone back into my pocket. My fingers brush against metal. Cleo's phone.

I take it out and press the home button. The picture on her home page surprises me. Camilla McCarthy's beauty was flawless as well as timeless but she never possessed her daughter's vivacity or traffic-stopping body. Plus she never smiled. Not like she's doing in this picture.

Also, Cleo never got on with her mother, Camilla's controlling nature constantly pushing her daughter out of the house. And more often than not, toward me. Which made Camilla hate me more than she already did for my blatant interest in her daughter.

In the months before Camilla and Michael McCarthy went to Boston never to return, Cleo and her mother fought constantly. Mostly about me. I made the mistake of trying to talk to her once to smooth things over. She told me she intended to leave Connecticut for good. Take Cleo with her. The conversation didn't end well. I may have threatened her a little. Or a lot.

In later years, I discovered that the McCarthys had gotten onto Finnan's radar because Michael McCarthy had been encroaching on Rutherford territory, doing deals with the Armenians, much like I am doing now. Only he hadn't been destroying the drugs. He'd been cutting them with other cheap and dangerous substances and selling them in his own clubs. Michael and Camilla fought about those clubs because Michael wouldn't let them go and because the girls in the clubs were being made compliant with drugs. General Courtland's transgressions arrived at a critical moment, a way for Michael to stave off retribution from Finnan by offering to share the private military contract deal.

But drugs started it all. It was the reason I kept my nasty little habit from Cleo. And the reason I kicked it to the curb the night after the Camaro incident. No way was I turning out like Bolton.

Luckily, I wasn't hooked enough for it to be a problem. Or maybe my addiction to her was stronger.

* * *

The phone goes dark, and I slide it back into my pocket. I return the remote to its slot, cast another glance at the blank screen, and grit my teeth.

What the fuck did any of it matter when my victims remain faceless? When my penance rings hollow?

Weariness drags through me as I stand. I'm halfway to the door when my phone rings. The caller is unknown. My hackles rise as I answer. "Axel."

"Mr. Rutherford, your request for a meeting is granted. Shall we say your club in one hour?"

The voice is different than the Bratva lieutenant's I met with the last time. This one holds more authority. Clearly, I've been elevated another rank.

"One hour. I'll be there."

"Very good," he replies solemnly, and then he hangs up.

I take one last look at the blank screen. The closure of knowing who my victims were might be blocked from me for now, but if I play my cards right, another opportunity might just open up before the day is over.

I return downstairs and slip quietly into the room. Cleo is still asleep, her dried hair a sexy, tangled mass on the pillow. The sheet has half slipped off her, and one breast is bared. The remembered taste of her fills me with fresh hunger. I clench my jaw and turn away. My hunger will need to be satisfied later.

I slip back out and head to my office. Because I've stayed in the club overnight on many occasions, I keep a stack of laundered clothes in a closet. I dress in a black shirt and black pinstriped suit and head for the parking lot.

It's still early enough for traffic to be bearable. I arrive at a deserted XYNYC ten minutes early and nod at the security guard at the door.

I'm not surprised when I walk into the empty club to find Sergey Yurinov, the head of the New York Bratva, seated in the booth at my private lounge, with half a dozen of his lieutenants fanned in a semi-circle around him.

I hold out my arms for the obligatory search before Sergey nods a dismissal at his men. Five of them stroll off, leaving the man I imagine is his number two.

I open my mouth to offer drinks but spot the five-thousand-dollar Stolichnaya Elite bottle and shot glass on the table next to him.

Sergey catches my gaze and shrugs. "You don't mind, I hope? It's still the middle of the night in Saint Petersburg."

I stroll up the steps and take a seat at the end of the booth. I don't hold out my hand for a handshake, and they don't hold out theirs. "Not at all. Feel free to keep the bottle."

He leans back, the half smile playing at his lips not diluting the look in the flint-hard eyes studying me. "Such generosity will aid us well in our negotiations, I think, Oleg, *da*?"

"*Da*," Oleg agrees, his shrewd eyes behind rimless glasses examining me as keenly as his boss's.

I stanch my premature anticipation of victory by cutting to the heart of the matter. For one thing, I don't intend to be away from Cleo longer than necessary. "Shall we discuss terms?"

Sergey picks up the bottle, pours the chilled vodka, and lifts the shot glass, unhurried, to his lips. "First, explain to me, as you did to my emissary, why you need guns to run your nightclub."

I take a breath, play the game, and give the answer he's already aware of. "I don't need guns to run my nightclubs. I don't need guns at all. I just don't want Finnan to have them."

The boss and his assistant exchange glances.

"And before you mention it, yes, it's personal. Will that be a problem?"

Sergey stands and strolls to the edge of the empty dance floor. "No, I don't foresee a problem."

I breathe easier. "Good. I propose a one-off payment of—"

"I'm not interested in your money, Mr. Rutherford."

Tension grips my nape but I force myself to remain calm. "What are you interested in?" I inquire.

"You are very successful in the nightclub business." He looks around, slowly spinning on his heel. "This one, for instance—"

"Is off the table," I interject before he can finish. "I'm not interested in letting it go. I also have a silent partner who might object to our arrangement."

Another exchange of glances. Oleg nods confirmation.

"The Punishment Club is also a noncontender," I add, sensing the direction of the conversation.

Sergey returns to his seat and pours another shot. "This conversation is not going how I intended, my friend."

I flash a mirthless smile. "You weren't expecting me to be a pushover. I'm trying not to disappoint you."

He laughs, but the humor doesn't reach his eyes. He downs the drink and straightens his pristinely knotted tie. "Okay, let's move further south. Viper Red."

"Viper Black," I counter. "You've done your homework. You know it's in a good location, and you know how much it's worth. It's yours, free and clear, along with a year's free consultation. In exchange for your agreement never to deal guns to my father."

I'm aware I'm throwing a very lucrative business away, but the recollection of Cleo's ugly bruises, and Finnan's glibness over his atrocities, has sparked renewed rage. The chance for payback sooner rather than later is too good to dismiss.

Sergey Yurinov takes his time to weigh my offer. He helps himself to two more shots of premium vodka before his eyes flick to Oleg. The second in command reaches for a leather binder I hadn't spotted on the bar and extracts a document, which he holds out to me. I take it from him and open it to find a transfer of ownership document. I suppress a smile.

"I'll have my attorney take a look at this and get back to you by noon."

Sergey dips his head and holds out his hand. When I shake it, he holds it firm, black eyes pinned on mine. "In return, you have my word that the business interests of your father and Bratva will never join forces."

I nod, dark elation expanding through me.

When they leave, I cross to the bar, pour a finger of Balvenie whisky, and toss it back.

The bracing liquor warms the dark spaces in me. I feel lighter than I have in years.

By day's end, Finnan's last bastion will be gone, and I can hammer the final nails into his coffin.

PART THREE
Us

Chapter Twenty

IT HAPPENED ON A RAINY NIGHT

CLEO

I lost my virginity in his bed.

I fell in love with him in his bed.

I charted the glorious life we would have together in his bed.

I named our children and imagined the grandchildren who would enrich our lives and bear testament to our love in his bed.

I found out the man I loved more than my own life was capable of murder...while I was in his bed.

It happened on a rainy night.

To my knowledge, Finnan Rutherford had not stepped foot in the pool house since his son moved in. Not until that day.

Axel is out picking up a pizza, our staple food after hours of marathon sex. I'm lying in his bed worrying about the college letters that are piling up on his nightstand. He put off college when his mother passed last year. I helped him mourn the mother who was never really there for him, while I was secretly overjoyed at having him to myself for a whole year. Despite our obsessive need to be with each other, he reapplied the moment his father started talking to him about joining the family business. I know he regretted his hasty decision the moment he posted the applications. Same as I know that this time around, *I'm* the reason he's putting off answering the acceptance letters that are pouring in from Ivy League schools.

I should be selfless. Think about the foundation we're laying for our future. Axel wholeheartedly supports my passion for interior design. I feel like the dirtiest bitch for not wanting him to leave me. He thinks it's because I haven't seen or heard from my parents since they flew out to a wedding in Boston four months ago. And that was partly true. My heart aches for the vicious argument my mother and I had the morning she left, when she once again mentioned moving back to Boston. The very idea of leaving Connecticut, leaving Axel fills me with dread, so secretly I'm glad they're not back.

But Axel's father reassures me that he'll leave no stone unturned until he finds my parents, and my almost seventeen-year-old self is consumed with Axel, so it's been easy to give my heart permission not to worry. To enjoy whatever time I have with Axel. My parents will always be around—once they rear up their heads from wherever they'd disappeared to. It's not the first time they've done this since we moved to Connecticut.

The love of my life, however, will be sequestered on a campus somewhere far away. Especially if he doesn't agree to stay in Connecticut and earn his business finance degree at Yale.

I don't need tarot cards to know he's refusing Yale out of hand because he doesn't want to be around his father.

Tracing my finger over the corner of one distinctive college logo, I bite my lip. My head wants to tell him to follow his dreams wherever he wants, but my heart wants to club my head with a baseball bat. The thought of Axel being away from me, even for a day, is giving me serious sleepless nights. Like the world's worst pessimist, my heart weeps even when I'm at my happiest in his arms.

Nothing short of a binding blood oath that we'll be together every day for the rest of our lives will shift my mood. Thunder booms from a storm-laden sky, adding to the melodrama of my melancholy. I hug the pillow that bears Axel's scent to my face and inhale deeply. Even though I'm wearing his favorite Yankees T-shirt, I can't get enough of his smell. I burrow deeper and sigh at my pathetically soppy state.

Turning my head, I see a flash of lightning. And a body silhouetted against the French doors.

I should have seen the devil for what he was. Should have jumped up and fled as fast as I could in the opposite direction.

Instead I sit up and pull the pillow into my lap as Finnan Rutherford raps his knuckles against the door and enters without waiting for a response.

I must look like a deer caught in headlights because he shakes his head. "You don't need to be frightened, Cleopatra. Not of me, at least."

My gaze tracks him as he strolls across the bedroom like he owns the place. Which he does, technically speaking, but still.

I purse my lips when he picks up and smirks at the stuffed bear Axel won for me at a fair two weeks ago. I want to jump up and snatch the toy from him, but that would mean leaving the safety of the bed, the safety of Axel's scent around me. So I sit, cross-legged, and wait for him to finish his casual examination.

When he turns and fixes his eyes on me, I want to cower under the covers. Instead I raise my chin. "Can I help you, Mr. Rutherford?"

"I hope you'll learn to call me Finnan. 'Mr. Rutherford' sounds like my church organist grandfather, the good Lord rest his soul." He attempts a coaxing smile.

My hackles rise higher than the tide beating itself to death on the beach. When he perches on the edge of the bed, I want to snap at him to move. This bed is our sanctuary from our families, although privately I envy Axel for the siblings he claims to loathe.

Ronan is super scary, no doubt there. But Troy, despite his caustic tongue, can be charming when it suits him. Although I haven't seen much evidence of it in the last couple of weeks.

But Bolton is a softie at heart. I frown inwardly. A big softie with a drug problem that will fuck up his life if he's not careful.

"Cleo?"

Finnan's voice jolts me into focus. He hasn't moved from where he sits but his gaze is drifting over me in a way that makes me uncomfortable.

"Yes?"

"I don't know how to sugarcoat this so I'm just going to come out and say it. News has surfaced about your parents."

My heart drops to my stomach. "What news? Are they okay?"

"That's just it. I don't know the full story yet but I have people working on finding out. You're not blind to the kind of businesses your father and I were aligned with in the past, but we've been taking strides to put all that behind us. Unfortunately, not everyone is receptive to that move."

"Are they okay? Are they...alive?" *Axel, where are you? I need you!*

He smiles a smile that is meant to be compassionate. It falls laughably short. "Whatever happens, be assured that I'll continue taking care of you. Like I have been taking care of you these last few months. We're not blood but I already consider you a part of my family."

I'm aware that he didn't answer my question. "I...okay. Thanks."

He nods and stands. Looks around. "And if anything should happen that upsets the status quo around here, know that it won't affect the promise I made to your father to look after you should anything happen to him."

My mind is reeling from what he's not saying. "What do you mean?"

"I told him returning to Boston wasn't the best idea. I was quite disappointed about that decision actually. But he wouldn't be swayed." He flashes a grim smile that bypasses his eyes. "And when he talked about taking you with them, I know not everyone around here was thrilled about that."

I frown "He talked about taking me?"

He nods. "Your mother wasn't too happy about your relationship with Axel."

My fists clench in my lap. For whatever reason, my mother took an instant dislike to Axel the moment they met. Years later, their relationship hasn't warmed. If anything, it's worsened. I'm not surprised that my mother's been pushing for it. "So why didn't they take me?"

He shrugs again. "I talked them out of it temporarily. Although…" he stops and looks a little pained. "I'm not sure if I made the right decision."

"Why not?"

"Axel has been a little…off lately."

"No, he hasn't," I defend hotly.

He reaches out a hand. I cringe from it. He sits back, his expression neutral.

"And what's that got to do with my parents? What's *he* got to do with them?" I press.

"Maybe nothing. Maybe, when you and I go to Boston next week, everything will be fine. I've heard your parents were in New Jersey meeting with the head of the Manzino family a few weeks ago but I don't think that's true. My contacts in Boston will clear everything up, I'm sure."

I don't want to think about going anywhere with Finnan. "I'm sorry, you mentioned Axel. What's this got to do with him?" I ask again, although my heart is banging against my ribs now. For what reason I don't know. No, that's a lie. It's banging because of the mention of New Jersey. Axel spent the better part of a day there three weeks ago. He grew cagey when I asked him why he went there with his brothers.

But doesn't he always evade when you ask about the "errands" he runs with his brothers?

I shake my head to disperse my thoughts and the images I once accidently found on Troy's camera. The horrible things Ronan was doing to that man made me lose my breakfast…

I jump when Finnan leans forward and pats my knee. My stomach takes a long dive. "It's nothing, I'm sure. You mean a lot to my boy. And I'm certain he'll do anything to hang on to you. Even if, with that temper of his, I sometimes wonder what he's capable of. He would never do anything to harm those you care about."

I'm grappling with the fact that he just implied Axel was capable of violence. Or more.

...you belong to me. I don't care who created you. You are mine. No one else is fucking allowed to touch you. No one is allowed to take you away from me, do you hear me?

I'm not sure why I'm recalling the words Axel said to me on the beach this summer. Sure, they excited me then. Now a different emotion punctures that excitement.

No. Axel loves me. He's a good guy. He loves me, and I love him. End of story.

"No, he wouldn't," I answer Finnan, my head held high.

He pauses then smiles. "You're a feisty young woman, Cleopatra. You're also loyal. I like that about you." He starts moving toward the door. "I'll finalize the arrangements for our trip to Boston in the next few days. I already have permission from your school. I'll let you know when to pack a bag."

He leaves with a similar ominous clash of thunder to the one he entered with. I sit in the middle of the bed, unable to stop shivering. I feel like a traitor for the fear I'm unable to dislodge from my heart.

Axel. My parents. New Jersey.

My parents have gone radio silent before. But only for a month or so when they went to Armenia. I never found out the ins and outs of that trip, although I guessed.

This time it's been months. And like every organized crime family knows, the first rule is to leave the authorities out of their affairs. Even in the case of a missing couple who haven't been heard from or seen in that long.

Lightning flashes again. Another silhouette against the door. My heart leaps into my throat. But it's Axel who walks in a second later, cursing and shaking the raindrops from his coat. He turns to set the half-sodden pizza box down, and my breath catches at the similarity in stature between father and son. Axel is very much his own person. And yet so much like Finnan it's scary.

"Shit, I hate these flash storms. They... Hey, what's wrong? You look like you've seen a ghost."

"I...Yeah, the stupid storm scared me a little. And you doing a Freddy Krueger impression against the door didn't help."

His face gentles immediately. Unzipping his coat, he drops it on a chair as he strides to the bed. A second later, I'm engulfed in his arms, and he's rolling me onto my back. "Sorry, baby. Here, let Freddy make it all better!"

I laugh. We kiss. We devour the pizza. Then we make love.

But the fears linger in my heart.

And two weeks later, they are confirmed.

Chapter Twenty-One

IMPASSE

The moment Finnan showed me the video and a photo of my father's body, my life slid on a downward slope to a permanent residence in the seventh circle of hell. In a state of numb disbelief, I read a copy of the autopsy report confirming he drowned. I barely heard or acknowledged Finnan's reassurance that he would take care of funeral arrangements or snapped out of my fugue state long enough to wonder why we were the only two people standing by my father's Boston graveside. Why, in a shockingly horrific twist of fate, the other two people I loved most couldn't be here.

Axel.

Mom.

Axel.

Axel.

Mom.

Finnan had no answers for me as to my mother's whereabouts. She wasn't found in the trunk of the Camaro with my father. I thought the possibility that her body wasn't found would bring me hope. Instead, all I thought about was what Axel would do when he found out I knew.

Will the man I love kill me too?

Will those hands that lovingly worshiped me snuff the life out of me when his secret gets out? It was an easy choice when Finnan cautioned me against letting Axel know we'd found and buried my father. The not-so-easy choice was returning to Connecticut to live under the same roof as my parents' murderer.

But at seventeen, as harrowing as it was going to be, I only needed to endure the nightmare for a year. Then I intended to put half a globe's distance between me and the man who was now the embodiment of every single horror I'd ever imagined.

So I agreed to Finnan's request.

Then the night before we were to return to Connecticut, he dropped his next bombshell. My mother was alive. For her to remain so, I had to hand over my life to Finnan.

That bombshell turned out to be one of many.

I inhale shakily and pull the cotton sheet more tightly around me as I walk to the wide window.

Although I've visited New York City many times, I've never spent an inordinate amount of time here. A few day trips for shopping or dinners where I played hostess at Finnan's business meetings are the sum total of my experience.

Now my whole existence is reduced to a two-hundred-square-foot bedroom in a club in Hell's Kitchen. My lips twitch at the appropriate location name. Unlike the house in Connecticut, I don't have security guards shadowing my every move, but I'm even more of a prisoner here than I was there.

I woke up half an hour ago, alone in bed. The only indication of Axel's presence was his scent lingering on the sheets. However, what he didn't imprint on the outside is very much branded on the inside. I can't move or take a breath without his possession registering, without the ache his cock left in my pussy making its presence felt. He's not in the room with me and I'm still claimed.

The door opens behind me and, as if conjured up from my thoughts, my jailor enters.

His dark hair is damp and finger combed, the black T-shirt and pants now replaced with stone-washed chinos and a dove-gray

T-shirt. I catch a tantalizing glimpse of the tattoos gracing his body.

His eyes zero in on me with unnerving intensity and intent. Even before he's halfway across the room, my belly begins to quiver.

My fingers convulse on the corners of the sheet and half-baked words of greeting wither and die on my tongue.

Good morning?

There's nothing remotely *good* about what's happening here.

How are you?

The vibes bouncing off his body are all the evidence I need.

He's in no mood for pleasantries either because, the moment he reaches me, he yanks the sheet from my body. My naked back meets the cool glass and I gasp.

His mouth devours the sound, his tongue licking deep into my mouth as he conquers what he's already claimed. The kiss is hot, dominating. Unapologetic and sizzlingly arousing.

The swollen tissue between my legs begins throbbing anew. Large hands slide down my shoulders and my sides to rest beneath my breasts. The sensation of them there fries my mind. A whimper escapes me before I can stop it. He eats that too, his hungry growls telling me each sound I make turns him on harder.

"Touch me," he breathes against my mouth, the command no less potent for being low voiced.

My hands, shamefully eager, slide beneath his T-shirt. Hot, muscle-tight skin greets my fingers as his hard abs ripple to my touch. I caress higher, over mouthwatering ridges to his pecs. When my fingers brush his flat nipples, I pause. Drag my nails over the tiny bumps. A full-body jerk before he's pressing his engorged erection into the cradle of my hips. Craving more of that reaction, I repeat it.

A feral sound rips from his throat. His hands slide up to capture my breasts, his thumbs mercilessly delivering double the exquisite torture. Hot arrows of need lance my sex, and my knees weaken.

Axel presses his lower body deeper into me, supporting my weight with one leg between mine. The rough material of his pants grazes my ultra-sensitive clit, and I cry out.

"Fuck. Cleo … *fuck.*"

The words aren't charged like his vulgar ones were last night. They're solemn, a little bewildered. Like a prayer. For what, I don't know.

His head drops to capture one nipple in his mouth, and my thoughts shatter. Hot, wet, hungry, his teeth and tongue ravage one peak then the other, his movements growing frenzied until he pushes the globes together and slides his broad tongue over both at once. He suckles until they're red and throbbing and ravenous. Then he takes my mouth again, his hands back to cupping and squeezing my breasts.

My hips pump his thigh, the hunger tearing through me needing satisfaction. My wetness soaks through, rendering the material coarser. Delivering more friction. "Oh!"

"Fucking hell, you're like the headiest addiction," he groans furiously against my mouth before he wrenches away. The brutal denial has my nails sinking into his waist before I register my action.

A hiss rips from his throat. He stares down at me with a touch of the bewilderment I heard in his voice moments ago. His gaze moves lower to my mouth. My breasts. The uncontrollable roll of my hip against his leg.

Lurching forward, he captures my nape and delivers another punishing kiss. "Christ, I have to fuck you. Need to." He releases me just as abruptly. One hand squeezes his cock, while the other one attacks his belt. The second he lowers the zipper he draws my hand to wrap around his steely length.

Dear heaven. His velvet thickness is a live, potent tool. Promising everything. Including temporary oblivion from fear and despair. I can't resist the urge to caress him from root to tip, enjoying the power of him.

Dragging his pants down, he pushes me back.

The cold glass reminds me where I am. "Axel, the…the window—"

"No one can see inside," he rasps, his voice edged in rough arousal and resolute ice. "And I wouldn't care if they could."

My breath hitches. The thought of people watching. Of seeing what he's doing to me. How he commands my body. When the thought doesn't immediately fill me with horror, another shudder rakes me. He lifts his gaze from the breast he's fondling, and a smile twitches his lips.

"That turns you on, doesn't it, my little exhibitionist?"

I shake my head. "No."

His eyes harden. "Liar. I should punish you for that. Maybe I'll take you downstairs tonight, fuck you in the lobby, in front of everyone," he muses cruelly.

"No!"

Rough hands yank me around, and my front is pressed into the glass. Cold meets heat meets the towering presence at my back, and my brain ceases to function.

His fingers slide through my folds, testing and finding my wetness for himself before he grasps my waist. With a guttural grunt, he plows into me, his cock hitting my end in one burning thrust.

My fingers claw at the windowsill as my feet leave the ground. "Axel!"

"Yes," he grates against my ear, his voice gravel rough. "Scream my fucking name so everyone on the street knows exactly who's fucking you. Tell them, Cleo. Tell them who owns this pussy."

He withdraws and rams back inside me.

Stars explode across my vision. I scream…something. His name most likely, if the unbelievable thickening of his cock is any indication. He feels sublime inside me. Saliva fills my mouth as bliss flames upward from my feet. The burn of his size hasn't abated. It probably never will, but my body is beginning to adjust to him. There is less pain and more incredible pleasure. Pleasure every cell in my body is screaming for.

"Oh God…Axel."

"You like that, baby? The way you're creaming around me, I'm guessing yes." The edgy smugness in his tone is accompanied by several butt-slapping strokes that hit me in exactly the right spot.

Ecstasy drowns me. "Y-yes."

Teeth sink into my shoulder, strong enough to leave a mark, before his tongue slides across my skin. "Louder, baby. Don't think that man in the suit at the stop sign heard you."

"Yes!"

A nip at my earlobe. "Want more?"

"Please...oh please!"

His head drops between my shoulder blades, his audible scenting of my skin pulling another layer of bliss from me. "Damn, I love hearing you beg. Again."

"Please. More...more. *Please.*"

I'm an incoherent mess, hurtling toward certain annihilation at the hands of an expert manipulator. And yet, all I feel is incomparable pleasure. Fatalistic craving for the orgasm headed my way. I ruthlessly hunt it down, pushing back against his thrusts.

A hoarse chuckle rumbles against my neck. "Look at you, fucking brave little thing, attempting to take more of me. You think you can handle it, baby?"

Probably not. Hell, I have no clue what I'm doing. All I know is the voracious ache inside me needs more. Of everything. Of him. So I buck my hips again.

His fingers dig into my waist.

Yes...oh God, yes.

I buck one more time.

"Fuck. Jesus, Cleo, I don't want to hurt you."

I've endured every imaginable horror in my short lifetime. Finding out what he did to my parents tore my beating heart from my chest. What he's doing to me now helps me focus on anything but that. He's my tormentor and my bogus deliverer.

"Do it. Hurt me."

He tenses like he's been shot. Then his hips explode.

A low roar starts from deep inside his chest. The higher it builds the faster he fucks me. My front slides against the glass as he rams deep. Deeper into me.

My screams fuse into each other, my throat as raw as my pussy by the time the most intense orgasm I've ever experienced rips through my body. Axel follows behind, his thickness pulsing long and hard and endless inside me. Furnace-hot, it burns everything in its path, and I melt into oblivion.

His nostrils flare wide. A muscle tics at his temple and even though his face pales a little, the mask of deadly rage doesn't dissipate. "Explain, and explain it well."

"I know what you did for Finnan. I *always* knew even though you lied every time I asked you. Those runs with your brothers? Bashing people's heads in? Destroying people's livelihood? I knew. It turned my stomach. I never thought…"

What the fuck are you doing?

I pull myself back from the brink. I note my shaking hands and brimmed eyes with a removed bemusement.

"You never thought what, Cleo?" One fist is balled tight within the other, the ferocious hold turning his skin pasty white.

He's barely holding himself together, this Beast Son formed from the rib of his father. I should be terrified, but terror is noticeably absent.

Maybe taking the beast inside of me, taking his cursed essence into my womb has rendered me immune? Numbed my instinct for self-preservation?

I shut my eyes and shake my head. This isn't about me. It never was. Everything I've done has been to ensure my mother's safety. "What does it matter? There was a time when I was foolish enough to believe I was in love with you. But that was before the scales fell from my eyes. Before I realized you're a Rutherford through and through. That every single one of you is incapable of change. You see what you want and you take it. The slightest wrong demands retribution the Rutherford way. It's that simple for you. No matter what the consequences for everyone else."

The breath that punches from his throat is searing and raw. The look that glazes his eyes threatens to stop my heart. Muscles thicken in his neck as if he's holding every single emotion he possesses locked down tight.

It's fascinating, this glimpse into the man I let fuck me not ten minutes ago. Fascinating and so hypnotic, his beautiful face frozen in that captivating, almost vulnerable mask. I could watch him forever.

"So you never loved me?" His voice is sandpaper rough, oddly subdued, as if each word chills him. I wonder if it's the worst bruised ego in history or whether he's reached the zenith of rage.

My tormented heartbeat screams that this isn't sustainable. Barely twelve hours after he claims me, my center is crumbling, my perspective shifting in the false quicksand beneath my feet. Because why else would I imagine I just caught a glimpse of the boy I knew in those gray eyes, heard the vulnerability of that same boy in his voice? "I loved a figment of my imagination who was never going to live up to reality. This room is both a reminder of that blinkered stupidity and a caution not to wear those particular shades ever again."

"And just so I'm clear on this, you made this earth-shattering discovery that you didn't love this particular Rutherford while you were in Boston those three weeks with my father?" he asks.

This one is easy. Heart-crushingly easy. "Yes."

His fists bunch tighter until I'm terrified his knuckles are going to pop. His frenzied gaze sizzles mine in the fraught silence. Searching. Searching. Then it drops, as if he can't bear to look at me. He stares down at his fists in fascination for a minute, his lips a thin, ruthless line. "Did you fuck him then too?" A hushed, white-hot demand.

I barely hear it over the hammering of my heart. "No."

His head jerks up, and he's back to probing my gaze again. Whether he finds what he's looking for or not, his fists unclench, and his torso straightens. "So you decided I wasn't a good bet on account of being my father's son. But my father was a better one?"

The shrug I attempt is probably one of the hardest things I've pulled off. "Something like that."

"I see."

No, you don't, I want to say. With Finnan, I walked into the devil's cesspool knowing exactly what to expect. With Axel, I never saw it coming.

"Are we done here? Is there something else you want to know or can I go take a shower?"

My questions draw his gaze down, over my throat, my chest,

the expensive but inadequate sheet covering my body. Even without looking down, I know my skin bears his marks from last night and this morning. In his own way, he's branding me.

His expression slowly morphs until he looks almost human again. Almost. The beast always lurks just beneath the surface.

"No, baby. You can shower later. For now, you stay right where you are. Until I'm ready to fuck you again, I want my sweat on your skin and my cum inside you."

I smash down the dizzying thrill and shake my head. "You can't—"

"I think we've established conclusively what I can and cannot do."

"And that includes keeping me permanently naked? Why?"

His teeth flash in a display of cruel mirth. "Maybe your clean, *un*-fucked body is my kryptonite. Maybe sullying you at every opportunity is how I'm going to deal with this fucked-up situation. I haven't decided yet, but let's go with that for now, hmm?"

"I still need clothes, Axel. And I need my—"

A knock on the door halts my speech.

Axel rises, his powerful frame dominating the room as he strides to the door and pulls it open. A short, muted conversation later, he's pushing a multi-shelved cart into the room. Without glancing my way or resuming our conversation, he starts lifting domed lids off dishes.

If I was told ten minutes ago that I would have an appetite following our conversation, I would've laughed. Instead, my stomach lurches in wild anticipation when aromas hit my nostrils. Tired of my body betraying me, I force myself to stay put in the middle of the bed.

"Let's see, we have hash browns, eggs Benedict, scrambled eggs, toast, Belgian waffles with whipped cream, coffee and juice. Or smoked salmon with watercress salad, seared lobster omelet, chicken Caesar salad." He stops and glances my way, eyebrows raised.

I should be shocked that his mood has morphed too. But just like I was fooled for a long time into believing in a different Axel, so I know that the man in front of me possesses many facets.

Right now, he's an alpha beast intent on feeding his prey before he devours it. "I'll have whatever you're having," I say.

Gray eyes scrutinize my face and body for a long moment before he shakes his head. "I doubt that, sweetheart. You're nowhere near equipped to deal with the magnitude of my appetite." He pours two cups of coffee, sets the sweetened one on a tray before he starts piling selections of food on a plate. Juice, water and condiments go on the tray before he lifts it and heads my way. He places the tray in my lap, then catches my chin in his hands, tilting my head. "Eat everything on that plate, and we'll discuss items of clothing."

I bristle. "I'm not a child to be offered treats for good behavior."

"No. You're mine. And I'll make you jump through as many hoops as I want. Even if some of them are for your own good."

"What's that supposed to mean?"

"It means you still have a mutinous little streak, when you're in a mood. Tell me you weren't dreaming up an excuse not to eat just now?"

A nasty bolt of surprise kicks me. "And how would you know that?"

A bleak look flits over his face, lightning fast and savage, then it's gone. "Not everything you imagine is altered *has* altered, Cleo. Now. Eat."

I stare at his retreating back as he returns to the cart. I pick up my cutlery, tossing the cryptic remark in my mind then discarding it. Everything I imagined altered. *Everything.* Wiped out of existence by a twenty-one-minute video that is seared in my mind and plays on an endless loop, awake or asleep.

If I didn't believe that, I wouldn't be here.

Chapter Twenty-Three

CONFESSOR, MY CONFESSOR

I jump at the sound of a champagne cork popping. I look up, certain with every breath in my body that we don't have a single thing to celebrate. But the Dom Pérignon is being poured into a flute containing orange juice. Shock punches through me. I'm unwilling to attribute the mimosa he's fixing to the memory that suddenly lances through my mind.

A stolen moment at my sweet sixteen birthday party where he pulls me into a silent corner and produces a bottle of champagne and two glasses. A sip of bubbly and comical choking when it goes down the wrong way. The loss of cool prompts his teasing laughter and my annoyed embarrassment. I declare that I hate champagne. Axel stops laughing, tells me to wait, and sneaks into the kitchen to grab a carton of juice. My first mimosa tastes like ambrosia. I beg for more and I drink until my vision blurs.

It became our drink of celebration.

A drink he's holding out to me now, his eyes steady and unnervingly direct. I don't want to take it. But I get the feeling *this*, more than the breakfast sitting in my lap, holds the power to determine my future.

With a not-quite-steady hand, I take it.

He goes back to fix a plate for himself, which he returns with to sit in the armchair. I barely manage to hold off rolling my eyes at the goodness of the cream-topped waffles. And the melt-in-your-mouth omelets. Everything on my plate tastes gloriously good. Halfway through eating, I risk a glance his way to find his gaze on me, a twisted little smile on his lips. Pursing my own, I go back to eating.

He wolfs his own meal down in silence then goes back for a second helping. "More?"

I look from his raised eyebrow to my plate, shocked that it's wiped clean. Frowning inwardly at my runaway appetite, I shake my head. He returns with the last waffle heaped with cream but, instead of the armchair, he sits on the bed, tantalizingly close.

He takes his time to arrange the perfect mouthful of waffle, cream, and strawberry and holds it against my lips. I shake my head. Piercing eyes narrow. "It's fucking okay to enjoy it, baby. There are many things I hold against you. Food isn't one of them."

Another remark to puzzle over as I open up and take the food.

When we're done, he disposes of the cart and returns to bed. Stretching out next to me, he tucks his hands under his head. The action rucks up his T-shirt, and I swallow at the mouth-watering inches of sleekly muscled, tattooed skin on display. He catches me watching, a slow, heavy gleam entering his eyes.

"Now, let's discuss the next item on the agenda." His tone is casual, but a hard knot threads through his words.

"I need clothes, including underwear."

He reaches into his pocket and pulls out his phone. His finger slides across the screen, and he hits dial, then speaker.

"Good afternoon, Axel," B's smooth voice greets him.

"Cleo needs clothes. Size four up top, six on the bottom."

I should be surprised he knows my size. I'm not.

A small pause. Then, "Okay, I'll take care of it."

He looks at me. "Anything else?"

I frown at him then at the phone. "Umm, I also need…birth control pills. I left the ones I had back in Connecticut, but you'll need a prescription—"

"B will take care of it. Won't you?"

A small huff. "Sure. B will take care of everything. Tell me what brand."

I tell her.

"You'll have them in a couple of hours. A little longer for the clothes. Anything else?"

I look at Axel. "Underwear—"

"No underwear," he overrules. "That'll be all, B. Thanks." He hangs up and tosses the phone on the bed.

I glare at him. "Why?"

"I don't want anything to get in the way of that kryptonite thing I mentioned earlier. It'll be wasteful to buy underwear I'll rip off you the moment it touches your pussy. Think about the environment," he drawls.

The punch of laughter is as unexpected as it is outraged. "I can't go out with no underwear!"

Both hands return to the headboard, exposing even more of his ripped stomach, his eyes raking my face with lazy possessiveness. "Since we've yet to discuss that, let's not be too presumptuous. I might decide to tie you to this bed for however long this thing takes."

I look around the room that I've inadvertently turned into my own prison. "I…you can't keep me here for…indefinitely."

"There's that challenge again," he murmurs. He looks deceptively calm, lying there with his hands behind his head, but the hooded eyes fixed on me haven't lost an ounce of their intensity.

"I'm not challenging you—" I stop when his phone pings. We both look down at the screen. Even upside-down, I can read the words.

Wardrobe ETA 5p.m. B.

When the screen goes dark again, I look up. "What's her story?"

One indolent eyebrow lifts. "Is that your way of asking me if I'm fucking the help, Cleo?"

A nasty little ball congeals in my stomach. I have no intention of investigating it so I shake my head. "It wasn't." I take a beat to congratulate myself for an even voice, biting my tongue to stop the other two words aching to burst free. They give me the finger as they launch out of my mouth. "Are you?"

"Not this particular one. B and I are strictly business."

Not this particular one.

No way are those four words biting into my skin. I'm just itching with...something. "But she runs clothes errands for you?"

"I haven't needed one until today. She will be adequately compensated. As to what her story is, I didn't ask. She didn't offer to tell me. We both like things that way."

I recall the phone call in the parking garage last night. Whomever she was talking to, she was more than holding her own. While not ashamed to let a trace of vulnerability show. "She reminds me of Jessica Jones."

One corner of his mouth twitches. "She's in charge of this place because she's a badass, and fortunately she doesn't have JJ's drinking problem or super-rage issues. Both of which I consider bonuses."

Discovering he knows about a favorite TV character prompts a dozen other questions. Mundane, boringly sane questions that shouldn't have even the tiniest platform in this space.

He takes a breath, and my eyes are drawn to his ink. It's not the safest subject but I choose it anyway because, hell, nothing is safe when it comes to Axel. "What does that symbolize?" I point to the yin yang tattoo at his navel.

"Harmony. Fucked up."

"I don't understand."

"I thought I had it. The perfect balance right there in my hand. Turned out I was wrong."

"When...when did you think you had it?"

"Time and dates no longer matter, but as these things tend to happen, it was right before my life turned to shit. After that, I hated the sight of it. It was either cut it out or burn it. I chose the burning flames of hell."

His scorching gaze suggests those flames are nowhere near abating. That the subject is still a precarious one. Leaving it alone, my gaze travels up his chest to the ink peeking from his collar. I want to know about those too, but I decide to leave them alone for now.

"Why a 'punishment' club?" I ask instead. That's more in keeping with the man he is. I tell myself that I'm not asking because I want to understand. There is no understanding. There never will be.

"Because everyone sins. Everyone deserves punishment. Why not make a killing off it?" Stark, soulless answers that should explain everything but are nowhere near enough.

"What are yours?"

His eyes meet mine, and all I see is an endless landscape of *nothing*. "Ah, baby, they're too many to count. But rest assured, I'm getting everything that's coming to me."

My breath catches, and my heart bleeds despair. "You sound sure about that but who are you to decide what your punishment should be? Surely, it's the right of the wronged party to decide what penance their tormentor gives?"

For the first time, he can't meet my gaze. His hooded lids sweep down and shut, and the muscles in his bent arms bunch until he's cradling his head, his breathing growing ragged as if he's fighting a demon from within. When his chest rises in a deep, long exhale, the sound is sub-human. "Not if they are no longer breathing."

The shock of hearing the admission fall from his mouth sucker-punches me so hard, I'm certain I'll never be able to take another whole breath. The blood drains from my head, and my hands fly to my mouth.

In every single way this played out in my mind on dark, rage-filled nights, not once did I imagine Axel confessing to his sins.

Now that it's out, now that it's writhing at my feet, I don't know what to do with it. I want to pick it up and shove it back into him, to have that obtusely hopeful kernel that never died inside me, the one that hoped that all this was one giant mistake, to have been worth me doubting his guilt.

I thought I hated him before. That emotion is nothing compared to what I feel for him now. And I'm agonizingly aware why that is.

Dear God... I feel sick. Bile rises, fast and acrid.

I jump off the bed, striking blindly for the bathroom. The sheet tangles around my legs, and I yank desperately at it.

Behind me, the bed creaks. "Where the hell are you going?" His voice is pulsing with something coarse and alien. I hope to God it's all the demons in hell flaying every inch of him.

"I'm going to the bathroom," I spit out without turning around. "And I'm going alone! Surely I'm allowed that dignity?"

Whether he agrees or not, he lets me go.

I slam the door, turn the lock, and rush to the bowl. But the nausea is gone. So are my tears. Everything is shut down.

I close the toilet lid and sit on it, shaky hands pulling the sheet around my trembling body.

What is wrong with me? I've known the truth for eight years. Have meticulously plotted an eye-for-an-eye reckoning while sitting at my mother's bedside, watching machines breathe for her.

And now I'm almost...*sorry* he confessed?

Chapter Twenty-Four

ATONEMENT: PART ONE

AXEL

She knows who I am. She knows *what* I am.

I know who she is.

Her sins have loomed very large in my mind for a very long time. But I never stopped to imagine how mine would look to her.

Never imagined what seeing myself in her eyes would do to me. I once dropped my guard during an illegal cage fight with a Filipino bruiser. His concealed kalis slashed my thigh wide open. The wound took three weeks to heal, each moment of that healing process hellish agony.

The pain I feel now is a thousandfold multiplied what I felt then. Sitting on the side of the bed with my head in my hands, I wonder in what dimension I imagined confessing would be okay.

Because it's good for the soul? Probably, if you believe in Sunday school stories and fairies. And if you believe you have a soul to redeem. I don't. And now she knows.

I raise my head and stare at the bathroom door. There's no sound coming from inside. She's been in there ten minutes. She wants to be alone. I should respect that.

The idea bumps around in my head like a clumsy puzzle piece seeking its slot. I'm not surprised when it doesn't find a landing.

Because fuck that.

When it comes to Cleo nothing is ever as it should be. Besides, we're not here, in this room, for the fun of it. We're here because, no matter what she thinks of me now, she's still mine.

I stand. Agonized but resolute.

My first knock receives no response. I try again. Harder.

"What?" Her voice is weak. Worn. *Heartbroken?*

The yearning to believe that last emotion sears through me. But hot on its heels...*I loved a figment of my imagination who was never going to live up to reality.*

I push my own imaginings to one side. "Time to come out, Cleo."

"Why?"

A dozen answers crowd on my tongue. I discard them one by one in favor of the bald truth. "Because you have to face who I am sooner or later. And because your time is mine, I vote for sooner."

She makes a sound that rips at something wide open inside me. Like the pain that lurks inside me, this new rip pisses me off. They all point to weaknesses I thought I conquered on the battlefield. The special black ops team I was assigned to following the Taranahar incident trained what extraneous emotions I had left after Cleo out of me. It taught me to divorce myself from everyday emotion. And yet I've never been rawer, felt more exposed, since she turned up at the club three weeks ago.

The sound of running water comes through the door for a few seconds. Then silence. I force myself not to kick the door open. And wait.

When she emerges, her face is paler than I've ever seen, her blue eyes dark and haunted. Not that she allows me to look into them for long. She slides past me and heads to the window where I fucked her an hour ago, her gaze fixed on the street below.

"Why did you tell me?" she finally asks, her voice husky and broken. "You could have kept it to yourself for…for the rest of your life. So *why*?" A raw, dejected demand.

My hands flex. Bunch. Flex. Words feel inadequate for the weight I carry inside. "Perhaps it was wrong but I needed…" *A confessor.* "If I could take it back, I would."

She rounds on me, her eyes wild pools of desolation. "Well you can't! You…you can never take it back." She shakes her head and storms back toward the bed. When I reach her, her mouth is pinched tight as if she's holding it together by a thread.

Jesus. How the fuck selfish am I? To dump this burden on her when she blatantly stated that the reason she left was because she couldn't handle the violence?

But then why take up with Finnan? What the hell does he have on her?

The questions blaze through my mind, but I coldly snuff it out. She wasn't inclined to tell me before. She most definitely wouldn't now. But this…her naked torment is down to me.

"I'm going to make amends, Cleo."

Her head snaps up, her eyes narrowing with incredulity. "*How?* How do you make up for…for killing someone?"

The wave of helplessness that sweeps through me is so debilitating, I stagger forward and drop into the armchair. She thinks it's only one. I can't bear to set her straight. My head feels heavy as I shake it. "I don't know. I haven't found a solution yet, but I'm working on it."

Her face clenches in a grimace of anguish and she throws her arms out. "How do I know those aren't just words? Here you are, living your billion-dollar life, driving your sports cars, getting to choose how many women to fuck in one night, and having minions on speed dial. How does any of it come anywhere close to making amends?"

"Those are useless trappings. Whether I give away every last penny I have or make another billion by Christmas, nothing is going to stop the endless cycle of hell that greets me every time I open my eyes and stays with me every single fucking second. Hell, sometimes I don't sleep at all. You know why? Because sometimes in dreaming there's hope. And you know what the fuck is worse than hope? It's hope based on nothing!"

Her eyes widen in alarm at my savage tone.

I take a breath. Look away. But I can't not look at her for long. She draws me back. *Fucking Christ.* She always will.

I can't read the emotion that weaves through her eyes, maybe because my every sense is churning in a life-size blender.

She walks forward and perches on the bed in front of me. "You want to make amends? Then let me go."

Let her... *What?*

The blender stops, and everything freezes. "Let you go...Hell no," I snarl.

Her bottom lip quivers until she firms it. "Axel—"

"He physically abused you, Cleo. I'm not fucking sending you back to him." My gaze drops to her midriff. I don't need to pull the sheet away to recall the ugly bruises on her skin. "I don't give a shit what he's holding over your head. He's *never* getting the chance to do that to you again."

She inhales sharply. "I'm going back. I have to."

"Tell me why you want to go back!" I don't realize I've surged to my feet until her head snaps up.

A second later, she looks away. A vise clamps my chest. Hard.

"It's not so easy, is it? Laying yourself bare? Opening yourself up to judgment?"

Her eyes are a little less haunted, a little more enraged, when she looks back up "I don't owe you any explanations, Axel. As you said before, I'm merely your pawn. So do with me what you will, but don't expect me to open up my heart to you just so you can inspect who lives in it. That is one satisfaction I'll never grant you."

The pressure in my chest tightens, the ferocity of it reddening my vision. I move without thought. Without focus. "Fine, then let's concentrate on other *avenues* of satisfaction."

The urgency to lose myself, now, pulls me under. She may not want to show me her heart—and just when did that become the single most important focus of my life?—but there are many other ways she can satisfy me.

I stare down at her, note her agitated breathing, the twitching of her fingers on the sheet. "The damn sheet is in my way again, Cleo. Make it so it's not." I sound like a being possessed. I feel like a beast owned. Chained by shackles she's not even aware she owns.

Her tongue swirls over her lower lip, her breath growing choppier. "Axel—"

My name on her lips produces a potent, unmistakable effect. My thickening cock roars to life, the urgent jerks already tenting my pants. "There's been enough talking for the day, baby. Time to shut that pretty mouth and put it to a different use."

I grab my cock to alleviate the teeth-clenching ache taking over.

Her gaze falls to the proud evidence, and a decadent shudder ripples through her small frame. Beneath the sheet, her nipples peak. My already altered mind slides further into madness.

She seems to debate with herself, her slightly glazed eyes going from the cock I'm gripping to my face and helplessly back again. I smile inwardly. If I had a heart, I would pity her. For whatever reason, destiny and chemistry colluded to give us bodies that insanely turn each other on.

"You can't help yourself, can you?" I mutter. There is no pleasure in my voice. No gloating. I'm just as helpless in this as she. But it's the only thing she is offering. And, from her, I'll take anything I can fucking get. And set the whole fucking world alight for a chance to have more.

The eyes that meet mine burn with lust and annihilate with censure. I reach out and brush a finger down her soft, warm cheek. Asking for forgiveness for the craving that has always been bigger than me? Maybe.

"You may have condemned my decayed soul and closed your heart to me, but in some respects, nothing has changed. Your body will *always* sing the perfect tune for me."

A ragged little moan rips from her throat, and depraved asshole that I am, the sound goes straight to my cock. I lower my zipper, slowly so I don't do myself an injury. My lack of under-wear aids my eager dick in springing free. It juts out, ravenous and throbbing.

Her mouth drops open and her nostrils flare as she scents me delicately. The drugged want in her eyes threatens to knock me off my feet. I remove my T-shirt, toss it away, and then lurch closer, of-fering myself to her.

"Take it, baby. It's yours." It always has been. I'm beginning to fear it always will be.

A hungry little swallow and she reaches for me.

"The sheet, Cleo," I bite out.

She raises the arm securing the sheets. The cotton slides down her tits, pausing for a cheeky second on the tight peaks before it drops to her lap.

Their gorgeous fullness makes my mouth water and sends mois-ture to other parts of me. Pre-ejaculate beads on my crown, and my cock bobs harder.

"Take me in your mouth. Suck me," I croak, barely recognizing my own voice.

Her hand closes over me. Tentative at first, it turns bolder when a thick groan rocks me. Slowly, torturously, she strokes upward, drawing more of my need to my crown. She seems fascinated by that drop of pre-cum. All I want is to feel her tongue taste it. "Now, Cleo."

Doe eyes sweep up my pecs to my face and hold my gaze. Then she brings me inch by excruciating inch to her mouth. She knows the power she has over me. And she wields it mercilessly. The first sweep of her tongue catapults me to heaven. The second plunges me to hell because it's not enough. My fingers claw into her hair, cradle her scalp. "More!"

Still she teases. Flicks and nips, up and down my shaft. My thighs tremble with the ferocity of need pounding through me.

"Goddammit, Cleo, suck me." I don't care that I'm pleading. All I want is to be in her mouth, her body.

She takes my crown and pulls it into her mouth with gentle suction, while her tongue teases my hole and her hand pumps me with firmer strokes.

The steady rhythm of suction and stroking threatens to blow my mind. Gradually, she takes me deeper, sucks harder.

My whole body is caught in a series of shudders I can't stop. Hell, I don't want to stop. Helpless words fall out of my mouth. "Fuck, that's so good. You look so gorgeous. Yes. Yes!"

My balls tighten, and my vision begins to blur. I blink hard and fast. I don't want to miss a second of what she's doing to me. Fire gathers at the small of my back, threatening a blaze I may never recover from. But I don't care. This feeling, this moment, here with her, is all I crave. Already it's going too fast. She's too fucking good at this. My gut clenches as I try to apply the brakes on my flailing control. Her mouth is the stuff of dreams but I want something more.

My hands move from her hair to catch beneath her arms. Surprise slackens her hold on me and I use the momentum to lift and toss her on the bed.

"I'm dying to blow my load in that glorious mouth of yours, and I will, soon. But right now, I want to finish in that tight pussy. So open up for me."

Her breath catches but her thighs fall open without protest. The sight of her pink, glistening cunt sends my heart rate through the roof. She's still wet with my release from before, but the swelling of her clit, the plumping of her pussy lips, is all new.

Doubly intoxicating.

Still mine.

I draw my tongue through her soft folds, the sound of her breathy moan music to my ears. I lick and tease, bite and suck, until the mingled taste of my cum and her juices is diluted with a fresh burst of her pre-release. Her clit fattens, and her thighs begin to shake. I insert one finger inside her. Then two. Jesus, I'll never get over her tightness.

I pump my fingers inside her, absorbing every response as she thrashes on the bed.

"Axel…"

"Come for me, baby. You're so hot. I want to watch you lose it. Let me see you explode for me." Her hands reach out blindly, find my shoulders, my hair. She clamps her fingers into it, as if she'll never let me go. I finger-fuck her harder, my thumb and tongue alternating in furious circles over her clit.

"Oh…oh God!"

Her hips roll into my pumps, her fingers dragging along my scalp. I close my eyes for a blind second to fight for control. Then open to the glorious sight of her body tensing a second before a scream rips through her throat. She flies high, and I'm bathed in her heady scent.

I want to watch. I want to drown in the beauty of her release. But I'm at my breaking point.

I climb up her body, barely stopping to taste her sweet nipples before I slide into her. I catch the tail end of her climax and pump through the ripples.

Her eyes pop open, wonder bathing her face as the convulsions gather intensity again. She grips my arms, her nails digging in as her back arches off the bed. "Oh God, I'm…I'm…"

I flick my tongue over one offered nipple, rolling the hot nub in my mouth. "You're coming again," I groan against her skin.

Her mouth goes slack, and her hips jerk into my thrusts. Her climax is quieter this time but not less sublime. No less mind-fucking-blowing.

I drop onto my elbows and tunnel my fingers into her hair, tasting her mouth as she shatters. But the more I kiss, the more I crave. The more I fuck her, the deeper my obsession grows. "Holy hell, I can never get enough of you. You're in my head, you're in my fucking blood. Sweet Jesus, Cleo, you're everywhere."

White-hot bliss flashes across my senses. Maybe I say more, maybe I don't. Maybe I'm spared the final defeat of spilling everything that my dark soul hides.

All I recall is surfacing to the sweet torment of her cradled in my arms, her head on my shoulder, her hand on the inked Japanese symbol for *penance*.

Her dark, solemn eyes meet mine. When I lower my mouth to hers, she receives my last kiss without hesitation. She closes her eyes. And sighs.

I sigh too.

Then contrary to my every expectation, I sleep.

Chapter Twenty-Five

RUM AND PERSPECTIVE

CLEO

It's been eight days since my unforgettable first day at the Punishment Club. Eight days where I've been fucked, fed, pampered by invisible staff, and fucked some more.

I'm not exactly a prisoner in the time capsule I created for myself, but there's an unspoken message in Axel's actions that tells me he would prefer it if I stayed put.

It's not a huge problem because the idea of venturing outside doesn't entice me. New York is an electrifyingly vibrant city with humanity plugged into life at super-high-octane speed. Nothing of that appeals to me right now. I prefer my temporary world of near silence.

Near silence and endless fucking.

That's our mode of communication since his earth-shattering confession. A confession that I still grapple with. With the hell I saw in his eyes when he spoke about making amends. I tell myself a symbol etched in his skin means nothing, but the strength of that belief is chipping away.

Axel rarely sleeps. The one time he fell asleep next to me, I woke to a man caught in the vicious claws of a nightmare. One from which it'd been nearly impossible to wake him. It happened on the second night when the arms clamped around me and the sweat pouring off his body in sleep told its own story.

Shaking him or calling his name didn't work. So I resorted to other means to pull him from his visible torment. Did a part of me want him to remain in that nightmare?

Maybe. Hell, I thought about it.

But the shuddering of my heart eradicated that feisty flame of retribution. Or perhaps it was the sensation of his hot, hard body nearly engulfing mine that prompted me to act. I captured his nape and pressed my mouth to his.

He stilled immediately, his eyes blinking open to pierce mine. I didn't need to tell him why. And he didn't relay his dream to me.

Instead he took over the kiss, his sexual expertise turning disturbed dreams into carnal reality the second he rolled onto his back and arranged me on top of him. Caught in the vicious hunger that never abated in his presence, I didn't need much encouragement to plant my hands on his chest and ride him. With my brains fucked out for a second time that night, I slept like the dead. And woke up alone.

That set the pattern for the following days.

Beneath the soft white linen tunic that drapes my body, my pussy throbs gently with the reminder of another charged Axel experience.

Halfway through breakfast, he grabbed me, pushed me onto my hands and knees, tore away the silk slip covering my rear, and rammed inside me. The hard and fast animalistic coupling left me spinning, my body a useless heap on the floor. Afterwards, he dragged himself off me then spent the next hour massaging and washing me in the Jacuzzi bath. Of course, true to his word to keep me filled with him, he fucked me again the moment we got out.

Reprieve arrived in the form of his ringing phone. The clipped conversation that followed ended abruptly with him striding for the door before he fully hung up.

"I'll see you tonight. We're going out. Eight o'clock. Wear something nice," were his terse instructions to me before he slammed the door.

Now, after a light lunch and midafternoon nap, I enter the walk-in closet filled with brand-new clothes, a half-drunk glass of water in hand. B hit the ball out of the park with her task. Had I been in a less distressed state of mind, I would feel giddy at the beautiful creations she managed to pull together on such short notice. Jumpsuits, sexy rompers, and cute sundresses in vibrant pastels took care of daywear. Sexy black, red and gray gowns took care of evening wear. A couple of silk nightwear pieces found their way into the collection as well, but as per Axel's instructions, no underwear made it through.

I move along the clothes rack, ignoring the saucy little voice inside that teases me for finding the absence of underwear surprisingly...freeing.

Or perhaps I'm turned on by Axel's hum of satisfaction each time he slips his hand under my clothes to fondle me and finds my bare flesh. I ignore my peaking nipples and select a black, sleeveless dress. The layered chiffon across the bodice will help hide my bra-less state while remaining classy. The knee-length hem will also aid in the no-flashing-private-parts area. The five-inch-wide, cinched-in waist also complements my figure.

I grab and set it to one side then open the shoe closet. B's penchant for fuck-me shoes is glaringly obvious in the sky-high heels carefully arranged in color blocks. None are below four inches, with the highest scaling an eye-watering six and a half. Unless I develop a burning desire to break my own neck, there's no way those stilettos are gracing my feet. I choose a pair of black-and-silver platform Ferragamos and move on to accessories. The silver hammered-metal choker is the obvious choice, and with my intention to wear my hair down, there won't be a need for earrings.

I'm finishing my water when I hear the knock.

Apprehension sweeps through me as I set the glass down. Axel cleared the whole floor after a member accidentally knocked on my door yesterday. Unfortunately for the guy, he interrupted another prelude to mindless fucking. If B hadn't stepped in, Axel would've ripped the guy's head off.

I approach the door with caution, keeping the chain on as I crack it open.

B is standing on the other side, her head cocked to one side, a half smile on her face. "Hey, it's only me. Promise, I'm harmless."

I don't believe that for a second, but I pull open the door, summoning a smile of my own. But she doesn't come in.

"You wanna come have a drink with me?" she asks instead.

"Uh..."

"Come on. You've been cooped up in here for too long. I understand that's probably the design but you're allowed to play hooky once. I won't tell the big bad wolf if you don't. Plus, I know a really cool place."

"Umm...sure." I look down at my dress. It's a little on the short side, no longer than a big shirt, really.

B waves a hand at me. "You don't need to change. We're not leaving the premises."

Nodding, I slip on a pair of comfortable wedges and grab the phone Axel returned to me a day after my arrival.

Thankfully, it's remained silent. Once Axel left me last night, I made my weekly Tuesday call and was reassured there was no change in my mother's condition.

I shut the door and follow B down the hallway to the elevator. Assuming we are heading down, I glance at her in surprise when she slides a card through the security panel and hits the button for PHR.

We exit at the twenty-fifth floor onto a stunning roof garden, complete with a water feature, miniature palm trees, sun loungers and an extensive bar. The space is unoccupied, save for a bartender and waiter manning the bar.

We pass three grouped sofas before she chooses a lounge chair. I pick the seat next to her and stretch out my legs.

After being in isolation for a week, the sunshine and fresh air are seriously awesome. I didn't think I wanted to go anywhere in the July heat, but the sun on my skin makes me sigh. I look around, stunned at the prime space most real estate investors would pay premium dollars to inhabit.

B slants a glance at me. "Interest you in a cocktail?"

"Sure," I reply with a smile.

She nods to the bartender and holds up two fingers.

"Is this place part of the club?" I ask.

She nods. "Only a select few are allowed up here during the day."

Her answer draws my attention to her clothes. Unlike on the nights when I've seen her in work mode, she's wearing dark gray palazzo pants and a white, body-hugging top. The combo shows off her toned arms and belly, with the customary stiletto pumps on her feet.

She intercepts my scrutiny. "It's my day off."

"And you're spending it here?"

She shrugs. "What can I say, I'm a workaholic."

Instinct tells me there's more but I don't pry.

Our drinks arrive. I accept the brightly colored cocktail and take a sip. Rum bursts through the refreshing taste of watermelon and pineapple, and I take another greedy sip.

B takes a few sips of hers before she glances at me.

"So, you doing okay?"

A part of me winces with disappointment. "I was hoping this wasn't a pity drink."

She holds up one hand. "It's not. But technically, everyone in this building is my responsibility, whether they're special guests of the boss or not."

Despite her answer, I can't help but think she has an agenda. "I'm fine."

Steady eyes remain on me for a long moment. "You sure? Because there's intense relationships. And then there's you and Axel."

I try a shrug. "It's just—"

"No honey, there's nothing 'just' about it. Not if you can't walk in a straight line in public."

Heat rushes up my neck into my face. A little irritated, I frown into my drink. "Why are you interested?" Was Axel lying when he said he and B were strictly business?

I stare at the brunette, trying to get a read on her.

She takes a sip of her drink, her eyes on me. "Don't try and figure me out, darling. Many have tried and failed."

"I'm not surprised. You're...intriguing."

A smile flashes across her face, gone too soon, but not before I glimpse the stunning beauty behind the carefully practiced badass demeanor. "Thanks, I try. And for your information and peace of mind, should you need it, no, Axel and I aren't sleeping together. Never have. Don't intend to."

A tight knot I was refusing to acknowledge eases in my gut. Enough to loosen my tongue. "Has he...done this before?"

She gives me a wry smile, despite the flash of sympathy I see in her eyes. "Sorry, honey. Cut me open and I bleed discretion. But I will say this. Axel likes his boxes. He keeps you here in this particular box for that reason."

I frown. "But I'm the one who created this one."

"Sweetheart, we both know who's in control here. If it didn't suit his purpose, you wouldn't still be here. I take it that room you re-created means something to you both? But something not altogether good for *you*, I'm guessing?"

She's ace at withholding stuff about herself while pumping me for info. I shouldn't indulge her. And yet I find myself nodding. "Yes."

"So he's enduring your punishment with you?"

I startle. Then frown. "I...I guess so."

"He owns the club. He could've moved you to any of two dozen other suites. He didn't." She keeps her eyes on me as she sips her drink.

I'm going to make amends, Cleo.

On the grand scale of wrongs that needed righting, this is a drop in the ocean. And yet the idea that Axel—despite his clear displeasure upon seeing the room—didn't move me is disconcerting.

I don't want to think about that while the woman with shrewd eyes continues to stare at me.

"Can we talk about something else?" I say.

She shrugs with effortless ease. "Sure, how about them Yankees?"

I laugh then glance at her sky-high heels. "How about them neck breakers?"

She laughs. The mood lifts. I decline another cocktail and settle for a soda on the next round. We spend another hour and a half on the roof bar before I head back downstairs. She leaves me at the door, and when I shut it behind me, I lean against it with a frown.

The swiftness with which my heart leapt at B's conclusion still worries me. What kind of person am I to be grasping at the flimsiest excuse to absolve a heinous crime?

And the sheer delight that stains my bloodstream every time he touches me?

What about telling me he won't let me return to Finnan? Did he mean forever? Or until he's done with me?

I drag myself from the door, my thoughts spinning in wild circles.

Chapter Twenty-Six

ATONEMENT: PART TWO

My thoughts are still spinning when Axel enters the dressing room just after seven thirty. My hands freeze as I'm slipping on the choker, and he stumbles to a halt.

"Fuck, you look incredible." The hoarse words burst from him, his eyes raking me with feverish intensity as he prowls forward.

"Thank you," I murmur. Through the mirror, my own gaze absorbs the animalistic dominance that seems infused into his drop-dead-sexy body. Dressed in a black dress shirt and pants, with a superbly cut jacket thrown over the ensemble, the figure he cuts is captivating, guaranteed to turn heads everywhere. Couple that with the stubble he's maintained all week—on account of it driving me wild when he grazes my inner thighs with it—and the lightly gelled, slicked-back look he's sporting now, and I fear brain damage if I look too long at him. It's how every woman out there will feel too when they look at him. I hate the dart of anxiety that accompanies the thought.

I hold my breath as he steps behind me and brushes my hands away to secure the choker. Then his hands drift over my shoulders to caress my bare arms. Beneath the chiffon, my nipples tingle and stand to attention, their shameless craving echoing through-out my body.

His hooded gaze locks on mine. "You ready?"

I nod.

Still keeping his eyes on me, he drops a kiss on my jaw then lower. My last-minute decision to wear my hair up gives him free rein over my neck.

I'm not surprised when he leans down and runs his nose along the curve of my shoulder, scenting me long and deep. Then his head snaps up, and our eyes clash in the long mirror. "You showered."

"Yes." My voice is already a breathy mess, and he's been in the room less than five minutes.

"So you're empty?" Anticipation throbs through his voice.

The urge to shout *yes* shocks me beyond measure. Thankfully, insane chemistry takes over, and I lose the power of speech as his hands drop to mold my hips. He rocks his hips into me, and my ass cradles the rod of his thick erection.

"Have you been waiting for me to come back and fill you up, baby?" he whispers in my ear. One hand creeps beneath my skirt, and his fingers unerringly find my center. In the mirror, I catch the reflection of my engorged clit, already screaming for attention. "Have you?" he probes.

"Yes."

He cups me harder, his whole hand working me into a frenzy. My knees weaken, and my hands land on the mirror to stop myself from falling.

"Christ, look at you. I want nothing more than to fuck you sense-less right now. But we need to go." With one last rub, he removes his hands.

My mouth drops open in shock. He's leaving me like this? "Axel..." His name is dangerously close to a whine. And I'm not even ashamed.

"I know, baby." He drops another kiss on my temple. "I'll make it up to you later." He removes a handkerchief from his pocket and wipes my essence off his fingers before he laces them with mine. "Let's go. Now, before I change my mind."

I want to say that he's free to change his mind but I'm suddenly plagued with the need to see Axel outside of this place. I want to see the man others see, to view how he interacts with others besides B.

What I'm hoping for with that, I'm not sure.

We pass B in the lobby. Her gaze drifts over me before she smiles and nods approvingly.

Axel's car is waiting in the underground garage but he bypasses it and heads for a limo idling a few spots away. He reads my surprise and shrugs. "I'm not in the mood to drive tonight."

The moment we slide into the sumptuous seats and the door shuts, I know why. I'm in his lap before the car hits street level.

A thorough kissing session later, he lifts his head. "Did you enjoy your drinks with B this afternoon?"

My eyes widen. "You know." Of course he does.

"She mentioned it."

His gaze demands an answer. I shrug. "It was fine."

"Just fine?"

"You want to know if we talked about you?"

One brow lifts.

"You may have come up in conversation for a minute."

A slight tension seizes him. "Anything I should know about?"

I recall my conversation with B and struggle to keep a neutral expression. "Only if you're interested in female gossip."

He stares at me for a handful of charged seconds before he takes my mouth again. When we part, he rests his head against the seat and slides his thumb over my bottom lip. "What's going on between us is no one else's business, Cleo." His words hold a clipped warning.

A trail of ice chills my spine. I attempt to shift from his lap. He holds me in place. "I'm not exactly shouting it from the rooftops."

"Good. There are some things you already know too much about."

"What things? You mean Taranahar?"

His tension increases, and his hand slides around my nape. "Yes."

I shake my head. "I don't know any more than what I saw on the Internet."

His jaw flexes. "Make sure you keep it that way."

"Is that a threat?"

Dark eyebrows gather in a frown. "Threat? Why would I threaten you?"

"I don't know, why would you?" I throw the question back, the claws of fear resurfacing after being shoved aside by days of mind-blowing sex.

"Dammit, I'm telling you this to keep you safe."

My heart lurches. "Why would I not be?"

He opens his mouth then clamps it back shut.

"If you really mean that, tell me," I push.

"I can't. Not yet."

Disappointment tightens around the fear, forming an even bigger knot of desolation inside me.

"We'll talk about this soon. Just not right now."

I don't respond. I can't. I may want to know more about Axel the man, but I don't know if I'm ready to deal with Axel the ex-soldier, and especially his involvement with the brutal massacre of a whole village. Not so soon after his confession.

The limo pulls to a stop. I look out the window and realize we're at XYNYC.

He steps out and reaches in to help me out. The bouncer manning the door, whom I recognize from last time, struggles to keep the surprise from his face as he holds the door for us.

The reminder of what happened the last time I was here ratchets up my tension.

Despite the early hour, the evening crowd is impressive. Axel cuts a dynamic, dominating figure as he leads me to his VIP lounge. A considerable number of female—and male—heads turn as we move through the buzzed crowd. The amount of eye-fucking shoved his way churns acid through my gut.

The moment we reach the roped-off area, I pull my hand from his.

He recaptures my hand, his eyes narrowed on my face. "What's wrong?" He has to raise his voice above the music, even with his mouth hovering close to my ear.

I fight my the shiver when his breath washes over my lobe. I fail miserably. "Who are you meeting? And why am I even here?"

"I'm meeting Quinn Blackwood. And you're here because I want you here. And you will behave," he warns.

My breath catches. "Excuse me?"

"You're showing me that stubborn little chin again. Whatever's gotten into you, contain it until I can take care of it."

I glare with every flame inside me. My offended chin rises higher. "And if I don't? Are you going to head out there and grab one of those dozen women who are eye-fucking you right now?" *Shit.* I bite my tongue. But it's too late.

He rocks back on his heels, his eyes flaring with surprise. An instant later, he yanks me forward and traps me against his body. "They can try all they want, but they'll go blind before any of them comes within a thousand miles of giving me what you can."

I catch my jaw before it drops. But the breath I was holding shakes out of me, along with a telling little whimper. "I...you..."

His thumb brushes over my lip, silencing me. "Let's get a drink, baby. Then I'm going to put you in my lap and grant you permission to give anyone who looks our way the finger."

My mouth twists. "And let them all think I'm a raging bitch? No thanks."

His hand traps my waist. Leading me toward the bar, he leans down to rasp in my ear, "Okay then, I'm sure I can find some other rewarding project for you to undertake in my lap."

Once again I'm overpowered by the absence of the man those twenty-one minutes of footage tell me he should be. My brain tells me it shouldn't be this easy to want to banter with Axel because he *is* that man. Yet playful words like those we used to indulge in when we were teenagers rise on my tongue. I bite them back and perch on the barstool.

He murmurs to his private bartender, who sets up the makings of a mimosa. A minute later, Axel slides the drink in front of me. "Enjoy it whiles it lasts. I'm cutting you off after two."

"I hold my liquor better these days."

A shadow crosses his eyes but it's gone a second later. "Says the person who passed out after one drink last night."

"That wasn't the drink. It was..." I stop, my cheeks flaming.

"Getting your brains thoroughly fucked out?" he supplies with an arched brow. "Well, drink up and expect a repeat performance tonight."

The recollection sends tingles up from my toes.

I grab the drink and take a large sip then watch him swallow a mouthful of his Balvenie whisky. Through the open neck of his shirt, I watch his strong throat move. Dear God, even watching him sip his liquor is sexy.

How? How can he be two completely different people? The desperate need to understand claws through me. I turn in my seat to look at him, *really* look at him.

But he's staring over my shoulder, his face set into serious lines. I follow his gaze, the hairs on my neck rising. Axel is staring at a couple two lounges over. The man is tall with dark hair almost the same shade as Axel's. Even from a distance, he's striking and chillingly sexy. His demeanor is forbidding to the point of arctic. Except when he looks at the woman he's with. She's petite, barely coming up to his shoulder, with caramel-blond hair, and yet there's a strength about her that I almost envy.

Axel stands, his hand pressing into my waist before he releases me. "Excuse me, baby. Quinn's here. I'll be right back."

The man looks up as Axel approaches. His expression turns from complete and utter absorption in the woman to guarded camaraderie.

They shake hands. He introduces Axel to the woman then they move to one corner of the lounge.

A faint memory strikes. He's the man I saw Axel talking to when I was forced to resort to texting Axel the last time I was here.

Quinn Blackwood.

The men are remarkably similar in height and build but, where Axel's face bears the shadows of his character, Quinn Blackwood's daunting personality lives in his chilling aura and eerie silver-blue eyes. I felt the power of it when he looked my way that night.

Unwilling to be caught gawking at the two most striking men in the club, I let my gaze drift over the crowd. And land on a redhead glaring at me from the side of the dance floor below the lounge. She was one of the many women eyeing Axel when we entered.

My middle finger twitches. I tighten it around the champagne flute, turn away, and take another sip. By the time I reach halfway, the light buzz in my belly is fizzing through my blood.

I rise from the barstool and move to the U-shaped booth. Tall and sumptuous, it gives privacy when needed without compromising full enjoyment of the club. I set my small clutch down and perch on the seat.

Dua Lipa's "Hotter Than Hell" throbs from the speakers. The sultry music pounds through me. Between my legs, the unsatisfied hunger Axel stoked earlier rears its head. I cross one leg over the other in a vain attempt to stem it but that only intensifies the ache. I drain my drink and jump up.

The lyrics wail about the devil, pleasure, heaven and sin.

My skin heats. My hips move before I fully connect with my actions. Across the lounge, Axel's gaze hones in on me. His lips move in conversation but his eyes never shift from me. My nipples tighten at the unholy gleam in the gray depths.

They finish talking, and he walks across the floor to me. With every predatory step he takes, my heart races, and the muscles in my belly quiver. He reaches me, towering over me like a dark overlord.

"Are you done with your meeting?" Shit, is that my voice? Needy and unsteady?

"I'm done with my meeting," he confirms, his voice pulsing with decadent intentions. "Now I can take care of you."

"H-how?"

"Take a wild fucking guess."

A different sort of tension mounts. Not-quite-steady hands trace my bare arms, down to my wrists. He raises them to drape over his shoulders, then takes control of my hips. The light material gives him the perfect geography of my naked body underneath. When he cups my ass, his breathing alters.

What that does to me...I shake my head.

He slides a finger under my chin and lifts my face. "What?" he demands.

"The way you sound, the way you look at me sometimes. Like...you're into me," I blurt, my tongue loosened by rum and champagne.

An almost sad expression washes over his face. "I'm so into you, you have no idea. I'm also aggressively into the sweet addiction between your legs. I love knowing that you're completely naked under that dress. I get hard as a fucking rock watching you walk across a room, knowing your pussy is wet with my cum."

I whimper.

"But you're not wet right now, are you?"

"N-no." The sound drags from me.

"Should we change that, baby?"

He doesn't wait for my answer. A nod at the bartender, and he leaves the lounge. Axel walks me to the booth at the back of the room. He sinks down into the farthest seat and pulls me crosswise into his lap. He presses a sleek remote nearby, and the lighting subtly dims.

We're partly obscured from view with only a corner of the dance floor and the VIP bouncer's broad back visible. The last strains of "Hotter Than Hell" pound the air, and I move my hips.

Hard hands clamp my waist. "Behave," he grits out.

"Or what?"

His eyes darken. "You wanna push me over the edge tonight? Is that what you're in the mood for, Cleo?"

Biting my lip, I shake my head.

"Are you sure? That frisky little ass is still moving, driving me fucking nuts." One hand slides down to grip my hip, the other moving to fumble between us. I hear the distinct tug of his zipper, and my breath strangles.

"Axel..."

"Put your arms around my neck," he instructs gutturally.

Refusal doesn't stand a chance against the hot thrill spiking through me. My arms curl over his shoulders, my lower half lifting long enough for him to pull the back of my dress out of the way. The front still covers my knees.

One hand caresses my bare ass, and a lusty shiver flays me.

"Are you turned on, baby? Do you like what's coming?" Against my hip, his cock is a thick, hot rod.

I bury my face in his neck, my head bobbing almost of its own accord.

"Tell me if you're ready? I don't want to hurt you."

"I'm ready," I groan. "So ready."

One powerful arm around my waist tips me against him then back down again. His hips roll upward, and I'm impaled on him.

My tiny scream meets his rough grunt. We both still to absorb the impact, my channel pulsing to accommodate him.

"Okay?" he rasps against my neck.

"Y-yes."

He huffs out a tortured breath. "Christ, you feel insanely good." His hips flex, seating himself deeper inside me. We both groan. "Perfect. So perfect."

We stay like that, my arms around his neck, face buried in his shoulder. His hands clamp on my waist and thigh. Then he begins to move. Slow, glorious strokes that build and build, relentlessly propelling us to our own pleasure heaven.

When he senses my impending climax, he grips my nape and tugs my face to his. Hot, wet, seeking, he tongues my mouth with the same sure strokes as his cock. The measured synergy sends me over the edge.

Half a minute later, he gives a hoarse groan. "Fuck, *fuck*, yes."

He jerks inside me, filling me with hot jets of creamy semen. His hands stay on me, stroking my body until our racing hearts quiet.

"I like this dress. Very, *very* much," he breathes in my ear.

An unexpected giggle catches me. "I think it likes you too."

His low, throaty laugh rumbles through me. The sound of it, the first genuine show of amusement I've heard from Axel, reaches inside and squeezes my heart. My breath catches.

"What's going on in that gorgeous head of yours?"

"Your laugh," I blurt without thinking.

His eyes turn wary. "What about it?"

"I haven't heard it for so long."

The light leaves his face. His jaw clenches tight. "A million reasons for that, baby."

And just like that, the easiness is gone. I don't know what comes over me. I slide my fingers down his cheek. Words I shouldn't feel, shouldn't accommodate, push against my vocal cords. With everything inside me I bite them back.

He sees my struggle. His haunted eyes meet mine, probing for a minute. Then he taps my waist.

"Time to go."

"Where are we going?"

His steel-hard jaw flexes. "To my next meeting. It's time to step things up."

Chapter Twenty-Seven

POSSESSION IS NINE-TENTHS OF THE LAW

AXEL

Thursday nights at the Punishment Club are what I've termed Vanilla Socials, although B chooses to slap a fancier term on it. But it's the night when the less adventurous club members socialize in the lobby.

It's the only night I allow Cleo in this part of the club. The only night when I can be assured some asshole won't try to draw her into his game.

Recalling the fucker who knocked on her door yesterday, my gut clenches in fury.

Why keep her here at all?

I'm giving her what she wants...like I always have. Because it's always been her.

Always will be...

My gut clenches for another reason. I push it aside and concentrate on the man in front of me.

Detective Malone's meerkat-like expression is almost comical. The moment he entered, I clocked his disappointment at the lack of a salacious orgy right here in the lobby. Since then he's been glancing around, waiting for the skin flick that is never coming.

I nod at the waitress, who delivers his beer, and glance to where Cleo sits at the bar, sipping her second mimosa as she listens to a man reading incomprehensible poetry to his wife. Every now and then, her gaze catches mine and skids away.

Something happened in that booth at my club. I saw questions in her eyes, questions I silently pleaded for her to ask, even though I was terrified I might not be able to answer.

It still hurts like an open wound to see her withhold them.

She catches my stare again, and her body freezes under the overhead bar light bathing her body. Fuck, she's gorgeous. And responsive. And strong.

And still closing her heart against me.

I exhale and redirect my attention to Malone. "The parameters of your assignment have changed."

Street-hardened eyes meet mine without surprise. "I had a feeling this was coming." He sighs. "So this is it? You're firing me?"

"No. I've found someone else who can do a better job on the Bearwood Lake thing. But I need you to concentrate on something else."

He perks up. "Sure. What is it?"

I slide the list of names on my notepad in front of him. He reaches for a pad and scribbles down the four names on it then looks up. "Who are they?"

"Ex-mercenaries employed by MMFR International on military contracts. There were twenty strong. They've all gone underground. But these men were in charge of the outfit."

"Something else to do with Finnan?"

My jaw clenches. "*Everything* is to do with Finnan."

He eyes me for a beat, carefully composing his words. "And you're hoping these men will further your...crusade?"

My mouth twists. "Crusades are not my thing, but...yes."

"And if they can't be found?"

"You buffering yourself against defeat even before you've taken a first crack at the job?"

"Hey, I'm a pragmatist. Bright sides are for Disney Princesses."

"Okay, here's a little pragmatism for you. Find the men within the week or you will be fired. How's that?"

"That's...fair."

I rise and button my jacket. He's back to doing his meerkat impression as I walk away.

Cleo is finishing her drink when I reach her. Intelligent blue eyes dart to Malone for a second. "He looks like a cop."

My knuckles trail her arm, the knowledge that I'm unable to stop touching her a living truth inside me. "Because he is. Not a very good one so far, but I live in hope."

"In hope for what?"

"That he'll find me the answers I seek."

Her eyes widen into watchful pools, and a trace of color leaves her cheeks. "An-answers to what?"

I open my mouth to tell her then caution myself. She still has a connection to Finnan. A connection she refuses to divulge. A connection that might put her in harm's way should he find out what I'm up to.

Arctic fury sizzles along my spine at the thought of Finnan harming her again.

"This will be over soon, Cleo. In the meantime, you're going to have to trust me on a few things."

A virtually impossible request if the look in her eyes is any indication.

"I...I don't know that I can, Axel," she whispers brokenly.

A wave of pain hits me like a body blow, knocking the wind out of me.

Jesus, what am I thinking, asking her to trust a murderer? Isn't it enough that she doesn't run screaming from me every time I come near her? That she allows me to touch her? Fuck her?

For how long though? Will there come a time when she won't? The very idea of that slashes me wide open.

I note the light tremble in my hand as I caress down to her wrist. When my fingers mesh with hers, I'm gratified that she doesn't pull away. "Fair enough. But know this: I'm doing everything I can to ensure that you remain safe. Is that good enough for you?"

Her eyes meet mine again. Searching. Like they did at XYNYC.

My gaze drops to her plump lips; I'm almost wishing for the questions I know she's dying to ask me. After a minute, she gives me a jerky nod.

I shouldn't breathe easier. I want to keep her. I've wanted to keep her from the moment she walked into my club four weeks ago. Hell, from the moment I set eyes on her seventeen years ago.

She was mine first. That gives me fucking rights.

But I'm finding out that holding on to her when she doesn't want to be held is going to be a problem.

"Axel?"

I refocus on her stunning face. "Yes?"

"You look...angry."

"Yeah, that fucking poetry is worse than Chinese water torture. It might be perfect for them, but I want to swallow a bucket of nails listening to that."

She probably doesn't buy it, but a twisted little smile curves her lips. "Don't look now, but one of them looks extremely constipated. So yeah, I'll say it's working."

"Let's leave them to it. Fancy a late-evening pizza?" I ask.

She blinks then nods eagerly. "God yes, I'm starving."

I hold out my hand. "Let's head upstairs. Delivery's already on its way."

She hops down from the barstool. "Is it—?"

"Half anchovies, half ham and pineapple thin crust, with a side order of buffalo mozzarella balls?"

Her eyes light up, her breath catching a little. "Yes."

I lean down and taste her lips. Because I can't help myself. "Yes."

Her happy groan goes straight to my cock. And the stupid jerking thing in my chest.

I keep her hand trapped in mine as we head for the elevator. Then draw her close the moment the door shuts. She kisses me back with enough fervor to makes me rethink a few things.

When we part, she looks at me with a touch of trepidation.

"Now you look…possessed."

I walk her down the hall and into the suite in silence. I don't want to confess what's on my mind for fear that I'll spook her.

Because I am possessed. By her.

She's mine. She's mine. She's always been fucking mine.

And regardless of the consequences, I'm keeping her.

Chapter Twenty-Eight

FULL DISCLOSURE: PART ONE

Six days later

Cleo's lying on the sofa in my office at the Punishment Club where I've temporarily moved my base of operations. One leg propped up, the other foot on the floor, she rolls the tip of a pin between her teeth as she frowns down at the *New York Times* crossword puzzle. Her hair is spread over the arm of the sofa, rippling with life from the bright sunshine slanting through the window. Her striped, off-the-shoulder blue sundress rides halfway up one thigh. From my position behind the desk, I can see the faintest outline of her bare pussy against the light fabric.

"A primal transaction..." she muses.

"*Fucking.*"

Her gaze swings to me, and she laughs. "You're obsessed with sex."

I'm obsessed with you. "Nothing wrong with a healthy libido."

One beautifully shaped eyebrow lifts. "There's healthy. And then there's super-charged. And then, there's *you*."

My gaze traces over her. Lingers on her kiss-swollen mouth, the nipples ripening beneath her dress. "What can I say? I have the perfect stimulus right in front of me. And I don't see you complaining."

Her exhale is as unsteady as mine. It pleases me that she needs to make a huge effort to redirect her attention to the crossword. "Anyway, it's fourteen letters." Her foot taps as her brow creases again.

I close the email containing Malone's abysmally disappointing report—he really needs to go—power down the laptop and walk around my desk. "I can tell you but it'll cost you. Big."

Her gaze darts back to me, the bright blue darkening to a perfect navy when it drops to my crotch. "Is there room for negotiation?"

I've started going commando when we're together. So much quicker to get inside her. Beneath my jeans, the power surging through my cock is plain for her to see. "No, baby. Payment in full. Upfront."

Her fingers convulse around the newspaper. "It's the last clue. I really need it," she pleads raggedly.

I nod. "It's easy, sweetheart. Give me what I want then you'll get what you want."

I reach her, drop onto my knees beside her, and flick a nail over one erect nipple. Her tortured moan is music to my ears.

"Y-yes…"

"What was that, baby?"

"Yes, I…accept your deal," she gasps.

Transferring my finger to her other nipple, I slide my other hand up one supple thigh, kneading and caressing her exquisite skin.

"Axel…" Her moan is needy. And yet the power of it weakens me.

I yank down the elastic bodice and bare her breasts to my greedy gaze. "Beautiful Cleo. So fucking beautiful." I drop my head to one globe, suck and lick until she's writhing. My upward caress reaches the outer lips of her pussy. Desperate to see her, I toss up her dress, exposing her perfect little mound. She's still wet from my fucking two hours ago. But holy fuck, I want her wetter. I want her wearing my possession on every inch of her body.

Her pen drops and rolls away, and her hand reaches down between my legs. The top of my head threatens to blow off when she fondles me boldly through my jeans. I roll my tongue over her velvet-soft nipples, hopelessly, fatally addicted to their perfection.

Her eager hips pump, searching greedily for my touch. I slide one finger inside her. Two. Her tissues are swollen. Fuck, she's probably sore. I need to throttle back this insane need to have her, every minute of every day.

But she loves it. And I crave it. It's the only time I am unequivocally confident that she's wide open to me.

And that fucking *gushing*? It's a new addiction I never want to deny myself. I plunge my fingers deep, stroke up to that sweet spot. Her flesh closes around my digits and she gives a tiny scream.

Fuck, there it is...

"Oh, A-Axel!"

I pull back and watch the convulsions rip through her, all while her hand is wrapped tight around my cock. I trail my nose over her skin, inhaling her intoxicating scent.

Her hand continues to stroke me until the red haze of lust completely engulfs me. Pulling my fingers from her, I stagger to my feet. "Need you, Cleo. Fucking need you."

"Yes." She lurches upright and scoots to the edge of the seat. I catch her tiny wince and change tactics.

"Your mouth, baby. On me." Complete sentences evade me, and I can barely breathe.

"Yes!" Her eager hands push my T-shirt out of the way and attack my fly. My heavy girth drops into her hands, and a second later, her mouth is on me.

"Oh, sweet Jesus," I groan.

I'm less than gentle when I fist her hair and pump into her mouth. She takes as much of me as she can, and fuck, it's more than enough to feel her tongue and mouth and throat spur me toward my fatalistic end. "I'm coming, baby. So hard. You ready?"

Her groan vibrates against my bulging head. The inferno I'm helpless to stop rages up my spine, shoots into my balls. I explode like a fucking fire hose, conscious I'm roaring incoherent words.

She swallows me. Every last drop, then collapses against the seat. I drop to my knees and take her face in my hands.

"God, that was..."

"Fucking amazing?" she supplies with a slightly smug, slightly drugged smile.

And I know, in that moment, that I never stopped loving Cleopatra McCarthy.

The depth of emotions rampaging through me terrifies the shit out of me. All I can do is lurch forward and seal my lips over hers.

Her arms creep around my neck.

We kiss until a knock jerks me from bliss. My thick curse makes her smile. I tug her dress down reluctantly before seeing to my jeans.

"What?" My query is less than cordial.

The door opens, and B pokes her head through a second later. Her gaze skates over me to Cleo. "You ready?" She smiles.

My hands tighten on Cleo's waist. "No. She's not," I growl.

"Jeez, lighten up, big guy. We're only going upstairs."

She's having lunch with B on the roof, a bonding routine that seems to have established itself without my permission. Something I've decided to allow. For now.

"Besides, your visitor has arrived. She's waiting in the bar."

Cleo's gaze snaps to me. "She?"

I kiss her on her scrunched-up nose, loving that she's not bothering to hide her jealousy. "Nothing to worry about, baby."

Even though what I'm about to do rams a spike of tension through me, I have no choice. Detective Malone keeps my secret because of the wads of cash I fling his way and also because he knows better than to cross me after getting a small glimpse of my military history.

This is new territory for me. But in a world where trust is a huge issue, Quinn Blackwood's word is one I'm prepared to risk a lot for. Nevertheless, I've done my homework. The feelers I put out for his contact have so far drawn a conspicuous blank, which perversely reassures me that the woman is the right person for the job.

I drag myself to my feet and help Cleo up. She looks satisfactorily just-fucked disheveled, and the glaze hasn't cleared from her eyes yet.

She's so beautiful. I smooth back her hair, press another kiss to her lips, and trail my hand down the side of her neck. God, I can't stop touching her.

"Come on guys, it's rude to keep people waiting," B grumbles.

"You're not people," I snap.

"Wow, you're all prince."

Cleo smiles against my mouth before she steps around me. "I'll see you later?" she asks softly.

B huffs. "You say that like you have a fucking hope of getting rid of him."

I spin around to glare at my intrusive partner. "Are you still here?"

She lifts an insolent brow. Cleo laughs and strolls to the door.

"Cleo?"

She looks over her shoulder. "Yes?"

"Monkey business."

She looks blank for a second before her gaze drops to the discarded newspaper. "Oh. Thanks."

My gaze travels over the body I'm hopelessly addicted to. "A deal's a deal."

They leave. I stare into space for a minute. Then every ounce of elation drains from me. I leave my office and head to the lobby.

My eyes zero in on the only woman sitting at the bar, nursing a spritzer. I stop for a moment to study her.

Nondescript hair. Slightly baggy but stylish clothes. She's chatting to the bartender, a ready and open smile bursting through every now and then.

The perfect camouflage.

I reach her, and she swivels in her seat. She looks me up and down, and I'm treated to a wider smile.

"Hi, I'm Fionnella Smith." She holds out her hand, and I take it.

"Axel Rutherford."

"Great to meet you." She hops down, grabs the largest, rattiest purse I've ever seen and stares up at me from her short height. "Okay, shall we wrestle this ferret into the bag?"

The bartender snorts. She throws him another smile over her shoulder.

It's an act. Or Quinn will owe me a serious explanation.

We head across the lobby. It's only lunchtime, but the crowd is healthy. And bracingly eclectic.

"This is…interesting." She indicates the room and the members.

I shrug. "Different strokes…"

She grins. "Hey, you don't need to tell me."

"What I want to show you is upstairs."

Her grin widens. "Aren't they all? Lead the way."

I head for the elevator and press the button just as Cleo and B emerge from B's office. Cleo sees me and stops, her eyes swinging from me to Fionnella and back again.

We start heading for each other at the same time. When we stop, her hand comes up to rest on my chest. On my heart.

"What are you doing down here?" Already a few male club members are checking her out. And setting unpleasant fires in my gut.

"B needed to grab something from her office."

"And of course she couldn't do that *before* she came to get you?" I glance past Cleo at B when she doesn't come back with a smart-assed reply.

She's staring behind me at Fionnella, a deer-in-headlights look on her face.

I glance back at Fionnella. Her gaze is on B, but her smile is still firmly in place. *What the hell?*

"Axel?" Cleo prompts me.

I make the introductions, my voice a little terse. They shake hands, Fionnella cheerily charming.

My nerves fray. Far too much attention is centered on our little party. On Cleo. "Go. Enjoy your lunch."

She nods, but her eyes are full of questions.

I draw her close, plant a hard kiss on her mouth, and turn to Fionnella.

She's watching me with half-sad, half-indulgent eyes.

That looks stays on me for a few floors until I ask. "What?"

One eyebrow spikes. "A McCarthy and a Rutherford? Two competing mob families? Really?"

I'm not surprised she knows about my history. I hadn't expected her to show her hand though. "Yes. *Really*. You have a problem with that?"

She carries on staring at me.

"*What?*"

"You remind me of my son."

"Damn, you have my sympathies."

She laughs, and she's transformed into a Sunday school teacher. I'm not fooled for a second. There's hardcore titanium behind the maternal demeanor.

"Ah, you all think you're badasses. Then you find the right woman and suddenly you're like adorable puppies."

A huff barks from me. "Jesus, I'm no one's puppy."

"Don't get me wrong. Your teeth are sharp when you need them to be, but I'm willing to bet you were happy to remain steeped in your...issue until recently? Am I wrong in thinking that ninety-nine percent of why I'm here is because of that woman downstairs?"

"And that makes me soft?"

"No. That makes you badass in a completely different way. A way that isn't headache free, but then where's the fun in that?"

I frown, wondering just who the hell Quinn saddled me with. "Tell your son he has my sympathies."

Her smile dims. "I can't. He's dead."

I inhale sharply. "Hell. Sorry."

She nods. "He would've liked you. And before you self-deprecate, trust me, I know a lot about you."

I believe her. "But not everything."

"Everything is a tall order, son. But try me."

The emotion expanding in my chest isn't one I feel often. It isn't one I trust well. At all. But it keeps growing as we leave the elevator on the sixth floor.

She stops a few feet into the room, her gaze taking in the austere chair, the chains and cuffs, the black walls, the multiple screens. "Now *this* punishment I understand. Not the frill-fest going on downstairs."

She moves toward the chair but doesn't sit in it. Instead she drops her purse on the floor and crosses her arms. "Whenever you're ready, Axel." Her voice is soft. Sympathetic.

As if she's already on my side. The side of evil.

I don't have time to ponder that. I lock the door, pick up the remote, and stand on the other side of the chair. Deep breath. Stomach clenched tight, I hit *play*.

She watches the video from beginning to end, her expression not once changing.

Then she turns to me.

"Jesus, son. You're fucked."

My fingers curl around the remote. "Is that your professional opinion?"

"Everything I say is my professional opinion," she quips. But her eyes are narrowed and fixed on the screen. "Play it again."

My chest tightens. "Is that necessary?"

"Yes, it's necessary." She holds out her hand for the remote. "But you don't need to be here. I think you've reached your permanent viewing quota."

Something about that makes my stomach roll in rejection. "No, I haven't—"

"You've tortured yourself enough for something you didn't do. I'm here. Let me help. Besides, I work better alone. Especially when there's all this"—she waves a hand over my body—"distraction in my way. Go *alpha* over your woman. I'll let myself out."

I stare at her, wondering if I've regressed into one of the handful of hallucinations I had when I dallied in coke. But almost without my will, my hand lifts and offers her the remote.

She nods at me, her smile infinitely kind. "Go, Axel."

I go.

"Oh, one more thing."

I stop with my hand on the door. "Yeah?"

"Fire Malone. Today. He's a drunk and a liability."

A twisted smile tugs my lips. "I knew that. But…"

Her eyes soften even more. "You were desperate. I understand how that works. But seriously, he's been knocking on doors loud enough to wake the dead. If you want to know about Taranahar, I'll get it for you."

I take in the soccer godmother in front of me and shake my head. "Will I find you on any...database?"

She laughs softly, understanding my meaning. "No, son. Same as I won't find you listed under that *extra*-special covert black ops program attached to a certain colonel's unit."

I nod and leave the room. I shouldn't feel lighter. No matter what she finds, I'm still responsible for ending those two lives. But the open, festering wound of not knowing will be over. I can finally make proper amends. And that eases the crushing weight I believed I would live under for the rest of my life.

On impulse, I hit the button for the roof when I enter the elevator. The need to see Cleo, right now, is a searing hunger inside me.

A few special guests are having drinks at the bar, others admiring the view from the glass-walled terrace. I see her immediately. Her hair dazzles in the sunshine, the curve of her cheek and chin pinched with laughter from whatever joke B is telling.

I pause and drink her in. I pause and entertain with audacity the idea that things could be salvaged, in some way, between us. That I haven't committed to loving a woman who may never love me back.

She flicks her hair over one shoulder then leans forward to take a bite of food. Her every movement is graceful, beautifully choreographed in a bundle of everything I desire.

Perhaps the power of my thoughts transmits to her. She can't possibly see me from her seat. But still her head swings around. Her blue gaze finds me. Over the seats and through twisted miniature palm trees, she finds me.

Downstairs, her eyes held questions first and welcome second. Now, there's a smile first. A wide, welcoming smile that radiates through me.

I stride through the seats, nodding here and there but not stopping to chat. Cleo tracks me the whole time, and when I stop next to her, her hand flutters up to mine. I grab it before she can change her mind. I take the seat next to her and kiss her knuckles.

"You done with your meeting?" She repeats the question she asked at the nightclub.

"I'm done with my meeting."

A pulse of erotic heat arcs between us. I turn her hand over, kiss her palm. Her breath catches softly.

"Thanks, Axel. Way to make me feel like a third wheel at my own lunch break," B grumbles.

I rest our linked hands on my thigh and glance at B. The snark is fully operational, but the corners of her mouth are pinched and her gaze is watchful.

Definitely something going on there. But our lines are clear and I'm not about to overstep.

"I'm not staying," I say reluctantly. "I have calls to make, a…long-term employee to fire."

Her eyes narrow at me.

I ignore her, and I lean over and kiss Cleo's cheek. "Don't overstay lunch, or *one* of you is getting fired too."

B snorts and rolls her eyes but again, her usual sassy comeback is lacking.

My journey from the roof bar is uneventful, but an overenthusiastic member who needs to be handled and reminded of the club's rules takes me to the fourth floor for far longer than I prefer.

Fionnella is waiting for me for when I walk into my office. I decide not to guess how she cracked the door's entry code. She still oozes harmlessness but her smile is considerably pared down.

My bubble of elation bursts. I grit my teeth and cross over to the drinks table adjacent to the sofas. "Drink?"

"Vodka tonic, thanks," she says.

I fix her drink and pour a whisky for myself. My legs feel decidedly leaden when I take the seat opposite hers on the sofa. She sips her drink. I down mine in one go, contemplate another.

"Well?"

"I was wrong. You're not doing all of this because of her. You want payback for yourself."

I exhale. "Yes. And?"

She shrugs. "Trust me, I understand that too. Tell me about your connection to Taranahar."

I relay the story, fast and emotionless.

She smiles. "Perfect."

"Excuse me?"

"I suspected you were in the area. I didn't know you witnessed it firsthand. Why haven't you handed this baby to anyone?"

Bitterness shoots up my throat. "No one seems in a great hurry to take it. The first judicial inquiry was half-assed at best. It didn't take much for it to fall apart."

She nods. "Don't worry, we'll get them in the mood this time around. After we've taken care of those responsible for the Bearwood Lake situation." For the first time, I catch a note in her voice. Fionnella is on her own path for vengeance.

I shake my head. "I appreciate the offer but all I need is their identities. I'll take care of the rest myself."

She eyes me, a touch disappointed. "You sure?"

"It needs to play out my way." Nothing else is acceptable.

"Fair enough. I have a few more questions, mostly to do with what happened after Bearwood." She pulls out a pen and giant pad.

I give her what she needs. She scribbles rapidly. Her eyes narrow when she stops to probe deeper into Cleo's Boston trip. Again when she asks about why I changed my mind and stayed at West Point following my decision to leave, I don't go into details about Finnan's video but she nods anyway.

Ten minutes later, she finishes her drink and stands. "Okay, that's all for now. I'll see what I can dig up, so to speak. I'll be in touch by the weekend."

"Three days? That's all you need?"

She shakes her head. "No, I mean I should know what I'm dealing with by the weekend. This thing could take weeks, months even.

But I have a little time on my hands now seeing as my employer is currently absorbed in other...matters."

I recall the blonde with Quinn at the club last week. Elyse. Not his usual type. But they looked...good together. Hell, it was more than that. They looked combustible.

Fionnella hefts her purse on her shoulder. "In the meantime..." She pauses, presses her lips together. "You can tell me to mind my own business, but I'm going to say it anyway." She ignores my crossed arms and raised eyebrows. "That room upstairs has its purpose in your life. But don't let it become your *sole* purpose."

"My choices are my own. I'm not going to debate them with you."

"Your choices are no longer your own. And you're already changing them for that sweet girl. By all means, let her see the monster you think you are. But it wouldn't hurt to show her another side. Who knows, you might achieve that goal you think is elusive much quicker than you expect."

My pulse continues to race long after she's gone. I can't ignore the impact of her words although I'm not completely certain what that impact is. So I shove it to one side and take care of the long overdue business of firing Malone.

The detective accepts his fate with more dignity than anticipated. "For what it's worth, I have a bit of news."

"Yes?"

"Two of the four have found their way into non-extradition countries in the last six months. Unless you have superpower connections, they're virtually untouchable."

"And the others?"

"I've drawn a blank so far." He clears his throat. "Do you want me to—?"

"No. Our association is at an end, Detective. Goodbye."

"Wait! One more thing. Your brother Ronan has been... uhh...stirring things up with the Armenians in the last few days."

My fingers tighten around the phone. "In what way? Be specific."

"I think he's planning a takeover of what's left of the kingdom. Whether it's hostile or not, I'll leave it up to you to figure out."

I hang up and stare into space, my mind churning. Picking up the phone, I dial again.

He answers on the second ring.

"Ronan, I told you to stay out of my way."

He laughs. "Who the hell are you to tell me what to do?"

"Twenty million."

He hesitates. "I don't want—"

"It'll buy you a lot of power. At a safe distance from my crosshairs. It's a good deal, brother. Way more than you deserve. Take it."

"Why the hell should I?"

My breath stalls for a moment before I speak. "Because I choose to believe we were all pinned under a yoke that was impossible to shift. We *all* have blood forced on our hands we can't wash away. But don't make things worse. That time is over. *His* time is over. But you won't be inheriting what's left of his fucked-up kingdom."

"Why? When you've never wanted any part of it?"

"Because it needs to end. You have forty-eight hours to accept. Then I'll offer the money to the Armenians to kill any deal you're hoping to strike with them."

I end the call.

He may be the firstborn son and by rights the heir. But I'm going to inherit the kingdom I never wanted.

And then burn it to the fucking ground.

Chapter Twenty-Nine

AXLE SHIFT

CLEO

He's quiet. Scarily quiet.

Has been for the last two days. Ever since he met with the woman who looks like Mary Poppins's middle-aged aunt but without the English accent. Something about her rattled me. B too, although for only an instant. I asked her what was wrong. She waved me away. I chose to let it be.

But Axel's dangerously brooding. The way he fucks me has changed too. There was always an edge to the way he took me, but that edge has intensified even more. And where he once left the bed shortly after we fucked, now he stays. All night. His arms tight around me, and with an after-sex tenderness that is slowly destroying me.

Because I realize I'm yearning for this part of him, while desperately bricking up monstrous parts of him I don't want to see. It won't end well for me because a secret part of me craves that monster too. It's part of who he is.

Which makes me…what?

"Are you ready?"

I glance up at the low, deep voice. He's standing in the doorway of the dressing room, his fingers moving over his phone. The phone that hasn't been out of reach for the past forty-eight hours.

I frown. "Are you...Is everything alright?" An absurd question considering our circumstances.

"Fine." His answer is clipped, but behind his eyes, I see a storm brewing.

"We don't have to go out if you don't want to."

He looks around the room before his eyes meet mine. "I don't want to. But you do. So we're going."

I turn away, and under the pretext of slipping on my shoes, I hide my turmoil. This prison is slowly strangling me. Especially since my conversation with B. Reliving it, I feel the crazy cascade of emotions again.

He's seriously obsessed with you.

A punch in my belly, followed by a frantic head shake. *He's not. He can't be.*

Her mocking laughter. *I'm pretty sure he can.*

No. You don't know what... You don't know him.

Oh honey, do any of us ever truly know another person?

Maybe not, but what he's...done...

Then why are you here? And don't give me a story about not having a choice. I'm not exactly prying you off the ledge when we have lunch on the rooftop. You laugh more with him than you do with me. And come to think of it, he's threatened to rip my head off every time I've come to get you, but he's smiled more in the last week than... shit, ever. What you're saying to me now may be a whole lot of truth, but even with a gun to your head, you still have a choice.

I don't.

Well, test it. See if what I'm saying is true. What's the worst that can happen?

My hands shook so hard I nearly dropped the glass.

Shit, forget that part. But a part of you is certainly enjoying... whatever this is. You fucking glow when he walks into the room. You may not think so but some part of you trusts him a whole lot. And please spare me the crap about sex. Every woman knows the difference between sex and love, regardless of what they may say. Think about it—

"Cleo?" God, *his voice.* Deep, coaxing. Dangerous to my... everything.

I compose myself and straighten. "I'm ready. Where are we going?"

Sharp gray eyes probe me for several heartbeats before he holds out his free hand. "Harlem. Dinner at my club. What happens afterwards is up to you."

Statements that give the impression that I'm in charge of my own destiny and not fully under his control. I dig deep to find the fury that lie should trigger. The effort it takes distresses me. Enough to keep me silent most of the way to Harlem.

Playhouse X is a jazz club featuring live bands. Revamped from an old warehouse, it's refitted with eye-catching tiered seats, clever lighting and excellent acoustics, evidenced by the stunning strains of a sax solo that greets us.

We're escorted to our private booth to the left of the stage and we order drinks and food. Axel pulls me close the moment we're alone. "Have I told you how beautiful you look tonight?" he rasps in my ear after dropping soft kisses along my jawline.

"Not that I recall."

A tense smile registers against my ear shell for an instant. "Probably because I've been trying to work out the logistics of how I'm going to get underneath this dress. I much prefer the black floaty one. And the blue one with the slit up the side. And the shorts-and-top combo—"

"The romper?"

"The romper. That's my favorite so far. Now this one..."

We both look down at the moss-green dress with black crystal detailing at the neckline and hem. Tight from neck to thigh, there's no way to fool around in it without earning myself a public indecency citation.

"I guess I'll just have to work harder to get in." Although his tone and expression are as powerfully sexy as ever, my senses continue to jangle.

"Or maybe tonight I'll take care of you," I say, the words falling out before the thought process is completely formed.

Narrowed eyes gleam down at me. A muscle twitches in his jaw. "You think you're up to taking on the challenge?"

I don't need a crystal ball to deduce the question extends beyond the giving and taking of public sex. My senses tumble even harder. "Maybe…"

A dart of disappointment chases through his eyes. "Be sure to let me know when you're sure." He goes back to kissing my temple, my cheek, the corner of my mouth.

The drinks and appetizers arrive. Axel pours and passes me a glass of Malbec.

Before I take a sip of the full-bodied red, he raises his glass to me. "Toast?"

I shake my head. "I'm…not sure what…"

A terse little smile twitches his lips. "Don't worry, I'll go. To 'maybes' in all shapes and sizes. To the possibilities they offer. To…being taken care of."

He clinks his glass to mine and takes a large drink. I follow suit, although the unwillingness to cloud my senses with alcohol slows my intake. If Axel notices, he chooses not to mention it.

Maybe he doesn't notice. His attention keeps darting to his phone.

"What's going on?" I finally blurt, unable to stand the tension seething through him.

He sets down the fork he's using to feed me the exquisite spicy crawfish served in bite-sized filo pastry. His fingers slide through my loose hair, arranging it over my shoulder. I'm fully prepared for a firm non-answer, much like I've received so far.

"I gave Ronan forty-eight hours to accept a deal I proposed to him. The time expired three hours ago."

Shock holds me still for a second before I dive through the open door. "What type of deal?"

"Financial compensation for abdication of a throne that will never be his," he states with dauntless arrogance.

"What did he say?"

"He postured. He swore. Predictably."

I shudder. He frowns. "What?"

"He...he scares me sometimes."

Axel's nostrils thin as he inhales sharply. "Did he ever hurt you?"

I shake my head immediately. "No, but I...sensed that he could."

He captures my nape and turns me to face him, his face set in granite. "No one will be allowed *anywhere* near enough to hurt you. You have my fucking word."

His words are harrowingly evocative of the words he said to me on the beach a long time ago. But now, like then, he didn't exclude himself from the equation.

My heart shreds as I stare at him. "Axel—"

"Trust me, Cleo. Please." There's a fever in his eyes that light dangerous fires inside me.

He's seriously obsessed with you.

In that moment, I almost believe it. Almost believe that, somewhere along the line, fate's black magic has selected us to be its puppets. That our destiny is inescapable. Forever intertwined. Set on a course of ultimate destruction.

"Yes, Axel. I trust that you won't allow anyone to hurt me."

A groaned breath shudders out of him. His forehead drops to mine, and his eyes shut. Deep breaths lift and lower his chest. I stare, fascinated by the Hyde of the heartless killer and the Jekyll of the sexy, caring man who will grant me the world. The man I'm beginning to believe *is* obsessed with me.

After several minutes, we go back to eating. His tension eases a touch, although his eyes remain dark and charged, almost frenzied when they run over my body.

We're distracted when the band starts again. But the young black singer who takes the stage is captivating, her deep, soulful voice keeping everyone's eyes glued to the stage.

When I refuse dessert, Axel rises and holds out his hand.

My thoughts churn some more as we exit the club. The thought formulating terrifies me a little but there's a wicked power thrumming through my veins that pushes me to go for it.

He activates the door when we reach his Spider. He cups my elbow to assist me in, but I draw away and place my hand on the low roof.

Narrowed eyes take in my defiant stance. A different type of tension sizzles in the air.

"Get in the car, Cleo." Soft. Sensual. Hideously dangerous.

I gird my loins. Then shake my head.

"What's going on here?" he breathes.

"I want…I want…" *Shit, use your words!*

He leans closer, his words for my ears only. "I know what you want. But if you don't get in the car, how am I going to drive us somewhere quiet so I can fuck you on top of it? And don't tell me you don't want that. You're fucking *caressing* my roof right now."

I snatch my hand away. "I want you to…fuck me. But not on the car. I want something else."

He pulls back. Stares at me. Watchful. "Whatever you want. Name it."

My heart shakes. My laugh doesn't come off as airy as I want. Which isn't surprising considering…"*Whatever* I want?"

"Yes, within reason. Tell me, Cleo."

Licking my lower lip, I gather the words to my throat. "I don't want to return to the Punishment Club tonight. I don't care where we go but not…not there."

His whole body goes taut. An animal poised to strike. "Why not?"

"Just for tonight…I don't want to live in the past."

"Why?" He probes harder, his gaze piercingly direct.

I stare at the can of worms slowly slicing open. "It's too hard."

"Life is fucking hard, Cleo. You can't run from it."

"But we can seek refuge for a while, can't we?" I plead.

Lightning flashes through eyes gone slate gray. "And you want me to be that? Be sure, Cleo."

"For … for tonight—"

His head shake dries my stream of words. His fingers slide up my cheeks to fist my hair, and he brings his whole being, vital and virile, to mine. "I can give you what you want, but I can't promise that I won't want more in the morning. Enough has *never* been enough with you. Are you prepared for that?"

"How about we promise to give each other as much as we can?"

His thumbs caress my cheeks, his eyes fixed, his breathing eerily calm. "There has to be an acceptable baseline. Mine is high. I don't want just your body, Cleo. I'm coming for all of it."

My breath strangles. "Axel…"

"Get in the car, baby. Let's go get your night started."

"Where are we going?"

"My place," is all he says.

I slide in. He shuts the door. I thought my head was spinning before. I had no idea.

Three blocks later, he catches my hand and raises it to his mouth. The open-mouthed kiss, followed by a slow lick of my palm, draws a low gasp.

And a curse from him. "We should've taken the limo. I could be balls deep inside you by now."

My free hand caresses the butter-soft leather of my seat. "I like this car."

White teeth flash in a carnal smile. "It likes you too. Very much." His voice throbs with torrid sex. He starts to raise my hand again. His phone rings.

His body goes rigid, and the thigh he lays my hand on is iron hard with tension.

Letting go of me, he answers. "Ronan."

He listens for a minute before his gaze finds mine. A subtle nod punches relief through me. "Glad to hear it. No, Troy will come around. And I'll take care of Bolton."

He stays silent for another minute before he exhales heavily. There's determination in there. But also regret. "I can't promise that, brother. So I won't." His voice is deathly rough. "I'll be in touch soon."

The screen goes black, and he shoves the phone into his pocket.

I'm almost too afraid to ask. "What did he want you to promise?"

His jaw flexes. "That everyone will come out of this...whole. Or at all."

Terror blazes through me. "What...what are you saying?"

"That I'm not making promises. To anyone." He reaches for my hand.

I snatch it away. "What happened to *wanting more*? To enough not being enough? Were those just words?"

He freezes for a moment before he traps my hand again. "I meant every single word. For however long we have, *I want it all.*"

However long we have.

I can't think beyond those fatalistic words. Can't think to a time in my future when Axel Rutherford won't be there when he's been at the front and back of my mind every single day since we met. Wanting vengeance kept him alive in my soul, searing him into the fabric of my existence in a way that bound us.

The thought that he won't be...

I remain silent as we roar through traffic toward the Upper East Side. His jaw is still set as we cross the breathtaking lobby of his Park Avenue apartment building. The concierge's deferential greeting is met with a tense nod. Axel's stride is almost punishing as he hustles me into the elevator.

He's on me before the doors are fully shut. Trapped against the elevator wall, I can only stare up at him as narrowed eyes rake my face to rest on my mouth. "The second I taste those lips I won't be able to stop. So let's deal with what's running through that head of yours first, hmm?" Despite his words, his hips push into me, the thick rod of his cock making possessive demands, promising immeasurable highs.

My fists ball on his chest, and I push. I succeed only because he lets me. "What if I want that promise?"

He exhales. A muscle jumps in his jaw. "There are only three things you want that I can't give you, Cleo."

My freedom. His innocence. His word on this.

The first I should be fighting tooth and nail for. The lack of the second had until recently fuelled my vengeance. But it's the third that's dominating my thoughts now.

I'm beginning to lose all perspective, and I can no more lay blame for that on Axel than I can stop breathing.

What is happening to me?

I breathe in. Out. My soul still flails.

"I understand," I say because I can find no other words. Fires I've kept burning on the coals of my hate are losing a vital ingredient—my will to keep them thriving. Instead, I yearn for impossible things.

But are they impossible? He's obsessed with you.

"Do you? Understand?" Axel demands.

I'm not ready for the pithiness in his tone. For the ravaged emotions swirling through his eyes. They speak to a torment that should be absent. He is a monster, after all. Except…

I shake my head, but the action is futile in restoring reason. And with my own bewilderment far too close to the surface, I open my fist and flatten my hand on his chest. His heart beats, strong and steady. And I blurt, "No. Not really. Make me understand, Axel."

The fingers cradling me tense, vibrating in a tight tremble. He stares down at me for the longest moment. "He *has* to be held accountable, Cleo."

I swallow. "For what…exactly?"

He starts to answer. The elevator doors open. He catches my hand and marches me down a wide, carpeted hallway to tall, carved double doors. A swipe of a silver keycard and an input code release the door.

My heels click on dark marble floors before they're muffled by the thick rug dividing the large, opulent space. Automatic lights illuminate the living room and I get an impression of gallery-sized windows, stunning views, and sumptuous furniture before I'm once against imprisoned in his arms.

"For what? For me. For us. For every *fucking* thing." Pure ice cuts through every single word.

My breath strangles. "For us? But Finnan didn't—"

The mouth he slams on mine is hard. Lethal. He withdraws just as quickly. "No! I can't tolerate hearing his name on your lips. I don't think I'll ever be able to—"

"Why?"

"Why what?" His voice is gravel rough.

"Why can't you tolerate it?"

"Because he's not fucking worthy of it! I don't give a fuck what he gives you that I...that no one else can." The eyes piercing mine are dark and stormy, his nostrils flaring with barely contained fury. But there's something else in there. A ragged entreaty that I can't look away from. "Tell me what it is, Cleo. Make me understand so I can stop driving myself fucking nuts about it. So it doesn't feel like my insides are being ripped every time I think about it."

"Axel—"

He propels me backward until my back hits the glass wall. He pins me with his body, traps my hands above my head with one hand, the other curving around my neck to completely imprison me. Gray eyes gone wild and fierce laser me. "Do you love him, Cleo? Is that it? Do you...*love* that bastard?" The questions fall at our feet like unpinned grenades, with their potential to annihilate in the seconds it takes for me to answer.

"No."

A deathly stillness shrouds us. He stops breathing altogether. Almost as if he's afraid to move. A single tremble twitches his lips before he speaks. "I...What?" he mutters.

"I don't love him, Axel."

He inhales at the words, his throat working. "*Again*. Say it again, Cleo."

"I don't love him."

A million questions flash from his eyes. Some bring torment, others fury. Each one blasts my skin. But it's his trembling hand that decides the next course of action. The mouth hovering a whisper from mine that tells me what's coming next.

The side zipper securing my dress rolls down, exposing me from armpit to hip.

"I have more questions," he says. His voice is barely audible. "Questions you'll answer when I'm done."

"Done with what?" I whisper.

"Done with imprinting my cock in that tight cunt. Done with making you come so hard you won't know whether to beg me to stop or scream for more."

The kiss he's denied us both finally arrives. Glorious, decadent, heart pounding, he kisses me like I'm heaven and hell. Like he's as addicted to me as I fear I am to him.

His hand slides through the opening to cup one breast in a bold, sizzling caress. He pinches my nipple between his finger and thumb, teasing, tweaking, tormenting until my knees give way.

One thigh slides between mine, propping me up. My dress hitches higher, and I go for a ride of my own, my aching, ravenous core demanding satiation, no matter how inadequate. Because nothing gets me off better than the power that sprouts from between his legs. Nevertheless, I pump then shake when my engorged clit drags against the woolen roughness of his pants.

He groans against my mouth. "Jesus, that greedy little pussy has a fucking mind of its own, doesn't it? Are you attempting to come without me, baby?"

A pathetic little whimper leaves my throat. "I need you. So much." The gravity of that statement stamps on my heart. The power of it freezes me in place.

Axel lifts his head and stares down at me. "Cleo…What's happening here?"

My eyes slam shut, squeeze tight. A childish move that shames me but my reality is spinning out of control. "I don't know."

His hand leaves my breast. "Open your eyes."

I shake my head.

"It's okay. Open them. Now."

I slowly pry them open.

"I can give you this. As often as you want it, day or night. You can have it while you work through what's going on up there," he taps my temple. "Deal?"

"Deal," I croak.

"Good." He lowers his head, tastes my mouth again. "Now, take my shirt off."

I fall on the manual task, desperate to stop myself from thinking about the turbulence raging in my head and heart. Unfortunately, undressing the virile man before me offers a fresh set of challenges. My fingers fumble, the heat from his skin fries my brain while making my mouth water.

"I don't want to be here all fucking night, baby. I need you too. So get a move on, hmm?"

"Don't…rush me. I want to take my time," I lie.

His low mocking laugh sees through my ruse. "I'd believe that if you weren't biting your lip and eyeing me like a hungry little bird." And just to compound my torture, he palms both breasts again.

A crazy fire blazes through me. Catching the two halves of his shirt, I yank them apart. Cotton rips and buttons ping across the floor.

"Fuck!" Axel's breath punches out, the tops of his hard cheeks heating with the insane pressure charging through the room. "That was one of my favorite shirts. I can't let that go unanswered. You know that, don't you, baby?"

He squeezes my nipples between his fingers with an expert timing that sends flames straight to my sex.

My moan is tinged with desperation as I reach for his belt. Undo his fly. "I'll pay…whatever you want."

A torn sound rips from his chest as I shove his pants down. He straightens long enough to step out of them. His shoes come off next. Then, with one hand on my belly to stop me from sliding down the glass wall, he tosses off his shirt.

A naked Axel Rutherford is worthy of so many accolades. None of which can definitively describe the perfection in front of me. All I can do is attempt to appreciate him with my hands. My mouth. My pussy.

"God, I love this." My fingers trail the twin thick veins that V from his abs toward his groin and the delicious crater running alongside it, loving the shudder that ripples up his frame. Reaching lower, I grasp his insanely thick penis and squeeze. "But I love this more."

His mouth drops open in harsh panting as I pump him. Beads of sweat are already forming over his brows and across his top lip. Leaning up, I lick his mouth.

"Sweet fuck, you're on a fucking mission, aren't you?" he croaks.

I lean back and smile. "Maybe…"

"Well, your mission will have to wait. I have one of my own." Strong hands tug my dress over my head. His mouth captures mine, and his fingers find my wet heat, test my readiness. He swallows my tiny scream. And just like that, between one breath and the next, the balance of power shifts.

"The heels stay on. Need the leverage."

He spreads my thighs wider and rubs his huge crown against my engorged clit. "Watch, Cleo," he instructs gutturally. "Watch me take you."

Foreheads touching, we both look down at the slow play of his cock between my legs. The sight is insanely hot. "God…Axel."

His gaze alternates between my face and what he's doing, as if he can't get enough of watching either. My senses scream with the urge to be filled.

"Please…fuck me, Axel. Fill me. Now. Please."

He takes me slow, his powerful drive sure and true, his abs clenched in tight, absolute control. I manage a single gasp of wonder at the unbelievable sensation before my vision hazes.

"Jesus, you look so *fucking* beautiful." The words are torn from a rough throat, his compliment tinged with a helpless vulnerability that prickles the backs of my eyes.

Because that's exactly how I feel.

Axel fucks me slow and deep until I come. Then he moves me to the couch and repeats the performance, his gaze absorbing my every gasp and shudder. He fucks me until I'm floating out of my skin. Until I'm drenched inside and out. Until his own skin is saturated with his exertions.

After a third climax, I open my eyes, watch a bead of his sweat slide down one cheek and land on my breast. I stare as the drop mingles with mine.

Seeps into my skin.

Then I look up into his devastatingly beautiful face. He told me to take the time I need to work things out in my head.

I don't need to work it out. The truth is savagely simple.

I'm in love with my father's killer. But despite my heart attempting to tear itself to shreds about it, my soul is shockingly okay with that admission.

Chapter Thirty

QUANTUM LEAP

Before we head into his bedroom, Axel calls B and arranges for my things to be moved to his apartment.

This is after I answer a hushed *no* to his "Do you want to go back?"

Now I'm lying in his king-size bed, my head on his chest and my hand on his heart. My sex still throbs from his possession.

"Tell me what I need to know, Cleo. If you don't love him, then why? What hold does he have on you?" His voice holds absolute determination. It also bleeds bewilderment.

This has been coming for a long time. My heart shakes with the leap I'm about to take, despite the insane leap it's taken all on its own. "He…I…" *What the hell are you doing?*

I shudder. Shake my head.

I have so much to lose.

Axel rolls me onto my back, levers his body over mine. "He will not hurt you. *I* will not hurt you." The look in his eyes shatters me. "Dear God, please trust me on that."

"You…you go first."

His brow clamps. "What?"

"Tell me about…" My mind freezes at the last second, the leap a step too far. I can't bear to know why he decided to take my father's life. But my need to delve beneath the skin of the man I shouldn't love, but do, pulses through me. "Tell me about Taranahar."

He tenses above me, his face devoid of all emotion.

"Were you there?"

A heavy, soulless sigh deflates his chest. "Yes and no."

My insides tighten. "What does that mean?"

His mouth purses then he exhales slowly. "I was on a special mission in a compound a couple of clicks—miles—from Taranahar. We were almost done when a private military contractor bombed the village. They got their intel wrong. They thought the wedding was taking place in Taranahar."

"Your special mission was to do…whatever at a *wedding*?"

His jaw flexes, and a chilling look weaves over his face. "I was a soldier, Cleo. I couldn't afford to get sentimental about my duties."

I don't have an answer for that so I nod. "Did you fulfil your mission?"

"Yes. I made it out in one piece."

Something in his voice tugs hard at me. I'm almost too afraid to ask. "Only you? You said 'we' before."

His eyes darken. "It was a two-man mission going out. It wasn't coming back."

My eyes prickle. "I'm sorry—"

"It shouldn't have happened. Crunch would still be alive if MMFR hadn't clusterfucked their intel."

Ice rams my spine. "MMFR? Finnan's and my father's company? They…*he's* responsible?"

"For every one of the people who died in Taranahar that night. All the evidence I've found so far on MMFR points to a sloppy operation. The mercenaries were barely trained. Taranahar wasn't the first mission they fucked up, but it was the worst. They were in it just for the money the contracts brought. They didn't care about human life. And now he wants me to help him get off scot-free."

"Oh my God."

"Do you understand now, Cleo? Why he has to pay?"

Despite knowing the cruelty that Finnan was capable of, the sheer amount of blood on his hands is shocking. But I also feel guilty relief that Axel wasn't involved. "But how are you going to make him? He's dangerous, Axel."

His small smile chills me to the bone. "I said I wasn't there when it happened. But I was there directly after. I have everything I need to end him with what he did at Taranahar."

"Then what are you waiting for?"

His face closes completely, a mask of desolation overtaking every other emotion. "Because dismantling his operations with the Bratva and the Armenians isn't enough. He needs to pay for everything."

"What—?"

"I've told you about Taranahar," he slices across me, one hand coming up to hold my chin steady. "Tell me why."

I can't tell him everything, not until I'm sure my mother will be safe from him. So I tell him the fraction of the horror that I can.

"When we went to Boston, he found out my father put a six-million-dollar trust fund in my name which I could access on my twenty-fifth birthday. If I waited, it would double on my thirtieth birthday. He wants the twelve million, and he's been...blackmailing me since to keep me in line."

Axel's face is a mask of unadulterated rage. "Jesus..." His voice trails off then he tenses as if he's been knifed. "How has he been keeping you in line?"

"Axel—"

"How?"

I would've been less afraid if he yelled out the word. The deadly cadence of his voice is chillingly terrifying.

"With...videos."

His face loses all color. "What videos?"

He doesn't know your mother survived.

My whole body is caught in a trembling I can't stop. "Videos that show his guards threatening people. There was one of...you. He had two of his bodyguards film while you were asleep. One had a baseball bat. The other held a vial of heroin. I was told to cooperate or he'd have you beaten and then injected—" I stop, shuddering.

Axel's lips are white with fury. "I get the idea. How many more were there?"

"Dozens. Of people I knew, people I didn't know. Some of them he actually hurt when things didn't go his way."

Axel rolls off me and launches to his feet. He paces the side of the bed, his body bristling with rage. I sit up and pull the sheet up over myself.

He stops abruptly, his face set in a painful grimace. "So all the times I sent you back empty-handed from the club?"

My gaze drops to my twisting fingers.

He paces to the side of the bed, his powerful body crowding me as he raises my chin and reads the answer on my face.

"Fuck!" He shoves his fingers through his hair and resumes pacing, his body growing more agitated until he stops.

When he starts to move toward me, there's a rabid look in his eyes that I want to recoil from. But there's also a ragged pleading that holds me in place.

His lips are bloodless white. They move for a few seconds before the words form. "You slept with him. I know you did. But...was it of your own free will?"

Shock plows through me. "You know? How?"

Gray eyes turned black and endlessly volatile pin me to the bed. "He sent me a video too."

My hand flies to my mouth. "No! Oh God...*oh God, no*..." My skin prickles with a thousand darts of shame and horror.

"Did he...did he force himself on you?"

My head feels heavy when I move it. "Yes. A week after my eighteenth birthday. Then a few more times...over the years," I whisper.

He lifts trembling fists to his face, his knuckles digging into his eyes, his forehead. The roar that charges from his soul is one I'll never forget. Whirling away from me, he lurches for the far wall, still cursing. Still shaking, caught in the deepest vortex of hell.

He drives his fist into the wall. Then again. And again.

Fear and concern drive me off the bed. "Axel, stop!"

But he's locked into a cycle of pain and rage. He pounds the wall again. Drywall flies.

I approach, heart in mouth. Lay a trembling hand on his back. "Axel, please stop."

He jerks around. Deranged eyes lock onto me then drop down my body to where Finnan's assault has faded from sight but not from Axel's mind. "I'm going to *bury* him. But not until I've ripped him into a million fucking pieces for everything he's done to you."

What about what you did?

"Jesus, I fucking hated you for so long…" He says the words almost to himself, but they zap through me like an electrocution.

I stumble back a step. Then another. "You…hated me?"

"In the video, you looked like you were enjoying it. You were making these…sounds." He stops and shudders.

"He took longer if I didn't—" Nausea punches up my windpipe and swallows my words. I turn and run for the bathroom, barely making it before I hurl. He's there, holding my hair out of the way. Caring for me. Loving me. Hating me. Oh God.

I bat his hands out of the way and stagger to the sink. I don't have a toothbrush so I rinse my mouth half a dozen times. He's there, dabbing my mouth with a damp cloth. Moving closer. Sliding his arm around me.

"Cleo—"

"You *hated* me." I can't get past that.

His chest rises and falls. "I hated you. And I *loved* you. I couldn't stop. It fucking tore me apart, knowing I couldn't turn it off. That it was taking over my life. Wanting you. Needing you. Craving you every single moment of every day. Knowing that no matter what hell hole I ended up in or how hard I worked to add more fucking zeros to my bank account, I could never close my eyes without wishing you were next to me. That I could hear you breathe. Hear you laugh. Make you scream with fucking ecstasy."

My heart lurches. I pull away and look into his eyes. "You… *love* me?"

"I love you, Cleo. I never stopped loving you."

A part of me is shrieking with happiness. The other part is curling up in a ball of agony. "You love me."

"I love you," he repeats, his voice pure and deep and strong. "So much. From the moment we met, every breath I've taken is for you. I'll lay down my life for you, Cleo, because it's worth nothing without you." He steps closer, his not-quite-steady hands reaching for me.

And that's when I see it. The ripped flesh on his knuckles. The blood seeping from it, coating his hand.

His blood.

My father's blood.

He pulls me into his body, wraps his arms tight around me.

Staining me with the blood.

"I love you."

Then why? I want to scream.

So much emotion. Too much violence. So much…*everything*. The sob tears out of me without warning. The dam bursts and I can't stop.

"Christ, don't cry. Please don't cry." Axel rains urgent kisses down my face, my neck, my mouth, his hoarse pleading doing nothing to stop the torrent and torment that gush out of me.

I faintly register when he picks me up and walks to the tub. The sound of powerful jets fills the room. Then he's placing me in the warm, scented water. He slides in behind and cradles me in his arms.

My sobs subside when I have nothing more to give. Drained, I let him wash me. When he's done, he just folds his arms around me, cocooning me in warmth.

In heaven and hell.

"I love you," he whispers fervently in my ear, kissing my hair, my jaw.

My heart kicks. Hard. Wanting to break the last, monumental shackle holding it. Falling back down when it can't.

And because I'm spent, because my world can't get any more desolate, I lay my head on his shoulder.

An eternity later, we leave the bath. Dry and clean, we return to a bedroom that looks the same but also so much different.

Once again, he pulls me into his arms. Once again, I go. It's where I fall asleep. Where I dream the dream of the damned.

Where I wake up to find his adoring eyes on me, his hands running down my body. Where I can express myself physically in a way I can't with words. When he slides inside me, fresh tears fill my eyes.

He brushes them away with his thumbs. "It's okay, baby. I know you can't love me because of what I am. But I swear, if you can bear me to love you, to worship you, that'll be enough for me."

"Oh God... Axel."

He places a soft kiss on my mouth. "Shh, just let me love you."

And because I'm weak, because the love I shouldn't feel for him burns just as strong, I let him.

* * *

One week slides into the next.

With the Bratva, the Armenians and the Albanians on board, it doesn't take much more for Axel to gain support in his campaign to isolate Finnan from every ally he can rely on, on the mob side of things. With the help of his brothers, he manages to pull the wool over his father's eyes. We remain on tenterhooks, knowing the hold won't last. Finnan is too shrewd to be fooled for too long.

Twice, I go with Axel to meet with Finnan's lawyers, and I'm stunned by his ability to calmly reassure and strategize while seething with deadly rage.

Even though Axel refused to let me into the room, I insisted on attending the meetings. I needed to see Finnan, to reassure myself that he believed I was playing the game too. Each time, his smugness reassured me that the ruse was working, that my mother was safe. For the time being.

But while Axel plots, I also make plans to move my mother. Now that I know the extent of Finnan's sins at Taranahar, I know he's preoccupied with saving his own skin. It's not an easy decision, but I risk calling my father's attorney and requesting the money I need to act when the times comes. Someday soon, Finnan will come face-to-face with the force of his son's vengeance. I can't afford for my mother to be caught in the crosshairs of their war.

Her doctors disagree with me, of course. Nevertheless, I quietly put them on standby and make arrangements with a private facility in Pennsylvania.

And I just…exist.

Axel's stunning penthouse is my sanctuary and my hell. It's where I'm saturated in his love and mourn my inability to embrace it.

I remain at the penthouse when he goes out. It's an easy choice given his concern for my safety and my own desire to stay put. A not-so-easy choice was finding a way to get through the hours without driving myself over the edge.

Because with time on my hands and the threat of Finnan temporarily held at bay, my brain gains the audacity to plot a future. A future I've never contemplated.

A future where I might learn to accept a killer as the love of my life? Possibly the father of my children?

For the hundredth time, I push the thoughts away. But they return, stronger than ever.

When my phone beeps, I jump on it. It's a text from Axel.

"Need to escape this madness. Lunch?"

My fingers tap out a *Yes* before I take my next breath.

"Great. See you in half an hour. Wear the yellow sundress."

The irony of distracting myself with the same man who dominates my thoughts isn't lost on me as I quickly shower.

By the time Axel walks through the door a whole ten minutes early, I'm ready and waiting.

He gives me the once-over, from my carelessly knotted updo, to the strapless heels complementing my dress. Striding over, he catches me in his arms. His mouth trails kisses along the curve of my shoulder before he breathes me in. "You look breathtaking, baby. Although I was hoping to catch you just out of the shower."

His hands mold my ass, and he uses the leverage to yank me into him. He's hard and ready to go.

My body revs to attention, a slave to its need. With no shame, I melt into him.

He groans and pulls away. "I'd love nothing better than to fuck you right now. But our ride is waiting."

Catching my hand in his, he kisses my knuckles and walks me to the door. When we reach the elevator, he hits the button for the roof.

"I thought you said our ride was waiting."

He smile is devastating enough to make me lose vital brain cells. "It is," is all he says before he pulls out a pair of stylish aviator glasses and slides them on.

We exit into the hot late-July sunshine and onto a roof on which perches the sleekest helicopter I've ever seen. Black with gold trim, the gleaming machine is even sexier than Axel's McLaren Spider. And that car is sexy.

The pilot spots us heading over, and the rotors begin to spin.

Axel helps me in and secures my headgear before he sees to his own.

When the aircraft lifts and I gasp, Axel grabs my hand. "Shit, I didn't ask. You're not afraid of flying, are you?"

I'm a little startled to hear his voice directly in my ear. When my gaze snaps to him, he points to the tiny mic attached to the headset.

"I...don't think so. I've only been on a plane three times."

He works it out, and his mouth flattens. "Connecticut to Boston?"

I nod.

"So you've never been out of the country," he says.

"No."

His face turns grim, but he squeezes my hand. "When this is over, we'll go on a world tour of my clubs. You'll enjoy Rio. And Paris. I'll fuck you in my ice hotel in Helsinki," he murmurs into the mic.

He laughs when I blush, but I turn away. The future plans I'm trying to run away from come screaming back, but luckily, the banking chopper scatters my thoughts when my stomach dips alarmingly with it.

My fingers tighten around Axel's. He leans over and puts his arm around me.

"You didn't say where we were going."

His lips graze my temple. "I have a place in the Hamptons. And a chef on standby to feed us. I also have a pool where I intend to get you very naked and very wet after lunch."

He keeps that promise an hour after the chef and staff are dismissed. In no time, my dress is discarded in one of the multiple rooms in the stunning three-story beach house that could easily feature in *Architectural Digest*. My hair falls down around my face as he scoops me up and strikes a steady path for the gleaming pool.

He allows me exactly one lap of swimming before he lays me out on the double-wide cabana-style lounger and proceeds to blow my mind. After three toe-curling orgasms, we doze in the shade.

I wake up first, a first in itself. Beside me, Axel's chest rises and falls in a steady rhythm, his face a little relaxed in sleep but no less ferociously dominant. My gaze drifts over his straight nose, sculpted cheekbones, the stubble on his jaw.

God, he's beautiful. So beautiful it hurts my heart just to look at him. I stare until I can't breathe. Until I have to tear my gaze away to stop myself from sobbing out the sorrow in my heart.

Shifting in his arms, I look beyond the pool to the private beach below. This time it isn't the future that haunts me but the past.

A similar beach. A girl who dared to dream of forever.

Of fairy-tale weddings.

Of bare feet and fat bellies.

Of plump, happy babies who grow up in the image of their father.

Babies.

Babies…

Oh shit.

Chapter Thirty-One

IT BEATS. IT BLEEDS.

AXEL

I should give her time.

I should keep my promise and let it be.

I should be thankful that my heart is beating again because of her.

That I get to cradle her in my arms every night.

But I see the terror in her eyes even when she's letting me love her.

And *Christ*, it hurts.

My heart started beating again only to bleed to death.

She doesn't love me.

I have to live with that.

But.

Fuck.

How?

Chapter Thirty-Two

PITTER PATTER

CLEO

"Open the door, Cleo."

Oh God.

Oh God.

Oh God.

Burying my head in the sand for two weeks after the Hamptons didn't work. Sur-fucking-prise. I hold the three pregnancy tests in my wildly trembling hand. Each one happily states I'm *3+ weeks pregnant*.

"Cleo, dammit, open the door!"

I'm pregnant.

Oh God.

My mind skates sideways, backward and forward.

The volatile cocktail of terror and joy and anguish surge through my blood. Hysteria bubbles up to fight with the tears clogging my throat.

I'll never be able to tell this child a cute little story of where he or she was conceived.

On the roof of your father's sports car in the middle of the forest where I thought he meant to harm me doesn't sound great.

In a replica childhood bedroom I staged in a punishment club sounds even worse.

"Talk to me, Cleo. Right fucking now or I'm kicking this door in."

"I'm...okay," I call out.

"Try that again. To my face. Once you open this door. You have ten seconds." The menacing power in his voice sends another shiver through me.

Even if I want to, there's no way I can hide this from him.

But I'm not ready to deal with...any of it.

"I'll be out in a minute."

"No, baby. You'll come out now. Rushing past me and locking yourself in the bathroom the minute you get back from lunch with B doesn't fill me with elation. In fact, it scares the living shit out of me. So...two fucking seconds."

I stagger to my feet, the tests clutched tightly in my fists. My legs feel like lead, my heart a rusty pump that barely functions. I'm about to tell my father's killer that I carry his child. Another golden nugget I'll never be able to relive with this child.

The moment I turn the lock, he pushes it open. Eyes ablaze with savage intent and dizzying worry meet mine. Rake my face. See my terror.

He exhales harshly as he grabs my shoulders. "Jesus. Baby, what's wrong? Did something happen at lunch?"

I shake my head numbly.

"Then what? Are you sick? I'll call the doctor—"

He stops when I hold up my hand. His gaze locks in on the tests.

He grabs my hand and turns the tiny screens to read the verdict for himself. He stops breathing for several long seconds, and then his breath punches out. Hard. "Cleo? Are you...is it real?" His voice is a hoarse, shaky croak.

Filled with elation. Hope. Apprehension. More elation.

"Yes, it's real. I'm pregnant." Emotions tumble from my own voice, but I can't name which one is paramount.

I watch stunned as his trembling hands cup my face. He rains kisses amid shocked laughter, harsh breathing.

Then he falls to his knees.

Gentle hands cradle my hips, tug me close. Reverent lips kiss my flat belly. When he looks up, his eyes are shining. "God, I love you, Cleo. I love you so much. And I love this baby. *Our* baby. I love…" he slows to a stop when he glances back up at me. "You're not happy."

"I…I don't know what I am," I reply honestly.

His face goes slack. Pale. He swallows and climbs back to his feet. "What does that mean?"

"I just found out. I'm thrilled you feel this way—"

"But you're not? You don't want the baby?" His voice is a charred mess.

"Yes, I do." That is a certainly that blazes in my heart.

But he goes paler. "But you're not thrilled about it because I'm the father."

Oh God. "No, that's not—"

"Try that again. And look into my eyes when you deny it."

My chest burns with love. With anguish. "Axel."

He staggers back a step. Then another. I can't work out how his eyes can be both desolate and fierce. His voice commanding but oh, so vulnerable.

"Okay, before we go further I need to say this. I love you. But it's not the kind of love that is selfless enough to let you go. My love is the fucking *selfish* kind. The kind that will demand to have you in my arms when I go to sleep at night. The kind that will insist on seeing your face every morning, no matter what. The kind that will shatter kingdoms for the right to be a father to this baby. I'm the selfish bastard who needs you to breathe. So tell me what penance you demand and let me pay it. I will spend the rest of my life paying if need be. Because we need to learn to live with this together. Because nothing but death will cut it for me."

My mouth drops open, but no words emerge. He stares at me for a rigid second before he veers away, his stride jerky with the same agony twisting through me. A second later, he leaves the room.

I sag onto the bed, the tests still clutched in my hand. Opening the nightstand drawer, I drop them in, then I lie back on the bed.

My hand finds my belly.

It's okay. It's going to be okay, I lie to my child. To myself.

Because what else can I do? I love Axel Rutherford with everything that I am. But I'm terrified that microscopic bubble of darkness that abhors what he's done will one day explode.

Can I live with that darkness? Smother it with the love fused with my soul for him? Buy us both time for a chance at the happiness that is owed to us?

Yes…yes. I swallow. Rise.

I find him in his office. He watches me cross the room, his face a twisted mask of hope and desperation as I crawl into his lap, my arms sliding around his neck. Strong arms bind me to him. His lips find my crown. And he stays there, shuddering, breathing me in.

"I love you," he vows. It's a promise and a sentence.

I bask in both.

We stay there for an hour. Or maybe it's a minute.

We have time.

We have time.

We have time.

Boy, am I wrong.

* * *

Axel is standing at the side of the bed when I emerge from the bathroom. The pair of low-riding sweatpants hugging his lean hips sends a pulse of electricity through me. It's good to know my sexuality hasn't up and died. Every other part of me may as well have. Axel hasn't fucked me in two days. I feel like shit, and I haven't stopped throwing up for forty-eight hours straight.

It's as if my body was waiting for acknowledgement of my condition before going to town. Because right on the heels of finding out I'm pregnant, I'm fully installed in Hurl Town.

Axel is out here only because I banned him from watching me

throw up over and over. What I don't know is why he looks like all the ghosts of hell are stabbing his soul with ice picks.

I shut the bathroom door behind me, leaving the room in semi-darkness. "Axel?"

The head he raises is heavy. The expression in his eyes rips me apart. "Why are you getting calls from Greenwich Memorial Hospital?"

My heart...stops. "What?"

"I put your phone on silent so you would get some sleep. I just un-muted it. It's eight a.m., and they've been calling since midnight. Why?" His breathing alters, shallow pants that stroke the edge of hyperventilation. "Is it...is it the baby? You said it was just morning sickness." His gaze flies over me, as if he's developed X-ray powers. They return to linger on my stomach, to my long-healed ribs. His face goes pale. "I swear, if he caused permanent damage—"

"I'm fine, Axel. It's not...The baby's fine."

He raises the phone clutched in his hand. "Everything's not fine or the hospital wouldn't have left you nine fucking messages! And why the hell would you book an appointment out of town when I've got you an ob-gyn right here in Manhattan?"

Terror and the shattering of my dreams rip through my soul. I stumble forward, hand outstretched. "Can you...give me my phone, please?"

His fingers tighten until his knuckles turn as white as his face. "Tell me why the hospital's calling, Cleo."

I shake my head. "No. Please don't make me. If I do, we can never go back."

Confusion furrows his brow. "Go back? Back where?"

"Back to this moment. Back to one minute ago, when I was okay with choosing your love over..."

He freezes. "Over what?"

I squeeze my eyes shut for a fatalistic second. "Over the darkness in your soul." The words are less than a whisper.

He hears them. His breathing stalls. The tendons on his neck stand out as his gaze goes from my face to the phone. Back again.

"Why would...I don't...Tell me why the hospital's calling."

"Because that's where my mother is!"

Silence. It sucks us into its grim chasm. I don't want to fight it. Surrendering to it would be so good right now. My knees weaken. I sag against the wall, slide down it, and attempt to wrap my arms around my grief.

He doesn't come to me. He doesn't scoop me up into his arms. He shakes his head. Denying us both the numbing blackness that will end all this.

"Your mother is dead."

The remnants of my ravaged soul refute that. So hard. "She's not dead."

"No. She and your father were officially declared dead two years ago."

My heart bangs against my ribs, every single scenario I've ever envisaged for this moment playing out in macabre Technicolor. "*Declared* dead, but not dead. At least not my mother."

"Why would you hide something like that—? Finnan? Did he threaten her?"

"He threatened her, yes, but with turning off her life support if I stepped out of line. He knew where she was because he was the one who paid for her care."

He breaks from stasis and begins to pace. "So...if Finnan knew she was alive and wasn't the one you were hiding her from, then—?"

"Stop. Please!" I realize I'm weeping when the hand I swipe across my cheeks comes away wet. "Are you seriously playing this game with me, Axel?"

He stops, looking at me like I'm an alien. "Why would I play fucking games at a time like this?"

I open my mouth. The penthouse's intercom buzzes loudly. I look toward it.

He steps in my line of sight. "We're not getting that until you answer me, Cleo."

"I made sure she was declared dead so *you* wouldn't know she was still alive! So you wouldn't find her and finish the job of killing her!" My broken voice joins my broken body and I lay my head on my knees.

The intercom continues to buzz. Our chasm grows wider. I shut my eyes against it all.

"You think...I tried to kill your mother?" His voice is a bleak, horrified rasp.

I'm spent. I don't answer. The buzzing stops. The bedroom phone rings.

"Answer me, Cleo!"

He's standing above me. Breathing hard. A sound tears from the beast within him. The phone continues to ring.

He lunges for it. "What?" A muffled voice at the end of the line. "No, I don't want to talk to anyone...Yes, okay. Who? Fine, send them both up."

He hangs up and returns to where I sit. I open my eyes and watch the fires of hell burn in his eyes. Bending, he lays my phone at my feet. His whole body is trembling. Without a word, he goes into the dressing room, pulls on a T-shirt, and leaves the room.

My hands shake as I place the call.

"Miss McCarthy, thank you for returning my call," Dr. Denker answers.

"Is...is everything okay with my mother?"

"Yes, I mean there's no change. The reason for my call is because we've had a query about your mother that I found a little odd."

"In what way?"

"I don't want to alarm you, but in light of what we talked about a while ago, about being ready to move her..."

"Yes?"

"Someone came to the hospital last night to discuss the same thing."

Finnan. I surge to my feet. Sway against the wall. "You didn't—"

"Of course not. She apologized profusely when she realized we wouldn't proceed without your express authorization."

"*She?*"

"Yes, she was quite gracious, actually. Very cheery. Dark brown hair..." Alarm bells scream at the back of my head. "Are you familiar with her, Miss McCarthy?"

"Yes. I am. Thank you for letting me know. I'll be in touch within the hour."

I hang up, my mind in a deeper level of turmoil than I would have believed possible ten minutes ago.

He knew. All along he *knew*. Otherwise he wouldn't have sent Fionnella Smith after my mother.

Going into the dressing room, I grab my tunic and drag it over my head.

It's time to meet Axel Rutherford's monster full-on.

* * *

AXEL

I made sure she was declared dead so you wouldn't know she was still alive! So you wouldn't find her and finish the job of killing her!

I thought the terror in her eyes was for my other sins. Now I know better—

"I'm sorry if this is a bad time, but this is the first opportunity I've had since my other employer's...issues. I thought you'd want to know immediately."

I drag air into my useless lungs and focus on the two people seated in front of me. Fionnella Smith. And Bolton.

I stare at my brother. He stares back at me. I can't even find the gear for confusion.

My gaze returns to Fionnella.

"What?" Is that my voice? It sounds like a stranger's.

Her eyes narrow, flicking to the empty hallway and back again. "Is everything okay?"

She's in there. In the bedroom where I thought my life could have meaning again.

Dear God. "You have a report to make. Make it." My eyes return to Bolton. His gaze is steady. Direct. He's either dialed down the drugs or he's found the perfect cocktail to help him fire on all cylinders. I don't have the mental capacity to decipher which.

She thinks I tried to kill her mother…

"I found out who moved the Camaro. And I…we know the identities of the victims."

"*We?*"

"I'll tell my part—it's the easiest—then let your brother tell his. Your father had it moved and burned. I figured he wouldn't use a local service so I trawled through nine hundred dredging companies on the eastern seaboard, and I lucked out."

"Just like that?"

She smiles. "No, son. But I won't bore you with the details. And this is where it gets interesting. According to the kind gentleman who manned said operation, there was only one body recovered from the trunk."

"There were two bodies on the video. You saw them."

She nods and glances at Bolton. "You wanna take it from here?"

My gaze shifts to my brother, every single hair on my nape erect.

He stares down at his balled fists for a minute before he exhales. "I didn't know what Pa had told them to do, Axel. I swear. Not until we were on our way to Bearwood Lake. When I realized what they planned to get you to do…I…I just couldn't. Knocking a few heads together for extortion money was one thing. Cold-blooded murder—"

"What did you do?"

"I told them I needed the restroom. They thought I was off my head—"

"You *were* off your head."

He shrugs. "Maybe I was, but what does that matter now? Ronan was glad to get rid of me, and you guys were so scared to attract attention, you were driving so goddamn slow. I made it to your side of the lake just as you were leaving."

"Then what?" I ask, but the puzzle is unraveling, faster than I can handle. I know what's coming. What's been coming for the last ten years.

I thought my life was over fifteen minutes ago.

I'm about to watch my own burial.

"The car was still sinking when I got to it. There was just enough daylight to see what I was doing."

I shake my head. "But the trunk was shut."

He shrugs. "Penknives aren't just for snorting coke. Plus I may not have been a high school swimming champion then, but I could still hold my breath for three minutes and eleven seconds."

Jesus.

"Why?" I ask my brother.

His face congeals with pain. "He didn't love any of us. I know that now. But the depth of his hatred for you…I didn't understand it. Still don't. Maybe he knew you would become the best of us."

Air shudders from my lungs. "Bolton—"

"It's okay. I'm fine with admitting that we weren't born equal. For what it's worth, I'm proud of the man you've become, brother."

The pain in my chest is expanding. I don't know that I've moved until the back of my legs meet the sofa. I sink onto it, clutching my pounding head. When I finally raise it, they're both staring at me.

"And for what it's worth, I can corroborate everything he's said," Fionnella adds.

"How?"

"Jeez, where's the trust? Okay, I know a guy at a cheeky little government offsite bunker that stores satellite archives. All he needed was a time and date."

I swallow. Nod. Then ask the question that will seal the nail in my coffin. "Who…who were they?"

"Michael and Camilla."

The torn gasp behind me sends me to my feet. Cleo stumbles forward from where she was leaning against the wall. Behind me, I hear Fionnella and Bolton charge to their feet too.

"Damn," Fionnella says under her breath.

Desolate blue eyes, brimming with tears, meet mine. She's deathly pale and won't stop shaking. The tears spill down her face, and I die all over again. "Cleo…"

Her gaze shifts to Bolton. "You saved my mother?"

"Yes. I'm…I'm sorry I couldn't save Michael."

"Why…why did Finnan want them dead?" she asks.

Bolton snorts. "Why does he do anything? The returning-to-Boston thing was a ruse. Michael was planning to do another deal with General Courtland behind Pa's back. I guess we all know the outcome." Bolton's gaze moves to Cleo. "I'm sorry."

Agony contorts her face, and she sways where she stands. I catch her by the arms and exhale in relief when she doesn't recoil from me. I walk her to a seat, and she sits but her attention remains on Bolton. "How did Finnan know my mother was alive?"

"He hit the roof when Ronan told him we hadn't torched the car like he asked. He had it dredged up a few days later. I didn't have a lot of options to save your mother's life besides CPR so I called nine one one. They took her to Saint Jude's. Tracking her there wasn't difficult. Sorry."

She nods, looking down at her linked fingers. "No. Thank you," she murmurs. "For…for saving her life." More tears fall.

I reach for her hands. She doesn't pull away, but she doesn't engage.

"Cleo." The eyes that meet mine are as dead as I feel. "I'm sorry, baby."

She returns to watching her hands.

"Cleo, you have to know that, if Axel had known, he would've never driven the car into—"

"Bolton—" I warn.

"What? She needs to know, and you need to stop torturing yourself to death with that thirty-seven-minute piece of film."

Cleo's head snaps up. "What did you just say?"

Bolton doesn't hear her. His gaze is still fixed on me. "You think you're the only one he sent that video to? Or the only one he uses any of his videos to blackmail?"

Fury finds a way through my ashen void. "Fuck."

"Wait…the video of my…the video was *thirty-seven* minutes?" Cleo asks.

"Yes," Bolton and I say in unison.

The sound that rises from her throat is all wounded animal.

I caress my hand down her arm. Again she doesn't react. "Cleo, what is it?"

"The video he sent me was twenty-one minutes," she replies.

Fionnella moves toward her. "And let me guess. The footage makes Axel look guilty as hell?"

Cleo's eyes meet mine. Shift away. Her mouth wobbles before she presses it tight.

Fionnella steps closer. "Just to be clear, you do know he's not guilty, right—?"

"That's enough," I snarl.

"Son, I'm trying to help you. You're not going to rest until this thing is behind you—"

"It'll *never* be behind me."

She mutters something under her breath about thick-headed alpha males with death wishes. "So, you'll defend your country against assholes who deserve everything you dish out to them, but you won't defend yourself?"

A rumble of acid builds in my gut. "I should've known it wasn't just picking up and delivering a car."

"So you're going to punish yourself forever?" Fionnella presses.

I stand and face her. She doesn't back away. Were my life not at the bottom of an abyss, I would smile at her fearlessness. "I owe you a debt for shedding light on this for me. If there's ever a way I can repay it, all you need to do is ask. But your work here is done."

She stares at me for an age before she gives a brisk nod. Going back to the sofa, she picks up her purse.

Bolton rises too. He looks lost for a minute before he clears his throat. "I'll see you around, brother."

I nod, too clogged up to respond. They both head for the door.

"Wait."

"What happened to Michael's body?" I ask.

Fionnella looks past me to Cleo, one eyebrow raised. "I have footage of that too. From Boston. But maybe you want to tell him?"

"Boston?" I jerk around.

Tears still falling, Cleo nods. "Finnan had him secretly cremated. He showed me the video. He...he and I buried his remains when we were in Boston."

"Sweet Jesus."

I barely hear them leave. But I watch Cleo slowly rise from the sofa. We stand feet apart, the universe between us.

Her eyes are huge pools of savage pain, regret and devastation. I want to take it all away, fold it into my own turmoil. But I'm not worthy to even touch her pain.

All I can do is will her not to fall apart. "I'm sorry, Cleo. So very sorry. God, if I could take any of it back..."

She shakes her head, her hand swiping at her cheeks. She sniffs and steps closer. "You...have nothing to be sorry about, Axel. Oh God, the things I accused you of. I ruined us. I ruined *everything*."

"I didn't look, Cleo! Compared to the other car we picked up, the Camaro was worthless, and yet we spent more time on it. I knew something was wrong, I just didn't trust my instincts. And your father died because of it. There's no coming back from that."

More tears fill her eyes. "No, don't say that. What happened is on Finnan. Everything that happened to us is on him."

"It's the truth. It's the truth that led me to do a lot more bad things after. There's no coming back from that either."

"What...what are you saying?"

"That you were right when you said we can't ever go back. I am what I am."

"No, we can. We can try and put it behind us."

I shake my head. "Not this. Not so much pain and suffering. It'll always be between us."

Her hand presses her flat belly. "So...what about the baby?"

Agonizing blades rip my insides to shreds, but the truth is a glaring beacon. "It's better off without me."

"God, no. Don't say that. Please!" Even crying, she's beautiful. So very beautiful it hurts.

I stumble toward her, ashamed of my one last act of selfishness. "I need...Can I...Please, let me hold you, one last time?" I beg.

"Axel...no. I don't want you to g—"

"Please."

"I love you!"

"I love you too." It's the only truth that makes sense. I cross the distance and take her in my arms. The kiss would be anointing if I were still alive. But I gorge on it, the way a man headed for his doom would. When I press her away, she looks at me with the most gorgeous eyes I've ever seen.

My heart kicks hard then somersaults just for the hell of it. I never dreamed I'd see her look at me this way again. I want to freeze her in time so I never lose that look. "Goodbye, Cleo."

"No." Strong hands dig into my arms. I grip her gorgeous body and gently set her away as the last chain to my anchor snaps free.

"You'll be okay without me. I promise. I'll always love you."

"Then stay."

"I can't."

The blood on my hands will never come off. She doesn't deserve that.

So I walk.

Chapter Thirty-Three

PENANCE. TOGETHER. FOREVER.

US

Finnan Rutherford is charged with war crimes two months later. I don't doubt that between Axel and his powerful allies, they orchestrated a process that could've taken years and reduced it to weeks. The trial takes three weeks and four days. He's sentenced to life imprisonment without parole.

For every one of those days, I sit in court two rows behind Axel. He knows I'm there. His shoulders tense every time I look at the back of his head. But not once does he turn or acknowledge me.

On the day he testifies, I catch my first real glimpse of his face. He looks as haggard as I feel. But he's strong and proud and ruthless when he puts the final nail in his father's coffin.

For my part, I feel little shame in rejoicing in the vengeance my father indirectly receives.

With the trial out of the way and the pervasive terror lifted from my life, I have room to think about the future. It's not the future I once dreamed of but it's one that still makes my heart lift.

My hand drifts over my belly as I exit the ground floor elevators of the offices of Mackey & Black Attorneys on Madison Avenue. My trust fund is back in my full control, and for the first time in my life, I'm financially independent.

I can buy a house.

I can plan a nursery.

I still have my interior design degree. I can apply for an internship once the baby is old enough. Or I can find a job I can do from home.

The world is my oyster. But I only want one thing.

Axel.

I step out into the fall sunshine, lift my face up to it. The chill that shrouds my heart doesn't dissipate.

Axel.

I thought him a cold-blooded murderer even when my soul screamed otherwise and craved him anyway. My head made excuses to not love him while my heart flew every time he touched me. I miss that touch. That touch he promised me would always be mine, whether I wanted it or not.

My steps slow, my thoughts whirling. When my heart skips a beat, I breathe through it. I find a coffee shop, order a decaf pumpkin spice latte. And I plot my course of action.

Half an hour later, I dig out my phone, and I dial. A short conversation and I have the information I need. I take a cab to XYNYC and ask the driver to wait.

Getting out, I walk up the black carpet to where the familiar-looking bouncer is vetting the early comers. He spots me and walks over to lift the velvet rope.

"You wanna come in, miss?" he says deferentially. "The boss is inside."

I look toward the silver steel doors, every cell in my body yearning to fling myself through them. But for what I'm planning, I need a quiet haven. Hopefully one he'll never want to leave.

I smile. "No, thanks. But could you give him something from me? But not right this minute. In about half an hour?"

He looks puzzled, but he nods. "Sure thing, miss."

I hand over the envelope, and I leave.

My hotel suite isn't as sumptuous as his penthouse but it's fit for this purpose. I figure I have forty-five minutes to an hour tops before he turns up. I jump in the shower, slathering myself in the expensive gel I treated myself to yesterday.

My dress is already laid out. I slip it on, tug on my heels and gather my hair in a topknot that leaves my neck bare. I'm slipping on silver chandelier earrings when I hear the firm knock.

Butterflies surge into my midriff. I slide a soothing hand over my belly. Leaving the bedroom, I open the door.

He fills my doorway. My world. Tall. Primitive. Proud. Fierce.

His eyes probe, *consume* me from head to belly to toe and back up again.

I clasp my hands behind my back. "Hi, Axel. You got my note?"

He walks into the suite and shuts the door behind him. "I got your note. *And* the picture. Please tell me that fucking tattoo isn't real."

"What if it is?"

His nostrils flare with barely controlled fury. "Then you'll be heading to a laser doctor to have it removed pretty fucking quick."

"Why?"

"Because that word has no fucking place on your beautiful body, that's why."

"You wear it on *your* skin."

He shoves a hand through his hair. "We're not doing this again."

"Why? Am I not worth your time, Axel?" I inquire softly.

He stops, his piercing eyes incredulous. "Not worth... What the fuck are you talking about? You're worth every—" His eyes narrow. "Why am I really here, Cleo?"

"Because I love you. And you love me. And whatever penance needs to be paid, we pay it *together*."

He pales. His whole body shudders. "No. God, baby, you can't—"

"Can't I?" Tears brim my heart, my throat, my eyes. "Tell me you're happy without me. Tell me you don't dream about me every night, and I'll let you go."

He blinks hard then shakes his head. "Cleo."

"Can you?"

"No. I can't. You know I *can't*." He sounds like a condemned man. My warrior.

I take a step toward him, not too close. But close enough for him to feel the edge of my torment. For him to miss me even more.

"You said yours was a selfish love. Well, mine is too. I demand your arms around me, your kisses on my face, my body. Your cock inside me whenever I want it. I demand you let me love you and worship you the way you do me. You told me you hated me once. That hurt me. A lot. But I was also ashamed because I hated you too. And you know what those are, Axel?"

"What?" he croaks.

"Wasted emotions that would've been better spent loving and trusting each other. So much wasted time. Years and years. Why would you want to waste more?" My voice breaks and tears spill over.

With a groan he closes the distance between us. He brushes away my tears, even as his own eyes mist. "I'm no saint, sweetheart. The things I've done, I'll never be clean, Cleo. Never."

I catch his wrist in my hand, look deep into his turbulent eyes. "You will. You know why? Because for all the bad things you did, you did a thousand more that were good. You saved a lot of people. You saved me. That has to count for something, right?"

"God, you count for everything. Without you, I wouldn't be alive. When I thought…" He stops, and his jaw clenches. He breathes through it. "When I thought you betrayed me, the only thing that kept me going was the need to understand. I had to know what I did wrong so I could try and fix it someday."

"Then do it. Fix us. Here, now. Let me be your Cleo. Do you want to be my Axel? The one who will never take no for an answer, never spend a night without me in his arms?"

He shuts his eyes, his breathing jagged. "Yes, I want to be your Axel again. Your Romeo."

I cradle his precious face in my hands, brushing my thumbs over his lips. "No, not my Romeo. I don't want to think about or talk about death. There's been enough of it for all our lifetimes. I just want you, my Axel. Mine alone and always mine."

"I've been yours from the moment we met. Every single second of every day. Even when you were lost to me, I loved you."

Uncontrollable tears fill my eyes. "I'm sorry I ever doubted you. So sorry. I never stopped loving you either."

With a groan, he gathers me into his arms, one hand passing reverently over my stomach. Back again. He buries his face in my neck and scents me. "Oh God. Living without you has been hell. I missed you so much. Missed the way you look, the way you smell..." He stops to smell me again. "Fuck," he groans again.

Oh, how I've missed that. "Kiss me, Axel."

He kisses me deep and long and hard, breaking away every few second to whisper his love. After long minutes, he lifts his head, grabs my hand, and inspects my wrist.

"Oh, thank fuck."

I smile at the cheap, stick-on tattoo I sent him a picture of. The word *penance* is already starting to fade.

"The moment this comes off, we leave the past in the past. Deal?"

He nods. "Fucking deal. I love you, Cleo. So fucking much."

My heart soars. "I love you too."

He starts to lower his head. I pull away. "Just so you know, that goodbye kiss killed me."

His eyes darken in pain. "Jesus, me too. I thought I was doing the right thing. I'm so sorry."

"Sorry's not gonna cut it, big guy. You'll have to pay for that."

"Whatever you want."

I take a few steps back and hold out my hand. "Take me to bed. Fuck me. Love me."

His eyes light up. With love. With primitive possession. Mine. All mine.

"With pleasure, baby." He eyes my sky-high heels. "But...should you be wearing those in your condition?"

"Which condition is that? The one where you bend me over the side of the bed and take me from behind with my heels on? Or the one where I climb on top of you and ride you all night long? With my heels on?"

He chokes on a breath, his eyes going wild. "Someone's been having naughty fantasies."

"I've had to live without you for almost three months. You don't know the half of it."

He exhales, strides to me, and sweeps me up in his arms. Touching his forehead to mine, he whispers, "I'll make it up to you. Whatever you want."

"I want you to never leave me again. I want you to have my heart and my love. Always. But right now, I want you to take me in the bedroom. And fill me up."

He shudders. "God, yes!"

"And Axel?

"Yes, baby?"

"If it helps you move faster, I'm not wearing any panties."

* * *

US

I didn't hold her firmly enough.

I didn't account for the world having the capacity to tear us apart.

She's back in my arms again. Her heart in my hands. Mine in hers.

I'll never make that mistake again.

This time I won't be her Romeo.

I'll be her whole fucking world.

And as long as the world spins, I'm never letting go.

Never.

DID YOU MISS QUINN AND
LUCKY'S STORY?

PLEASE SEE THE NEXT PAGE
FOR AN EXCERPT FROM
BEAUTIFUL LIAR.

1

CASTING

April 2015

There's no reason for me to be here. I don't need to do it.

Not another one.

I have more than enough to work with. I should end it now.

It's what I've been telling myself for months now.

Shit, who am I kidding?

Enough will *never* be enough. He has to pay for what he's done with absolutely everything I can take away from him.

Besides, I have big enough balls to admit it's become a rush. The delayed gratification is part of the game. It's an addiction. In my jaded world where everything comes to me with a snap of my fingers, risky highs like these are to be treasured.

They'll be gone in a blink of an eye. Just like every other pleasure in my life.

I peer at my watch.

5:58 p.m.

I rise from my sofa, walk down the wide hallway and enter the empty room. It's not completely empty, but it might as well be. I haven't bothered to decorate since acquiring it six months ago when my time in Boston was done and I moved back to New York. It's as if my subconscious knew I'd need it just for this purpose.

In the middle of the room, I grab the remote on the table and hit the power button. Three screens flicker to life. I sit down in the leather chair I'd placed in here earlier. Three faces stare back at me. The darkness and mirrored glass means they won't see me as clearly. Even if they do, my mask is in place. My black clothing and leather gloves take care of the rest of my disguise.

Anonymity is key. I'm too well-known for anything else to be acceptable. Or acceptable for now, at least. Who knows what'll happen a month, two months from now? Every day I fight my impulse. I might wake up tomorrow and decide the time has come to give in, unveil my plan.

I'm not ashamed of taking this route to achieve what I want. Far from it. In fact destroying myself in the process is exactly what I'm aiming for. I want there to be absolutely nothing left to be sustained or redeemed by the time I'm done.

For now, though, my public role is integral to my grand plan. And since my sins are already numerous, I don't have any qualms about adding vanity to them and admitting I love my other life. Keeping my identity secret adds to the thrill.

It's all about the thrill for me. Without it, I risk prematurely succumbing to the dark abyss. The abyss my shrink keeps warning me I'm rimming.

She thinks it's a revelation, that morsel of news she dropped in my lap three years ago. Little does she know I've been staring into that abyss since I was fifteen years old. I've stared into it for so long, it's fused with me. We are one. We haven't done our final dance yet, but it's only a matter of time.

I'm twenty-eight years old.

I won't live to see thirty.

It's an immutable inevitability, so I take my pleasures where I can.

"You each have scripts in front of you. When I tell you to, read them out loud. You go first, Pandora." I use a voice distorter because my natural voice contains a distinctive rasp that could give me away. Because of who I am, I've had cameras shoved in my face more times than I've had sex. And that's saying something.

Pandora—fucking idiotic name—giggles, and her golden curls bounce in an eager nod. I suppress a growl of irritation and relegate her to the *possibly maybe* list.

"*May I feel, said he.*" She giggles again.

Ten seconds later, I place her firmly in the *hell no* list and press the intercom. She's escorted out, and I switch my gaze to the next girl.

The redhead is staring into the camera, her full mouth tilted in an *I-was-born-to-blow-you* curve. I admit the lighting is better on her, but her eyes are a little too wide. Too green.

I adjust the camera and scrutinize her closer. "What color are your eyes? And don't tell me they're green. I can see the edges of your contacts."

She flushes. "Umm...they're gray."

I check the notes on my tablet. "Missy, is that your real name too?"

She nods eagerly.

"Did you read the brief?"

"Umm...yeah," she answers, her voice trailing off in a semi-question. This one is clearly dim.

"What did it say about lying?"

The *blow-you* expression drops. "They're just contacts." She leans forward, nearly knocking out the camera with her double Ds. "Here, I can take them out—"

"No, don't bother. Your interview is over. Leave now, please," I command in my best non-psycho voice, and press the intercom again.

I may be slightly unhinged, according to some spectrum my shrink keeps harping on about, but Mama, God rest her pure soul, taught me to be a gentleman. Mama's worm food now, but that's no reason for me not to honor her with a touch of politeness.

Missy's lips purse, then part, as if she's about to plead her case.

The burly guard who enters the room and taps her on the shoulder convinces her words have lost their meaning at this point.

I turn to the last screen.

Her eyes are downcast. Her lashes are long enough to make me wonder if I have another fake on my hands. I sigh, then take in the rest of her face. No makeup, or barely any if she made the effort. Her lips are plump, lightly glossed. I use the controls on the remote to zoom in. There's a tiny mole on the left side of her face, right above her upper lip. Not fake.

I zoom out, examine the rest of her that I can see. Her gray T-shirt is worn to the point of threadbare, and her collarbones are a little too pronounced. Malnourishment wouldn't be a crowd-pleaser, but that problem can be easily taken care of.

Unlike the previous stock from which I plucked my prior subjects, she doesn't seem like the BDSM club–going type. For a second, I wonder where my carefully placed adverts unearthed this one.

Beneath the T-shirt, her chest rises and falls in steady breathing, although the pulse hammering at her throat gives her away. I zoom in on the pulse. The skin overlaying it is smooth, almost silky, with the faintest wisps of caramel-blond hair feathering it.

Something about her draws me forward to the edge of my seat. I like her pretended composure. Most people fidget under the glare of a camera.

My gaze flicks to her skeleton bio. "Lucky."

Slowly, she raises her head. Her eyelids flick up. Her eyes are a cross between green and hazel with a natural dark rim that pronounces their vividness. I can't pinpoint it exactly, but something about that look in her eye sparks my interest.

Hell, if I had a heart, I'd swear it just missed a beat.

"Is that your real name?"

She shrugs. "It might as well be," she murmurs.

Fuck, I have another liar on my hands. "Cryptic may be sexy if you're auditioning to be the next Bond Girl. It's not going to work here. Tell me your real name. Or leave."

"No." Her voice is a sexy husk, enough to distract me for a second before her answer sinks in.

"No?"

"With respect, you're tucked away behind a camera issuing orders. I get that you hold the cards in this little shindig. But I'm not going to show you all of mine right from the start. My name, for the purposes of this interview, is Lucky. It may not officially be on my birth certificate, but I've responded to it since I was fifteen years old. That's all you need to know."

Well…fuck. I note with detached surprise that I'm almost within a whisker of cracking a smile.

I rub my gloved finger over my mouth, torn between letting her get away with mouthing off to me this way, and sending her packing.

Sure, she intrigues me. And whatever relevant truth I need would be dug out before she signs on the dotted line, should it come to that. But for this to work, she needs to obey my commands, no questions asked.

"Stand up. Move away from the camera until you reach the wall."

She rises without question, restoring a little goodwill in her favor. Moving the chair out of her way, she backs up slowly. The hem of her loose T-shirt rests on top of faded jeans. Even before she's fully exposed to the camera, I catch my first glimpse of the hourglass figure wrapped around the petite frame. She's a fifties pinup girl dressed in cheap clothes. Her breasts are full but not quite double Ds, her thighs and calves shapely enough to stop traffic, with a naturally golden skin tone denoting a possible Midwest upbringing.

She's knock-out potential—subject to several nourishing meals. But I've seen enough and done enough in this twisted life of mine to know her body isn't what would draw attention. It's the look in her eyes. The secrets and shadows she is trying hard to batten down. They're almost eating her alive.

I don't really give a shit what those secrets are. But the chance to fuck them…to fuck *with* them, expose them to my cameras, sparks a sinister flame inside me.

"Turn around, let your hair down."

Her fingers twitch at her sides for a second before she faces the wall. One hand reaches up and pulls the band securing the loose knot on top of her head.

Caramel and gold tresses cascade down her back. Thick enough to swallow my hands, her wavy hair reaches past her waist, the tapered ends brushing the top of her perfectly rounded ass.

I watch her for a few minutes, then speak into the mic distorting my voice. "Do you have any distinguishing birthmarks I should know about, Lucky?"

The question sinks in. Her back goes rigid for a second before she forces herself to relax. "Yes."

"Where?"

"At the top of my thigh," she responds.

"Show me," I reply, although I don't really need to see it. My carefully selected stylists can disguise any unseemly marks.

Slowly, she turns around. I expect her gaze to drop or a touch of embarrassment to show, but she stares straight into the camera as her fingers tackle the buttons of her jeans. The zipper comes down and she shimmies the denim over her hips. Her white cotton panties are plain and the last word in unsexy. All the same, my eyes are drawn to the snug material framing her pussy lips.

I also see the hint of bush pressed behind the cotton.

I shift in my seat, but don't reach for the hardness springing to life behind my fly. Hand jobs are a waste of my time. I either fuck or I don't. It's that simple.

She lowers the jeans to knee-level and twists her right leg outward. The round red disk just on the inside of her thigh is distinctive enough to need covering up. I make a mental note.

"Thank you, Lucky. You may put your clothes back on."

A hint of surprise crosses her face, but she quickly adjusts her clothing. When she's done, her hands return to her sides.

"It's time for your screen test. Sweep your hair to one side and come closer. Place your hands flat on the desk, bend forward, but don't sit down."

She follows my instructions to the letter. I adjust the camera so it's angled up to capture her face.

"Are you ready?"

She gives a small nod.

"You've just walked into a bar. You don't know me. But you see me, the guy in the corner, nursing a bourbon. And I see you. All of you. Every fantasy you've ever had. I want to give it to you. You've found me, Lucky, the guy who wants to fuck you more than he wants his next breath. Do you see me?"

Her nostrils quiver slightly. "Yes."

"Good. Look into the camera. Don't blink. Show me what I want to see. Convince me that you're worth fucking. Convince me you're worth *dying* for."

Her lids lower, her face contemplative, but she doesn't blink or lose focus. Slowly, her expression drifts from disinterested to captivated. Her lids lift and she's a green-eyed siren. Her attention is rapt, unwavering. Her bruised-rose lips part, but she doesn't swirl her tongue over her lips as I expect. She just…breathes. In. Out.

She swallows, a slow movement that draws attention to her neck, then lower to her breasts. Mesmerized against my will, I watch her nipples harden against the thin material of her top. Her fingers gradually curl into the hard wood and every inhalation and exhalation becomes a silent demand.

In…fuck…out…me…

In. Fuck.

Out. Me.

I remain still, even though my fingers itch to twitch and my muscles burn with a restlessness I haven't felt in a long time.

I watch her command the camera, her body rigid with lustful tension. Her eyes widen with the need to blink, but she doesn't.

She stays still, hands curl into fists and she just breathes sex. Her eyes water and a tear slips down one cheek. The sight of it is curiously cathartic, a tiny climax.

I subside into my seat. "That was convincing enough. You may sit down, Lucky."

She blinks rapidly before she sinks into the chair. A quick swipe and the tear never existed. Neither does the promise of the fuck of a lifetime that was on her face a moment ago.

Her acting skills are remarkable. For a second, I'm not sure if that's a good thing or a bad thing. I don't want her to be too polished. I dismiss the notion and glance down at her notes.

"You list your address as a motel?"

The address in Queens is unfamiliar to me, but the motel chain is notorious for being exceptionally bad. I hide my distaste and wait for her answer.

"I arrived in town recently. I don't have a permanent address yet."

The secrets in her eyes, the threadbare clothes, the unkempt hair and unshaven pussy begin to tell their own story. She may be brave enough to sass me when she risks losing a job that promises a once in a lifetime payday, but she's also desperate.

How desperate is the question.

"Are you currently working?"

She nods. "I work on and off for a catering service. But it's nothing I can't work around, if needed."

"So you'll be free to do this if I want you?"

The desperation escalates, then a hint of anger flashes through her eyes. "*If*? You mean I did all of this for nothing?"

I give a low laugh at her gumption. "You didn't seriously think you'd waltz your way into a million dollars on a simple three-minute screen test, did you?"

The anger flees from her eyes, although her mouth tightens for a moment before she speaks. "So it's true? It's not a con? This job really pays a million dollars? For…sex?" she rasps.

"You think I'd admit it if it was a con? What did the ad say?"

Her delicate jaw flexes for a second.

"*One million uninhibited reasons to take a leap.*
One million chances to earn a keep.
One million to give in to the carnal.
Are you brave enough to surrender,
For a payday to remember?"

It speaks even more to her desperate state of mind that she remembers the ad *verbatim*.

I remain silent and wait for her to speak.

"So...assuming it's *not* a con, how will this work, then?"

"If you pass the next few tests, and I decide you're a good fit, you get the gig. You'll receive one hundred thousand dollars with each performance."

"So...ten performances...over how long a period?"

"Depending on how many takes are needed, anywhere between three weeks and a month. But I should warn you, it's hard work, Lucky. If you think you're just going to lie back and recite the Star Spangled Banner in your head, think again."

Her fingers drum on the table, the first sign of nerves she's exhibited. "I...I won't be doing anything...skanky, will I?"

"Define skanky."

"This is going to be straight up sex. No other...bodily stuff? Because that would be a firm no for me."

My mouth attempts another twitch. "No water works, waste matter or bestiality will be involved in the performances."

Her fingers stop drumming. "Okay." She waits a beat, stares straight into the camera. "So when will I know?"

I hear the barely disguised urgency and I rub my finger over my lip again. "Soon. I'll be in touch within the week." I'm not sure exactly why I want to toy with her. But I sense that having her on edge would add another layer of excitement I badly need.

When she opens her mouth, I interrupt. "Goodbye, Lucky."

A passing thought about the origin of her name is crushed into oblivion. I press the remote to summon the bodyguard to escort her out, and I leave the room.

In my study a few minutes later, I bring up the screen on my desk and activate the encrypted service I need. I open the application and within minutes, the members of my exclusive gentlemen's club are logging in.

My email is short and succinct.

The next Q Production is scheduled for release on May 20, 2015.

Limited to ten members.
Bidding starts in fifteen minutes.

I start the countdown and rise to pour myself a neat bourbon. I swallow the first mouthful with two prescribed tablets, which are meant to keep me from going over the edge, apparently, and stroll to the floor to ceiling window. I look down at Midtown's bumper-to-bumper traffic. This mid-level penthouse is one of many I own in this building and around New York City.

Technically, I don't live here. I only use it when volatile pressures demand that I put some distance between the Upper West Side family mansion and myself. I would never stray far for long. For one thing, I've accepted that my family would never leave me alone.

I know what I know. So they've made it their business to keep me on a short leash. But with over three hundred properties in my personal portfolio, and a few thousand more under the family firm's control, there are many places to disappear to when the demons howl.

Today, the Midtown penthouse is my temporary haven.

I turn when the timer beeps a one-minute warning.

I return to my desk and adjust the voice distorter. When the clock reaches zero, I click the mouse. "Gentlemen, start your bids."

My words barely trail off before the first five bids appear on the screen. Sixty seconds later, the total bid is at a quarter of a million dollars. I steeple my fingers and wish I were more excited. The money means nothing. It never has. It's the end game that excites me.

My mind drifts back to Lucky. I turn the gem of her elusiveness this way and that and admit to myself she has potential.

I want to take a scalpel to all her secrets, bleed them and soil my hands with the viscera. I also want to fuck her until her body gives out. Right in this moment, I'm not sure what I want more.

So I concentrate on the numbers racing higher on the screen.

Half a million. One million. One point five.

My phone beeps twice. I pick it up and read the two appointment reminders on the screen.

7p.m.—Dr. Nathanson. My shrink.

9p.m.—Dinner with Maxwell.

I re-confirm the first and delete the second.

Cancelling dinner with Maxwell will bring a world of irritation to my doorstep. No one cancels dinner with Maxwell Blackwood. For a start he's one of the most powerful men in the country.

He's also my father.

Yeah, my name is Quinn Blackwood, heir to the Blackwood Estate, only child of Maxwell Blackwood and Adele Blackwood (deceased). My family owns a staggering amount of property across the eastern seaboard of the United States and a few in the west. According to the bean counters, I'm personally worth twenty-six billion dollars.

But tangling with my father in hell is what I live for. Have done since I was fifteen. So I ignore his summons and watch the stragglers fall away until I'm left with the top ten bidders. The bids wind down, and within the space of half an hour, I'm just under two million dollars richer.

I spot the familiar name of the top bidder and I sneer. Taking his money on top of everything else is darkly satisfying.

Once bidding ends, I close down the application and call up another list. Dozens of charity websites showing pictures of starving children flood my screen. Within minutes, fifty charities are the grateful recipients of two million dollars.

I may be Quinn Blackwood, occasional user of prescribed meds to keep the demons in check, who moonlights as Q, porn star to an exclusive few who pay millions for my work.

And I may be an unhinged asshole with serious daddy issues.

But no one said I wasn't a giver.

I was a wife, once. Had hoped to be a mother, too. But that all came to an end, and then there was only Killian. Arrogant, dangerous, undeniable. I submitted to the fire that blazed between us—and I got burned. Now I should hate him. Maybe even fear him. But I don't. I still want him. And so, I run…

A PREVIEW OF *ARROGANT BASTARD* FOLLOWS.

Chapter One

KILLIAN

I've found her.

After four years and two months.

I stare at the screen, my blood pumping relief and shock and fury and joy through my veins. The cocktail of emotions paralyzes me for several minutes.

Then I force myself to analyze what I'm seeing.

Her hair is different. Longer. Darker. Pin-straight and rigid where soft, friendly waves used to be. The curve of her jaw captured by the camera lens also shows the difference. She's leaner. Meaner. Even from this obscure angle, I can tell any trace of softness has been wiped clean. Eroded by sin and tragedy.

To anyone else, the picture would seem ridiculously vague, the image nothing more than a blurred black and white pixilation of chin and shoulder.

It's the reason my algorithm spat it out almost reluctantly, a last batch of possibilities in the dregs of to-be-discarded possibilities, and then dumped it in my supercomputer's equivalent of a spam folder, the code scrolling impatiently as it waited my command to *delete, delete, delete.*

But I know it's her. Despite the black leather cap pulled low over her forehead. Despite the bulky jacket designed to hide her true shape. Her evasiveness speaks volumes.

It's her. The Black Widow.

My hand shakes as I hit the zoom-in key. My gut churns, and I feel a little sick as my ever-helpful brain supplies me with all the ways she could've continued to elude me—if I'd turned away, for a second, to stare at one of the other three screens on my desk. If I'd trusted my super-smart computer and accepted the prompt to delete without reviewing the content. If I hadn't tweaked the code yet again last night to capture just such an obscure image.

Hell, if I'd blinked at the wrong time. I torture myself with infinite possibilities as I stare at that mesmerizing combination of chin and shoulder.

A chin I've trailed my treacherous fingers over.

A shoulder I've rested my guilty, weary head on.

There's so much more to her. And I treasured every single inch of her forbidden body, fucked her at every opportunity she granted me. Until she systematically erased herself from my life.

But why New York? And why now?

I know how good she is. Hell, she's the best or she wouldn't have eluded me for this long. The thought of another four years without her punches a cold fist through my gut.

The Black Widow.

I can't see her eyes. But I don't fool myself into thinking they'll hold an ounce of softness. What we did changed us forever. And not for the better.

I lean back in my chair. Exhale slowly. Terrified of blinking in case she disappears from my screen. It doesn't matter that I've copied and stored the longitude and latitude of her location in a dozen vaults on my server and memorized every single piece of data on the screen.

New York City. East 53rd Street. CCTV camera. A one-in-a-billion shot.

Without taking my eyes off her, I reach for my phone and press the voice activation app. "Good evening, Mr. Knight."

"Nala, how many times do I need to tell you to call me Killian?"

"You have yet to change my default settings, Mr. Knight."

My lips twist but a smile doesn't quite form. "I changed them last week. You reset it, didn't you?"

"I assure you, I'm quite incapable of doing that."

"Yeah, right. Fine. Place a call for me. Pilot. Home."

"Dialing, pilot. Home," the female AI obliges me.

Nelson, my LA-based pilot, picks up on the second ring. It's 3 a.m. but he answers as if it's normal working hours. Which it is, to be fair. Everything is normal for me in my line of work.

"Good morning, sir."

"How soon can you get to the airport?" I snap.

"As soon as I put on my trousers and chuck a bucket of water over my son to wake him up," he replies with a dark chuckle.

My fingers fly over the keyboard as I save her information in a few more electronic vaults. "Give William my apologies," I say.

"No need. He's been chomping at the bit to take the new girl for another spin." The new girl being the Bombardier Global 8000 I added to my collection of private jets last month.

"In that case, I expect to see you at Van Nuys within the hour." At this time of the morning, traffic from their Santa Monica apartment should be light enough.

"We'll be there." He clears his throat. "I expect the paperwork regarding out of curfew flights—"

"Will be taken care of. I'll text you the details but we won't be straying far from the usual parameters."

"Very good, sir. Destination?"

My gaze tracks that chin. That shoulder. The hair. Four years' worth of emotion threatens to rip free. My chest burns with it, but I contain it. "New York."

"And do I need to file a return flight?" Nelson asks.

"Not yet. I anticipate being there for a while." *Until I find her. Until she's back in my arms. She won't come willingly, but that's another problem for another day.*

"Got it."

I hang up, staring at the picture for another minute before I blink and turn to the next screen. It takes less than five minutes to hack the database I need and input the relevant information.

Russell, my driver, is waiting when I sprint downstairs. The advantage of owning homes around the world is the ability to pick up and go at a moment's notice. All I need are the clothes on my back, my computer, and other clandestine electronics.

"All set to go, sir?"

I nod but don't answer as I slide into the back seat. I'm already itching to power up my computer again to make sure her picture is still on my home screen. When it flares to life, I breathe easier.

There's very little traffic at this time of night, but I stare at the screen for the short drive to the airport. The photo has got me whipped. I can't look away from it. Just like I couldn't look away from her the first time I saw her.

God, was that only five years ago when I almost didn't make it to her fateful birthday party? When I dragged my darkness through the side gate of a house in the middle of Xanaxville and felt the earth shift beneath my feet?

I feel like I've known, and lost, her through several lifetimes. She wishes she'd never met me in even one of them, I know. But that matters very little now.

It happened. We happened. And this time…I don't plan to lose her again. My fists clench as I debate the lengths I'm prepared to go to make it that way. She'll fight me. That's her nature. I might even lose this particular fight. But there's a reason the phrase *Or die trying* is more than mere words to me. To us.

"Another medical emergency, Mr. Knight?"

I look up from the screen. I have no recollection of leaving the car and entering the terminal building reserved for private flights.

"Unfortunately, yes," I respond, my gaze already sliding away from the uniformed officials gathered around and back to the screen.

"Damn, you must have the worst luck in the world, huh?" The customs guy is standing next to the immigration guy. They're both staring at me. Because what...they think I'm going to fuck up and confess that I hacked into their system to input the information that is allowing me to fly outside the aviation curfew?

"These things can't be helped," I reply insincerely.

He laughs, and we both shrug. He follows me across the reception area, and I slip him a couple of hundred-dollar bills although he's getting paid triple time for half an hour's work. We part ways, each feeling marginally satisfied but a little screwed over and a little dirty. The money means less than nothing to me, and although nothing would make me feel bad about faking an excuse to fly outside curfew hours tonight of all nights, I detest the lies I have to tell to achieve what I want.

Which is beyond laughable considering what my chosen profession is.

I hurry toward my plane, the grip of anticipation getting tighter with each step. Nelson, trim and tall and much younger-looking than his early sixties age implies, emerges from the plane first, followed by Will. The father and son piloting team have been in my employ for three years. Between them they have forty years of experience, which gives me one less thing to worry about in the grand fucked-up landscape of my life.

"We're ready to hit the skies as soon as you are," Nelson says as he signs the requisite pre-flight papers and hands the clipboard back to the official. "I've been informed your doctor will be on stand-by at Teterboro," he adds, tongue firmly in cheek.

"That's excellent news, Nelson. I'm assuming my doctor is also capable of doubling as my driver?" I ask as I follow him up the steps into the plane.

"He's willing to be whatever you need him to be, sir. He has a helicopter license if you want him to be your chopper pilot. He's very versatile that way."

"Remind me to add a little extra to your Christmas bonus this year, Nelson."

"Don't worry sir, my email will be right on time."

I allow myself a little smile, but it's soon eaten away by razor sharp memories, acid guilt, and churning anticipation. I wave the flight attendant away as she arrives beside me with my usual pre-flight shot of Hine cognac.

She quietly retreats, and when I'm finally alone, I dare to glide my finger over the screen, across her cheek. One artificial touch and my insides go into free fall.

The shaking could be from the power of the engines thrusting me and my crew into the sky. Or it could be the cataclysmic chain reaction that has only ever come from her.

It's a universally held belief that you can't help who you fall in love with. There are a fuck-load of textbooks expounding that theory.

I call bullshit.

I could've walked away that day. Waited another three years to see the brother who hated my guts twice as much as I hated his. The half continent I had placed between us was no problem for me, especially since he chose to continue living in the house of horrors we grew up in, long after my parents' death.

I should've walked away when the crackle and flash and roar of flames warned me the fires of hell were consuming what remained of my pathetic soul.

I could've stopped myself from soiling her goodness. From falling ass over feet in love. But I carried on walking. And with each step I took, I knew we were doomed. Because with each step, I glimpsed her potential, absorbed her genius and her beauty and her flaws.

She was everything I'd been waiting for without even knowing it.

And somewhere between the sparkling pool and the shitty Tupperware strewn on the floral-clothed table where she stood cutting her birthday cake, I decided to just...take.

The only problem was that Faith Carson, the woman I eventually turned into the Black Widow, the woman who fucking conquered the world, wasn't mine to take.

She belonged, legally, according to the laws of Idaho anyway, to another man.

Did I change course? Retreat?

Fuck, no.

Chapter Two

The first step was easy.

I'm a spy. Albeit a reluctant one. But I'm fucking great at it. Or I was. Until I met the Black Widow. She made me think recruiting her was easy. I soon discovered the truth.

She was way better than I was.

I wasn't even upset when I found out. She *is* a genius, after all. Beauty and brains are an insane combination in any given scenario. With her it was lethal. When she wasn't slaying me with her mind, all I thought of was her killer body and the new and inventive ways I could fuck it.

That day, even while I walked by her side through the introductions to people I would never willingly mingle with again, even before I finished the slice of too-dry chocolate cake I didn't want, I knew our destinies were already aligned. And it wasn't because my utter preoccupation with her insulated me against the quiet vitriol spilling from my older brother's smiling lips. Before I became a spy, I often wondered how he could do that—smile so affably to everyone else while ripping me to shreds with his words. I wondered why he bothered when anyone with a lick of sense could tell we hated each other with a vengeance.

Two things became clear soon enough. Matthew Knight was a born politician, right down to the sleaze running through his veins. And becoming a spy opened my eyes to the existence of smiling assassins.

But I digress.

The Black Widow. She was the only recruitment I actively campaigned for, gleefully ignoring the shrieking alarm bells that spy school taught you to heed. I had no problem ignoring them. She was supposed to be my last, my reluctant victory lap before I retreated into the cave the government had dug me out of. At the ripe old age of twenty-eight, I was done serving my country or, more accurately, letting it chew me up and spit me out.

Hell, who am I kidding? She was supposed to be the present I gave to myself.

Until it all went wrong. Until we went too far.

My shaking finger drops from the screen. The deep breath I take barely hits my lungs before it ejects itself back up again. Agitation spikes through me, and I finally release my death grip on the laptop long enough to dump it on the sofa beside me. I head for the cockpit and pull the door open.

Father and son glance over their shoulders, a little startled by my presence. I should say something boss-like and reassuring.

Fuck it.

"How long before we land?" I snap.

They exchange glances. "We took off forty-five minutes ago, sir?" William says.

I raise an eyebrow.

He clears his throat. "Not for another four and a half hours, sir."

"Is there any way to shave some time off that estimate?"

Will frowns. "Uhh…"

"Are you sure we can't get this tin can to go faster?" I look down at the controls, make some quick calculations. "We're not doing anywhere near our top speed."

"That's correct, but we need permission from the aviation authorities for that."

"Get the permission. Bribe someone if you need to."

Nelson stares at me for a beat before he shakes his head. "I don't advise doing that, sir. Not without getting our knuckles severely rapped. And frankly, I'd much rather not rekindle memories of Mrs. Butterworth and her wooden ruler."

Will sniggers under his breath. The look I send him dries up the sound, and he clears his throat.

"But you are welcome to keep us company," Nelson offers after an uncomfortable few seconds.

I drop into the jump seat behind the copilot's even though every particle in my body is straining to return to my laptop.

"Can I get Stacy to bring you something to eat or drink?" Will asks.

"No, but you know what I'd like?"

"No, sir."

"For you to nudge that throttle lever up a fraction. Think you can do that?"

Father and son eye each other again and then turn resolutely to face forward without replying.

I close my eyes, slam my head back against the wall, and grit my teeth to keep from unleashing the demons of frustration running rampant through me.

Five hours. New York City.

The Black Widow needs to be there when I land.

Any other scenario besides her in my arms at the earliest fucking opportunity is more than I can bear right now.

She needs to know that a small part of me never meant to drag her to hell with me. I won't be insincere and confess a wholehearted regret I don't feel. But maybe that small admission might achieve…fuck knows. Something. Enough for her to let me in? Enough for me to touch that goodness again, to calm the ravaging nightmares that are eating me alive?

Or just drag her back down because hell wasn't such a lonely place when she was right there beside me? The truth doesn't cause me discomfort. There had to be a degree of moral bankruptcy to do what I do, achieve what I have achieved.

And if I need to exploit it for the sake of getting her back. Well…fuck it, I'm already damned.

Acknowledgments

My thanks to the usual suspects who make this writing journey a heady ride: my Minx Sisters, you know who you are. To Helen Breitwieser, my agent, for your awesome support and enthusiasm for this series! To Alex Logan, my editor, for making this story shine, shine, shine! Thank you so much. To all the bloggers, reviewers, Goodreads readers, FB groups, Twitter and Instagram followers who selflessly share my stories, I love you all hard. Thank you for all you do.

Finally, to my husband and kids. Thank you from the bottom of my heart for every single moment of love and support you lavish my way, and for your enthusiasm for what I do. I couldn't do this without you.